MW01087870

Balance Due

An Alexis Parker novel

G.K. Parks

This is a work of fiction. Names, characters, places, events, and other concepts are the product of the author's imagination or are used fictitiously. Any resemblance to actual persons, living or dead, places, establishments, events, and locations is entirely coincidental.

No part of this book may be reproduced in any form or by any electronic or mechanical means including information storage and retrieval systems, without express written permission from the author.

Copyright © 2024 G.K. Parks

A Modus Operandi imprint

All rights reserved.

ISBN:
ISBN-13: 978-1-942710-39-4

For my dad

BOOKS IN THE LIV DEMARCO SERIES:
Dangerous Stakes
Operation Stakeout
Unforeseen Danger
Deadly Dealings
High Risk
Fatal Mistake
Imminent Threat
Mistaken Identity
Malicious Intent
Controlled Burn

BOOKS IN THE ALEXIS PARKER SERIES:
Likely Suspects
The Warhol Incident
Mimicry of Banshees
Suspicion of Murder
Racing Through Darkness
Camels and Corpses
Lack of Jurisdiction
Dying for a Fix
Intended Target
Muffled Echoes
Crisis of Conscience
Misplaced Trust
Whitewashed Lies
On Tilt
Purview of Flashbulbs
The Long Game
Burning Embers
Thick Fog
Warning Signs
Past Crimes
Sinister Secret
Zero Sum
Buried Alive
Trouble Brewing
Balance Due
Hostage Situation

BOOKS IN THE JULIAN MERCER SERIES:
Condemned
Betrayal
Subversion
Reparation
Retaliation
Hunting Grounds

BOOKS IN THE CROSS SECURITY INVESTIGATIONS SERIES:
Fallen Angel
Calculated Risk
Light Them Up

ONE

"Are you seeing this?" I asked, nodding toward the window at the man pacing in front of the coffee shop. "I'd say another two passes, and he's going to hold this place up. Gun's in his left pocket."

Detective Derek Heathcliff put his cup down and sighed. "You're bad luck, Parker."

"I've been telling you this since the day we met. Are you just now figuring it out?"

Heathcliff rolled his eyes and reached for his radio. "Be advised, potential robbery in progress." He gave them the address. "Roll a few units to this location."

I felt the weight of my nine millimeter resting in my shoulder holster, concealed beneath my jacket. "Do you want me to go outside and have a friendly chat with him? I could tell him there's a police detective who's trying to enjoy his afternoon cup of joe and would prefer if he wait until tomorrow to rob the place."

"We agreed to meet for lunch today. I won't be here tomorrow."

"That's exactly why I'm going to tell him to wait."

"You're not funny." Heathcliff watched the guy pass in front of the door again.

This time, the would-be offender yanked a frayed beanie over his face, one in which he'd cut out his own eyeholes. It barely came down far enough to cover his nose. Strings hung from the fraying edges of the knit material around his eyes.

"Looks like it's showtime." I moved to intervene, but Heathcliff grabbed my wrist.

"You're a private investigator. This is a police matter. Stay put." He headed for the door just as Fraying Eyeholes got up the nerve to enter.

If the homemade robber costume was any indication of this guy's level of criminal genius, there was nothing to worry about. But fear made people do stupid things, and Heathcliff was one scary son of a bitch. Ten bucks said Fraying Eyeholes would shit himself. But another ten said he'd open fire. I didn't like the fifty-fifty split. Those weren't great odds.

I glanced around the coffee shop. Three-quarters of the tables were occupied with young professionals, students, and the occasional screenwriter. The barista, the sandwich artist, and the woman working the register were oblivious to the potential danger. Any one of them could get hit by a stray bullet or turn into an easy hostage. That's why Heathcliff wanted to keep the problem outside the shop, except Eyeholes was nearly through the front door.

Heathcliff remained directly in front of Eyeholes, who had paused in the doorway while he surveyed the coffee shop. At first, I thought he realized he was in trouble, but that wasn't it. He was looking for something or someone.

A man across the room caught my eye. He had just stepped out of the bathroom. He wore a dark hoodie with a suspicious bulge in his front pouch. Since this wasn't one of those coffee shops, I had to assume the lump was a gun. The probability that two guys decided to rob the same coffee shop at the exact same time had to be extremely low. They had to be working together.

Ignoring Heathcliff's instructions to stay put, I picked up his coffee cup since mine was empty and headed for the bathrooms. Hoodie hadn't moved. He was waiting for Eyeholes to do something.

Before I reached my target, Heathcliff shifted his jacket to the side, revealing his weapon and badge. The detective didn't say a word, but Eyeholes stumbled backward. He tripped over an artificial potted plant and banged into the door as it swung closed, causing everyone inside the shop to turn and look at him except Hoodie, who busied himself with studying the creamers and sugar packets near the pick-up area.

I popped the lid off Heathcliff's half-full cup and reached for some sugar packets, wondering what Hoodie planned to do now. "What is up with that guy?" I asked Hoodie, jerking my chin toward the door. "Hasn't he ever used a door before?"

Hoodie kept his face down. "It takes all kinds."

"I guess so."

Eyeholes' sneakers squeaked against the tile as he scrambled out the door, and Hoodie cursed. "Freaking chicken shit."

"What?" I turned to look at him, realizing he wasn't as smart as his friend.

Hoodie yanked the gun from his front pouch and aimed it at me. "You shouldn't talk to strangers."

"So I've been told." I raised my hands to shoulder height, the half-full coffee cup in my right. "Derek, gun," I shouted, throwing the coffee in Hoodie's face and grabbing for the weapon.

The firearm discharged into the ceiling tiles, showering us in dust and fiberglass. Someone screamed, and the patrons stampeded for the door. I fought to get control of the robber's gun, but he was several inches taller. Even on my tiptoes, the weapon was almost out of my reach.

I kneed him in the stomach, hoping to get him to hunch forward, but that only irritated him. He attempted to headbutt me, his forehead cracking down on my cheek, just beneath my eye. The force and sting knocked me backward, my eye watering. He shoved me to the ground and pointed his gun at me.

"Don't make me hurt you," Hoodie warned.

"Police," Heathcliff announced, pushing his way through the sea of people running toward safety. "Out of my way."

"Ditto." I pulled my piece, aiming with one good eye. At this distance, I wouldn't miss. Unfortunately, Hoodie had me in his sights. And I didn't think he'd miss either. After all, he had two good eyes.

"Drop it," Heathcliff commanded.

Hoodie edged backward, his eyes darting from left to right before grabbing the tip jar and running for the rear exit.

"Parker, you good?" Heathcliff asked, waiting long enough to hear my affirmative before he charged after the second fleeing suspect. By now, Eyeholes was long gone. We couldn't let his partner get away too.

I climbed off the floor, finding two people hiding in the back corner and the staff hunkered down behind the counter. "Where does that door lead?" I asked the barista, who peeked out from her hiding place to see what was happening.

"To the dumpsters outside."

"Does the alley cut through?"

She shook her head.

I rushed out the door after the men. The booming pop of gunfire echoed in the enclosed space. Sticking to the walls, I hurried toward Heathcliff, who had taken cover behind a large green dumpster on the left side of the alleyway.

Finding a smaller black dumpster on the right, I crouched down beside it, pushed my back into it, and rolled it forward until our cover positions were almost even. Heathcliff kept his eye on the man hiding behind what looked like an old refrigerator and firing potshots in our direction. When the gunfire stopped, I cautioned a look around the side.

"He's trapped," I said.

"I know." Heathcliff gave me a look. "This is the last time you get to pick where we meet for lunch."

"Agreed."

Heathcliff peered around the side of the dumpster. "This is the police. You're surrounded. Throw down your weapon and put your hands up."

Hoodie cursed. Most of it was too low for me to make out, but the few phrases I caught made me think he was pissed his accomplice had gotten away.

"Derek, let me try something." I took a breath and spoke loud enough for Hoodie to hear me. "The way I see it, you have two choices. One, you surrender. Tell us about your accomplice, and we cut you some kind of deal. Two, you keep shooting at us until you run out of bullets. Then you better hope we believe it isn't a trick, or you end up shot to death in this gross alley. I don't know about you, but this isn't where I'd want to take my last breath."

I peered around the dumpster. Another shot rang out, this time whizzing much closer to my head. Apparently, the only thing my speech did was make him realize he needed to aim.

I pressed against the dumpster and turned to Heathcliff. "Shouldn't backup be here by now?"

"Yeah, but they're not. Feel free to file a complaint."

Another few shots flew in our direction. I ducked down, cringing as they rattled the metal dumpsters. "He should be running low on ammo by now. Once he's out, we can take him. It's a good thing you have me for backup."

"No. I'll handle it. You stay here." Heathcliff gave me a stern look. "I mean it this time, Parker."

"We both know I'm terrible with instructions."

He fought not to smile. "Don't you think this can wait until we aren't taking fire?"

"You started it."

He chuckled. "Damn. I missed you."

"I knew it." Another shot flew in my direction. This one banged against the side of my dumpster, ricocheting and hitting Heathcliff's at an angle. A few more inches, and one of us would have exceeded our daily allotment of lead. "Hey, asshole, do you mind?" I shouted to Hoodie. "We're having a moment here."

"Shut up, bitch." Hoodie tried to fire again, but the gun clicked empty.

It's about damn time, I thought.

"Cover me." Heathcliff charged the offender, tackled him to the ground, knocked his weapon away, and cuffed him. By the time he finished patting him down, finding a switchblade and a pair of brass knuckles in the guy's pockets, a patrol car had arrived.

"Freeze," an officer said from the mouth of the alleyway.

Heathcliff held up his badge. "Detective Heathcliff, major crimes division. What took you so long?"

Officer Franco stepped closer. "Sorry, we've had a busy afternoon. Is that the suspect?" He indicated the handcuffed man on the ground.

"Shooter," I corrected. "He shot at us."

"Detective?" Franco hoped Heathcliff could elaborate on the situation.

"He and his pal tried to rob the place. The first one got spooked and took off. But this guy wasn't as smart." Heathcliff handed Hoodie over to the officer. "Make sure you read him his rights and get statements from everyone inside the coffee shop."

"Yes, sir." Officer Franco did as he was told while Heathcliff pulled out a latex glove and evidence bag and retrieved the discarded weapon. Franco tightened his grip on Hoodie's arm when he jerked and bucked, hoping to get free.

"Be careful," I warned Franco. "He likes to headbutt. I think he has anger issues or maybe abandonment issues."

"Bitch," Hoodie hissed. "She burned me. I need a hospital."

"Burned you?" Franco raised an eyebrow. "Ma'am?"

"Don't call her that," Heathcliff said. "She doesn't respond well to it."

"He had a gun. I had a coffee cup. Things happened," I said.

Hoodie gave me a look that made the hairs on the back of my neck stand at attention. "You shouldn't have done that."

"You're just mad you were left holding the bag." I indicated the tip jar beside the discarded fridge, which Heathcliff was slipping into a second evidence bag. "Make sure you check his pockets. He had to stuff the cash somewhere." I returned Hoodie's icy stare. "If you have trouble finding it, order a cavity search."

Heathcliff's expression warned me not to antagonize the wildlife. Then he grabbed the offender by the other arm and helped Franco wrestle him into the back of the waiting patrol car.

"What do you want us to do with him?" Franco asked. "He doesn't look injured, but—"

"Run him by the hospital to get checked out anyway. He complained about burns. Let's make sure there's nothing to it," Heathcliff said.

Officer Franco nodded before turning to me. "I'm going to need some information." He pulled out his notepad. "What's your name? How do you figure into any of this?"

"Alexis Parker," I said, "bad luck magnet."

"What?"

"She's a witness." Heathcliff gingerly touched my cheek, which felt sore and a little swollen. "Actually, she's a victim. He assaulted her before attempting to flee."

Franco clicked his pen. "Would you mind telling me what happened, Ms. Parker? Do you need an ambulance?"

"I'm fine."

"You always say that." Heathcliff poked at my cheek again, and I slapped his hand away.

Franco looked confused. "You know each other?"

"I'd hope so since we were meeting for lunch," I said, "and I don't do blind dates."

"Oh." Franco looked at Heathcliff. "*Oh.*"

"She works private security. She used to be a Fed," Heathcliff said. "Go get him squared away. I'll make sure to get her statement. Once you get back to the precinct, find me, and I'll make sure you have everything you need."

TWO

I stretched and checked my phone messages. No one at Cross Security cared that I never showed up after lunch. More than likely, they didn't notice. I'd have to keep that in mind the next time I wanted to play hooky.

"What happened to your face?" Detective Nick O'Connell asked, spotting me at the empty desk in front of Heathcliff's.

"Someone got a little testy over the half and half."

O'Connell reached into his drawer and pulled out an instant ice pack. After shaking it a few times, he tossed it to me. "Weren't you meeting Derek for lunch? Did he hit you?"

"No, but he wanted to." I told O'Connell what happened.

"Let me make sure I have this straight." He rocked in his chair. "You stopped an armed robbery at a coffee shop."

"Almost. He fired one shot into the ceiling before using the rest of his bullets on us. Besides stealing the tip jar, no actual robbing occurred."

O'Connell chuckled. "How'd you know it was going down this afternoon, Parker?"

"She didn't." Heathcliff returned to his desk, fastening his cuffs back in place now that they'd been returned.

"Are you sure about that?" Thompson asked, winking at O'Connell. "Parker doesn't believe in coincidences. She may have had intel. Did she suggest you meet there? Or did you pick the place?"

Heathcliff glanced at me. "Tell me this wasn't a Cross Security thing."

"It wasn't." I glared at Thompson. "What kind of Cross Security thing would involve the world's dumbest criminals?"

"Sounds like one of those reality TV shows. You and Cross did spend an awfully long time in Los Angeles. He may have signed a deal with a TV studio for something like that," Thompson said.

"Cross has a lot of celebrity clients," O'Connell added. "But wouldn't you have to disclose and get the cops to sign waivers?"

"It's not a show. Eyeholes and Hoodie were in the wrong place at the wrong time," I said.

"Likely story," Thompson teased. "Are those their stage names?"

Ignoring him, I asked, "How much did the guy in the hoodie even steal?"

Heathcliff checked his notes. "A hundred and seven dollars and thirty-five cents. It would have been a misdemeanor if he hadn't been armed, opened fire, or assaulted you." He sat down, typing something into the computer. "The register didn't have very much either, a few hundred bucks tops. Split two ways, that isn't much of a payday."

"People do lots of stupid things. Like they say," O'Connell said, "crime doesn't pay. They must have been desperate or thought it'd be an easy in and out."

"It was for one of them." I thought about the man who ran away. "Have any other calls come in? Maybe Eyeholes decided to hit somewhere else. Maybe the coffee shop was the first stop on their spree."

"Now it's a spree?" Thompson asked. "Are you sure you don't know more than you're letting on, Parker?"

"I'm speculating."

"That makes it worse," Thompson said. "Now you're doing our jobs for us."

"She always tries to do our jobs for us," O'Connell said.

Heathcliff picked up the paper in front of me. "Except I still can't get her to write my reports."

"I've got that problem with this one." Thompson indicated O'Connell.

"Keep that up, and I never will," O'Connell said.

While O'Connell and Thompson bickered, Heathcliff scanned the computer screen.

"What's wrong?" I asked.

"It's been a while since we had one this easy. I'm not used to it. I forgot what it's like when someone does something stupid and gets caught red-handed. It's actually kind of nice. No one got hurt. We caught one guy. We have a BOLO out on the other. Easy peasy."

"This is why it pays to eat breakfast at noon. That's when the lazy criminals are most active."

"Did you even finish your breakfast? All you ordered was a piece of pound cake and coffee."

"That counts." I nodded at the precinct swill in his mug. "I'm sorry you didn't get to finish yours. You should have let the barista make you a cup to go."

"I'm just glad the hospital gave our suspect a clean bill of health." Heathcliff keyed in the suspect's name, Wayne Savage, shaking his head at the screen. "I can't believe we have nothing on him."

"Are you sure that's his real name? Guys like that usually have priors."

"I checked. His fingerprints aren't in the system. Maybe the guy's been lucky up until now and has never gotten caught."

"Or he usually runs out the door first."

"Yeah, maybe. Or this was their first time. Given how quickly his partner ran, I wouldn't doubt it."

"Do you think he'll roll on Eyeholes?"

"I have no idea. Officer Franco can sort it out. I've already got plenty of open cases to keep me busy. He can have the collar."

"Is there anything you need help with? It doesn't look like anyone's missing me at work, so I have some time." I reached for the stack of files on his desk, but he gave my hand a gentle slap.

"You've done enough today, Parker. Thanks for having my back."

"Are we still on for poker Friday?"

"As far as I know. Do you think you can stay out of trouble until then?"

"No promises." I got up and waved goodbye to Thompson and O'Connell. "I'll see you boys Friday."

"I thought we were going out next week," O'Connell said.

"We are, unless you can get us out of the symphony. But I wasn't talking about double-date night. I was talking about poker night."

O'Connell's eyes brightened. "How about you get Martin to give you the tickets, which you'll bet and lose in the poker game?"

"Do you think Martin or Jen would believe that story?" I asked.

"I'll keep working on it."

"How about you get that two-bit criminal you helped arrest to steal them? It seems like the kind of dumbass thing he'd do," Thompson chimed in. "Tell him you'll put it on the TV show."

"There is no TV show," I reminded him.

O'Connell rubbed his chin. "Y'know, that could work."

Shaking my head, I headed for the door. It was a miracle they ever got anything done.

By the time I made it back to the office, it was almost time to call it quits for the day. No assignments were waiting in my inbox. I'd completed my investigation on a cheating spouse for a pending divorce case yesterday, and Cross had given Bennett Renner my only other assignment, which was to gather intel on a potential insurance fraud case.

Since it was a little after four, I thought about calling James Martin to see what time he planned on leaving the office, but ever since we returned home from California, he'd been working late every night to catch up on all the things he'd missed. After drumming my fingers on the desk until the sound annoyed me, I performed a search on Wayne Savage. Even though Heathcliff had decided it was open and shut, I had nothing better to do than look into it.

Wayne Savage had no priors. His credit history was a

mess. His employment history was spotty. From what I gathered, he had an addiction problem.

While I was checking his social media, hoping for leads on identifying Eyeholes, Kellan Dey knocked on my open office door.

"Hey," Kellan indicated his own cheekbone, "what happened there? Were you in a bar fight?"

"Coffee shop fight. The lunch crowd is brutal."

"It looks like it." He narrowed his eyes at my computer. "Are you busy? I'm in the middle of a client meeting, and I could use your help."

"Who's the client?"

"New guy. His name's Landon. He goes by Don. I think he might be a con artist."

"That's never good." I pulled a tube of concealer and a compact out of the top drawer and dabbed on the makeup to hide the reddish-purple bruise. At least my cheek wasn't swollen anymore. "Has he been vetted?"

"That's what I'm trying to do now. He never made an appointment. He was a walk-in."

"Okay." I put the makeup away. "Has he said why he wants to hire us?"

"He's looking for his daughter."

"So it's a missing persons case."

Kellan shook his head. There was something he wasn't saying. "She's not missing. They're estranged. He said he hasn't seen her in years. He hired another P.I. firm to handle it, but they sent him to us."

"We are the best, or so Cross keeps telling everyone." I slipped into my blazer. Cross didn't like it when new clients could tell we were armed. I turned, finding the look on Kellan's face disconcerting. "What am I missing?"

"I need you to take a look at him. Let me know if you think he's full of shit. Maybe you'll recognize him."

"Why would I?"

"He says he's your father."

"My what?"

"Yeah, see, I didn't buy it either. You look nothing alike. The guy's clearly playing some kind of game."

"What else did he say?"

"Nothing, except he wants to reconnect with you. I'll contact security. Obviously, he poses a threat."

"You have no idea." My heart banged against my sternum. I hadn't seen Don Parker since I left for college. At the time, my adoptive parents made it very clear their obligation to me was over and they never wanted to see me again. I couldn't come up with a single scenario to explain why Don would show up now or how he found me. "Where is he?"

"Conference room A."

Every cell in my body told me to hide or run in the opposite direction, but I had to know if it was him and why he was here. "Okay." I went down the hall to the conference room closest to the reception area with Kellan at my heels.

THREE

The blinds were closed, so I couldn't see inside. Based on Kellan's reaction, he hadn't expected that either.

"Alex, you don't have to go in there."

"I have to know if it's him."

"Why can't you just call your dad and ask?"

"Because we haven't spoken in years. I wouldn't even know how to get in touch with him."

"Shit." Kellan ran a hand down his face. "You think he's here."

"Honestly, I hope not."

"In that case, stay out here." Kellan opened the door, revealing a man with the beginnings of a bald spot. The guy had his head down while he read one of the Cross Security brochures. Kellan glanced at me for confirmation, but from this angle, the guy could have been anyone. Kellan gestured that I wait while he entered the room.

"Sir," Kellan said, "is there anything else you can tell me about your daughter?"

The man held up his pointer finger while he finished reading the brochure. "I don't know much. I told you everything I know."

I knew that voice. It sent shivers through me, like nails on a chalkboard, only worse.

"You only gave me her name and age," Kellan said. "Is there anything else you can tell me about her?"

The man closed the brochure and looked up.

"Shit." The word left my mouth without permission.

Don Parker turned to look at me. "Alexis?" He moved to stand, and I edged backward, my jacket snagging on the door handle. This must have been how Eyeholes felt. "Little swan, it's me. It's Dad."

"Alex?" Kellan asked.

But I couldn't explain. Not now. Maybe not ever. "Why are you here? What do you want?"

"I wanted to see you," my adoptive father said.

"Why?" A tumbleweed lodged in my throat, and I struggled to swallow.

Don Parker moved toward me, and I tried to move farther away, my snagged jacket holding me in place.

Kellan intervened, gesturing at the chair Don had vacated. "Why don't you sit down, sir?" Kellan turned to find me pressed against the door, contemplating fleeing the scene. "Are you okay, Alex? Would you like some privacy?"

The last thing I wanted was to be trapped in a room with the first person who ever crushed my soul. But I nodded, my eyes on Don. "What do you want?" I asked. "We're not related. So if you're looking for a kidney, I can't help you."

"I don't need a kidney." Don chuckled. "I just wanted to see you. Look at you. You're so beautiful. You look just like you did the last time I saw you."

"A lot's changed."

"I know." He offered a tight smile. "Have you spoken to your mother? Did she tell you what happened?"

"I talk to her as often as I talk to you. She's not my mother any more than you are my father."

Anger flashed across his face. "Like it or not, we are your parents."

"No, you're not. You made that abundantly clear."

Don's expression softened. "Don't say things like that, honey. You're our little girl, our little swan, always."

The light pulsed with my heartbeat. It was too hot. Every cell in my body wanted to run, but I didn't. "Really? Because I haven't seen or spoken to either of you since I left for college. I don't remember getting a birthday card or invitation to come home for the holidays."

Don ignored me, continuing with his story. "I hate to tell you this, but your mother and I got divorced. It's still fresh." He held up his left hand to show he hadn't taken off the ring yet.

"It couldn't have happened to nicer people."

"Don't be like that." Don sighed dramatically. "I always loved you, Alexis. I shouldn't have let your mother's drama get in the way. I messed up. I let her dictate my actions. You know what it was like in that house. You know how she was. I want to make up for it now. That's why I came looking for you."

"So you get divorced, and the first thought that went through your head was *I should go look for the kid I adopted and tossed out like yesterday's trash*? Do I have that right?"

"Of course I'd come looking for you now that I don't have to answer to her."

A million thoughts raced around my head. A million arguments. A million emotions. And no matter how much I wanted to believe that was true, I knew it wasn't. "Regardless, you made your choice. This is the result. Have a nice life."

"Stop being so dramatic. We didn't throw you out. We gave you everything."

"Do you want a thank you?" I asked.

"It wouldn't hurt." He stood, and I stepped away, my back pressing against the blinds, causing them to rattle. "At least tell me how you're doing," Don said. "Let me take you out to dinner. It's early. I'm sure you haven't eaten yet."

"I'm fine." Even if I was on the verge of a panic attack or seizure.

"I heard you went to law school. Are you a lawyer?"

"I work here," I said. "But I'm guessing you already knew that."

Don smiled. "This is a lovely office. You must be doing very well for yourself. I'm proud of you."

I fought to keep my anger in check. "Don't insult my intelligence by pretending you care. Why are you really here, Don? What do you want?"

The sudden cold shift transformed his face from doting

father to hardened professional. I'd seen it happen so many times when I was a kid. I never understood how he could flip that switch so suddenly. Now, I wondered if he was a sociopath. That would explain a lot.

"Your mother took everything from me. I'm trying to get back on my feet, reclaim the things she stole from me. That includes you."

"She didn't steal me."

"She destroyed our relationship."

"What relationship? You pushed me just as hard as she did to perform. I was nothing more than a wind-up toy meant to amuse you."

"It was never about amusing us. You could have been a great ballerina. You had such potential. You trained hard. You were built for it. Even now, you still look like a dancer. You could have done it if you focused, really tried, but you never did. You wasted it. All that time. All that money. My money. Gone."

A contemptuous smile curled my lips. "That's why you're here. You want money. This is nothing more than a shakedown." I sucked in a breath, surprised at how close to the surface the tears were. But I was angrier than anything. "How much do you want? My college tuition? Because I don't have that. But hey, at least now I can stop telling people how you generously paid for school. After all, that was the only nice thing you ever did for me. I wouldn't want anyone to get the wrong idea about you."

"I did plenty for you, but you were always so ungrateful," he spat, forgetting himself. "Those ballet lessons and equipment costs added up, and you walked away from all of it. It's such a shame. You could have been one of the premier ballerinas. By now, you'd be world-renowned. That's what we wanted for you. That's the life we hoped to give you. We wanted the best for you. You would have had nothing if it weren't for my generosity. My love. My devotion."

"You never asked what I wanted. You never cared what I wanted. And you sure as shit never cared about me." I was shaking so hard my teeth chattered. "You made that clear the moment I failed you."

"You never should have failed. You were supposed to be better."

Kellan returned to the room and grabbed my elbow, afraid I'd do something that would land me behind bars. "Alex—"

"How much?" I eked out through clenched teeth. "For the lessons?"

"I have no idea." But the truth flickered behind Don's eyes. "If I had to guess, somewhere in the ballpark of a hundred thousand."

"My savings account won't cover that either, but I'll give you whatever I have so you can be on your way." I pulled out my phone and logged into my bank account. "What's your routing number?"

"Alexis, I'm not here for your money," Don insisted. "I'm here for you."

I slid my phone across the table to him. "Are you sure about that? Because I'm not available, and I never will be. But if it's the money you want, take it."

Don didn't speak. Instead, he eyed my account balance. My savings contained thirty-eight thousand. It was everything I'd held onto from my time at Martin Technologies to my severance from the OIO, to working for Cross Security. I'd been squirrelling away as much as I could to pay Martin back, which I knew he'd never take unless it came in the form of an expensive present, like a watch or car or really nice paperweight.

"You can see how much I have. That's everything. Take it and leave," I said.

"Alex, don't," Kellan hissed, but I waved him off.

"Little swan, why are you always so difficult? I want things to be pleasant between us."

"None of our previous interactions ever were," I said. "Why change now?"

"I gave you a good life," Don insisted. "It's not my fault you squandered it."

Memories of him and my mother telling me I wasn't good enough, that if I had been their real daughter I would have been better, played through my head. Instead, they'd been wrong to pick me. They should have picked someone who was worthy of their generosity and love, that I was selfish and ungrateful and didn't deserve any of the things they did for me. Obviously, his opinion hadn't changed.

Locking my jaw to keep my chin from trembling, I folded my arms over my chest and waited for Don Parker to rip away that last tiny shred of hope that I never realized was there. This was the stupidest game of chicken I'd ever played, and I knew before it even began that I'd lose.

"Forget it. I don't know why I bothered." Don stared into my eyes. "I expected more from you. But you always disappoint. Nothing's changed."

"Great, then stay the hell away from me. I never want to see you again." I stormed out of the room, fighting to hold back the tears.

FOUR

After security escorted Don out of the building, Kellan found me curled in a ball on the couch in my office. "I'm sorry," he said. "I didn't know."

"It doesn't matter."

"Get up. We're going out for drinks. And we're not stopping until we hit the bottom on the bottomless rum punch pitcher."

"There is no bottom," I said.

"That's the point."

After what just happened, I didn't have an ounce of argument left in my body. So I went with Kellan to the Mexican restaurant not far from our office building. Once we were situated at a table, Kellan ordered the bottomless pitcher and appetizers. Then we sat in silence for the next twenty minutes drinking.

Kellan poured more rum punch into my glass. "I know you said you don't want to talk about it, but at least tell me you were never actually going to give him the money."

"I don't know. I just wanted him gone. I still think he would have taken it if there had been more in my account." I sipped the pineapple concoction and reached for a tortilla chip.

"You wanted what he said to be true. You were hoping he had turned over a new leaf and wanted to start fresh."

"What I want has never mattered to him." I turned my head and stared across the room, angry with myself. "I should have known nothing had changed. I guess he was right about that."

"I told you the bastard was a con artist. He tried to extort you."

I drank more punch, wondering how much I'd have to drink before I stopped caring about this. I didn't think there was enough rum in the world. "I don't see why this bothers me. Nothing's changed. Maybe I should get checked for brain injuries. That bastard at the coffee shop hit me pretty hard."

"It's not your fault. Some things we can't get over. We always hold out hope that things will be different."

"Hope is a four-letter word. I know better. That smack to the face I took earlier today must have knocked my common sense loose. Why am I so surprised by this? I knew he'd do it. I knew the second he started talking about the divorce that all he wanted was money."

"Maybe not."

"You didn't see his face. He's trying to hide it, but that's what he wants. And I didn't have enough, so as usual, I disappointed him. He must regret making the trip here."

"I'm sorry. I never meant for you to get crushed."

"I shouldn't be. Don's been out of my life for almost fifteen years."

"It doesn't matter how long it's been. He's still your dad."

"No, he's not."

Kellan tried another approach. "I didn't know you were adopted."

"Neither did I until I failed to make the cut for some prestigious ballet school. That's when Don and Lydia dropped the bomb on me, saying I would have done better, been better, if I was really their child."

Kellan poured more punch into my glass. "I should have asked them to bring a long straw instead." He gestured for the waiter. "Did you even want to do ballet?"

"No."

"Then you shouldn't have to pay for that. You shouldn't have to pay for any of it. Don and his wife decided to be parents. The unrealistic expectations and financial responsibility rests on them, not you."

"They didn't exactly get the kid they wanted."

"No one does. Ask my father. He was in denial for years after I came out, and I have half his DNA."

"I'm sorry." I crunched on a chip and reached for the file Cross Security had compiled on Don Parker. I'd already skimmed it twice since we arrived at the restaurant. Don's finances had been turned upside-down since before the divorce, but they got worse afterward. The paperwork had been finalized four months ago. Don must have been looking for an easy payday. That had to be what made him come here. Too bad I wasn't rich and famous, like he wanted.

Lydia Parker, my adoptive mother, had gotten the house and car when they split. More than likely, he blamed me for the dissolution of their marriage and wanted to get payback. After all, they wanted a prima ballerina, and when I wasn't good enough, things had gotten rocky between them. Apparently, they never got over that rough patch. They should have tried counseling or called it quits a decade ago. I had no idea why it took them so long to realize they despised each other. Maybe they'd been too busy despising me to notice.

"I never should have let you go in there. You didn't need to confront him." Kellan played with the napkin. "I didn't think he was actually your father, Alexis. That's why I wanted you to get a peek at the guy before you went in there, but he closed the blinds." He drained his glass and poured another.

"He knew I'd run for the hills if I saw him coming. He's pathological."

"Clearly."

"Yeah." I rubbed my eyes, which reminded me my face hurt.

"At least we know he won't be showing up at the office again. Building security will make sure of that, and they'll be happy to escort you to your car when you leave every day, just to be on the safe side."

"He's not dangerous. But I don't want to see him ever again. I'd gotten used to the status quo. Things were good.

I want to go back to that. I'd like to pretend he doesn't exist and what he said doesn't matter."

"It doesn't," Kellan said.

"You're right."

The waiter placed a tray of nachos fajitas in front of me. I couldn't tell if I was hungry or nauseous. In fact, I couldn't feel much of anything. So I rubbed my cheek again, relieved when it stung. At least that was something.

The waiter rested his hand on Kellan's shoulder. "Is everything okay?"

Kellan sighed. "Work was rough today, but the food looks great. And the punch is perfect. Do you want another pitcher, Alex?"

"Not unless it'll make today disappear."

The waiter peered into the half-empty pitcher. "Maybe if I fill it up with straight rum."

"Go for it." I choked down a few bites of our appetizer to soak up some of the booze since my head was spinning.

When the check came, Kellan paid. "I can update Lucien on the situation, if you don't want to deal with it tonight."

"Thanks."

"Yeah." Kellan walked me back to the office. "Is that handsome fiancé of yours picking you up?"

"His driver is." I had texted Marcal after we finished the pitcher of rum punch and I realized driving home was out of the question. The familiar town car pulled to a stop out front a few seconds later. "Speak of the devil."

"Hey," Kellan called, causing me to turn at the door, "are you okay?"

"We'll see."

Marcal opened the back door for me. "Should I even ask?"

"Probably not," I said.

He got behind the wheel, eyeing me through the rearview. "Mr. Martin wasn't planning on leaving work for a while. He said he'd let me know when I should pick him up. But, if you'd like, I can take you to the MT building. He won't mind a surprise visit."

"I'd prefer that Martin doesn't see me like this."

"As you wish." We were halfway home when Marcal

spoke again. "When I stocked the freezer after my last shopping trip, I moved the ice packs to the door. I believe they are still there."

"Does my eye look that bad?" I'd been pressing on my cheek throughout dinner as a way to ground myself.

"No, but Mr. Martin will be concerned. I can stop at the drug store if you need to pick up some concealer or foundation."

"I have it covered."

"Literally and figuratively?"

I cracked a smile, and Marcal nodded at me through the mirror.

"I'm here if you need anything," he said.

When he pulled to a stop in front of our apartment building, I opened the door before he could fight with the doorman over who should have the privilege of helping me out of the car. I wasn't drunk enough to need that kind of assistance. "Text me when you drop Martin off, so I'll be ready."

"He won't like that," Marcal said.

"He doesn't need to know."

By the time I made it upstairs, reality hit hard, making me feel as if I were stone-cold sober. After pouring myself a glass of coconut water and grabbing the ice pack from the freezer, I paced the length of our apartment. There wasn't much to it. Kitchen, dining area, living room. Repeat. I thought about going out on the balcony, but I never liked it out there. Too high up and too many pigeons. The only reason I'd go out there was to jump, and I had no desire to give Don that kind of satisfaction.

I thought about running the stairs in the building, but the up and down would make me dizzy. More than anything, I wished we were spending the night at the estate instead of the apartment. Then I'd have the treadmill and boxing equipment in Martin's home gym to work through some of these feelings. Maybe I could get a day pass to one of those twenty-four hour gyms.

My phone chimed while I was browsing for the closest one, and I read the message. Martin was on his way up. It wasn't midnight. It wasn't even close.

Tossing the ice pack back into the freezer, I went to the sink to wash my glass and whatever dishes I could find. When Martin came inside, I was emptying the dishwasher.

"Alexis?" He put his briefcase down on one of the stools, shedding his jacket, and working to loosen his tie, which he normally had off by the time he got home. "Are you okay?"

"Marcal ratted me out, didn't he?"

"I sign his paychecks." He left his tie on the counter and tugged open the first two buttons on his shirt, leaving his vest fastened. "Tell me what's going on."

After wiping my hands on a towel, I turned to find him behind me. His fingertips brushed against my upper arms. "Don paid me a visit."

He zeroed in on my bruised cheek, gently brushing his thumb against it. "Who's Don? Did he do this?"

"No. His sucker punch didn't leave a visible mark, but it hurts a hell of a lot worse." I sucked in my bottom lip while I collected my scrambled thoughts.

"How did this happen?" Martin asked, sensing that was a safer question.

"Heathcliff and I stopped an almost robbery-in-progress." I smiled. "At least I know I'm good at something."

"Sweetheart," he lifted me onto the counter and closed the space between us, "talk to me. Who's Don?"

"Mark didn't tell you? I figured when he spilled the beans about my history, he would have mentioned the names of my adoptive parents." I swallowed, finding the tumbleweed had returned. "Don's my adoptive father."

Martin pressed his lips to my forehead and wrapped his arms around me. "What does he want?"

"Money, I think. I'm not sure. I offered him my savings, but he didn't take it. I don't know what he wanted besides a chance to ruin my day."

"What? Why?" He tensed, giving me a squeeze before easing back to look me in the eye.

"He said he wanted to reconnect, but it sounded more like he decided I owed him." I pressed my palms against Martin's chest, feeling his heart beating faster than it should. "You didn't need to come home. I'm fine."

"You're not. How could you be?"

"It doesn't matter. I don't want to talk about it. I don't want to think about it. I just want it to go away. Maybe when I wake up, I'll find out this was a bad dream."

Martin kissed me. "I love you," he stared into my eyes, "fully, fiercely, and completely. You are incredible."

"Are you hoping to get lucky? Nightmares usually don't turn into sex dreams for me, but there's a first time for everything. I'm game, if you are."

He didn't smile or laugh. His expression remained as serious as I'd ever seen. "You are everything to me."

His sincerity would break me, if I wasn't careful. "Can I ask you one favor?"

"Anything, gorgeous."

"Tell Jen the symphony was sold out."

FIVE

The only thing that got me out of bed the next morning was my promise to Bruiser. Ever since the accident, I'd stop by his place before work, bring him lunch and some form of entertainment, and see how he was doing. That's why I hadn't been showing up at the office particularly early and why Heathcliff and I met for breakfast at noon. My obligation to Bruiser trumped everything else, including my desire to wallow in self-pity.

"Parker." Bruiser put the crossword puzzle down and eyed me. "Damn, first you replaced me as Martin's bodyguard, and now you're trying to steal my nickname too."

"Correction, you replaced me as Martin's bodyguard. And this," I pointed to the now much darker blackish bruise beneath my eye, "is why it isn't safe for me to leave the house." I put the takeout bag on the table beside him, along with my personal stack of puzzle books, and picked up the thick variety puzzle book I'd brought over yesterday and flipped through it. "Seriously, why do you always start with the number puzzles? They're torture."

"They're my favorite."

"Why?" I sat down across from him, glancing at the chart. He had physical therapy at two.

Given how severe his injuries were, Bruiser was making good progress. It wouldn't be long before he made a complete recovery. His cognitive impairments had made leaps and bounds. His speech had improved. He hadn't slurred his words in weeks, and he had regained full vision in his right eye. His bones were still healing, which made walking difficult since both legs had been compromised, along with his pelvis and back. But he had feeling in his legs, so it was just a matter of time before everything sorted itself out.

"It makes sense. It all adds up," he said.

"That's the problem. Each damn line has to add to whatever number, horizontally and vertically. I can do that, but I can never figure out the order so the other lines have the right number."

He laughed. "That's what makes it fun."

"Since you think so, I brought you all my old books since none of the number puzzles have been filled in. I have enough trouble getting my checkbook to balance."

"Next, you're going to bring me that."

"I might." I stared at the massive big screen Martin had bought him which had a nature documentary about lions playing in the background. "If I ever have the urge to go on a safari, this would suffice."

Bruiser hit mute. "You don't have to keep checking on me, Parker. I have enough people doing that already."

"By letting me hang out for a while, you're doing me a favor," I said. "But I'll stop if I'm bothering you."

"You're not." He nodded at my bruised cheek. "Let me guess, you were hoping we could go a few rounds since you're in need of a sparring partner."

"I am, but my ego wouldn't be able to handle you kicking my ass in your current state."

"We both know that wouldn't be much of a fight now that I'm a cripple."

"You aren't. You're going to be fine."

Bruiser's expression soured. "I don't know when I'll be able to come back to work. I can't even walk on my own yet."

"Martin said to take as long as you need."

"He also said if I wanted to resign, he'd understand."

"You know his track record with bodyguards. It's lucky either of us survived. I quit. You can too, if you want. But you don't have to. It's your decision. He loves you. He wants you to do what's best for you. You know that."

"I don't like him waiting for me. I told him to hire someone else. But he won't."

Martin and I had gone a few rounds over that subject. I understood why my beloved didn't want to hire anyone else, but I worried about him. However, until he hired me, he never had a bodyguard, and now that we were home, he didn't think he needed one, unless Bruiser came back to work.

"Martin's stubborn," I said. "And he's scared what will happen to the next person he hires."

"I should have done better."

"It was a car accident. Martin was driving, not you. There was nothing you could have done."

"Still." Bruiser shook his head a few times and exhaled. "I know you, Parker. My guess, you've been filling in for me in the interim. Is that how you got the black eye?"

"No."

He studied me more closely than his number puzzles. "Something's up. What's going on?"

"Nothing for you to worry about." I gestured at my face. "Are you sure you don't want to go a few rounds? After all, you are Bruiser. I'm just bruised."

"Is that your way of saying my nickname is safe?"

"It is for as long as you want it."

"Good."

I met his eyes. "Does that mean you want to continue as Martin's bodyguard?"

"As long as he'll have me."

"Even though I've put you through hell?"

"You're not that bad." He winced as he stretched his legs. "But that's only if I can walk again."

"You'll get there." Noticing the time, I climbed off the couch. "What can I bring you tomorrow for lunch?"

"There are apps for that."

"And deprive you of my company?" I grinned at him. "Never."

"Fine." He opened the takeout bag I'd dropped on the tray table beside him. It contained a grilled chicken sandwich, a baked potato, a garden salad, and a fruit cup. "Falafel and a salad." Bruiser jerked his chin at the stack of books and movies piled on the coffee table. "I finished those, but I wouldn't mind a few more of those spy novels, if you're offering."

"You got it."

I was almost to the door when he called out, "Hey, Parker, be careful. Whenever you look like this, trouble isn't far behind. Keep an eye out. Both eyes. And tell Martin he doesn't need to stop by every morning for breakfast. I can fend for myself. Cereal's easy enough."

"Did he make you oatmeal again? I told you to hold out for pancakes or French toast."

"I like oatmeal," Bruiser said.

I shook my head. "Just like those damn number puzzles. Unnecessary torture." I opened the door. "Remember, if you need anything else, let me know. And unlike Marcal, I won't rat you out to Martin."

"The eye?" Bruiser asked.

"Of course."

He chuckled. "Figures. You should have seen that one coming."

I should have seen a lot of things coming. Yesterday started on a high-note when I spotted the would-be robber outside the coffee shop, but it all went downhill once we discovered he had an accomplice. And the hits just kept on. Today had to be different. I had to be more vigilant.

Already on edge, I kept my head on a swivel as I approached the office building which housed Cross Security. Luckily, Don Parker wasn't camped out in the garage or waiting inside the elevator for me. Kellan said building security would make sure he didn't return, but that didn't make me any less jittery.

When I found my office door open, I hesitated before entering. Lucien Cross was seated on the couch with a stack of files on the glass coffee table in front of him. "You're in the wrong office," I said. "Yours is upstairs. It has a window with a view."

"You're mad." He turned to look at me, his head cocking to the side at the sight of my black eye. "Did he do that?"

"No."

"If your father is anything like mine, I apologize for allowing him into the building. But you never warned me. You should have."

"I didn't know I had to. I never expected to see him again." I put my things down. "I'd prefer if we don't discuss this. It's over."

"I've never seen family matters resolve that easily."

I reached for the top file. "What is this?"

"A case. If you'd attended the morning briefing, you'd be up to speed."

"I have other obligations."

Cross scowled but kept the commentary to himself. "The law firm, Reeves, Almeada, and Stockton, needs us to do some digging. They have a client who may be heading to trial. They'd prefer to avoid that if possible, so they need to know how solid the prosecution's case is. They need you to see what evidence the police have and how reliable witnesses are. Since your friends bleed blue, I thought this would be easy for you."

"What's the crime?"

"Hit and run."

I flipped through the police report. The victim, a seventeen-year-old, had been struck by a vehicle and left to die. Surveillance footage had clear shots of the driver, Teddy Gibbs, and his vehicle, a classic American muscle car. When police arrived at Gibbs' home, they found blood and hair in the grill of the car and dents consistent with the hit and run. They arrested him on the spot for vehicular manslaughter.

"This looks open and shut to me. What does Almeada hope we'll find?"

"A defect with the vehicle, another driver, a traffic light malfunction, that the victim had suicidal tendencies, that the police conducted an illegal search, that the witnesses were drunk, that there was an issue with the surveillance footage, things like that." Cross eyed me. "Almeada is a defense attorney. His job is to pick apart the prosecution's case, starting with the police department's investigation. Is that going to be a problem for you?"

I didn't like it, but that's how the legal system worked. "No, but I don't think there's anything to find."

"Then look harder." Cross indicated the files beneath. "Mr. Gibbs had work done on his car, automating and computerizing a lot of the systems and bringing them into the current age. He even had driver-assist software installed. Read his statements. He said he didn't have control, the brakes wouldn't respond, and the wheel had locked. I have several calls into experts, mechanics, and engineers to see if this has happened before. As soon as the information comes in, I will have the research forwarded to you."

I skimmed the accident report. "They didn't find anything wrong with the car. In fact, the car was parked at Gibbs' house hours later. It wasn't anywhere near the crime scene. Gibbs didn't call 9-1-1 or report an accident. I'm guessing he didn't call his mechanic either." I narrowed my eyes. "The only call he made after it happened was to Almeada."

"Parker, we don't pass judgment. We do our jobs and remain unbiased. I thought you'd like something to get your mind off other things, but if you'd rather deal with your family drama, by all means."

"I told you that's over."

"We both know it isn't." He gave me a hard stare when I didn't cave. "Fine. But if you find this is beyond your capabilities, I can reassign the case."

"I'll take it. But I want you to look me in the eye and tell me you didn't know Don Parker came here because he was looking for me."

"I didn't. He was a walk-in."

"Okay." I reached for the police report, looking to see who caught the hit and run. It belonged to Detective Alloway. I'd never met the detective, so I'd need an introduction. I sunk into the chair and grabbed a pad, jotting down notes while I skimmed the police report.

Cross cleared his throat. "Alex?"

I looked up, surprised to find him squirming, all his anxious tics on display. "What?"

He considered what to say. "Make sure you cover up

that eye before you go anywhere. I don't want people to get the wrong idea about Cross Security."

"Whatever you say, boss."

Once he left, I put the notepad down. Concentrating shouldn't be this hard, but I had too many unanswered questions concerning Don's appearance. Cross was right. Family issues never resolved that easily.

Don didn't live in the city, which made me wonder how he tracked me down. How long had he been looking? If he'd shown up a month earlier, I wouldn't have been here. Was he waiting for me to return?

"This doesn't matter," I mumbled, but until I had answers, I wouldn't be able to work on Almeada's case. And I'd be damned if I called to ask Don what was going on until I'd done my own research. I didn't trust him, and I wanted to be prepared for our next encounter, if there was a next encounter.

Kellan had told me everything he could the night before, which had been limited. The two-page client information form Cross Security had put together didn't include much of anything. Don's current address was listed as the house where I'd grown up, but that belonged to Lydia now. And I didn't think she'd let him sleep in the guest room.

If I'd been older when her dreams for my life as a ballerina came crashing to a halt, she would have thrown me out on my ass. But since I was just a kid, barely even a teenager, she'd been stuck with me for a few more years. She wasn't stuck with Don anymore.

Instead, I ran every background and social media check I could think of on the two of them. Besides the divorce, the only other red flag I found were constant withdrawals from Don's account. He'd been hemorrhaging money for almost a year prior to the divorce. At first, the withdrawals were small, a few hundred every couple of weeks. But then it turned into thousands. And then it became more frequent. He'd been careful to keep everything under the ten thousand dollar mark to avoid scrutiny, but I knew that trick. Was he gambling?

Curious, I called the accounting firm where he worked as a CPA. He hadn't been fired. There hadn't been any complaints. And with tax season around the corner, Don had taken this as his last chance to get out of the office before things got crazy.

"Is Mr. Parker on vacation?" I asked.

"He's taking some time," the woman in HR said.

"What does that mean?"

"Just what I said. He's taking time."

"Is this about his divorce?" I asked. "Or his daughter?"

"Daughter?" Her tone told me she had no idea he had a kid, which was fine by me. "I don't know. What did you say this was about?"

"Routine background check." I hung up once I was sure this wouldn't lead to anything. But there was one other place I could go for answers.

SIX

"Where's Mark Jablonsky?" I asked.

Agent Eddie Lucca peered up at me from his desk. "Hi, Eddie. It's nice to see you. I meant to call when I got back from California, but things have been crazy. How are you?"

"Lucca, I don't have time for this. Where's Jablonsky?" I repeated, pointing to Mark's empty office. "I need to speak to him."

"Did you try his cell?"

"This isn't the kind of conversation I can have over the phone."

Lucca rolled his chair backward, crossing his arms over his chest. "You've got my attention." He glanced around and lowered his voice. "Is this about you going to work for the DEA?"

"I am not working for the DEA."

"That's not what I heard."

"That's over. And I wasn't really working for them. It was complicated." I gave Mark's empty office one last look before perching on the edge of Lucca's desk, knowing what I had to do to get my old partner to cooperate. "Hi, Eddie. How are you?"

He grinned. "Great. Thanks for asking. What brings you by?"

"I need to talk to Mark."

"Jablonsky's in D.C., dealing with the fallout of whatever happened in San Diego. He should be back in a couple of days."

"Dammit. I don't want to wait a couple of days."

Lucca centered his keyboard on his desk. "Is there something I can do?"

"I need some information, but I'll wait for Mark. The last thing I want is you quoting the rulebook to me."

He clicked the mouse a few times, bringing up the search box. "What kind of information?"

"Someone's been hell-bent on finding me. I'm trying to find out why."

"You pissed someone off again?"

I shook my head. "This is personal."

"So was last time."

"No. Not like that. The guy's a CPA. It looks like he's been having money problems for a while."

Lucca sighed dramatically. "Did your accountant embezzle from you or your rich boyfriend?"

"This reads more like a gambling problem, but it could be something else. Though, I'm not sure what would require so many cash withdrawals."

"Sex addiction. Drugs."

"Possibly." Neither had been cited in the divorce proceedings, but that didn't mean anything. "He doesn't have a criminal record. He strikes me more as a white collar criminal, anyway, if he were to turn to a life of crime. After all, he tried to extort me yesterday." At least, that was Kellan's conclusion.

Lucca froze. "Name."

"Landon 'Don' Parker."

"Parker, as in..."

"As in I wanted to have this conversation with Mark instead."

Lucca hit enter and waited for the results to populate. "Nothing's coming up. He's not a person of interest in any federal investigations." Curious, Lucca conducted another search, against regulations, bringing up Don's information. I read over his shoulder, but the details listed were the same as what I had. "What did he want from you?"

"I'm not entirely sure. Money, maybe."

"Maybe? You said he tried to extort you."

"Extort might be too strong of a word, but he showed up out of the blue, claiming to be looking for his missing kid. Then he implies that I owe him somewhere in the ballpark of a hundred large plus my college tuition. I offered him my savings to see what he'd do, but he didn't take it. He said he expected more from me. I bet if I had every dime he gave me for my college tuition and those damn ballet classes he would have taken it in a heartbeat."

"Does he know about James Martin?"

"I don't know."

"If he does, that might explain why he's looking for a handout. A former OIO agent turned private eye doesn't usually scream out money, unless he's aware of Cross Security's reputation, and if he's done that much homework, he'd have to know you haven't been working there long enough to have substantial savings." Lucca reached for his phone. "Hang on a second."

After checking to see if anyone had called looking for me, he put the phone down. We'd gone through this dance routine once before. But Lucca wanted to make sure we weren't missing anything.

"Thanks for trying, Eddie. I'm gonna get out of here and let you get back to work."

"Are you okay?"

I stared at the wall, seeing the gold letters hanging for the Office of International Operations. "Yeah."

"Really?"

"Uh-huh, just tell Jablonsky to get in touch when he gets back from his trip. And don't mention this to him or anyone."

"Why not?"

"It's personal. I'll fill Mark in myself."

"You got it. But now you owe me, Parker."

"Don't I always?"

I had just gotten into my car when another idea struck me, so I called the office. Don had provided his phone number, so there'd be no harm in pulling his phone records and seeing to whom he'd been speaking. When I passed the request on, I was surprised to find the records had already been pulled.

"Mr. Cross asked us to get that together last night," the tech said.

"Send me a copy." I stared out the windshield, watching traffic creep past the federal building. "Did Cross ask you to get any other information pertaining to that particular client?"

"No, Ms. Parker."

"What about additional information pertaining to me?"

"You?"

"Yes. Did Cross ask you to pull any information on my background?"

"Not since you were hired."

"Thanks." I hung up, unsure if I believed the tech. After all, Cross signed her paycheck, and money talked. I'd learned that lesson the hard way from Marcal yesterday evening.

When I got back to the office, I found the phone records waiting in my inbox. I didn't recognize any of the numbers. Despite being raised by the Parkers, I didn't know anything about Don Parker or his life.

It didn't take long to run through his phone records for the last year. Work, his attorney, Lydia, and several other innocuous numbers filled the pages. However, one number stuck out. Ace Investigators.

They were a local private eye firm. Theoretically, they were our competition, but they were small potatoes. Two guys ran the place.

"Hey, Kellan." I leaned against the doorjamb to his office. "You said another private investigator firm passed Don off to us. Was it Ace?"

"Uh-huh." He frowned. "I thought you washed your hands of this."

"I need to know what he wants."

"Didn't you say it was money?"

"I have to be sure. I don't like it when people come looking for me. I've had way too much of that happen lately."

"Alex, I don't think—" Kellan clamped his mouth shut when he saw the look on my face. "Yeah, all right. What do you want me to do? I can come with you."

"No. I should handle this myself. But Cross gave me a case. It's for Almeada. Do you mind putting together some background for me? I'll take whatever shit assignment you don't want to make up for it."

"You got yourself a deal."

* * *

"Can I help you?" Ace Darrow wiped the crumbs off his Hawaiian shirt and put the bag of chips down on his desk. He wiped his hand on his cargo shorts, leaving a greasy stain behind.

Turning on the charm, I tucked my hair behind my ear and sat down in the plastic lawn chair situated in front of his desk. Obviously, he didn't waste a ton on the overhead. "I sure hope so. I was told you were the man to see."

"What can I do for you, darlin'?"

"Don Parker," I said, "do you know him?"

"Can't say that I do." He reached for a toothpick and worked to get something out from between his two front teeth. "But I'm sure I can track him down for you."

"Oh yeah?" I held the hopeful smile. "That's pretty damn impressive."

"Ace Investigators can do all sorts of things." He put the toothpick down and grinned at me. "But it'll cost ya. I got a two-fifty per diem plus expenses."

"Two hundred and fifty dollars?"

"You want this guy found, right?"

"How long do you think it'll take you to track him down?"

He rocked a little in his chair. "That really depends. A common name like that, we could be looking at thousands of possibilities. I'd have to narrow it down by other things. It'll depend on how much you can tell me about him. Why are you looking for him, anyway? Does he owe you money or something?"

"Something."

Ace squinted, suspecting I said something clever but not quite sure what it was. "Something?"

"Uh-huh." I unfolded the copy of Don's phone records

and placed them in front of Ace. “That highlighted number, that’s you, right?”

Ace leaned forward, reading the number. “Huh? What do you know?” He looked back at me. “Are you his wife or something?”

“Something.”

“Again with the something.” He shook his head. “What do you want, lady? I got things to do here.”

“Those chips won’t eat themselves.”

“Damn straight.”

“How about we make this simple?” I pulled out my business card and put it down beside the copy of Don’s phone records. “It’s my understanding you referred Don to Cross Security. I want to know why. What did he hire you for?”

“I didn’t refer him. You’re in the business. You know what it’s like. Our clients never listen. I told him the person he was looking for worked at Cross Security.” His eyes moved back and forth as he read my name on the business card. “He was looking for you. Did he find you?”

“Why was he looking for me?”

“That’s confidential. But for you to be here, he must have found you. Why don’t you ask him what he wanted?”

“Because I’m asking you.” I glanced around the office. “How much did he pay you?”

“Two-fifty a day, plus expenses.”

“What was the total?”

“Two grand.”

“What did you tell him about me?”

“That’s confidential.”

“Not when it’s about me,” I said. “Did you ever think maybe I’m here to fact-check you?”

He snorted. “Five grand.”

“What?”

“I’ll tell you what I told him, but I want five grand.”

“He paid you two.”

“Yeah, well, Cross Security can afford it.”

“Twice in two days. Jeez. Enough with the shakedowns.” I shook my head and reached for my purse. “Do you take checks?”

"Cash and money transfers only."

The bell above the door chimed, and Lucien Cross stepped inside, not surprised to find me. I'd forgotten how much he liked to track the company car and keep tabs on me. "Ace," he said.

"Lucien, to what do I owe this displeasure?" Ace folded the chip bag and used a paperclip to close it.

Cross turned his attention to me. "Did you pay this asshole?"

"Not yet."

"Good, because he owes us a favor. And I'm here to collect." Cross flipped the open sign to closed on the front door and pulled down the shades. "I see not much has changed." My boss eyed the plastic lawn chair with disgust before taking a seat beside me. "Weren't you wearing that same shirt the last time I saw you, Ace?"

"It's my favorite. It makes me look like Magnum." Ace pushed my business card away. "Women love it."

"No one loves it," Cross said.

"Lucien, I'm in the middle of something," I hissed.

My boss gestured that I should go ahead. "I'm a silent observer."

I gave him an uneasy look and turned my focus back to Ace, who was sitting up straighter and sucking in his stomach as he attempted to imitate Cross's expression and mannerisms. "You were about to tell me what Don Parker wanted."

"He wanted to find you," Ace said, suddenly all business.

"Why?" We'd already gone over this.

Ace shrugged, his belly expanding with the motion. "It's not my job to ask. I only do what my clients want. And Don Parker wanted to find you."

"What else did you tell him about me?" Now that Cross was here, Ace may be more forthcoming, though I wasn't entirely sure why.

Ace shrugged, rubbing his palm roughly against his nose and sniffing as he fought back an itch. "The basics."

"Like?"

"Where you work. What you drive. Where you live."

"Where I live?"

"It's public record, cupcake," Ace said. "Property records are available to everyone."

Cross got up and went to Ace's filing cabinet.

"Hey," Ace protested, but one look from Cross shut him up. "Yeah, the apartment you bought. That's where you live, isn't it? That's the only property record I could find on you. Before that, you had a lease agreement, but the building burned down." He looked from me to Cross. "Was that a hazard of the job?"

"It'd be a shame if your office met the same fate," Cross muttered, thumbing through the stained and yellowing files in the cabinet.

"Hey, I'm telling you what you want. You can't threaten me like that." Ace glared at Cross's back.

"It's not a threat." Cross closed the drawer and opened the next one.

"What else did you tell Don?" I asked while I kept an eye on my boss as he searched for the relevant files.

"I think that was it. He just wanted to get in touch. He said you were estranged." Ace scrunched his face together. "I'm not really seeing the resemblance."

"Did he say anything more than that?"

"Nope." Ace picked up the used toothpick and went to work on his back teeth. "Again, that's not my business. I didn't ask. He didn't tell."

Cross pulled a file out and handed it to me. Then he yanked Ace's chair backward, nearly dumping the private eye onto the floor in the process. Cross plugged a USB drive into the side of the computer and clicked a few keys.

While Cross did whatever he was doing, I skimmed the pages. It didn't look like Ace had dug much deeper than a public records and internet search, but I still didn't like it.

"What about my phone number?" I asked.

Ace shook his head. "All I gave him was your work number. I don't want to make it too easy for my clients. Then they wouldn't need me."

"Lovely." Though, in this case, I didn't mind.

"Get away from that." Ace slapped at Cross's hands. "You're going to mess everything up."

"If you'd prefer, I'll take your hard drive with me," my boss replied.

"You can't. That would be stealing. I'll call the cops."

"Go ahead. I'm sure they'd love to hear why all these amateur adult films are on your computer."

"My clients hired me to find out if their significant others were cheating," Ace insisted.

"I wouldn't imagine these dated videos are still relevant." Cross clicked a few more keys. "Oops."

Ace shoved him aside. "What did you do?"

"I may have accidentally set your hard drive to reformat. You might want to do something about that." Cross tucked the USB into his pocket. "Ms. Parker, if there's nothing else, we should get going."

"One last question," I said. "Where's Don Parker staying while he's in town?"

SEVEN

I watched the hotel from my car, drumming my fingers against the steering wheel. It wasn't one of the nicest places, but it was decent for a chain. They had a business center in the lobby with workspaces that could be rented for the day or were complimentary for the guests to use. They also had free coffee and juice and continental breakfast every morning. The one thing they didn't offer was a clear view into Don Parker's room.

Cross returned from the lobby with a paper cup in each hand. He took his time getting into my car, placing one cup on the roof while he opened the door. Once he was settled, he gave the hotel entrance another look, but no one cared we were parked in the check-in area.

"Don's staying in room 213." Cross took a sip, making a face. "You don't want to drink that."

"When did he check in?"

"Four days ago."

"How long is he staying?"

"I have no idea. He didn't make reservations. He just showed up and paid cash for the room. That's why I didn't see any record of it in his recent transactions."

"I thought you had to use a credit card at reputable establishments."

"They have it on file, but they won't run it unless he incurs additional charges," Cross said.

"He's hiding. He didn't want me to know he was here."

"Maybe."

I pulled out the file Ace Investigators had put together for their client. Most of it was basic information about me. But it contained a few facts on Don. Unfortunately, they weren't nearly as specific with their billing as Cross Security. No dates were listed as to when Don hired them. But he'd paid for the information when he picked it up. Again, in cash.

I checked Don's phone records. He first spoke to the private investigators several weeks ago. Then there was nothing but radio silence until Ace called him back six days ago.

"How did he know I was in the city?" I asked. "When I left home, I never looked back. No birthday cards. No nothing. He and Lydia never tried to contact me when I was in college, even though they knew damn well where I was. After I graduated, I don't see how they would have had any idea where I had gone."

"The FBI must have reached out to them when you applied. They run background checks and conduct interviews on all their candidates." Cross glanced at me. "Don't law schools do that too?"

"No, but the BAR would have. However, I didn't bother taking the exam."

"Do you have the same phone number?"

"No. I didn't even have a phone when I left home. Do you really think my so-called parents would have wanted to spend any more money on me?"

"And you never called them after you got a phone?"

"Why would I?" I shook away the question.

"You had to earn everything yourself. That explains a lot." Cross sipped the coffee again, grimacing. "You really don't want to drink that."

I grabbed the cup away from him and tossed the brown liquid out my window. "Problem solved."

"Correct me if I'm wrong, but when we spoke earlier, you said this was over. I'd like to know what the hell you're doing. Have you already found the silver bullet for Almeada's case?"

"Kellan's working on it." I peered out the rear window

into the lobby. "Did you ask if Don was in his room?"

"I didn't have to. I spotted him at one of the workstations to the left of the doors. He's got a spreadsheet open. From the looks of it, I'd say he's assessing P&Ls. He told the desk clerk he needed access to a fax machine and printer. I'm not sure why, but I wonder if it's so he doesn't create an electronic trail. If he used e-mail or text, I could get a look at it."

"It's probably for work," I said.

"No one faxes anymore, so I doubt it."

"Did he see you?"

"Possibly, but it wouldn't matter. He doesn't know who I am. We've never met."

"He could have looked you up."

"He didn't see me." Cross cleared his throat, anxious to ask a question. "Why do you hate him? Did he do something to you?" A fire burned in Cross's eyes, one that I had rarely seen. "Was he abusive? Assholes like that have a special place in hell."

"He never laid a finger on me. If he had, I would have broken it."

"No doubt. So why the animosity?"

"It's complicated."

"Family dynamics often are." Cross watched as I picked up the cup of coffee he'd gotten for me and took a sip. "How can you drink that?"

"It's not that bad. The stuff at the precinct is worse, and I've ingested gallons of that. At this point, I'm immune. Your espresso maker has spoiled you, Lucien."

We sat in silence for an uncomfortable twenty minutes while I sipped the coffee and stared into the lobby. Eventually, another car pulled up behind me, so I circled around to the reserved spaces and parked next to Cross's car. From here, I had a clear line of sight into the hotel lobby, but I still couldn't see Don.

"Are you sure he's at one of the workstations?" I asked.

"Yes." Cross's voice held an irritated undertone. "I thought you wanted to confront him and find out why he came looking for you."

"He's here for money. That's the only thing that fits. But

when I accused him of that yesterday, he denied it. I hoped to find something that would tell me why he's in desperate need of a cash infusion, but I haven't come up with anything, which is why I don't want to confront him yet. I'd like to know what's going on, and I can't trust a word that comes out of his mouth."

"How long are you planning to sit here?"

"Until I decide what to do."

Cross looked at his watch. "You have another case to work."

"I know." I glared at him. "Fine, you want me to go back to work, I'll go back to work."

"No, Alex. I want you to take care of this. I wanted you to take care of this when I spoke to you this afternoon, but you were in denial. Care to explain why this man has you so freaked out?"

"I'm not freaked out, and I'm definitely not afraid of him."

"You are." The fire returned to his eyes. "I can take care of this."

"I'll do it."

"Then do it." Cross jerked his chin at the door. "We have other things on the agenda. We have actual cases with actual clients who deserve our time and attention. I don't want to turn into some second-rate hack with a Hawaiian shirt and dingy lawn chairs. But that's where this is heading if we waste any more time out here."

"Fine." I pushed open the car door. "But I never asked you to help. I was handling this on my own."

"You weren't. When I arrived, you were about to shell out money to Ace Darrow for pointless intel. According to Kellan, you almost gave your bozo father your entire savings yesterday afternoon. What the hell are you doing, Alex?"

"I'll give that bastard whatever he wants if it'll make him go away."

"Why?"

"Because no matter what shit he's done, I owe him and Lydia. No one else wanted me. No one would have taken care of me. No one gave a damn about me. Look at the statistics. We know what happens to most of the kids who grow up in the system. Sure, the Parkers are shitty people and worse parents. But that's because I disappointed them. I failed to become what they wanted. But without them, who knows where I would have ended up. I wouldn't be here now. I'd probably be dead. So I should just give him the money and hope he walks away. That's the only way I know how to handle this since I can't figure out why he suddenly decided to pay me a visit or why he's so strapped for cash. But if I help him with that, then he'll have no reason to stay. Right?"

"That's a bad idea, Alex."

"What else can I possibly do? He's here for a reason, and no matter what he says, it isn't because he wants to get to know me. It's because he wants something. And we haven't figured out what that something is. But it has to be money. It's the only thing I have or he thinks I have. So I give him my nest egg and hope that ends this."

"What's to keep him from coming back for more?"

"I don't have more."

"Not yet, but what about in six months or a year? What if he wants monthly payments? Are you going to give him that too?" Cross fixed me with a hard stare. "Think about what you're doing."

"I am." But we both knew I wasn't thinking clearly.

"Let me fix this."

"How?"

It was a good question. But Cross didn't have an answer.

I slammed the car door and strode toward the hotel lobby. My breath shallowed, and my heart beat faster. Panicking would get me nowhere. So I decided I didn't care. Don Parker lost the right to call himself my father a long time ago. He couldn't hurt me or disappoint me anymore. I knew his true colors.

Once inside, I spotted him in an oversized office chair, working at what was meant to look like an expensive table but was probably something cheap with a fancy finish. "Don, I have questions that need answers."

He looked up, a surprised smile emerging on his face, but it never reached his eyes. It was an act. Everything about this man was phony. "Little swan, I'm so happy to see you. How did you find me?"

"I'm a private investigator. It's my job."

He gestured to a nearby chair, and I sat on the edge. "I was just getting some work done. Hang on one second." He hit a few more keys on his laptop before shutting the lid. "I'm sorry about yesterday. I wasn't expecting to see you again so soon. I wanted to give you time to cool down. But I planned to call, to see if we could start over."

"I looked into your finances. I know you're broke. For once, be honest with me. Is that why you came here?"

"Not entirely. I mean, yeah, I figured if you could help me out, that'd be great, but that's not why I came all this way. Alexis, I meant what I said. I want to have a relationship with you."

"That's not an option."

"Why not?"

A million words came to mind, but I didn't utter a single one. "Are you in trouble? Do you owe someone money?"

"I owe a lot of people money." He shook it away. "Let's not talk about that now. Let's talk about you. You graduated with honors and went to law school. Why didn't you become a lawyer? How did you get into private security?"

"Who do you owe?"

"Everyone. I have to find a place to live, which means rent and car payments, utilities, credit cards, all of it." But there was more to it.

"I couldn't find an address for you. Where are you living?"

"At the moment, a friend from work is letting me stay at his place. But I can't do that forever." He reached for my hands, and I pulled away. "Tell me about you. I want to know everything. I've missed so much, little swan."

"Stop it," I said.

"Stop what?"

"Pretending you care."

"I do care."

I shook my head, deciding arguing would cause me to remain in his presence even longer. "Why are you working here? Your office said you were taking some time off."

"You spoke to my office?" Anger flashed across his face, but he regained his composure almost instantly. "We had a lull, so I said I wanted to take some time to see you. That doesn't mean I can't finish up a few projects for clients remotely."

"Projects?"

"Tax prep, business planning, portfolio projections." Don cocked an eyebrow at me. "You never cared about my work before."

"I'm trying to get to know you." And figure out why you're here.

He smiled, pleased. "That's precisely why I came. We don't know each other, not as two adults. A lot has changed. You've changed." He waved his hand in my direction, like a magician indicating his lovely assistant before she disappeared inside a box. "I want to know everything about you. Ace Investigators didn't come up with much. Are you married?"

"No."

"No significant other?"

Maybe he did know about Martin. "Who could ever love me?"

His forehead scrunched together. "Don't say that, Alexis. You've always been special."

"That's not what Lydia said. It's not what you said." My chin quivered, and I turned my head to see Cross lingering in the middle of the hotel lobby, his hands tucked in his pockets, his jaw clenched. Even though he was irate, I was glad he was here. Swallowing, I shook my head. "It doesn't matter."

"Clearly, it does." Don reached for my hand again, so I folded my arms over my chest. "That's why you're so angry? You're still upset about the way we told you you were adopted? That was a bad day for all of us. Your mom was so disappointed. We were all disappointed. I guess we could have handled it better. Is that why you pulled away from us?"

"Stop with the revisionist history. I know what happened. I was there. I didn't pull away. The two of you stopped pretending to love me. You stopped pretending to care about me. You treated me like a squatter, who you fed on occasion."

"We paid for your school. We provided everything you needed."

"I'm sure it's on that itemized list of things I owe you."

"Dammit, Alexis."

"If you cared so damn much, why didn't you reach out before now?" I was amazed my voice remained even when I was feeling so unsteady. "What has made you so desperate that you sought me out? You had to know this wouldn't be a pleasant reunion. Tell me what you want, so we can get on with our lives."

He licked his lips, absently running his finger over the insignia on his laptop. "I wanted to see how you were doing."

"I know about the withdrawals. What have you been doing with the money?"

"Why?" A dark wickedness came over him. "Afraid I'm hiding it from Lydia?"

I hadn't considered the possibility, but Cross was thorough when it came to finances. If there was an offshore numbered account, Cross's experts would have found it, or so I liked to believe. "I couldn't care less if you screw her over. But I don't think it's about that."

"What do you think it's about?"

"I think you need money. I just don't know why or how much."

"A lot more than you're offering. Thirty-eight won't get me far." He shook his head. "It's hard to start over. I spent everything I could to keep it away from her. Now I can barely make ends meet. It was stupid. Impetuous. I have nothing left."

"So you came here to collect, just like I said."

"I want more than money, Alexis. I want your forgiveness. I want to play a role in your life from now on." Again, he slipped back into the doting father role. No wonder I had trust issues. This was why so many people in my life thought I needed therapy. After this, I might have to give it another shot. "Let me take you to dinner, and we can talk this out," he said.

"Dinner won't change my bank account. All I have is thirty-eight. If that's all you're after, save us both some time and take it and go."

"I was hoping I could stick around for a while. I can work remotely. It's not like I have a place to live. Maybe I could persuade you to let me stay at your place. The city might have more opportunities for me. What do you say? I took you in when you had nowhere to go. How about returning the favor?"

"I was a baby."

"You became my baby girl."

Again, Don Parker had spun everything around, including my head. I pulled out my checkbook, signed the bottom, and tore off the blank check. "I can't. But take whatever you need. You provided shelter for me. This won't buy you an apartment, but it'll cover your cost of living for a few months. It's the best I can do. I hope this makes us even. Please don't contact me again."

EIGHT

Cross hadn't spoken to me since the hotel incident. I wasn't sure why he was mad. But I didn't have the energy to figure it out. I was knee-deep in the case he had assigned me, which wasn't going anywhere fast. Almeada's client, Teddy Gibbs, was guilty as sin. The seventeen-year-old he killed in that hit and run was a star student. He volunteered at nursing homes and animal shelters. He'd received early acceptance to a prestigious university and was set to receive an academic scholarship. He'd never been in any trouble. His family and friends were devastated.

"The victim might as well have been a saint." Kellan rubbed his eyes and stretched out on the couch in my office, putting his hands behind his head. "No wonder Almeada passed this off to us. He knows he's got a losing case. This is what he does every time. It's his version of a Hail Mary."

"Does it usually work?"

"Rarely."

"He should know we aren't miracle workers," I muttered.

"Except Lucien expects us to be."

"Lucien needs a reality check."

Kellan turned to look at me. "What about the police angle? Did you find anything hinky with the arrest?"

"I've gone over the records, watched the surveillance footage, and checked everything that's been admitted into evidence. It looks solid. I haven't spoken to Detective

Alloway yet, but I did talk to the responding officer and the EMTs. It's clear this was a hit and run. Teddy Gibbs didn't step on the brakes. He plowed into the kid and drove off. He didn't even try to stop."

"Was he drunk?"

"He refused to submit to a blood test. By the time he was compelled to give one, it was hours after the accident. He was no longer drunk. His BAC showed he'd had a drink at some point, but Gibbs said it was after the accident, not before."

"Almeada can use that," Kellan said.

"It's not much. And given how erratic his driving was, I don't think that excuse will sway a jury." I rocked in my chair, reading the reports Cross Security received about the automation and computer systems installed in the vehicle. "Nothing malfunctioned. There have been no reports or instances of software or hardware glitches with this vehicle or any other. The mechanics signed affidavits saying everything is in proper working order, so mechanical failure is not to blame."

"So it was driver error," Kellan said.

"I don't know if Gibbs meant to mow down the kid or if it really was an accident, but he was in control of the car at the time. There's no question about it."

"Have you looked into motive?"

"The DA's going for vehicular manslaughter. They aren't pushing for homicide, so I didn't bother."

"That could change if new evidence comes to light. You should look into it, just to be thorough."

"Don't you think I have enough to do?"

Kellan laughed. "Almeada's going to ask."

"Shouldn't he be investigating this himself?"

"He is, by having you do it for him."

"Maybe I should have become a lawyer instead." Maybe that would have made my father proud.

"You would have been bored to tears." Kellan rolled onto his side and watched me work. "Should I ask how things are going on the other front?"

"Fine."

"Really?"

"I took care of it." The bank had called to verify I'd written a check for thirty-five thousand dollars. Frankly, I was surprised Don left anything in my account. But it was over. We were done. "Which means I have to take care of this." I checked the time. "I have an appointment with Detective Alloway in an hour. I should get going."

Kellan dragged himself off the couch. "Have fun with that."

"Yep."

It didn't take an hour to get to the precinct. It took twenty minutes, which left enough time to pop into the major crimes unit and remind the boys about our poker game tonight.

"What's wrong?" Heathcliff asked.

"Nothing."

He knew better. "Did Franco call you?"

"Franco-American?"

"Wow, that's a dated reference. How old are you?" he asked. "They haven't sold that stuff in decades."

"And yet you still understood."

"Because you made me watch old TV shows with the original commercials." He gave me an exasperated look. "I meant Officer Franco."

"Why would he call?"

"To follow up." Heathcliff lowered his voice, glancing around to make sure we had some privacy. "Hey, what's going on with you?"

"What do you mean?"

"I know you, Parker. Something's wrong."

"I'm digging up dirt on a case for Almeada. It makes me feel icky."

"It should. Almeada's the enemy. He's a defense attorney. We bust our humps to take trash off the streets, and he does everything in his power to toss it back out there."

"Yeah."

Heathcliff narrowed his eyes. "What case? It's not one of mine, is it?"

I shook my head. "Hit and run. Detective Alloway was primary. What can you tell me about him?"

"You won't find anything. Alloway's always by the book."

"That's what the case file suggested, but I thought I'd talk to him anyway."

"Go easy. Most cops around here don't take kindly to private eyes, and he doesn't know you or the things you've done for the department."

"My reputation doesn't precede me?" I batted my eyelashes at him. "Could I convince you to talk me up a little and ask him to play nice?"

"On one condition."

"You want me to help you cheat at poker?"

"No, Parker. I don't need help winning. I know all your tells, which is why I know something else is bothering you. I can see that storm cloud hanging over your head, and it's not about your job with Almeada. Spill."

"I don't want to get into it."

He eased back, giving me some space. "When's the last time we went to a grief counseling meeting?"

"Are you trying to kill me? I already had my spirit crushed and stomped on twice this week. I can't take any more hits right now. And I already said I don't want to talk about it."

"All right, but know that I'm here."

"Thanks." I looked around, finding O'Connell's and Thompson's desks empty. "Why'd you think Officer Franco called to follow up? Did something happen? Did you ever identify Wayne Savage's accomplice in the attempted robbery?"

"No breaks yet. Savage won't give up his buddy. He claimed he panicked when he realized I was a cop, and that's why he grabbed the tip jar and ran. He said he was working alone, but no one buys it."

"It doesn't explain why he shot at us."

"He doesn't like cops." Heathcliff shrugged. "Since that morning, there have been two other armed robberies in broad daylight. One was at a grocery store. The other at a gentlemen's club."

"They robbed a strip club in broad daylight? Who was even there?"

"The place was packed. They have a lunch buffet."

"Seriously?"

"They have really good buffalo wings, or so I hear."

"You heard they have good wings?" I gave him a look. "Puh-lease."

"I may have been there once or twice. Rossdale had his second bachelor party there. The appetizers stand out."

"Let me guess, besides wings they also had thighs and breasts on the menu."

Heathcliff resisted the urge to smile. "I can't recall."

"Bullshit."

He led me to the double doors. "Come on, I'll take you to meet Alloway. You can bust his chops for a while."

After convincing Detective Alloway to go over the arrest and the case he built against Teddy Gibbs, I thanked him for his time, warned him Almeada would have a trick or two up his sleeve, and left the precinct. It was still early. The guys weren't supposed to show up at my apartment until eight. Even though Martin said he'd try to make it, I knew he wouldn't be there. Jen, O'Connell's wife, agreed to sit in since we were short a player. But I doubted an ER nurse would get out of work on time either, so there was a good chance it'd just be the four of us.

I was almost to my car when someone called out, "Hey."

Turning, I spotted Officer Franco jogging toward me. The door to the precinct swung closed behind him. I waved, reversing course and heading for him. He came to a stop in front of me, a little out of breath. He put his hands on his thighs and sucked in some air.

"Man, I need to get back to the gym. You're fast on the stairs." He looked around, but no one was nearby. He appeared much friendlier and more relaxed than during our previous encounter. Maybe he was hoping to score an invite to the poker game. "I've never been good with stairs."

"Me neither until I got an apartment on the twenty-first floor. For exercise, we like to run up and down."

"Doesn't your building have an elevator?"

"Yeah, but what fun is that?"

He shook his head. "I need you to sit with a sketch

artist."

"Why?"

"You saw the second suspect, the one Detective Heathcliff said changed his mind and left the coffee shop."

"I already gave you a description. If you need more, why can't you ask Heathcliff?"

Franco's expression hardened. "I'm sorry for the inconvenience, Ms. Parker. But this is important."

"You don't believe Heathcliff?"

"It's not that. But he's a cop. We have to be sure."

"Didn't you look at the surveillance footage? The guy should be on camera."

"He wasn't pacing in front of the cameras. He was too close to the building. All we can see is the top of his head going back and forth at the bottom of the screen. We can't determine anything except hair color based on that. Frankly, we can't even be sure it's the same guy."

"It's the same guy. All the back and forth is what caught my attention."

"I'm sure it did, but we need a description. The only footage we have is after he fled, and that's from a neighboring shop's security camera after he had the ripped-up beanie pulled over his face like a reject superhero."

Franco's word choice gave me pause. "He's not a hero. He had a gun. That usually makes them villains."

"Did you see the weapon? Can you identify what kind of gun it was?"

"I didn't see it. But it was there."

"Detective Heathcliff said the same thing." Franco held up his palms, cutting me off by saying exactly what was on my mind. "I know. You recognized the outline of the weapon beneath his clothes. We've been conditioned to notice, but unless you saw the actual gun, we can't prove it wasn't some other object. And even if he had a weapon, that's not a crime. He never used it. He never threatened anyone. He left before the attempted robbery took place. Unless Wayne Savage implicates this mystery man, we can't arrest him for a crappy hat choice or having a suspicious bulge."

"Why do you want me to talk to a sketch artist? It sounds like Eyeholes is in the clear."

"For the coffee shop, yes. But he may have played a part in two other recent robberies." Franco came to his full height, looking more like the cop I'd met in the alley. "I want to compare your story and the sketch you come up with to what other eyewitnesses at these other robberies have said. You saw this unsub without his mask, Ms. Parker. That makes your recollection valuable."

I checked the time. "Yeah, okay. But I need a minute to call my office."

After asking Kellan to e-mail my report to Almeada since my talk with Detective Alloway hadn't resulted in anything useful for the defense attorney, I returned to the precinct. Officer Franco was waiting for me near the front desk.

"Who's assigned these cases?" I asked as I followed Franco through a door near the back and past several desks and offices.

The first floor looked a lot different from the specialized units upstairs. This was where press conferences took place and the police staged massive operations. I'd sat in on a few of them as a federal agent, but it had been a while. Since then, they'd painted and updated the fixtures, or I'd been away so long I'd forgotten how everything looked.

"I am. Didn't Heathcliff tell you he gave me the collar?"

"Yes, but I figured an investigation involving multiple robberies would be higher up the food-chain. No offense," I said.

"None taken. Usually, it would be, but we don't have enough yet. That's why I need your help. The detectives in robbery and grand larceny need something solid before they open a case. Right now, the three hold-ups don't connect for them, particularly when the prime suspect from the first hold-up remains in police custody."

"They don't believe you," I said.

"They need proof."

He led me to an office near the back where a tech had his computer equipment and drawing tablet ready to go. The tech introduced himself and brushed off the seat on a nearby chair before offering it to me.

While he asked me to describe the suspect, Officer Franco asked a few other questions about the robbery and resulting firefight. I told him everything I could, which wasn't much. After I finished describing the suspect before he put on his DIY mask, we went over the same process again as to what he looked like with the makeshift mask. If Heathcliff and I had been smarter, we would have taken a few photos of the guy while he was casing the coffee shop.

"Print those for me, Kennedy," Franco said. Once he had hard copies in hand, he turned his attention back to me. "If you have a few more minutes, I want to show you something. Detective Heathcliff said you used to be on the job and you've consulted with the department on several occasions."

"Guilty."

He led me into one of the IT rooms, where all the department's A/V geeks were hanging out. I recognized a few of them from previous cases.

"Hey, Parker," one woman said. "I haven't seen you in a while."

I searched my memory for her name. *Bex*. "I've been out of town. The LAPD needed my help."

"Seriously? They asked for you specifically?"

"Only when arresting me."

Franco looked uncomfortable. "You were arrested in Los Angeles?"

"Details." I waved my hand as if to brush the question away. "That's not important. It was a misunderstanding. A catch and release. In my current line of work, it happens every now and again."

"Okay." But uncertainty lined his face. "Heathcliff vouched for you, so I'll blame him."

"That's always my plan too." I winked at Franco. "Now what do you want to show me?"

He had footage brought up from the other two recent armed robberies. The grocery store security cameras had gotten several good shots of Eyeholes.

"That's him. Same mask. Same jacket. There's no doubt. That's the same guy," I said.

Franco switched to some blurred footage from the gentlemen's club. No security cameras were inside the club. The only ones outside covered the parking lot. He let the video play. "Do you see the suspect anywhere?"

I studied the footage carefully. "Can you clean this up?"

Bex shook her head. "Not with the low-res shit they have. I'd even go so far as to say the elements did a number on the lens because it shouldn't be this blurry."

"That might be him." I pointed. "But I really can't tell. Did you speak to the witnesses inside?"

"They said it was a three-man team," Franco said. "That's the only detail eyewitnesses agree on. The rest of the details vary. When you stopped Savage at the coffee shop, did you notice anyone else with him?"

"No, but I don't think the coffee shop would have required a four-man crew."

"We have to be sure," Franco said.

I studied the blurry footage from the strip club again. "Did you ask witnesses what the girl on the main stage was wearing?"

"Neon red thong, clear heels with red poofy feathers, and sparkly silver pasties with tassels that spun," Franco said.

Bex grunted. "And not a single person can agree on what the robbers looked like. They all provided different descriptions, except for what she was wearing."

"Too bad the robbers weren't in pasties and a thong," I said, returning my attention to the grocery store hold-up. "How big was the team at the grocery store?"

"Just the one guy," Franco said. "The man you call Eyeholes went on the express lane, held up the register, and ran out the door. No one remembered seeing him with anyone else, and security cams didn't show him interacting with anyone."

"Maybe the two robberies aren't related," I said. "The coffee shop and grocery store seem similar. But the strip joint was different. Limited exits, no centralized location to rob. They would have needed a team to pull it off."

"That's what the robbery detective I spoke to said too, which is why he doesn't think the crimes are connected.

But one of the dancers said she remembered a guy with the same ripped-up beanie over his face. Unless this is some new fashion statement or some kind of internet sensation, I'm guessing the same guy's working with a crew. If they've hit three different places, it's just a matter of time before they knock over even more."

NINE

It had been months since our last poker night. Usually, we had five or six players, but Mark Jablonsky had just gotten back from D.C. We hadn't spoken yet, so I didn't get the chance to invite him. Martin texted to say he was running late, like I knew he would. Luckily, Jen had arrived early with a tray of sandwiches, giving us five players. While we got everything set up, I updated O'Connell, Thompson, and Heathcliff on the rest of my day.

"That's what Franco said?" Heathcliff grabbed a handful of pretzels from the center serving bowl and put them on the napkin in front of him.

"You shouldn't have passed off the case." Thompson put his cards face down and pushed them toward the middle of the table. "Don't you know by now Parker never does anything simple? She drags you into the middle of this, and you think it's an open and shut armed robbery. You need to have your head examined."

"Hey." I picked up my beer bottle to take a sip, disappointed when I found it empty. "This isn't my fault. I had nothing to do with these knuckleheads showing up in the middle of breakfast."

Heathcliff nodded down at my poker chips, urging me to call or fold. I tossed two more chips into the middle. "It was lunch, not breakfast," he insisted.

"Maybe it was your lunch, but it was my breakfast. It was my first meal of the day."

"It was noon. Does Cross have you working late nights again?" O'Connell asked. "Are you back on the cheating spouse brigade?"

"I check in on Bruiser before I start my day. That always puts me behind schedule, that and being stuck on West Coast time."

Jen brought over the platter of sandwiches and placed them at the far end of the dining room table. "How is Bruiser doing? Has he made any progress?"

"He'll be okay." I wasn't willing to accept any other possibility. None of us were.

"You should have invited him to poker night," O'Connell said. "At least then we'd have something to talk about besides work." He nudged his wife. "Someone hates it when we do that."

I got up to get another beer. "Getting around isn't easy for him. I don't think asking would make him feel better."

"It's still recent," Jen said. "He might need incentive to push himself a little. Getting out to do something fun might help."

"Maybe." I grabbed a few more bottles for the guys and sat back down at the table.

"Gin," Jen announced, laying out a full house.

"That's not gin, honey." O'Connell tossed his cards into the center.

"I know." But she liked to say it, anyway.

"Ah, fuck." Heathcliff tossed in his cards and leaned back.

I gathered the cards and shuffled. "I offered to help you cheat, but you didn't want my help," I said to Heathcliff as I dealt the next hand. "Jen brought sandwiches. That automatically makes her my favorite to win."

"Mine too." O'Connell gave her another peck.

"Hey," Thompson picked up his cards, "I thought I was your ride or die, Nick."

"Only at work."

"I hate that phrase," Jen muttered.

"Me too," I said.

Conversation turned to other things, like my trip to California and the things I'd missed while away. We played for another hour before the sandwiches disappeared and my chips dwindled to nothing. Tonight wasn't my night.

"Buying more chips?" Thompson nodded to the case of poker chips, but I shook my head. "Come on, Parker. You're making that private sector money. What's another hundred bucks among friends?"

"Someone already cleaned me out this week." I got up to clear away the empties and refill the pretzel bowl. "Does anyone want tortilla chips? We've got some lime flavored ones stashed around here."

"Nah. Pretzels are good," O'Connell said.

"I can order a pizza."

Jen gave me a stern look. I'd forgotten she'd been on a health food kick.

"Never mind." I put the bottles into the recycling bin and opened the fridge. "How about some fruit? Grapes and apple slices?"

Jen raked in her winnings. "Sure."

I arranged the fruit on a serving board and brought it over to the table. Thompson narrowed his eyes at it, finding it in opposition to what poker night stood for, but he'd never bitch about his partner's wife. He knew better.

"I'm out too." Heathcliff joined me at the kitchen counter. After popping the top on another beer, his fifth if I wasn't mistaken, he lowered his voice. "You said Officer Franco thinks Eyeholes is running with a crew. That would mean Wayne Savage is part of the same crew."

"If it's true. Franco doesn't have proof yet."

"He doesn't work investigations, but that is the gig he's been vying for. It's possible he's hoping to find something big that will give him the bump he needs to have a shot at detective."

"He's not making it up," I said. "I saw the footage from the grocery store. Eyeholes held one of the cashiers at gunpoint and emptied the register. Again, it wasn't a very big score. A couple hundred bucks."

"The same as what he and Savage would have gotten from the coffee shop."

"Yeah, but the strip joint was different. That was a much larger score. It's mostly a cash business. The team that knocked over the gentlemen's club got everything from the establishment, plus the tip money the strippers earned and whatever pocket change the men still had on them."

"Not to mention phones, watches, and jewelry," Heathcliff said.

"You looked into it after I left?"

"Of course. I'm guessing you did the same, so what did you find?"

"I spoke to the stripper who claimed Eyeholes was part of the crew and got her to give me a description of the man. It sounds like the same guy we saw at the coffee shop. She described him exactly as I remembered. So I went back to Cross Security and looked into the gentlemen's club."

"Did you find anything?"

"No, so I did more digging on Wayne Savage. If this is a crew, he must have had interactions with the other members of the team."

"We've looked at his phone records, but it didn't lead us anywhere," Heathcliff said.

"I looked a little deeper than that."

"I don't want to hear it. Arresting you isn't on my list of things to do tonight."

"You wouldn't arrest me."

He raised a challenging eyebrow. "I don't want to know what you did, but I want to know what you found."

"It was computer work. Mostly looking at files, social media posts, and documents. Nothing someone with time and access to public records couldn't find."

"Uh-huh," he said, unconvinced. Motioning that I move the story along, he took another sip of his beer and waited.

"It's not much, but Savage had a loyalty card to that grocery store and ATM transactions at the gentlemen's club in question. He had visited both a week prior to his arrest."

"Do you think he was casing them?"

"I don't know, but he may not have been alone. We can't find anything online that connects him to Eyeholes, at least not yet, but the stripper provided a description of the other two men involved in the hold-up. One of them looks a lot like Savage's brother, Kelsey. But that's just one witness.

She didn't ID him from the online photo, so there's not much the PD can do with it. But it could be worth pursuing. Maybe set up surveillance or assign a unit to tail him. After all, we caught his brother Wayne red-handed. If they were at the grocery store and gentlemen's club together, that might mean something."

"Show me what you found."

Crossing to the chair where I had dropped my things when I came home, I moved my purse and looked inside my duffel, which doubled as a go-bag, but my laptop wasn't inside. "I left my computer in the trunk."

I looked back at the dining room table where Jen had a growing mountain of chips in front of her. Thompson looked determined not to give up, and O'Connell seemed happy doing nothing more than eating pretzels from the bowl.

"I'll be right back," I said. "Don't lock me out."

Thompson chuckled. "If only."

O'Connell looked up. "Do you need help with something?"

"I got it." Heathcliff waved him off, putting his beer down and joining me at the door.

"I am capable of walking to my car alone," I said.

"It's dark," Heathcliff said. "Plus, I could use some fresh air." When we got outside, he inhaled deeply. "Where'd you park?"

"In Martin's spot." I indicated the garage across the street.

"Where's he going to park?"

"Marcal will drop him off."

"Has Martin driven himself anywhere since the accident?"

"Every once in a while. He usually doesn't drive when he's working. It takes too long to find parking. With the way his lunch and dinner meetings are, it makes more sense to have a driver."

"No reason not to, if you can afford it."

"Right?" I popped the trunk and looked inside. "If you're expecting a smoking gun, I didn't find one. I didn't find much of anything, but I think Officer Franco is on to something."

"I do too. But I don't understand why Savage won't give up his partner, unless it's one of his relatives. Still, he's looking at attempted murder charges. Even if Eyeholes is family, most people aren't that loyal. Charges like that usually get people to talk, but Savage won't."

"Savage only has the one brother. Eyeholes could be a cousin or uncle."

Heathcliff's phone rang, and he reached for it, distracted as he read the display. "Give me a sec." He hit answer and stepped away from my car.

I leaned over, practically climbing into the trunk while I searched for my computer sleeve. Since it was black, it made finding it in the dark even harder. I felt around, but all I felt was the rough carpeting. Maybe I left it in the back seat.

Carefully, I stepped backward before straightening, not wanting to hit my head on the trunk lid, which I had done on more than one occasion. I'd just stepped back when I bumped into someone.

"Who was on the phone?" I asked, turning and expecting to find Heathcliff behind me.

Instead, I saw a claw hammer swinging toward my face. My arm shot up to block. The assailant's arm knocked hard against my forearm, but the hammer fell short of making contact with my skull.

Whoever wielded the hammer wore a dark jacket, maybe green or navy, with the hood pulled up and tied tight, leaving a small circle from which to see and breathe. It wasn't the best disguise, but it was effective.

I pivoted, throwing my hip into a right cross. My punch landed squarely on the guy's jaw. He took a step back, shaking it off as he swung with the hammer again.

The momentum propelled him forward, but my hit and the weight of the hammer knocked him off balance. I easily sidestepped while the hammer crashed into the inside of my open trunk lid with a resounding crunch before getting stuck.

I delivered a high kick to the side of his chest, wanting to put some distance between us. The last thing I needed was to have my skull crushed with that damn hammer. The force of the kick pushed him backward. He lost his balance, his arms flailing as he tried to keep himself from crashing to the ground.

He skidded in a backward duck-walk, dropping the hammer as he struggled to balance and regain equal footing. The hammer made a loud, echoing clang.

"Alex?" Heathcliff yelled from twenty feet away.

"A little help," I replied, closing on the guy.

The assailant glanced at the dropped hammer, but it was too far from his current location. He remained in a low crouch, hands in front of him as he circled like a wrestler. I'd left my gun in the apartment. I never expected to need it.

"Police," Heathcliff announced, jogging toward us.

The guy darted to the side. After three steps, he raced toward the exit as fast as his legs could carry him. I charged after him, listening to Heathcliff's footfalls behind me. But the guy was fast. Faster than me.

At the exit, I peered left and right. But he had vanished. I studied the ground, but it didn't provide any indication of which way he'd gone. With minimal traffic and few pedestrians at this time of night, his escape left no discernible trail or wake for me to follow. No angry voices or beeping car horns. He was just gone.

"Wait." Heathcliff grabbed my shoulder before I could take off in a random direction. "Be smart. You'll never find him."

I glanced down, realizing Heathcliff had left his off-duty piece in my apartment too. We were quite the pair. But unlike me, he had brought one useful piece of hardware with him. His phone.

"I'll call it in," he said. "Are you okay?"

I nodded as I made my way back to my car, more on edge now than before. Normally, I paid more attention to these things, but I hadn't felt the need. This was supposed to be a safe neighborhood. I had a police escort. What was that asshole thinking attacking me?

Heathcliff requested units to our location, provided a vague description of the suspect, where he'd last been seen, and hung up. After sending a quick text to O'Connell to let him know about the fun he missed, Heathcliff turned his attention to me. "Any idea who that was?"

"No."

"He was built like the guy from the coffee shop."

"Eyeholes?"

"Was it him?"

I thought about it. "That would be one hell of a coincidence. I don't see what he'd be doing out here. And he wasn't wearing that stupid mask, so I can't say for certain."

Heathcliff looked around, taking in the nearby cars. Most were much nicer than mine. "You know what I'm going to ask next."

"Cross doesn't have me assigned to anything dangerous. I haven't made any new enemies. I have no idea who'd want to come at me with a hammer." I indicated the dropped weapon. "He had gloves, but you might still want to check it for prints."

Heathcliff crouched beside the hammer, using the flashlight on his phone to examine it. "Do you have any gloves?"

"Hang on a sec." I opened my car door, tossed him the evidence collection kit I kept on hand, and retrieved my laptop from where it had slid beneath the passenger's seat.

"I don't see anything on the weapon, but the lab might get lucky. I'll have them test it for blood too. If this was a random attack, he may have had other victims," Heathcliff said.

"What do you think? We have a rogue bludgeoner on the loose?"

"Possibly."

I went to the rear of my car and examined the hole he'd made in my trunk lid. The thin aluminum didn't stand a chance against the heavy hammer. "Maybe you should check with the mental hospitals and see if anyone escaped who believes he is the god of thunder."

"Thunder?"

"The hammer." I nodded at the tool in the evidence bag.

Heathcliff hefted it. "It's a little small, don't you think?"

"Not when it's coming at my head."

"Point taken." He looked around. "At least this place has plenty of security cameras. We should be able to get something useful from them."

"I'm sure we will." I spotted O'Connell and Thompson crossing the street with a few members of building security behind them. Even though the garage was a separate structure, the spaces were rented exclusively to residents in our building.

"Are you guys okay?" O'Connell asked.

"Yeah," Heathcliff said. "The lunatic went for Alex, not me."

"Lunatics are drawn to Parker," Thompson said. "She's like catnip to them."

"Where were you?" O'Connell asked.

"Taking a call," Heathcliff said.

"You know better than to leave Parker alone for a second. She always gets into trouble. First, coffee. Now, the garage. Once we get this straightened out, I'm going to find some normal people to introduce you to," Thompson said. "She's a bad influence on us."

I stuck my tongue out at him. "You're just jealous you missed the excitement."

"The last thing I want is to be on your TV show."

I rolled my eyes, scoffing. "There is no TV show."

Thompson looked at the hammer in Heathcliff's gloved hand. "With these theatrics, there should be."

TEN

We rode the elevator up to the twenty-first floor. Heathcliff had gone silent, his thoughts mirroring my own. When we emerged, I found my apartment door open. O'Connell didn't wait before rushing inside, but his wife was safe. She was with my fiancé.

"Alex?" Relief relaxed the tension on Martin's face. "I saw the police cars outside. I didn't know what happened. Are you okay?"

"I'm fine. My trunk now has air conditioning."

Martin resisted the urge to hug me. Instead, he looked at the detectives. Thompson packed up his poker set while O'Connell and Jen put the dishes in the sink and scooted in the chairs.

Heathcliff put his jacket on. Thompson was giving him a ride home, so I didn't have to worry about him driving. "Twice in one week," he said. "Are you sure it wasn't the same guy?"

"I don't think so. Since we don't know who he is, how would he have any idea who I am?"

"He wouldn't," Heathcliff admitted, though he sounded about as convinced as I felt. "But it's weird we'd run up on another crime in progress."

"I'm sure the guy with the hammer would agree. After all, he had no way of knowing I'd need to get something out of the car. It's probably a coincidence." But even saying the word left a bad taste in my mouth.

"You don't believe in those," O'Connell said.

"How else would you describe tonight's events?" I asked.

"More bad luck," Thompson volunteered.

Heathcliff zipped his jacket. "Tomorrow morning, I'll call Franco and see what he's got. Maybe we missed something at the coffee shop."

"Find out if Wayne Savage has been in contact with anyone. He heard my name. He could have sent his buddy to check up on me," I said.

"Do you think this connects to the other morning?" O'Connell asked. "Or are you just covering all your bases?"

"It doesn't hurt to rule it out. I didn't recognize the guy with the hammer, even though I only saw this much of his face." I made a circle with my hands and held it up to my eyes. "I'm guessing he was some random loser looking for an easy score with incredibly bad timing."

Heathcliff nodded down at my laptop. "You never showed me what you found on Wayne Savage's brother. Maybe we should be looking into him as a possible suspect."

"I'll e-mail you everything I found, but the chances are slim."

"It depends on who Wayne Savage contacted. Hopefully, I'll have some answers for you by the morning."

"Great."

Heathcliff nodded to Martin. "Patrol will be keeping an eye out tonight. Building security's been briefed. However, if you go out, take a few precautions. It wouldn't hurt to pay attention. You see something, say something."

"Almost learned that the hard way," I said.

Heathcliff's lip twitched. "I'm sorry, Parker. I shouldn't have stepped away. I should have noticed."

"Don't beat yourself up. I didn't see him either."

Thompson grasped Heathcliff's shoulder, pushing him toward the door. "Thanks for another exciting night, Parker. But remember, you can't show any footage of me working the scene until I sign a waiver, and I'm gonna need some compensation first."

"Ask Jen. She cleaned house tonight." I smiled, returning her hug automatically before she stood on her tiptoes to give Martin a friendly kiss on the cheek.

"Enough of that, woman." O'Connell hooked his arm around her shoulders. He shook hands with Martin. "We'll catch up next week at the symphony."

Martin didn't miss a beat. "I hate to say it, but I couldn't get tickets. We'll find something else to do. There's a new pop-up we could try."

"Aww, that's okay," Jen said. "A pop-up sounds fun."

O'Connell winked at me. "You need anything, call me. I'll make sure to stay on top of the canvass and have the techs comb through the security feeds to see if they can get an ID on this guy. But for now, stay out of trouble. We," he indicated himself and his wife, "will see you next Friday for date night. We're looking forward to it."

As soon as they left, I locked the door and bolted it shut. Martin ran a hand through his hair. "What the hell happened?" he asked.

"Some whack job was breaking into cars. Heathcliff and I interrupted him, and he came at me with a hammer."

Martin grasped my face and ran his thumb across my cheek. "Are you okay?"

"He didn't have the best aim."

He searched my eyes. "Yet, you look like you wish he hadn't missed. Whatever's going through your head is scaring me, sweetheart."

"Kiss me," I said, which he did.

"Alexis, you can't distract me that easily. Are you upset about this guy or everything else that's happened this week?"

I backed away from his touch. "Both. The evidence suggests the guy we bumped into tonight has nothing to do with anything, but there have been a lot of weird robberies lately. It seems strange that it's unconnected. Mark would have something to say about that. He doesn't believe in coincidences."

"Except when they happen." Martin followed me into the kitchen, separating the recycling from the trash while I loaded the dishwasher. "What does your gut say?"

"I don't think it was the same guy who bailed on the coffee shop robbery. If it was, he had a costume change and an attitude change. Last time, he didn't attack. He ran. This time, he attacked first. Even at the strip joint, he wasn't the aggressor. He was the grab-and-go guy, just like at the grocery store. No violence. No yelling. He asked for what he wanted. He only used the gun as a prop to get the cash quickly and easily. He didn't wave it in the clerk's face or hit anyone with it. In fact, no one else in the store was even aware a robbery happened until the clerk reported it after he left. But the guy tonight wanted to fight."

"So it's not the same guy?"

"No, but Heathcliff thinks it might be." I rubbed my eyes. "I'm off-kilter this week. I went outside without a gun, without paying attention to my surroundings, without doing any of the normal things I do. It was stupid."

"You felt safe. Heathcliff was with you."

"That doesn't matter." I chewed on the inside of my lip. "My head is twisted around."

"Because of your adoptive father?" Martin asked, but it wasn't a question. He knew the answer.

"I handled Don a couple of days ago. But I'm reeling from the final blow."

"Final blow?"

I hadn't told Martin what happened because I didn't want him to think less of me or pity me. But now I'd backed myself into a corner. "I gave him what he wanted and sent him on his way."

Martin washed his hands and leaned his hips against the counter while he dried them. The look on his face said he already knew what happened. "You gave that bastard your savings."

"Did Lucien tell you that?"

"Bruiser did."

"Remind me to stop running my mouth to your staff."

Martin offered a playful smirk. "Bruiser also mentioned he's thinking of trying French toast with a side of scrambled eggs for breakfast."

The smile overtook me. Martin was the only person on the planet who could occasionally shake me out of my foul moods, and he'd done it again. "It's about time you fed that man something besides oatmeal."

"I brought him steak with baked sweet potatoes, asparagus, and a salad for dinner. Doesn't that count?"

"You didn't cook it. It only counts if you cook it."

"I thought you only wanted me to cook dinner for you."

"I never said that, and Bruiser's the exception."

"You don't have to stop over there every day," Martin said.

"Neither do you."

"Yes, I do."

"Same," I said.

Martin pulled out his phone. "I'm texting to tell him I won't be there for breakfast, but I will make sure something gets delivered. After tonight, I don't see any reason why we need to venture out that early tomorrow."

"You read my mind."

ELEVEN

When I woke up, I found Martin standing in front of the balcony door. “Morning,” I murmured, wrapping my arms around him and kissing his shoulder blade. “How long have you been awake? The bed was cold.”

He turned to give me a good morning kiss. “I woke up early and thought I’d get my workout and shower in before you got up.”

“Stairs?” I asked.

“No. I went for a run.”

“You ran? Out there?” I pointed out the glass door, narrowing my eyes. “Didn’t you say we shouldn’t leave the apartment?”

“I had things to do.”

“You went to look at my car.”

“I thought I should. I also spoke to building security. They promised to pay closer attention to the parking garage. The police canvassed everyone in the building and have been given copies of the surveillance footage. According to what I was told, the guy with the hammer only vandalized four cars, not including yours. The owners weren’t sure what he stole, probably cash or change they had lying around. Nothing major.”

“That doesn’t make a lot of sense. It’d be understandable if he’d taken phones or credit cards.” I stared across the street at the parking garage. It didn’t look any different than it normally did. The police had finished collecting evidence, so no one was barred from entering or leaving. It was just another lazy Saturday. My fingers itched to dial Heathcliff's number. "Did building security have any theories on who this guy is or what he wanted?"

"They figure he's an opportunist who spotted a few expensive cars and hoped to hit the jackpot."

"Maybe he would have if Heathcliff and I hadn't interrupted him."

Martin didn't argue, which meant he didn't disagree. "What are your plans for today?"

"Besides a trip to the precinct, stopping by Bruiser's for a few minutes."

"But nothing pressing?"

I raised a suspicious eyebrow. "What did you have in mind?"

"How about we grab an early lunch or late breakfast, check in on Bruiser, stop by the precinct, and catch a movie?"

"You're offering to take me to the movies? Now I know something's up."

"We've been to plenty of movies. It's the weekend. Isn't that the quintessential Saturday night activity? We can even call it a date." He fake gasped, smiling at the absurdity of us doing something normal.

"The precinct could take a while. It depends on what kind of progress Heathcliff and O'Connell have made. There may not be time for a movie."

"Since your phone hasn't been ringing off the hook, I'm guessing they haven't come up with much of anything. I'd also go out on a limb and say that some random guy breaking into cars shouldn't require too much of your time." He brushed my hair behind my shoulders. "But you hope it does." A question mark formed on his face. "Why?"

"I'm not convinced this was a random guy. The more I think about it, the more I wonder if he wasn't breaking into those cars for a specific reason. The cops said the only cars that were broken into were silver sedans."

"Like yours."

"Nicer than mine, but yeah, like mine."

"What would be the point? You don't keep sensitive

material in your car."

"Not usually." I had before but never overnight in the parking garage. "Maybe he wanted to scare me or see if he could track me down. My name would be on the car registration, and from what we saw, the guy could have been breaking into cars to check names."

Martin didn't comprehend why someone would go to the trouble, and going into the details of why someone would want to ID and track me sounded far too paranoid for this early in the morning.

"Ignore me. I'm grasping at straws here. Last night was disconcerting. I'll feel better once they ID and arrest the guy."

"Everyone in this building will feel better." He turned me toward the bedroom. "Go get dressed. I want to take you out, and I'm starving."

Twenty minutes later, I was showered and dressed in casual clothes which went with Martin's loose fitting black t-shirt and jeans. Since he had called it a date, I clasped the necklace containing the engagement ring around my neck. After slipping into my shoulder holster and covering my nine millimeter with my leather jacket, I met him at the front door.

"You never told me how bad my car looks," I said. "Do I want to know?"

He eyed me as we waited for the elevator doors to open. "You'll need a new trunk lid. There's no way to buff out the hole. In the meantime, I covered it with plastic and duct tape and called your insurance company. They want a copy of the police report and the receipt for the bodywork. After that, they'll cut you a check."

"Without seeing the damage in person? How did you get them to agree to that?"

His green eyes sparkled. "I have my ways."

"You flirted with the insurance agent."

"I did not."

"You totally did," I teased. "You flirt with everyone. Last night, Nick was ready to take a firehose to you and his wife."

"For the record, Jenny doesn't do a thing for me."

"Nick will be happy to hear that. If she did, you'd be in a gutter somewhere."

Martin moved closer, his lips brushing against my ear. "She has nothing on you. No one does."

"You don't have to lay it on so thick."

He intertwined his fingers with mine and brought my hand to his lips. "It's true."

When the elevator doors opened, we were still holding hands. Martin led me through the lobby, tossing out options on where we should go for breakfast. The doorman smiled as he saw us coming, wishing us a good morning as he held the door for us to exit. Martin let me go first and nearly collided with my back when I stopped short.

"What's wrong, sweetheart?"

I tugged my hand free from his grip and hastily tucked the engagement ring into my shirt. A cold chill traveled up my spine. "Get building security."

He tensed. "What is it?"

The man sitting on the bench a few feet away smiled and waved. "Funny running into you, little swan."

"Go," I hissed before stepping forward, hoping to put as much distance between Martin and me as possible. "What are you doing here, Don? I said my piece. I gave you what you wanted. I thought I made it clear that I'm done. We're done."

The phony smile faltered. "I changed my mind. It's not enough. I want more."

"The three grand you left me?" What was wrong with this guy?

"No, honey. I left that for you. The cost of living is astronomical. I didn't want to leave you short for the month."

"So what do you want?"

"Let's get a cup of coffee, so we can sit down and talk about this."

"Talk about what? I don't have anything left to say. And whatever you have to say, I don't want to hear. It's too late. Too much time has passed."

Don's eyes flicked to something behind me. *Martin.*

"You heard the lady," Martin said, his voice low and

lethal. "She doesn't want to talk to you. I suggest you go on your way."

Don stood, sizing up Martin's six feet of toned muscle that said don't fuck with my girlfriend. He looked Martin in the eye, a snort escaping his lips. Obviously, my father wasn't only a sociopath, he was also suicidal.

"Property records pointed me to your apartment, little swan." Don turned his attention back to me. "Someone else's name was on the deed." He stared at Martin. "I take it that's you."

"Who are you?" Martin asked.

"Don Parker. Alexis's father."

Martin moved closer. I could feel the heat of his body against my side. "You have no right to call yourself a father. A father wouldn't withhold love. A father wouldn't turn his back on his kid, and he sure as shit wouldn't abandon her."

I put my hand up to stop Martin. His chest heaved against my fingers, his body trembling with pent-up rage. He'd rip Don limb from limb.

"You don't know me," Don said. "But you shouldn't talk. That ring on your finger says you're married. Alexis is not. That tells me you don't have the moral high-ground here."

"You don't know anything about us," Martin said. "You lost that right. Now get away from her."

I pushed harder against Martin's chest with the back of my hand, my eyes still on Don. "Get security," I repeated. "Now."

Martin fumed, like a dragon preparing to spew fire, and then he stepped back. "Get going, unless you have a death wish, because I'll fucking kill you."

Don didn't move, but Martin retreated. I could hear him speaking to the doorman before his voice disappeared back inside our apartment building.

"This could be construed as stalking," I warned. "Building security could detain you until the police arrive. You should leave while you still can."

Don didn't acknowledge that he heard a word I said. "Your boyfriend's protective. He looks like he could handle himself in a fight."

"You don't want to find out."

"I'm sure I don't, but I didn't come here to fight. I came here to have a civil conversation. You visited me. It's only fair that I visit you this time." Don looked up at the luxury apartment building behind us. "For someone with pennies in the bank, you have an awfully nice apartment. So I'm thinking I'm going to need the rest of what you owe me. It's the only way I'm going to get my life back. Please, little swan, I wouldn't be asking if I had any other choice, but I don't. I need the money I paid for your college tuition. Consider the ballet lessons a gift."

"*A gift?*" I nearly choked. "I don't have the money. You saw my bank account."

He gestured at the building. "Clearly, you could get it. The apartment was paid in full. You had the money to blow on that."

"It wasn't my money."

"Oh?"

I never meant to let that slip. "I don't know who you think I am, but I don't make a lot of money."

"He does." He nodded at Martin who was leading four members of building security toward us. "I suggest you find a way to get it before things get ugly. I don't want you to get hurt, Alexis. I love you. But I have no other choice. I need that money. And I'm going to need it sooner rather than later." He turned and walked away.

TWELVE

"Sweetheart," Martin ran his hands up and down my arms, "are you okay?"

I turned, but Don Parker was gone. If he knew what was good for him, he'd stay gone. But his words told me otherwise. I didn't know why he was so desperate. All I knew was that I didn't have that kind of cash. It'd take me years to save that much. Lucien was right. I was stupid for opening the door. "Dammit."

"It's okay. He's gone. Building security will make sure he never gets inside the building. If they see him loitering outside, they'll call the cops." Martin tried to hug me, but I shrugged away.

"He knows who you are," I said.

"I didn't introduce myself." Martin's eyes kept darting in the direction Don had vanished. "He's lucky I didn't introduce my fist to his face." He fought off the scowl. "What did he want?"

"Money. More money."

"How much?"

"It doesn't matter. I don't have it. Truthfully, he has no right to it. He chose to pay my college tuition. I didn't ask him to do it. He never said it was a loan." But I would have given him all of it if I had it. Anything to ensure he stayed far away from Martin and me.

"I remember you mentioning that, but I thought you also had scholarships and a work study," Martin said.

"I did. But Don didn't know that. He set up an account

at the university with enough to cover tuition for all four years. The extra went for my room and board and summer classes, since I had nowhere else to go."

Martin pulled me into his chest. I was shaking so hard I couldn't even manage to pull away from him.

"Easy," he whispered, but the tension radiating off of him did nothing to calm my nerves or assuage my anger. "I'll make sure he never comes near you again."

"What are you going to do? Hire a hitman?"

Martin chuckled. "I bet we know a few people who'd be happy to help."

I laughed into his chest, mostly from the tension and nerves. "Don't even joke about that. This is my problem. I'll take care of it. I don't want you going near him."

"How are you going to handle it?"

I had no idea. "I'll get a TRO. That should be enough." But a sheet of paper wouldn't solve the problem. Don Parker threatened me. It might have been the ballsiest thing the CPA had ever done.

Perhaps, Don had friends at the IRS who could have me audited. But I wasn't worried. Martin's company and finances were in order. Even if they came after him, there was nothing to find. But I had to know why Don was so desperate. This felt like more than calling in old debts to recover from his divorce. He made it sound like life or death. Could the idiot with the hammer be connected to my adoptive father?

That made even less sense than my other theories, but I couldn't be sure. Don must have owed someone. Did that someone come looking for me?

"Have you talked to Jabber?" Martin asked. "Does he know this asshole expects a handout?"

"Mark's been in D.C. I haven't told him any of this yet."

Martin held me with one arm while he fished his phone out with the other. "How about I invite him to join us for breakfast?"

"We don't need to worry him. This will blow over. Don's just...I don't even know."

Martin stepped back so he could look me in the eye. "You're worried, which has me worried. We should let

Jabber join in on the fun. You know how much he hates being excluded."

I didn't have the energy to argue. In fact, the only thing I wanted to do was crawl back under the covers. But that would have to wait. "Fine."

While Martin extended the invitation, I pulled out my phone and scanned my contacts. My pride had taken enough of a beating this week. I didn't want Cross to know he'd been right by asking one of his accounting experts to do some digging. So I texted Kate Hartley, an FBI forensic accountant, and asked her to find out where every penny Don Parker spent had gone.

I'll do what I can, but if you want to get down to the nitty gritty, I'll need clearance, she replied.

Wait an hour and ask Jablonsky. By the time we finished breakfast, my former boss and the man who felt more like a father to me than anyone else would be more than happy to help. I just wished I could have taken care of this quietly on my own. But now that everyone was involved or about to be, I knew it'd only get worse from here.

* * *

"I can't believe that son of the bitch had the nerve to ask you for money after all the shit he and his bitch wife put you through." Mark slammed his coffee cup down hard enough that the liquid inside sloshed over the sides.

"They aren't together anymore." I pushed the food around on my plate, too upset to eat.

Mark's eyes narrowed. "What the fuck is wrong with you that you gave him your savings?"

"I wanted him gone. I never would have done it if I realized he wasn't going to leave."

"Why would he leave when he figures he'll mooch off of you for the rest of his life?"

"I don't think that's what this is." I didn't want to talk about this anymore. If Martin wasn't blocking my exit from the booth, I would have left. Perhaps, I could fake dropping my silverware, crawl underneath the table, and escape.

"Don's desperate. First, he shows up at my office. Now, he shows up at my apartment."

"How'd he get the address?" Martin asked.

"He hired an investigator to track me down." I focused on Mark. "I spoke to Lucca about it. No one came sniffing around the OIO."

"We don't hand out intel on our agents, current or former," Mark said. "But at least you know he hasn't inquired." He wiped up the spilled coffee. "What investigator did he hire? If you tell me Cross Security, I will shove my foot so far up Cross's ass—"

"Ace Investigators," I said. "Cross already took care of it. He wiped Ace's hard drive and took whatever files he had pertaining to me."

"That you know of. There could have been duplicates. A backup drive."

I exhaled, realizing property records hadn't been included in the files Cross pulled. Ace had mentioned it during our chat, but he didn't keep a copy. I wondered what else he handed over that he failed to tell me about. Resting my elbows on the table, I put my face in my hands. "Can we change the subject?"

"That's not an option," Mark said.

"Make it one." I glared at him through my fingers. "I never wanted to talk about Don or Lydia before. Why would you think I'd want to talk about them now?"

"He's here, and he's making your life miserable. We should talk about it," Mark said.

Martin rubbed my back, but I scooted closer to the wall. Right now, I didn't want to be comforted. I wanted to escape this conversation.

"Do you want to hear about the guy who tried to crush my skull with a hammer last night?" I asked.

Mark narrowed his eyes. "Did that really happen?"

"Yeah."

"Did Don put him up to it?"

"I don't know."

"Would Don send someone to hurt you?"

"I never thought he was dangerous. Now, I'm not sure."

"You never said much about him," Mark said. "Are you

sure he never tried to contact you?"

"He didn't." I put my hands down on the table. "He only bothered to show up because he wants money. He's underwater. He lost most things in the divorce, or so he says. All I know is he's looking to collect. Apparently, my balance came due."

"You don't owe that bastard anything," Martin said.

"I'm not so sure."

Mark narrowed his eyes at me. "To make the threat he did, I'd guess someone's looking to kneecap Don or worse."

"That's what I was thinking, but I don't know who he owes or where to start looking." Again, my thoughts went to the assailant with the hammer. Would Don send someone after me to save his own skin? Every cell in my body said yes, which brought about a fresh wave of melancholia. The Parkers had never physically harmed me. It was the one line I thought they'd never cross. Now, there were no lines left.

"He must owe a lot if he thinks he can squeeze six figures out of you," Mark said. "Do you think he's hoping you'll get the money from Marty?"

"He implied that I should try."

"Are you sure the threat he made wasn't a ploy? Don should assume you deal with dangerous people. If he wants to get solvent again, he may have exaggerated the danger, hoping you'd jump to a few conclusions and give him what he wants," Martin said. "I'm sure he knows you'd never let anyone you care about get hurt if there was something you could do to prevent it."

"I don't care about him."

Martin pressed his lips together, not wanting to argue.

"You'd still pay to protect him if you could," Mark said. "I know you would. My gut says Don knows that too. Some things are ingrained in people, and that's always been ingrained in you."

I put my hands on my head and stared up at the ceiling. "I don't know why he wants the money or that much money. When I spoke to him at the hotel, he asked if he could stay with me. I don't know what his game is or why he's doing this. Maybe he wanted a place to hide out, or he figured Martin would have some expensive things around the apartment he could steal."

"You're spinning," Mark warned. "Let's get back to the facts."

"Don is broke. He said he tried to spend as much as he could before the divorce, that's why he had so many withdrawals from their account, but I don't buy it." I replayed the threat Don made to me. "Cross Security didn't turn up anything. I was hoping Kate could find something, but I don't want any of you taking the hit on this."

Mark reached for his phone. "I'll open an exploratory investigation and make sure she has the necessary resources. No one threatens an agent, former or otherwise." He sent a text and put his phone down. His eyes bore into me. "Tell me everything. What am I missing?"

"I don't know."

"What about from before? When you were a kid, do you remember your parents fighting about money? Maybe Don has an addiction. Maybe he gambles."

"I don't know. Nothing was cited in the divorce petition."

"Why did Lydia get everything?" Martin asked.

"I don't know anything besides what I told you. We haven't been in contact. Reaching out to me had to be a long-shot. For all Don knew, I could have been living on the streets somewhere."

"He knew that wasn't the case," Mark said. "Ace Investigators told him as much. That's why he made the trip to see you. I know you don't want to hear this, but maybe you should go for that cup of coffee. It's the fastest way to get answers."

"I'd rather give him every last cent than spend another minute listening to him rewrite the past."

"You already tried paying him off. That's what got us here," Mark pointed out. "Plan B will save you a lot of money in the long run."

"I'm compromised when it comes to him. There's too much hurt, too much baggage. I lose it every time. I can't question him. I can't even be in the same room as him." My chin quiver betrayed me, and Martin put his arm around me, which nearly made a tear roll down my cheek. But I scrunched up my face, forcing it to remain where it was.

"I hate to see you hurting," Martin whispered, pressing his lips to the side of my head.

"If there was abuse," Mark said, "we'd have grounds to—"

"There wasn't. I've told you that before."

"Then why are you acting like this? You've gone face to face with killers, people who've tried to kill you, and you didn't bat an eye."

"It wasn't always terrible. He wasn't always terrible. That's why it hurts so damn much. I remember the attention Don and Lydia would give me, the hugs, the kisses, the encouragement. Sure, it had to do with ballet and performing, but I didn't get that. I thought they loved me. All the pretty pink dresses and accessories, fussing over my hair, making sure I had the ballet bag I wanted and the things that went with it. Don would bring me flowers after every recital. But when I didn't get into the proper school, when I didn't get picked, he and Lydia flipped a switch. Instead of doting on me, they despised me. It was my fault. I wasn't good enough. I let them down. Even now, with Don coming to me with his hand out, I can't get those two versions of him out of my head. The man's psychotic. Emotionally stunted. Something. But I just..." I pulled one leg up onto the seat and hugged my knee, staring at the wall.

"You want him to turn back into the man who brought you flowers," Mark said. "You want him to be your dad. To love you no matter what."

"It's so stupid. I hear it. And I know it. And I can't stop it."

"That's why you hate flowers," Martin mumbled.

I wiped my eyes and stared across the table at Mark. "I'm a mess."

"Nothing new there." He winked. "I'll see what we can dig up, but give some thought to what I said. I'd be more than happy to go with you when you speak to Don."

"I told Alex I'd handle it," Martin said.

Mark pointed at Martin. “You stay the hell away from this guy. Do you hear me?”

“Yeah, fine.” But Martin’s tone was far from convincing.

THIRTEEN

Heathcliff watched as I dropped into the chair across from his desk. Martin and Mark were at Bruiser's, but I needed to get away from them. I had half a mind to take a cab to the airport and get on the first flight out, regardless of where it was going. The farther, the better. Instead, I took a cab to the precinct.

"You look like dog shit someone stepped in." Heathcliff slid a file across the desk toward me. "Are you ready to tell me what's going on?"

"I'm tired of talking about it." I flipped open the file, which contained photos of the man with the hammer. I didn't recognize him. "What do you want me to do with this?"

"I figured you'd want to see it." He sat up straighter, tugging on the cuffs of his sleeves. "The assailant from last night appears to be unconnected to the recent string of armed robberies. I checked the call logs, but Wayne Savage didn't contact anyone after he was arrested. It's unlikely he could have sent someone to seek revenge on you."

"I told you that was farfetched."

"You didn't seem quite so convinced last night."

"Things change."

"Like what?" Heathcliff eyed me. "Do you have a lead on who this guy is?"

"Not exactly, but I'm looking into a few long shots that aren't worth mentioning. I'll let you know if anything pans."

"I spoke to Officer Franco about his suspicions concerning the armed robberies. He can't get anyone else to take him seriously, so I told him to bring everything he's got to me. Major crimes will look into it. We'll let him assist."

"How nice of you."

Heathcliff met my eyes. "I forgot how abrasive you can be. If you're going to keep this up, I won't tell you what I was going to tell you."

"I'm sorry, Derek. Really. I'm dealing with family drama and kind of spinning out."

"Family? You never mentioned them before."

"There's a reason for that. My dad's in town. It's not ideal."

"Copy." Heathcliff glanced at Lt. Moretti's office door. "How full is your schedule? You look like you might need a distraction."

"Does the department want to hire me to consult?"

"Moretti thought it was only fair. Half of this case is yours."

"Half? I pointed out Eyeholes, and I confronted Savage."

"I arrested him."

"With my help."

Heathcliff smiled. "Do you want in on the investigation?"

"Yes, please."

He nodded at Moretti's office. "Paperwork's waiting for you in there. I'm glad I could cheer you up."

"That's why you're my favorite." I went around the desk and gave him a quick hug.

"Are you sure you're okay?" he asked, surprised by the unexpected affection.

"I am now."

Lieutenant Moretti didn't look up as I entered his office. Instead, he pointed to the chair across from his desk, the highlighter still in his hand from whatever he was reviewing. I took a seat, and he grabbed a pen from the cup before placing it on top of the official forms. Only after I was halfway through did he finally look at me.

"It doesn't matter where you are. You always find a way to cause trouble for me, Parker." But Moretti's tone was teasing.

"Didn't Jablonsky warn you about that?"

"Many times." Moretti didn't crack a smile, but his eyes twinkled. "As long as you continue to be less trouble than you're worth, I'm willing to put up with it."

"Thank you, sir." I finished signing and initialing.

He took the forms from me, made sure I didn't miss anything, and slid them onto the top of one of the piles. "Before you get started, I have some questions. Tell me about the lunatic from last night. Heathcliff said you didn't recognize him, that you didn't think his appearance had anything to do with whatever it is you do at Cross Security."

"As far as I know, it doesn't. Heathcliff thought it might have been the man who changed his mind about robbing the coffee shop, but he'd have no way of identifying me."

"The canvass failed to turn up any relevant information. No one saw the guy. The victims were a random scattering of your neighbors. We didn't find any particular motive. The guy was targeting silver sedans, and you drive a silver sedan. Other than that, it appears to be random. No prints or blood were found on the hammer. It's unlikely he attacked anyone else or intended to attack you. He may have gotten spooked and reacted badly. Do you have any inklings or gut feelings about who this unsub is?"

"No."

"Have you received any threats recently?"

"Nothing credible," I said, which may have been a teeny, tiny fib.

"Okay." He shut the folder and tossed it onto another pile. "Moving on to more important issues. What can you tell me about the robbery at the coffee shop?"

"I gave my statement. That's everything."

Moretti glanced in the direction of Thompson's desk. "I heard rumors you knew it was going down."

"That's not true. Those are the guys busting chops."

"I take it you heard about the other two recent robberies which Officer Franco believes could be related."

"They are related. I saw the footage from the grocery store. That's the same man who Heathcliff scared off at the coffee shop. Apparently, one close call with the cops wasn't enough to dissuade him from trying again. I also spoke to one of the dancers at the club that was held up. She described the robbers. One of them matched the description of the man who fled the coffee shop."

"I'm not going to ask why you took it upon yourself to look into this matter before we asked for your assistance."

"It's initiative," I said, "or boredom."

"Heathcliff said you found a possible connection between the robber we have in custody and the crew who hit the club."

I told Moretti what I'd told Heathcliff yesterday and directed him to Wayne Savage's social media account and the photos of him with his brother, who roughly fit the descriptions a few of the eyewitnesses from the gentlemen's club provided. Then I directed his attention to Wayne Savage's ATM transactions, his loyalty card at that grocery store, and his recent financial transactions. "I haven't followed up yet, but I'd say he bought a burner phone two weeks ago. That electronic shop is notorious for selling them, and as far as I can tell, he's never been there before or since."

"That may be a stretch, but I like the work you've put in on this. It's something else we can question Savage about."

"You're still holding him?"

"He couldn't afford bail, so he's ours until his court date." Moretti looked up. "The guy's flat broke. A couple hundred bucks must have looked pretty appealing."

"That's what his work history suggested. It was spotty. He may have an addiction or some other impediment that caused him to fail to retain gainful employment."

Moretti jerked his chin at the door. "Heathcliff's running the show on this. I just wanted to make sure I wasn't missing anything that could get my guys jammed up or placed in unnecessary danger."

"I'm an open book when it comes to this stuff."

"I sure hope so, Parker." He indicated the door. "Shut that on your way out."

Heathcliff had a cup of coffee waiting for me at the empty desk attached to his. I sat down and took a sip. Even though Cross Security was where I worked, consulting for the police department felt more like home. And since this was one of the few places Don Parker hadn't been, I was glad to spend as much time here as possible.

"Wayne Savage is broke," I said.

"No kidding. He used to work at the container yard. He got laid off ten months ago. No wife. No other income. He got evicted from his apartment four months ago. His brother Kelsey, which you were going to show me photos of before things went sideways last night, is his closest relative. He's been staying with him a lot since it happened."

"They were tagged together in a few photos online. I didn't get a chance to run a full background on Kelsey, but from what I've seen, he and his wife have a baby. I'm not sure what she does, but he's a delivery driver."

"What does he deliver?"

"Packages."

Heathcliff glanced up from his screen, wondering if I was being my usual sarcastic self. But I wasn't. After a few clicks of the mouse, he leaned back and read aloud. "Kelsey Bartholomew Savage, twenty-eight, married six months ago to Breann Blackwood, they share one child, two years old. He was arrested nine years ago for vandalism. Judge dismissed the case. He was arrested a second time at twenty-two for joyriding. He got probation and paid a fine."

"Anything else?"

"That's it. Those aren't violent crimes."

"I'd say they are leaps and bounds away from armed robbery. His brother Wayne has no record at all. But he needs money, and that can make people act out of the ordinary, like show up out of the blue after a decade and a half of radio silence."

"Are you sure you don't want to talk about whatever's going on with you?" Heathcliff asked.

I shook my head. "How's Kelsey's credit?"

"It looks like he and his wife are scraping by. No major

debts, besides a few grand on a credit card. No missed payments. They have steady jobs, even if they aren't making what they should."

"What does she do?" I asked.

"Waitress." He typed furiously, his eyes moving from left to right as he read the screen. "She has no connection to that gentlemen's club, the grocery store, or the coffee shop."

"Her husband shops at that grocery store, and from Wayne's social media posts, we know Kelsey's been to that particular strip joint at least once. I'm sure he only went for the wings. But a witness described a man with his build and facial features as one of the armed robbers. That's why I think he's involved. That and we have his brother in custody for committing the same crime."

Heathcliff opened his desk drawer and pulled out a folder. "The men who held the place up wore masks. How did you get a description?"

"One waitress remembered him. Everyone else's description was vague, but she was able to give a partial description since the guy who fit Kelsey's profile only had on a *Zorro* mask. Most of his face was still exposed."

"*Zorro*?"

I used my pointer finger to draw an oval around my eyes. "A black mask that only covered this much of his face. The kind *Zorro* wore. His nose, mouth, and jaw were clearly in view."

"What about his ears?"

"Ears?"

Heathcliff turned his monitor. "Kelsey Savage has a skull and crossbones earring he always wears. It's in his DMV photo, in all his social media photos, in everything. I don't think he ever takes it out."

"In that case, it sounds like we should find out if any of the witnesses remember seeing that earring."

FOURTEEN

"That was a bust." Heathcliff climbed behind the wheel. "Franco said the eyewitnesses weren't helpful. I should have listened to him. Even when I flashed around Kelsey's photo, no one seemed sure it was him."

"I told you that already."

"I have a badge. I thought the result might be different."

"Yeah, less cooperative," I said. "Too bad Kelsey Savage wasn't wearing a thong and pasties."

"What?"

"As a rule, most people know not to pay too much attention to crooks with guns. Being able to identify someone is a good way to get killed. That's why the descriptions I got from the staff and witnesses wouldn't be admissible. They were vague, but I think they fit, particularly given the facts." I peered out at the neon sign. Half the bulbs were out, but the board beneath boasted a special deal for the all-you-can-eat lunch buffet. Sex and food ruled everything, and this place had devised a way to combine them. Personally, that made both prospects unappetizing to me, but the packed parking lot meant I wasn't in the majority.

My phone chimed, and I glanced down to check my messages. Martin was spending the day with Bruiser since I ditched them, and Mark had gone back to the office to dig into Don. I put the device in my pocket and stared out the windshield.

"When I confronted Wayne Savage in the coffee shop, he seemed desperate. He wanted that money badly. Even though things had gone south with his accomplice, he wasn't willing to throw in the towel. He could have walked out of the shop without either of us being the wiser."

"You already spotted him," Heathcliff pointed out.

"Maybe, but I made small talk. He could have taken his cup and walked out the front door. You didn't have grounds to detain him. All of this could have been avoided. He needed that money. If this was the only way he could get it, I feel bad for him. But then I remember how he tried to kill us, and I don't feel quite so bad anymore."

"That's why this case makes no sense." Heathcliff turned the car around and headed back to the precinct. "We have to start at square one because we're missing a lot."

"No kidding."

When we got back, Heathcliff assigned me to research recent robberies, figuring the Savages and Eyeholes might have been doing this longer than we realized. But I didn't come across anything useful.

"You should call it a day." Heathcliff nodded at the double doors.

I spotted Martin talking to someone in the stairwell. "Hey," I tapped on Heathcliff's desk, "thanks for convincing Moretti to give me the gig. I needed this."

"It didn't take much. He likes having you around." He exhaled, working up the nerve to ask, "Are you sure you don't want to talk about whatever's on your mind?"

"Thanks, but I'm okay."

After grabbing my things, I met Martin in the stairwell. I didn't recognize the person to whom he was speaking, but the ESU emblem on the man's shirt tipped me off that this was one of the men who'd taken Martin through the training course.

"It was great seeing you again, James. Take care." The ESU guy bounded down the steps before Martin could introduce us.

"What are you doing here?" I pulled out my phone, but there were no missed calls or texts. "I thought you and Bruiser were going to watch that space exploration docuseries."

"We did until Ann showed up. After that, I thought I should make myself scarce so he could spend some time with his sister. She's staying until Monday morning, so she's got breakfast, lunch, and dinner covered for tomorrow." Martin checked the time. "That gives us the day off."

"Bruiser is tired of seeing us," I said.

"Possibly."

"I hope you're paying him for dealing with our drama even though he's on medical leave."

"Absolutely." Martin pointed to his watch. "After everything that happened today, I didn't know if you still wanted to see a movie. We could do something else, or nothing. Whatever you want, sweetheart. The sky's the limit."

"How about a Caribbean cruise?"

"If I thought you were serious, I'd make it happen."

Outside, Martin's town car was waiting in a visitor parking spot for us. Marcal got out and opened the rear door. "Ms. Parker."

"Remind me not to talk to you."

He smiled. "Yes, ma'am."

I pointed at him. "You're not funny."

He winked. "No, ma'am."

"Enough, Marcal," Martin said, unsure of my current mental state. He turned to me. "Where did we land on the movie idea?"

"Not tonight, handsome."

"Okay." Martin waited, but I continued to stare out the window. "What would you like to do instead?"

"Like isn't the right word. I'd prefer to do almost anything besides the one thing I have to do." I shook myself, catching Marcal's eye in the rearview. "Can you drop me off at the federal building before taking Martin home?"

Marcal nodded.

"Mark's right," I said. "I can't run away from this no matter how much I want to. I'll see what he dug up in the last six hours, and then I'll take him with me to confront

Don. Once we finish up, I'll meet you at home."

"Let me come with you."

"Don and Lydia destroyed my life once. They blew everything up. I know it's irrational, but I'm terrified he'll find some way to take you away from me too."

Martin grasped my chin. "No one could ever do that." He ran his thumb against the faded bruise on my cheek. "You don't have to face him alone."

"He wants money. I don't have it, but you do. Tempting him is the last thing I want. Desperate people do crazy things." I thought about Wayne Savage. That would explain his actions in the coffee shop, but if his goal was to empty the register or steal the tip jar, he didn't need a weapon to do it. The threat of a weapon was usually enough, and experience told me the only ones who came prepared with a weapon planned to use it.

"Sweetheart?" Martin used his other hand to brush my hair out of my face. "Are you sure you're okay? You don't have to do this tonight. Maybe you should wait until tomorrow."

"If I don't do it now, it'll fester. It's been getting to me ever since Don showed up at Cross Security. I can't hide from it, not after this morning. Mark's right. Lucien's right. Everyone's been right about this. I have to sit down with Don and find out what's going on. If I let him set the terms, let him rewrite the past, play along with his mind games, maybe I'll get to the bottom of this."

"Then what?"

"I wash my hands of this mess."

"Listening to him won't get him the money he wants," Martin said. "If that's the only reason he's hounding you, you shouldn't subject yourself to more torment."

"It might give me enough leverage to reason with him or help him find a reasonable solution."

"You owe him nothing."

That was debatable, but it'd be easier to agree than spin myself in circles like I had when Lucien said the same thing. "You're right, but it's the only way I'll be able to put this behind me. Put him behind me."

"I don't have to go inside with you. I could wait in the

car."

"Go home. Not to the apartment. I'd like to avoid that for a while, if I can."

Marcal pulled in front of the federal building. At this time of day, there wasn't much traffic.

Martin kissed me. "I'll swing by and pick up whatever we need from there before going home, but if you change your mind, I'm a phone call or text message away."

"Thanks." I squeezed Martin's hand before catching Marcal's eye again. "That goes for you too." Then I opened my door and stepped onto the curb. Hopefully, Mark had found something I could use as leverage in my conversation with Don.

I texted Mark and paced in the lobby while a nervous probationary agent kept a careful watch on me. A few minutes later, Mark appeared.

"It's about time you came to your senses. I was afraid you'd skip town," he said.

"The thought may have crossed my mind." I let him lead me to the parking garage and got into the passenger seat of his SUV. "Did you find anything?"

"Not a damn thing. Don was careful. He withdrew cash. There's no paper trail. Kate looked. I looked. We got nothing."

"That does not help me."

"I know." He worked something out of his back tooth. "It's possible he told you the truth. He could have blown his savings on stupid shit. Hookers, blow, baseball tickets, whatever. We have no way of tracking it. What was his exact wording when he threatened you?"

"Find a way to get it before things get ugly. I don't want you to get hurt." I tugged on the seatbelt. "That sounds ominous to me."

"It's too vague. We need something concrete. If it were a direct threat, you could have him arrested."

I'd already considered that, but throwing fuel on the fire was never in anyone's best interest. "Did Kate find out what he did with the money I gave him?"

"He cashed the check."

"Dammit. The divorce settlement is final. Why is he still

hiding his funds?"

"Ex-wives can be vindictive. He may be trying to keep her from getting wind of it. At one point, they both had access to the account. Even though she's been removed, she may have a friend in the bank who'd tell her these things."

"The last thing I need is Lydia showing up." I watched the buildings pass, my anxiety increasing the closer we got to the hotel. She'd know what was going on, but I couldn't fathom making that phone call.

"It's just us, kid. I remember everything you've ever said about your parents. You don't have to put on a stiff upper lip."

"I was drunk."

"You were honest. They tortured you with those practices, making you perform through injuries and pain and punishing you for eating junk food, for watching TV, and trying to be a kid." He licked his lips. "I get why seeing him is hard. But you've got us now. Me. Marty. Those knuckleheads at the precinct you call your friends. We're your family. Nothing will ever change that. Do not let this asshole get in your head."

Mark parked in the check-in lane, and I peered into the brightly lit hotel lobby. It looked warm and inviting, which was not what I expected this encounter to be.

"Let's get this over with." Reluctantly, I pushed open the door and went inside.

Don Parker wasn't at a workstation, so I pushed open the stairwell door. Lucien had gotten his room number, 213. Mark remained a few feet away as I knocked on the door. My heart pounded so loudly I couldn't hear movement inside the room.

I knocked again, relieved my hand wasn't trembling. "Don, it's me. It's Alex. Can we talk?" I waited, but the door remained closed. The light patterns beneath didn't change. I pressed my ear against the heavy door, but I couldn't hear anything inside. "Don?" I waited a beat. "Dad?"

Mark joined me, giving the door a careful look. "Are you sure this is his room?"

"That's what Cross said."

"Let's make sure."

We returned to the lobby where Mark flashed his badge at the desk clerk. She typed in Don's name. "He checked out first thing this morning."

"This morning?" I asked.

"Yeah, he had breakfast and handed in his room key."

"Did he have luggage with him?" I asked.

She looked bewildered. "I can't say for certain, but I'm sure he did."

"Did he leave a note or anything? Maybe something for Alexis or his little swan?"

She checked the cubbyholes on the wall behind her. "No, sorry."

"Can we see inside his room?" Mark asked.

"It's already been cleaned. If he left anything, housekeeping would have turned it in. There would be a note, but there isn't."

"I'd like to see the room anyway," Mark said. "If it's not too much trouble."

"You're lucky it's still vacant." She reached into the drawer and pulled out a key card. After coding it for the room, she handed it to Mark.

We returned upstairs, and he unlocked the door. "Maybe you should wait here."

"Afraid we'll find him dead inside?" I snorted. "Housekeeping would have reported it."

"Fine."

We searched high and low, but the room was pristine. It looked like all the other rooms. Nothing had been left behind. On a whim, I took the hotel provided stationery. If Don wrote something on it, the lab at Cross Security could recover it based on the indentions.

"Don't you have his cell phone number?" Mark asked. "You could call him."

That was a can of worms I hoped to avoid. Even though Ace claimed he gave Don my work number, we hadn't used that to communicate either. Opening up those lines seemed like a bad idea. But I had no idea where Don had gone, and I wasn't optimistic enough to believe he had returned home with his tail between his legs.

“Here,” Mark held out his cell, “use mine.”

The call went straight to voicemail. Don’s message was professional, saying he was out of town and would get back to the caller when he returned.

I shook my head and handed the phone back to Mark. “His phone’s turned off.”

“Odd.” Mark made a call, requesting a location on Don’s cell phone. The last place it pinged before he shut it off three hours ago was the airport. “It looks like he gave up and went home.”

“Let’s hope so.” I bit my lip, replaying everything from this morning. “But if he came to see me after checking out of the hotel, where was his luggage?”

“Maybe he didn’t have any.”

“He’s been here a week. The three times I’ve seen him, he had on different clothes, and he had a laptop. When I found him on that bench this morning, he didn’t have anything with him.”

“Could it have been in the car?”

“As far as I know, he didn’t have a rental, and I doubt he’d trust leaving his belongings in a taxi or rideshare for an unknown amount of time, particularly when he’s strapped for cash and wouldn’t want to leave the meter running. Plus, he walked away. He didn’t get into a car. As far as I could tell, he was headed for the train.”

“He could have parked a few blocks away. I’ll check with the car rental agencies in the morning, but it looks like he got what he could from you and left. Maybe this morning was a last ditch effort. Perhaps, he thought Marty would write him a check on the spot.”

“Yeah, maybe.”

FIFTEEN

The next few days were quiet. The notepad I found in the hotel didn't contain even the slightest hint Don had used it. Mark and I checked with car rental agencies, but no one had any record of Don renting a car. I called every hotel and motel. No Don. The techs at Cross Security pinged his cell phone a few times. He had yet to turn it back on.

Part of me wondered if he was lying dead in a ditch somewhere. Knowing Don, he would have left a note that blamed me for it. So I made sure I read my mail every day. But I didn't find any suicide notes or threatening letters. Don had vanished. I didn't want to look a gift-horse in the mouth, but every cell in my body was telling me something was wrong.

"Parker," Heathcliff waved his hand in front of my face, "did you find something?"

"Huh?"

He came around the desk to see what I was doing. "I thought you were looking at the grocery store security footage for the last month. Isn't that footage from outside your apartment building?"

"I was hoping to see where that guy went."

"We already looked." He folded his arms over his chest. "Didn't we agree the car vandal was unrelated to the armed robberies? Did you find something to the contrary?"

"No, but Cross Security installed the security cameras around my building. I thought with the additional access, I might be able to find something we missed."

"That's the morning after." Heathcliff pointed to the timestamp in the corner. "Do you think he returned to the scene of the crime?"

"That would have been something." I closed the video before Heathcliff spotted me on the screen. "I already went through the grocery store footage. Wayne Savage went to that store with his brother ten days before Eyeholes robbed the place." I pointed to the timeline I'd stuck to the corkboard. "The interior cameras see the two men talking to two other men in the freezer section. Unfortunately, we never get a clear look at the other two because they are both wearing baseball caps. One even had a hooded jacket on over it."

"The freezer section's cold," Heathcliff said.

"Not that cold."

He went to the board where I'd printed out blown-up stills of the two unidentified men. "The one with the baseball cap could be Eyeholes. He's shorter than Wayne Savage. From what I remember at the coffee shop, that fits his profile. Have you tried a side-by-side comparison of this photo and the footage we have of Eyeholes holding up the register?"

"It's impossible to tell anything. The angles are bad. These guys are very much aware of the mechanics of this store. They did a good job staking it out. I'm guessing they did the same thing at the gentlemen's club."

"They didn't do such a good job with the coffee shop," Heathcliff said.

"It's hard to say. That was supposed to be a two-man job. Only one man showed up."

Heathcliff gave me a look. "Why do I get the feeling you're going to make a joke about screwing in a lightbulb?"

"You're just hoping, but I don't have any jokes. However," I brought up every loyalty card membership and charge I could find for both Wayne and Kelsey Savage, "they have a few places they go all the time. It's the places they've only visited once or twice that worry me."

"You think the crew has another job planned?"

"Maybe. Wayne being in custody didn't stop Eyeholes or

the crew from hitting the strip club. I don't think they're going to stop because someone got caught. Wayne didn't stop when Eyeholes backed out. They're on a mission. I just don't know what it is."

"Probably to get as much money as possible."

I maximized a tab I had minimized. "On a related note, have you seen this? Kelsey Savage opened a crowd-funding campaign to raise enough cash for his brother's bail. So far, the only pledge is from an anonymous donor for fifty bucks."

"I'm frightened he's trying this, but I'm relieved random strangers aren't offering to help put a violent offender back on the streets."

"In this case, I agree. But we both know there are plenty of innocent people who spend years behind bars waiting for their day in court because they are too poor to afford bail."

"The system's not perfect, but Wayne Savage would have gladly left our corpses to rot in that alley, so I don't think the bail set for his release was unfair or astronomical."

"Anyway, the point I'm making is Kelsey wants to get Wayne out. Unless he can take out a loan, he's going to need a big score. I've been tracking the places they visited, figuring they may have planned these smaller robberies as practice for something bigger."

"Did you figure out their next target?"

"I've come up with a few possibilities, but none of these places would have enough cash on hand to cover Wayne's bail."

"Kelsey would only need ten percent if he found a bondsman to front the rest."

"Ten percent would be doable." I scanned the list of potential targets. "This doesn't help us identify Eyeholes or the other man involved in the strip club robbery, but that won't matter if we catch them in the act."

Heathcliff looked at the list. "That's assuming you're correct in thinking they'd risk tying themselves to these locations by making a purchase."

"It's hard to go into a restaurant or store and not buy

something without looking suspicious. And nowadays, most people don't carry cash." Don may have been the only exception.

"Tell Franco to run these and see if any of them keep enough cash on hand to cover the ten percent. If they do, we'll check them out." Heathcliff sighed. "I'd love to bring Kelsey in for questioning, but we don't have proof yet. We need more. I don't want to spook him or put him on the defensive until we're sure."

"I'm on it, captain."

Heathcliff shook his head and returned to his desk. Unlike me, he had other cases that needed his attention. I just had the one personal issue that I didn't want to acknowledge.

Taking the list, I went downstairs to see if I could find Officer Franco. He was out on patrol, so I asked the desk sergeant to pass the message along to Franco when he returned.

I'd just settled back behind my desk when my phone vibrated across the surface. *Cross.*

"Hey, boss," I said. "What's up?"

"Where are you?"

"At work."

"I'm standing in your office. Try again."

"I'm at the precinct, working on a case."

"Didn't you finish looking into the police department's investigation for Almeada? He said he received your report. Did you find something else?"

"It's not for that case. This is an armed robbery thing."

"I don't want to know, but make sure you keep track of your billables. I expect my cut."

"Is that why you called?"

"No. I've been looking into your father. The last place his phone pinged was the airport, but he never purchased a ticket to depart or arrive. He didn't fly here, which makes me think he wouldn't fly home. I was considering paying Ace another visit."

"Don lost the car in the divorce," I said. "Jablonsky and I couldn't connect Don to a rental car. So I don't think he drove either."

"He could have taken a bus," Cross said, "or the train. It's far more common to purchase those tickets with cash without arousing suspicion."

I'd been failing miserably at putting this behind me. I never wanted to see Don, and now that he was gone, I had this sinking feeling. If he hadn't shown up outside my apartment, I would have been content writing him off. Now I was worried. I just wasn't sure if I was worried about him or me.

"Do you think Ace Darrow's going to help us after the stunt you pulled with his computer?" I asked.

"He will if he knows what's good for him."

* * *

Broken glass crunched beneath my feet as I pushed open the door to Ace Investigators. The blinds on the front windows had all been drawn. From outside, there was no way of seeing the damage inside. The filing cabinets were overturned, the files scattered. Dirt from the potted plant made a straight line across the thin carpet. Ace's desk was overturned, as was his associate's. The drawers had been removed and broken, leaving splinters everywhere.

Lucien Cross stood in the center of the room, his gaze scanning the ceiling.

"What did you do?" I asked, appalled by the destruction.

Cross didn't answer. Instead, he pointed to the bashed in security cameras in two corners of the room. One had been hit, probably by a piece of the broken drawer. The other had been yanked off the wall so hard the cord had ripped through the ceiling tiles, leaving a serpentine line above and a matching one in fiberglass dust below. "The computer's gone. I'm guessing the backup hard drive, modem, and router are also missing. But I haven't checked. Ace kept them in the ceiling."

"Did you do this?"

He turned to look at me over his shoulder. "No, Alex. I did not."

"Where's Ace?"

Cross pointed to what looked like blood spatter. "If he

was here, he's not now."

I reached for my phone to call the police.

"Not yet," Cross said.

"Lucien, he could be dead or kidnapped. We have to report this."

"Not yet." He pulled on a pair of leather gloves and moved carefully through the room, making sure not to disturb the patterns on the floor. He righted one of the plastic lawn chairs and stepped onto the seat. Carefully, he slid the memory card panel open on the security camera. "The card's gone."

"If that's wired to a hard drive, there may not have been a card," I said.

"Ace always had backups for his backups." Cross rocked a little on the chair, struggling to maintain his balance while he lifted one of the few undamaged ceiling tiles. "Hand me a flashlight."

I pulled the tiny light from my keychain and did as he asked. "Do you see anything?"

"The wires that would have connected to the equipment. Like I said, everything's gone." He replaced the ceiling tile and stepped down from the chair.

"Any idea who did this?"

"With Ace, the possibilities are endless. The man is a real piece of work. Just another one of my mistakes I'd prefer not to think about."

"Your mistake?"

"We used to work together." Cross narrowed his eyes at the tiny air vent near the top of the wall. Carrying the lawn chair to the vent, he climbed back on top and used a dime from his pocket to remove the screws. "Whoever destroyed the place didn't expect Ace to have another backup." Cross pulled out a tiny camera and checked the display to find it still recording. After popping out the memory card, he wiped the internal memory and reset the recording. Then he replaced it in the vent and screwed it back in place. "Now that we have what we need, you can call the police."

SIXTEEN

I was already back at the precinct when the police brought a battered Ace Darrow in for questioning. Ace had an ice pack pressed to his swollen lip. Blood dribbled down his chin, which he kept wiping away. The officer who'd brought him to the station asked if he needed medical attention, but Ace refused.

"Stay here." The officer pointed to some chairs near the main desk. "I'll get a detective to take your statement."

"Sure." Ace eased into a chair. From the way he moved, he was hurting.

I took a seat beside him. "Who'd you piss off?"

He looked surprised to see me. The officer must not have told him who had made the call which resulted in the wellness check at Ace's apartment. "Get the hell away from me."

"Take it easy." I looked around, but no one seemed concerned by his panicked tone. "What happened? Who did this to you?"

"Ask Lucien. He probably ran his mouth about my video files and sent a pissed off ex-husband to pound on me."

"Why would he do that?"

Ace snorted. "As payback for handing out the dirty deets on you."

"What dirty deets? Who did you tell about me? Did someone else come knocking besides Don?"

"I don't want to have anything to do with any of this,

okay? You, your dad, your boss, you all need to stay the hell away from me. Do you understand that?"

"Tell me what happened."

"Nothing. Someone showed up at the office, trashed my place, and took everything. I have to start over." The extent of that hit him like a ton of bricks. "My clients aren't going to be happy when they find out what happened."

"What does any of this have to do with me?"

"I don't know, sugar pop, but I didn't have any of these issues until you showed up. That tells me this is all on you."

"In that case, I need you to tell me everything you know about Don Parker."

"We've been over this. I don't know shit."

"How much do you want?"

"Nothing," Ace spat. "Because I don't know a thing. And I don't want to. No amount of money is going to change my mind on that."

"When Don first contacted you, where was he?"

"How would I know?"

"Did you ask? Trace the call? Do anything?"

"I assume he was at home. He said once I found something, he'd make the trip."

"How?"

"How what?"

"How was he going to make the trip?" I asked. "Did he fly? Take a bus? Drive?"

"He clicked his fucking heels three times and made a wish." Ace glared at me. "How should I know?"

"Do you know where he is now?"

"If he's smart, he's as far away from here as possible." Ace made sniffing sounds and spit up a glob of bloody phlegm. "Hey," he hollered at the desk sergeant, "what's taking that detective so long? This bitch is bothering me."

I held up my palms and stepped away. "I found his office ransacked and called it in. I was just asking him what happened."

"A detective will do that. Why don't you wait in that meeting room for someone to take your statement?" The look on the sergeant's face told me not to argue.

"Sure, just let Detective Heathcliff know I'll be up to see

him as soon as I finish down here." I moved toward the meeting room the sergeant indicated. "Have you finished interviewing Mr. Cross?"

The sergeant knew what game I was playing. "Not yet. He should be done soon. I'll let Heathcliff know where you are."

"Thanks."

A few minutes later, the door opened. Heathcliff sighed. "I leave you alone for a few minutes, and you get yourself into more trouble. How is that even possible?"

"I was following up on something unrelated, and Cross and I walked into a crime scene."

Heathcliff sat down, shoving the familiar forms and legal pad toward me. "You know the drill. While you fill that out, you can fill me in."

I told him everything except the part about Don hiring Ace Investigators and Cross taking the memory card with him. The last thing my boss would want to face was evidence tampering or obstruction charges. More than likely, the police wouldn't even check the vent, not with all the other destruction inside the office. But if they did, they'd find the hidden camera and could question Ace about why it was there.

Taking the paperwork from me, Heathcliff tapped the sheets against the edge of the table. "While you were gone, another call came in. Armed robbery. Three men. They had *Phantom of the Opera* masks on."

"Do you think it's the same crew?"

"I think it's a possibility. Officers are securing the scene and questioning witnesses."

"Shouldn't we get going?"

Heathcliff's expression hardened, and he tapped the pages again. "What is this about, Parker? Don't tell me it's another case or a Cross Security thing. I need details."

"Someone hired Ace Darrow to look into me. His place got ransacked, and I'm wondering if it had anything to do with the information he pulled on me or the person who asked him to pull it."

"Do you think it does? Do you think someone's out for revenge?"

"I don't know enough yet."

"The asshole with the hammer could have been looking for you."

"It's too soon to jump to conclusions. But I had the same thought, just no proof."

"You should have mentioned this sooner." Heathcliff stared at me. "Has Cross attempted to ID Mr. Hammer?"

"Too much of his face was covered. After he left the garage, he disappeared into a blind spot. We got nothing."

"That would explain why you've looked like shit the last few times I've seen you and why you were looking at security footage from around your building. Why didn't you tell me any of this?"

"It's not important. I'm probably just paranoid."

He thought for a moment. "Do you know who hired Ace Investigators to look into you?"

"That would be my father."

"Why would he hire a private eye? Why wouldn't he just call you?"

"We don't keep in touch, not since my parents kicked me out when I turned eighteen."

Heathcliff didn't ask questions or offer sympathy about what happened back then. "Do you think he intends to harm you?"

"Not physically." Again, Don's words played through my head, but I pushed them to the back of my mind. "But someone might be looking to harm him and may have gotten confused about the dynamics of our non-relationship."

"Look, if you need time to handle that, I'll understand. Moretti will understand. We can offer resources to help."

"It's too soon to assume anything. The last I heard, my father had left town. I went to Ace Investigators to see if Ace had a current address or any idea where he might have gone, and that's when I found the place trashed. Ace had files on his computer that he could have been using to blackmail his clients. More than likely, one of them got wind of it and came for revenge. What happened to him probably doesn't have anything to do with me."

"But you don't know for sure."

"Not yet."

Heathcliff looked torn. Finally, he said, "Grab your things. We have a crime scene to visit."

* * *

The trio had held up a check-cashing establishment. The place hadn't been on my list, but it was across the street from a dollar store that Wayne Savage had shopped at a month ago. The store had been included on my list, but if this was Savage's crew, I'd been wrong about the location.

Unlike the other places that had been robbed, this place had bars on the windows and security cameras covering the entire store. Beneath the desk was a panic button. The clerk had tripped it, which triggered the silent alarm that notified 9-1-1 of the robbery in progress. By the time units arrived, the robbers had escaped.

The clerk sat on the sofa, the vinyl cushions creaking as he trembled and rocked. "All three of them came in together. At first, I didn't notice the masks. I wasn't looking at the door. A woman had just handed me her paycheck, and I had the safe open so I could take out more money. It was the worst time possible for them to show up. The next thing I know, she's screaming. I turned to look, and I didn't see her. They'd knocked her to the ground, and the business end of a sawed-off is inches from my face."

"A sawed-off shotgun?" Heathcliff asked, jotting down a few details.

"Yes, sir." The clerk sucked in a shaky breath. "I think that's what it was. It could have been something else, I guess. I'm not sure what, though. It all happened so fast."

"They came in from there?" I pointed to the front door.

The clerk looked at the door behind me. "Yeah."

I went to the door, seeing the two cameras which covered the doorway and the other camera which covered the rest of the shop.

"How would you describe them?" Heathcliff asked.

"Scary," the clerk said.

I examined the room. It was a straight shot from the doorway to the desk. On the desk was a register. Behind it was a safe. Off to the right was a door which presumably led to a back office and a rear exit. “Where were they standing?” I asked.

“The main guy, the one with the sawed-off, he was right there.” He pointed to one of the black tiles which formed the checkerboard pattern on the floor. Blood had dripped onto the six tiles closest to it, the red contrasting sharply with the white while leaving nothing but a wet look on the black spaces. “That’s where the woman had been, so he had shoved her down and took her spot.”

“And the other two?” I asked.

“Um...”

There wasn’t a lot of space. The vinyl sofa stood on one side of the room as a sort of waiting area. On the other side were a few chairs and a small cabinet set up with a complimentary coffee station and a pen on a chain for anyone who’d forgotten to sign his check. It reminded me of a bank.

“Was anyone waiting for service?” Heathcliff asked.

The clerk shook his head. “No, but I thought the three men were going to wait. Two of them were near the chairs. I don’t think they sat. I don’t remember them sitting. I just remember guns.”

“Guns?” Heathcliff asked. “They had more than one?”

“One of the other guys, the tall one, had a revolver. It was a big thing. Didn’t look like it held many bullets, but it looked like it could put a hole in something.”

“That’s what guns do,” I muttered.

Heathcliff glanced at me, communicating with his eyes that he didn’t think my comment was helpful. “Did either of the other men speak?”

“Not that I recall. I just remember the one in front of me. He wanted everything from the safe and register.”

“How much did he take?” Heathcliff consulted the intel the uniforms had already collected.

“Everything.” The clerk pointed to the empty safe and opened drawer on the register. “He cleaned us out. It had to be close to fifty thousand dollars. We’d just gotten a fresh infusion last night since it’s the first of the month and we know a lot of people are getting paid and would be showing up."

"Shouldn't you have armed security?" Heathcliff asked.

"We do, but the guard got food poisoning and went home early. His relief was supposed to show up, but he's not the punctual type."

Heathcliff made sure he had contact information for the two security guards while I gloved up and examined the contents of the trash can. I had to sift through a lot of empty coffee cups and receipts before I found a bag from a Chinese takeout place.

I held it up. "Is this where the guard ate lunch today?"

The couch cushion squeaked as the clerk turned to look at me. "I'm pretty sure that's the place. It's pick-up only. It's a block from here."

I recognized the name. It was on my list of possible target locations since Wayne Savage had been there once before.

"Did any of the men have distinguishing features?" Heathcliff asked. "Tattoos? Scars?"

"I didn't get a good look at any of them. Between the guns and the masks, I didn't notice much else."

"What about an earring?"

"Maybe. I don't know."

Heathcliff clicked his pen. "What were they wearing?"

The clerk gestured at the cameras. "Wouldn't it be easier to look for yourself?"

SEVENTEEN

Photos pulled from the security cameras had been printed and were circulating. The man with the shotgun had an earring, but it had been obscured by the edge of his collar. All we knew was it was shiny and round at the top, like a silver skull and crossbones.

Uniformed officers were checking the nearby shops to see if anyone had seen anything. Instead of helping with the grunt work, Heathcliff and I decided now would be a good time to pick up some takeout.

"The only camera is at the order window," I said. "They don't have anything near the pick-up window."

I watched as several people milled about inside the tiny restaurant. Most had their faces glued to their phones. No one paid much attention. The only time anyone looked up was when the bell dinged and a number was called.

Heathcliff examined the health department's score posted on the middle window. It read A-. "The place was checked last week."

"I didn't believe the restaurant was responsible for giving the guard food poisoning," I said.

"The lab will be analyzing the remnants inside the container that you found to make sure."

A woman looked up. "Did you say food poisoning?"

Heathcliff flashed his badge. "Do you eat here often?"

"At least twice a week. It's on my way home from work, and they have the best dumplings. Please tell me it wasn't the dumplings."

"Have you ever gotten sick from eating here?" Heathcliff asked.

She shook her head. "I always thought this was one of the better places." She pointed to the glass where you could see the cooks preparing the meals. "It always looked much cleaner and less cluttered than what I've seen at other places with boxes of sauces and fortune cookies everywhere. Was I wrong to think that?"

"The health inspector doesn't think so." I pointed to the restaurant's rating.

"Would you mind looking at a few photos?" Heathcliff showed her the stills printed from today's armed robbery. "Have you seen any of these men?"

She shook her head.

"What about these men?" I brought up ID photos of Wayne and Kelsey Savage and held them up so she could see.

"No. Sorry." The bell dinged, and she went to the counter. "This is safe to eat, right?"

The restaurant worker gave her a bewildered look. "Yes." He tossed a handful of fortune cookies and a few packets of soy sauce and mustard into her bag. "Have a nice day."

She gave me a look as she headed for the door. But I kept my mouth shut. Although I didn't think the food was contaminated, I didn't know for certain and didn't want to risk giving her my word under the circumstances.

A moment later, the bell dinged again and a number was called. This time, the restaurant worker left the bag on the counter and disappeared back into the kitchen. A man who'd been tapping furiously on his phone got up from where he was waiting on one of the benches and trudged over, his eyes still on his screen. Blindly, he grabbed the bag with his left hand and headed toward the door. Only when he bumped into the glass did he look up, push the door open, and put his phone away.

"It wouldn't be impossible for someone to have slipped something into the guard's food before he picked it up at the window," I said.

"That's assuming he wasn't paying attention."

"Do you think the guard was in on the robbery? A job like that should have required more than three guys."

"I checked with the hospital. The guard left work and went to the emergency room. They have him on fluids, but he's been puking his guts out since he arrived. An officer is waiting to question him further, but they haven't made much progress with all the interruptions."

"That doesn't mean he didn't poison himself on purpose."

"Most people wouldn't be that committed to the idea."

Heathcliff had a point. As soon as there was a lull, one of the restaurant workers opened the door and allowed us into the kitchen to question the staff. No one recognized the men involved in the hold-up, but that may have been because of the masks.

"I'll get you the security footage," the cook said. "Maybe we overlooked them. When we get busy, we don't pay attention, and we're busy a lot."

"Do you remember the security guard?" I asked.

The cook smiled. "Ned. He comes here almost every day. He's one of our best customers. Always orders the same thing, moo goo gai pan. He's watching his weight, so he asks us to go light on the sauce."

Another order was up, and one of the other cooks marked the takeout box with a red marker, indicating what was inside, before putting it in the window and ringing the bell. If Ned always ordered the same thing, it'd be easy for someone to lace his food. Unfortunately, without evidence, this was nothing but speculation.

"Thanks for this." Heathcliff palmed the USB drive that held the footage.

"One last thing," I found a photo of Eyeholes on my phone from the grocery store robbery, "do you recognize this guy?"

The cook squinted at my screen. "I'm sure someone was in the shop today with a ripped knit hat." He called to one of the other cooks to take a look.

"He was here today," the other cook said. "I recognize that jacket and hat. It must have been around lunchtime, maybe one o'clock. All he got was an order of egg rolls."

"Can you tell us anything else about him?" Heathcliff asked. "How did he pay for his order?"

"I don't remember. Let me check the receipts." The cook went through a stack of order tickets until he found one with nothing on it but egg rolls. "It was 12:52 when he placed the order. He paid with a credit card. That information gets encrypted, but we have the last four digits of the card."

Heathcliff took the restaurant's copy of the receipt. "What time did Ned place his order?"

"12:48," the cook said.

"Is there anything else you can tell us about the man with the ripped hat?" Heathcliff asked.

The cook shook his head, turning when another customer stepped up to place an order.

The receipt indicated the egg rolls were bought with a VISA. It could have been a debit or credit card. But we had the last four digits. That had to be enough. "Do you think you can track down the owner with this?" I asked.

"We should be able to. But it'll take some time." Heathcliff reached for his phone and made the request. Now we had to wait for the numbers to be run and narrowed. At least we'd know we had the right man if there was a charge for Chinese food timestamped at 12:52. "The footage might be able to tell us something faster."

"When did you become the optimistic one?" I asked.

"Did that sound like optimism to you?"

"It did."

"You need to get your ears checked." Heathcliff led me back to his cruiser and plugged the drive into the computer. "The cooks narrowed everything down for us, which should make this a lot easier." He moved the time bar until we were within minutes of Ned the Guard placing his lunch order.

Ned entered and stood in line. By the time he made it to the order window, I could see the familiar beanie on top of someone's head. Tufts of hair stuck out of the two ripped holes, making the robber hard to miss.

When the woman in front of him stepped to the side to

get a better look at the menu board, the camera caught sight of the man's face. "That's Eyeholes," I said.

"Yep." Heathcliff paused the video, wrote down the timestamp, and hit play. A moment later, Eyeholes looked down and kept his head down until he made it to the order window. Heathcliff paused it again. "If this is one of the *Phantoms* from the check-cashing place, he changed clothes. No one was dressed like this. We would have recognized the ripped beanie from their footage."

"Maybe he ditched the jacket and tossed the beanie." I unpaused the footage, but since the cameras were only focused on the order window, we couldn't tell what happened after Ned or Eyeholes walked off screen. Neither reappeared on the footage. "Ned would have walked here to pick up his lunch. Do you think Eyeholes followed him back to work?"

"He wouldn't have had to follow him since he knew where Ned was going, but someone must have been set up outside the check-cashing place in order to time everything just right. I don't think the robbers happened to get lucky with the safe being open when they decided to strike. They must have been watching from somewhere with a clear view inside." Heathcliff looked around.

Getting out of the car, I headed back to the shop. Two squad cars remained parked out front. Not many places provided a clear view of the safe. Whoever had been watching the shop must have been directly in front of it. I crossed the street and continued in a straight line while Heathcliff went inside to see if the latest victim remembered seeing Eyeholes in or near the check-cashing place.

In an alcove where one storefront ended and the next began, I found a half empty duck sauce packet on the ground. Given the lack of insects surrounding it and the unmarred plastic packaging, it couldn't have been there long. This was the best place to maintain eyes inside the check-cashing place. Eyeholes must have stood here while he waited for Ned to leave and the safe to open.

When Heathcliff joined me outside, I pointed to the duck sauce, resisting the urge to pick it up. "I think I found something."

Heathcliff liked to do things by the book when possible, so I let him handle the evidence. He crouched down and examined the packet closely. "It looks like you may have found us a usable print."

EIGHTEEN

Cross was waiting for me when we returned to the precinct. He gave Heathcliff a wary look. “We have things to discuss, Alex. In private.”

“I’ll meet you upstairs,” I said to Heathcliff.

We’d already dropped off the evidence we’d collected. Hopefully, the techs could match the nearly perfect thumbprint on the duck sauce packet to a print in the database or determine Eyeholes’ identity from the credit card receipt or the image we pulled off the takeout restaurant’s surveillance footage. But since Wayne Savage had no priors, I wasn’t sure Eyeholes did either. But that had to be his duck sauce packet. At least, I assumed it was. For all I knew, it could have belonged to any of the dozens of people who went in and out of that restaurant this afternoon.

“Alex,” Lucien grabbed my elbow and led me to a spot beside the door, “how much did you tell them about Ace Investigators?”

“The basics. Ace Darrow has enemies. He may have been involved in blackmailing schemes. Tons of people would want to hurt him.”

Cross glanced back at the front desk, but no one cared we were here. Still, he forced me closer to the wall. “Keep your voice down.”

“You’re letting your paranoia get the best of you. Can’t one of your medics prescribe something for that?”

"I'll ask if you're interested in a prescription of your own."

"Forget it."

He gave the desk another look. "I told the police what I could without mentioning your issues or our previous visit. I'd prefer if you keep those details to yourself."

"Agreed."

He gave me a look. "You already told Detective Heathcliff about this."

"I mentioned a family member may have hired Ace to dig into me. That was it. No more. No less. I won't rat on you, Lucien." I jerked my chin toward his pocket. "Did you get a chance to look at the footage yet?"

"Do you see me holding a computer?"

"You have your ways."

My boss smiled. "The man who broke in wore basic black, mask, gloves, what you'd expect from someone with two functioning brain cells. Given his build and the way he moved, I don't believe it was your father. I'd say the assailant is younger, taller, and more athletic. He's tall and burly. Between 6'2 and 6'4."

"Big guy, so definitely not Don. Do you think the big guy's a professional?"

"I have Justin looking into the possibility. But I'm of the opinion a professional wouldn't have left Ace breathing. The beating was only part of an interrogation."

"What did the big guy want to know?" I asked.

"Audio was garbled due to the heat running. I have my techs working on it. They should be able to clean it up, but it may take several hours. Until then, the only thing I'm certain of is the big guy was looking for something. That's why he searched the office and took the hard drives."

"Do you think he found whatever it was?"

Cross tilted his head from side to side. "I'm not sure. It's possible whatever he wanted was already destroyed when I reformatted the hard drive. But he took the hard drive with him. Some files could be recovered."

"Ace told me this had to do with me."

"Did he tell you how he reached that conclusion?"

"He said he didn't have any trouble until he started

looking into me."

"That's Ace. He never understood correlation and causality." Cross made sure the cops at the front desk hadn't decided to eavesdrop on our conversation. "This may have had nothing to do with any of that or us." He wagged a finger in my face. "I don't want to hear that shit about coincidences. These may be two unrelated events. We'll know once the audio is finished. In the meantime, the police sent Ace home. They'll keep units on his place, but I'll check on him. Maybe bring him some soup."

"Don't spit in it."

"I wouldn't waste perfectly good saliva." Cross buttoned his jacket. "I'll call as soon as I know something. Your time would be better spent at the office, but I doubt I'll be able to convince you of that."

"Sorry."

"You're not." He pulled open the door. "I will keep you informed of any progress. If you learn something, I hope you'll return the favor."

"This isn't your problem, Lucien."

He stepped closer until his lips were near my ear. "Landon Parker came to my office and threatened my investigator. That makes this a Cross Security problem."

"As far as we know, he's long gone."

"Once that's been confirmed, we'll get back to business as usual."

I wanted to thank him, to tell him how much I appreciated him looking out, despite the way we often butted heads, but he was out the door before I could utter a word. "Thanks," I said to the lingering scent of his aftershave.

"What did Cross want?" Heathcliff asked when I met him at his desk.

"To remind me I have other obligations as a Cross Security investigator."

"Do you have to go back to work?"

"You mean this doesn't count? Isn't this what you call work?"

Heathcliff chuckled. "Point taken." He indicated the printed stills of the three robbers he'd hung on our corkboard. Beneath one of the robbers, he placed the photo of Eyeholes from the Chinese restaurant. "The clerk didn't recognize Eyeholes, but the robbers wore masks and were dressed differently, so we can't assume anything." Heathcliff pointed to the only unarmed member of the robbery crew. "Eyeholes had a gun in his pocket when we spotted him at the coffee shop. If this is the same guy, why wasn't he armed at the check-cashing place?"

"Are you sure it's the same guy?" I moved closer, squinting at the photos. "It's hard to tell. The hair's the same color, but the cameras don't get a close enough look at his face to make out eye color. We know the clothes don't match. Maybe Eyeholes acted as the lookout. He stood across the street and ate his egg rolls while he let his pals do the heavy lifting."

"That would mean we're looking at a four-man crew. If Wayne hadn't been pinched, that'd be five. How come only three hit the strip club?"

"When we figure out who Eyeholes is, you should ask him." I looked at the photo of Kelsey Savage with the question marks surrounding it. "You should question Wayne's brother concerning his whereabouts from this afternoon." I pointed to the earring the ringleader wore. "Twenty says Kelsey took the lead on today's robbery. Given everything we know, you must have grounds to bring him in."

"They're a little shaky, but Moretti will sign off, if for no other reason than Kelsey may have information on what other crimes his brother had planned." Heathcliff went back to studying the photos. "The *Phantom of the Opera* masks make it hard to tell who's who, but the techs are using other physical markers to make comparisons between the robbers and our list of potential suspects. Eyeholes is within the height and weight range of the unarmed third man, which is why I'm not sure he didn't pull a costume change and help rob the place." Heathcliff flicked the photo. "Eyeholes could have poisoned the guard, waited for Ned to get sick and leave, and once the safe was opened, he changed his jacket, ditched the hat, and joined his buddies inside."

"Kelsey had the shotgun," I said. "He had the strongest motive for robbing the place. He wants to bail out his brother. But we still don't know who the other armed man is, and frankly, I'm not convinced the unarmed man is Eyeholes. We could be looking at a crew of four."

"Why do you want to make this harder than it is?"

"Martin asks me that all the time."

Heathcliff ignored me, flicking the photo of four men in the freezer section of the grocery store weeks before the robbery. "It's basic math. Wayne's in custody. That's his brother Kelsey. This one could be Eyeholes, and that leaves one unknown. They may have had a crew of four to start, but they're down to three."

"They could have found a replacement."

Heathcliff sat down, sorting the papers on his desk. Once things were organized, he reviewed his interview notes. "Three men entered the shop. The main guy threatened the clerk. The other two didn't speak, and they didn't approach the counter. They were working in a support capacity in case other customers entered. Luckily, that didn't happen, or we could be looking at a bloodbath."

"The clerk said the three of them left together and headed east out of the shop. Someone must have seen something."

"No one spotted three *Phantoms* heading down the street."

"What about the customer?" We hadn't questioned her, so I didn't know what she had to say.

"The woman who'd been cashing her check was no help. The *Phantom* with the shotgun hit her from behind and made sure she stayed down, facing the floor. She didn't see anything."

"Dammit."

Heathcliff pointed at the photo display. "The leader concealed the shotgun beneath his jacket before and after the robbery."

"That's not easy to do, especially with the cops approaching and a heavy bag of loot over his shoulder." I tried to recall every shop and alleyway to the east of the check-cashing place. "They could have tossed their weapons. After all, we know the robbers had gloves on. Prints wouldn't have been a concern." I thought about the duck sauce. "Why wasn't Eyeholes wearing gloves when he got lunch, assuming he's the source of the fingerprint?"

"The gloves would have been suspicious when he paid. Plus, have you ever tried to open a sauce packet with gloves on? It's nearly impossible to do."

"The trick is to wear leather gloves. That stops the plastic from slipping," I said.

"Eyeholes didn't have leather gloves. His gloves were the same knit material as his beanie."

"He could own more than one pair of gloves."

"That's doubtful when he only has one beanie."

"Do you think he's homeless?" I asked.

"Probably not, but since we know the Savages are strapped for cash, I'm guessing everyone in their crew is in the same boat."

"I'll go over Kelsey's and Wayne's work records and social media profiles again to see if I can find any groups or message boards where they posted about financial difficulties or asked about job searches. Maybe that's how they connected with Eyeholes and whoever else is in the crew."

"In the meantime, I'll see if there's anything else on this footage we overlooked. Officer Franco's searching the area for evidence. If they tossed the shotgun, revolver, or their masks, he'll find them."

NINETEEN

By the time I left the precinct, not much progress had been made. Everything was still in the works. Surely, by morning, there would be something concrete. In the meantime, an unmarked car had Kelsey under surveillance. Heathcliff and I would pay him a visit in the morning.

I returned to Cross Security and checked to see what kind of progress we had made. The audio had been cleaned up, but I didn't recognize the assailant's voice. He demanded files from Ace. He didn't specify which files, and, as expected, Ace Darrow played dumb. That's when things took a turn.

"He whispered something to him." I pointed to the footage of Ace, who'd been held at gunpoint and zip-tied to his desk chair. "Right there."

The masked man leaned in while securing the second zip-tie. His face was to the side of Ace's head and even though his mouth was covered by the mask, I could see the fabric moving.

Cross's resident expert shrugged. "It didn't make it to the recording." He showed me the track, but the words weren't loud enough to register over the humming of the heating system. "There's nothing I can do."

"Ace won't talk," I said.

"Has Lucien spoken to him?"

"He said he was going to bring him soup, so maybe that's what he's doing now."

The tech snorted, a knowing grin on his face. "We will know what was said soon enough."

"I hope you're right." I exhaled, unsure if I wanted to know the lengths my boss would go to get answers.

Cross didn't seem like the torture type, and with the police out front, I didn't think he'd risk getting arrested for assault. But I could never be sure what he was thinking or how he'd act.

"Did that phone number I asked you to ping ever turn back on?" I asked.

"No."

"Any financial activity on the accounts I gave you?"

The tech slid his chair to another work terminal and hit a few keys. "Sorry."

"Thanks for checking."

"That's why Lucien keeps me around."

Unsure what to do now, I returned to my office. I'd already gone over the Savages' social media pages and internet activity with a fine-tooth comb. They were careful. They didn't have any radical or inflammatory posts indicating they planned to go on a crime spree. And their contacts appeared to be just as innocent. Could we be looking at this all wrong?

Wayne Savage didn't have a criminal record. His brother's record was the result of youthful indiscretions. And with the way Eyeholes acted outside the coffee shop, I doubted he'd ever done anything like that before. He may have been gun shy, which is why I didn't think he'd gone inside the check-cashing place when the leader of the crew was brandishing a shotgun and assaulting innocent bystanders. But Eyeholes had been inside the gentlemen's club when that robbery occurred, and those robbers had also been armed. Heathcliff was probably right. Eyeholes served as lookout, changed his jacket, lost the hat, and went to back up his crew.

Every one of my instincts said Kelsey Savage had been the *Phantom* with the shotgun. Besides the earring, there was something about the way that particular *Phantom* moved that made me think it was him. But I couldn't put my finger on it.

While I went back over every media file Kelsey had posted, from photos to videos, I thought about the surveillance footage. After an hour, I found one of his social media posts where he was singing a lullaby to his baby boy. He cradled his son in one arm as he swayed. With his left hand, he tapped a rhythm on his thigh using only his ring finger. That was it.

Rubbing my face, I grabbed my phone and called Heathcliff with the update. The detective had gone home for the night, same as me, but I knew he wouldn't mind the interruption. He answered on the second ring.

"I thought you and Martin made a pact not to bring work home," he said.

"We did no such thing. And I'm not at home. I'm at Cross Security. There was something familiar about the shotgunner from today's robbery that reminded me of Kelsey Savage."

"They're the same height, weight, and have the same hair color."

"Besides all that."

"I'm listening."

I sent the video to Heathcliff. "It's the tapping. I've never seen anyone else use only his ring finger. The shotgunner tapped the same way on the side of the gun."

"That doesn't hurt, but it's not irrefutable evidence."

"I wouldn't want to overstep. This is your rodeo. I'm just one of the clowns. But all these little things add up."

Heathcliff laughed. "Actually, it's Franco's rodeo."

"Does that mean he found something?"

"He called ten minutes before you did. In a dumpster, three blocks from the crime scene, he found the *Phantom of the Opera* masks inside a Chinese takeout bag."

"Did he find the shotgun?"

"No, but forensics has the masks. They didn't find any prints on them, but they should be able to pull epithelial cells, maybe hair, maybe more. It'll take forever to get the DNA results back, but it doesn't take nearly as long to run a comparison."

"Do you have enough to compel Kelsey Savage to cooperate?"

"You don't think your tapping observation is enough on its own?"

"No, Derek, I don't."

He was enjoying giving me a hard time. "In that case, tomorrow's interview should be enough to seal the deal. As long as he doesn't have an airtight alibi for the time of the robbery, getting a court order shouldn't be that difficult."

"Again with that optimism thing?"

"Get your ears checked, Parker. I'm a realist. And the facts are on our side. Worst case, we find out Kelsey Savage isn't involved, and we turn our focus elsewhere."

"What about the fingerprint on the sauce packet?" I asked.

"Lab hasn't gotten in touch, so I'm guessing they're still working on it. If I get a text at four a.m., do you want me to call and tell you?"

"Only if you think you should."

"Night, Parker."

"Good night, Derek."

At least something was looking up. I dialed Cross's extension. After two rings, his assistant, Justin, answered. I asked if Cross had returned to the office, but Justin told me he had not.

"Is there anything you can tell me about Ace Darrow?"

"Enough to fill volumes," Justin said. "But none of that will help you. Ace knows how to find dirt. He also knows how to hide things."

"You're not making me feel any better."

"That's not why you're asking these questions. Is there still no word on your father?"

"He left town."

"You don't think so. Do you think the man who ransacked Ace Investigators is looking for your father?"

"Don asked me for money. He said he didn't want to see me get hurt."

"But you paid him."

"He wanted more."

"Should I start calling hospitals and check with the morgue?"

"No." I'd already done that earlier today before things

got exciting at the precinct.

"Would you like a security detail to watch your back? If Don said you'd get hurt, he must have figured whoever he owes may come to you for payment."

"Or Don was being dramatic and hoping I'd cave."

"Do you think that's the case?"

"I wouldn't doubt it." I wondered if my father would go to the lengths of faking his own death to avoid paying back his debts or to freak me out enough that when he resurfaced I'd gladly find a way to hand over every cent he ever spent on me on the off chance he wasn't lying. "I don't need a security detail. Ace Darrow might."

"Lucien will take care of that."

"Are you serious?"

"It's getting late, Ms. Parker. Is there anything else?"

"No."

After setting a reminder to show up to tomorrow's morning meeting before heading to Bruiser's, I collected my things and drove home. Since my car had a hole in it, I took the company car to Martin's estate and pulled into the garage. His town car was parked in its normal spot. I hadn't expected him home so early.

Once the security system reengaged, I went up the stairs to the second floor. "Honey, I'm home."

A grunt came from the vicinity of the kitchen.

The wet bar had a fresh bucket of ice and a dribble of scotch on the surface. As I entered the kitchen, I found Martin standing near the back door. He had the blinds pulled up so he could see the pool. The lights reflected off the water and rising steam.

He held the glass down by his side. Condensation dripped from the bottom, but he didn't notice. The knuckles on his right hand were cut and bruised.

"Tough day at work?" I asked.

"You could say that."

"Do you want to talk about it?"

He shook his head and turned, offering a smile. "No. I'm good."

"You don't look good."

"It must be the t-shirt and jeans. You were expecting me

in a suit."

"Where is your suit?"

"Upstairs."

"Did you get blood on it?"

"What?"

"Your hand."

He put the glass down on the counter and examined his knuckles. "Oh, I uh...came home and decided to work some things out on the heavy bag. I didn't bother with the wraps."

"What about the gloves?"

"I wasn't in the mood."

I moved closer, gently running my fingers up the scruff on his jaw. "Are you okay?"

"Yeah." He held my hands in his before bending down to kiss me. "I'm fine. It was just a bad day. Work stuff. The bag took the brunt of it."

"Bruiser?"

He shook his head, a familiar spark returning to his eyes. "He's fine. PT went well. He took a few steps with his crutches today."

"That's great."

Martin smiled, but it didn't look quite right. "Yeah."

"Are you hungry? I'll cook."

"I ate with Bruiser."

"You must have left work early."

He pulled away. "Let's not talk about work. I don't even want to think about it right now."

I held up my palms. "No problem." But Martin never acted like this.

Opening the fridge, I was surprised by the lack of takeout. Normally, Martin brought something home for me to eat, not trusting that I could be bothered to feed myself, which was often true. When I turned back around, he was staring out the door again.

"It's a bit cold, but with the heaters, we could swim. We may freeze when we get out, but hey, I'm game if you are." I ran my hands down his shoulders.

He tugged on the cord, releasing the raised blinds. With a flick of his fingers, he closed them. With an all-too familiar glint in his eye, he turned to face me. “Don’t you want dinner?”

“Not really.”

He moved closer, like a lion stalking a gazelle. “Is there anything else you have to do tonight?”

“You.”

TWENTY

Even after Martin fell asleep, the ferocity didn't dissipate. He wrapped his arms around me, cocooning me. He knew I hated that, but it didn't stop him. And it was the only way he could fall asleep.

I tried to relax, but the tension radiated off him. Why wouldn't he talk to me? This must have been how he felt every time I avoided talking to him. Eventually, my eyes closed, and I drifted into dreamland.

When I awoke, I found the blankets tucked around me. Martin had done it intentionally so his absence wouldn't wake me. What was going on?

"James?" I called, freeing myself from the warm blankets.

The bathroom was empty, his towel wet from his morning shower. Instead of getting ready for my day, I went down the stairs, checking each floor on my way to the bottom. He wasn't in either home office, the kitchen, or using the home gym. His town car was gone, and the security system was fully engaged. He'd already left for work.

The gnawing in my stomach grew worse as I went back up the stairs. By the time I was ready to leave, I could barely keep down a few sips of coffee. It was for the best. Caffeine on top of anxiety wouldn't mix well. And the last thing I needed was to have a full-blown panic attack during

Cross's morning meeting or while interviewing Kelsey Savage.

When I entered the conference room, Kellan Dey gave me a cockeyed look. Cross barely glanced in my direction, but from his lack of sarcastic remarks, he must have expected me to show up. As usual, he passed out new assignments and got updates on current cases.

"Alex," Cross waited for me to meet his eyes, "how is your consulting for the police department going?"

"Fine." Normally, he didn't ask about jobs I took on the side.

"When do you think it'll wrap?"

"Hard to say. We have an interview scheduled in a couple of hours. It's also possible the lab found a concrete piece of evidence or IDed an accomplice."

"So you're close?"

I hadn't realized it, but if we could prove Kelsey Savage was involved and convince him to talk, the police could arrest the entire crew and this would be over. "Possibly."

"All right. Good." Cross rocked in the chair. "If no one has anything else, you can get to it."

The rest of the investigators filed out of the room, chit-chatting amongst themselves.

Kellan nudged me when I didn't move. "Are you coming?"

"Not yet."

Kellan glanced at Cross who was skimming details on one of the files he hadn't passed out. "All right. If you need me to pick up any more of your slack, let me know."

"I already owe you." I noticed the papers in his hand. "Were you hoping to cash in on that favor now?"

"Not yet. I'm waiting for something really terrible before I pull the trigger." Kellan winked and went out the door.

"Is Ace Darrow still alive?" I asked.

Cross snickered. "That would explain my curiosity as to whether you'd be at the precinct later today. But no, I did not harm a single hair on that man's head." Splaying open the file, he pushed a few sheets of paper in front of me. "I made him an offer he couldn't refuse."

"That sounds a little *Godfather*-y." I read the top page.

"Ace Darrow lied."

"Of course he lied. That's the only thing the man is capable of. He dug up everything he could possibly find on you. Some of the material dates back over ten years. Graduation announcements, news articles, your dating history."

I flipped to the next page, finding a copy of the *Page Six* photo from when I served as Martin's bodyguard. "Shit."

"After that, Ace dug deeper. He made an entire separate portfolio on Martin. His research almost puts mine to shame. Almost."

"Your research?"

"You know how long I pursued a partnership with Martin, how long I tried to woo him, how I stumbled upon you while looking into him."

"Ace did it in reverse."

"Uh-huh. However, he had little interest in Martin's business or what he does. All Ace was concerned with was figuring out Martin's net worth, his assets, how liquid he is, and what his weak points are."

"Me."

"You're not a weak point. There is no dirt to find. James Martin is no slouch. Whatever dirt that may have existed was professionally and carefully handled, not even Ace's connections and contacts could bust a hole in that perfect, shiny exterior."

"That's because Martin's clean."

"Whatever you say."

I flipped through the pages, getting more agitated as I went. "What was the point? Why was Ace looking into it?"

"I assume your father put him up to it."

"Why?"

Cross's expression soured. "Landon Parker came here to bleed you dry. You were stupid enough to open a vein for him."

"Do we know why? I don't buy his bullshit story. He has to owe someone. But your people couldn't find out who he owes or how much. The FBI's forensic accountants didn't come up with anything either."

"That remains a mystery. Landon—"

"Don," I corrected.

Cross looked like he wanted to argue but decided not to waste his breath. "Don didn't say. But Ace said when he first spoke to your father on the phone, Don sounded desperate, like a man whose child was taken. He begged and pleaded with Ace to look for you. For the first half of the conversation, Ace thought it was a child abduction or custody issue with the way Don went on about everything. Given the circumstances, Don's level of desperation was beyond the norm. That's why Ace got curious."

"So he looked into Don too?"

"He did, but he is not better at this than I am. He didn't find anything that I have not. However, when Don showed up to collect the files, Ace noticed a car outside his office. It arrived with Don and left with Don. Ace is pretty sure the same car pulled up before the big guy came into his office and knocked the shit out of him yesterday."

"Did Ace tell you what the big guy wanted? The assailant whispered something that didn't get picked up by the recording."

"Ace stuck to the same story he told the cops. I'm not sure I believe him, but I couldn't get him to change it. It might be true. Ace may not know who the man is. But the big guy threatened his life if he didn't hand over every copy of his files."

I waved my hand at the papers on the table. "How'd you get these?"

"Ace doesn't do what he's told. That's always been one of his problems. In this one instance, it appears to be for our benefit." Cross rubbed his chin. "When we went to Ace Investigators the first time, I thought we got everything. The big guy thought the same thing. But Ace knows a few tricks. He has another device he uses for what he considers sensitive research. The relevant bits, the pieces he hands over to clients, he copies to his work computer and puts printed copies in his filing cabinet. The stuff he holds on to for a rainy day stays hidden in a floor safe in his home."

"Did you know about that?"

"If I knew about that, I wouldn't have wasted my time at his office." Cross swiped a hand through his hair. "No one knows about that. That's why the big guy didn't follow Ace home. You're lucky. So are Ace's other clients."

"How much intel is he keeping?"

"You don't want to know. He's done a lot of opposition research. He's just waiting for politicians to be of use before he pulls out the intel and dusts it off, which means the big guy could have shown up for any of dozens of reasons."

I flipped through the pages again. "Are these the only copies?"

"I'd say yes, but I can't guarantee it. The good news is this was stuff Ace kept hidden. When I asked Ace how much he gave to your father, he said none of it. I don't believe that. What I believe is he upped his asking price."

"And I gave Don the money to buy this intel."

"I told you not to pay him."

"You were right." I got up, needing to move to keep these facts from crushing me. "But it still doesn't explain why Don needs a six-figure payday. Maybe it's greed, but that wouldn't explain Don getting into the car with someone else, someone Ace thinks could have been the big guy who assaulted him."

"I'll make some calls and see what I can learn about Don's whereabouts. Whatever this is must have begun around the same time he started withdrawing funds from his bank accounts. We've tried figuring it out through our usual methods, but Don didn't leave a paper trail."

"Who are you going to call?" I asked, knowing the answer. Lydia was the one person on the planet I wanted to speak to even less than Don Parker, which was why I hadn't already called to ask these questions myself.

"I'll be discreet. She'll never know this connects to you."

"You're going to call my adoptive mother?"

Cross nodded. "I'll take care of it."

"Okay." I didn't want to stick around. "I should get going."

In my anxiety-fueled daze, I forgot to stop by Bruiser's. But since it was too early for lunch, I'd swing by after Heathcliff and I spoke to Kelsey Savage.

With my consulting credentials prominently displayed, I

went up the steps to the major crimes unit and pushed through the double doors. O'Connell and Thompson were at their desks, a bag of bagels sitting between them. When O'Connell spotted me, he pointed at the bag and the drink carrier.

"Cappuccino and a bagel?" he asked.

"No, thanks."

O'Connell gave me a quizzical look. "Are you feeling okay?"

"Not really."

"Is it the stomach flu?" Thompson asked. "Jennings has the stomach flu. It's going around. If you've got it, stay the hell away from us."

"Thanks for the concern, but I'm not sick."

"The security guard from that check-cashing place can't say the same." O'Connell waved the lab report at me. "Someone dosed his food with ipecac."

"So it was intentional." I skimmed the report. "Has Heathcliff seen this?"

"Yeah. He's anxious to question Kelsey Savage about Wayne's friends since it looks like one of them has no issue poisoning people."

Thompson reached into the bag and pulled out a poppy seed bagel. "Speaking of poison, I thought you got sesame, Nick."

"Keep digging."

Thompson put the poppy seed back into the bag. "Yeah, it's at the bottom, with all the other bits and bobs stuck to it."

"I didn't pack the bag." O'Connell hadn't taken his eyes off me. "I got the coffee especially for you, Parker. Are you sure you don't want it?"

Picking up the cup, I lifted the lid and inhaled. "Since you twisted my arm." I winked at him. "Thanks."

Heathcliff stepped out of Moretti's office. The look on his face sent chills through me.

"Derek, what is it?" I asked.

O'Connell and Thompson fell silent, turning to see what was going on. Heathcliff shook his head at them and took me by the arm. Carefully, he took the cup from my hand

and put it on the desk I'd been using.

"Let's talk for a second." He led me into the break room where another cop was helping himself to a croissant from the pink pastry box. "Irving, I need the room. Take the box and get out of here."

Irving looked at the box and then at Heathcliff. "That's fine by me. Anyone else has a problem, I'll direct them to you."

"Yeah, you do that." Heathcliff kicked the doorstop out of the way and shut the door.

"What's going on?" I asked. "Why the sudden need for privacy?"

"Sit down."

"Hell no." I fought to keep myself from trembling. "Tell me what's wrong."

"Last night, patrol received reports of an assault. They found a man brutally beaten outside a restaurant. He was unconscious. It wasn't a robbery. He still had his wallet. His ID gave us his name – Landon Parker. Your father."

My throat went dry. "How is he?"

"He should make a full recovery. He's been in and out of consciousness, so we haven't been able to thoroughly question him. But he's said a few things during the fleeting moments when he's been lucid. Things that aren't making a lot of sense. Things that he probably shouldn't be saying."

"Do you know who attacked him? Or why?" The gnawing increased with a vengeance, threatening to rip a hole through my insides. Martin's bruised knuckles and odd behavior played through my head. How had my beloved found Don? Why didn't he tell me?

Heathcliff pressed his lips together. His eyes searched my face. "Landon Parker was found a few blocks from the Martin Technologies building. He said James Martin assaulted him. We found Martin's business card in your father's jacket pocket. Eyewitnesses said they saw a man who fit Martin's description punching your father in the face outside a restaurant."

"When did this happen?"

"Around eight o'clock last night."

"Have you pulled security footage from the area?" I

forced my face to give nothing away. I'd spent enough time undercover to know how to hide things. And it was imperative I hide this.

"Restaurant employees verified your father and Martin dined together, but the altercation allegedly occurred afterward, outside the restaurant. The security footage didn't catch it. But it did show them together at a table prior to the altercation. Did you know they were eating together?"

"It must have been spur of the moment."

Heathcliff went to the vending machine and gave it a look before resting his hips on the table and tucking his hands into his pockets. He didn't want to come off as threatening or interrogative. He wanted to keep me from becoming defensive. "Did Martin have any reason to want to harm your father?"

"Martin's far too civilized. He'd never do anything like that." But I'd seen Martin's violent side. The shattered coffee cups, the holes in the wall, the way he'd fought with people who had tried to harm us. And Don Parker had done plenty to hurt me. I didn't doubt Martin would attack him if provoked.

"What time did Martin get home last night?" Heathcliff asked.

"Early. He got home before I did. It must have been right after they had dinner."

"He didn't tell you they ate together?"

"My relationship with Don is complicated. Martin knows I don't like to talk about him."

"In that case, why would he have had dinner with him?"

"Martin knows I've been worried about Don. I already told you how he disappeared. He must have reached out to Martin, and Martin went as my proxy to find out what was going on."

"But he didn't tell you he saw Don or that they had dinner together?"

"Derek, it's complicated."

Heathcliff sighed. "Simplify it. You said you thought someone wanted to harm Don. Now it looks like that someone is your fiancé."

"You know that's not true. Don owes someone money. I'm guessing that's who attacked him."

"But you don't have a name?"

"No."

"Would Martin know? Maybe Don told him."

"I'm sure Martin knows nothing about any of this."

"How can you be sure? You didn't even know they were together last night or that Don was in the hospital."

"Martin didn't do this, and if you keep asking these questions, he's going to get dragged into the middle of the investigation. I don't want to see that happen. If Don had told Martin something important, Martin would tell me. We don't keep those kinds of secrets from one another anymore." Until last night.

"It doesn't matter what I ask you, Alex. Right now, the only thing we have to go on is the victim's declaration and eyewitness accounts. Both point to Martin as our suspect. Unless something changes, we'll have no choice but to bring Martin in for questioning. That's why I'm asking you what is going on."

"Derek, please don't do this."

"It's not my case. Moretti told me about it, so I'd break the news to you. But we're cops. We go where the evidence leads. We can dismiss your father's statements for now. He's not in his right mind with the concussion and pain meds. But as soon as the doctors give us the all-clear, his statement will hold a lot more weight. Hopefully, his mind will clear and he'll be able to point the finger at the actual culprit. But right now, the facts suggest it might be Martin. The lead detective will want to follow up on that."

"Am I allowed to see Don? Maybe I can get him to tell me what happened."

"You're his daughter. There's no reason you can't be there," Heathcliff said. "How about I drive you?"

"I can drive myself."

He nodded at my shaking hands. "You shouldn't drive when you're that upset. I'll take you."

The last thing I needed was Heathcliff tagging along when I spoke to Don. "I have to bring Bruiser lunch afterward. And you have that interview with Kelsey Savage.

I'll be fine. I promise."

TWENTY-ONE

Calling Don Parker family didn't come with perks, but getting an update on his condition from the doctors came damn close. Don had two broken ribs and a fractured cheek bone. He'd sustained bruises over twenty percent of his body, had a few lacerations, and a mild concussion. The hospital had given him pain medications and antibiotics while they continued to monitor his condition. But they were sure he'd make a full recovery and planned to release him the next day.

I entered his room, finding the lights dimmed. His eyes remained closed, his face swollen and bruised to the point he was nearly unrecognizable. The monitors beside the bed showed he was stable. Steady heart rate and decent blood pressure.

Moving closer, I assessed his hands, which were on top of the blankets, a pulse monitor stuck to one of his fingers. He didn't have any bruises or cuts on his knuckles. He hadn't fought back. From what I could see of his palms, they were slightly scraped, as if he'd tried to catch himself from falling.

Martin was more than capable of inflicting this much damage, but I didn't think he would. Don Parker was sixty. He had more than two decades on Martin. And while Don didn't appear feeble or brittle in any sense, he looked soft. It wouldn't have been a fair fight, and I didn't think my beloved would have gone to these extremes. Then again, rage had a way of taking hold. So I couldn't rule anything out.

"Wake up." I gave the side of the bed a shake.

Don looked around, as if confused where he was. But I saw the glimmer of recognition and the tiniest bit of smugness. If I held a pillow over his face, the hospital might think he died of natural causes.

"Little swan," he said, a smile gracing his grotesque features, "I knew you'd come."

I checked the door, but I'd shut it tight when I entered. "Who did this to you?"

"Your boyfriend."

"Try again."

"It's not a lie, Alexis. James joined me for dinner. We exchanged words. Things got heated. When we left, he hit me. Right here." Don indicated his left cheek. "Plenty of people saw it."

"Then what happened?" I glanced at the monitor, using it as a rudimentary lie detector.

Don's eyes narrowed. "That depends on you."

The pillow was looking more appealing by the second. "What does that mean?"

"I warned you what would happen. I told you to give me the money. I didn't want to see you get hurt."

"You're the one hurting me. You always hurt me."

"That's your own fault." He maneuvered the cords and wires around so he could sit up. "James Martin did this. He attacked me. He tried to kill me. I bet the doorman or those security guards from your building will recall him saying how badly he wanted to kill me. It's not my fault he didn't accept my apology at dinner. It's not my fault he got so angry he put me in the hospital."

"Careful, or I'll put you in the ground."

"Don't talk to me like that. I'm your father. You owe me everything. And since you don't have what I need, I found another way to get it. This is what's going to happen, honey. You and your rich boytoy come up with the cash, the whole $200,000 plus enough to cover my medical costs, and I'll change my tune. I tell the cops I don't want to press charges. That I made a mistake. That a homeless man assaulted me. They'll never find him, and this goes away."

"More blackmail." Forget the pillow. Maybe I'd shoot him. But that was too quick. I could inject a gas bubble into his vein and hope that'd do the trick. It'd be untraceable. Natural causes.

"You can continue to fight me on this. But the longer you deny me what is rightfully mine, the faster I'll make sure your boyfriend ends up behind bars. Since you went to law school, I'm sure you know that winning a civil trial is easier when there's already a criminal conviction. I'll sue him for at least six figures, maybe seven. Y'know, pain and suffering."

"I choose option C."

"Let's hear it."

"You already did. I'm going to bury you."

"Little swan, you know better than to call my bluff. When has that ever worked in your favor?"

I was going to kill him. Maybe Martin did put him in the hospital. I understood the impulse.

Calmly, I pushed the recliner in front of the door, so no one could interrupt us.

"Are you trying to scare me, Alexis?" The monitors showed the slightest blip. Don Parker was getting nervous.

I played up the theatrics, taking the pulse monitor off his finger and clipping it to mine. When I tried to remove the leads from his chest, he slapped me.

"What are you doing?" he asked, the tiniest bit of fear creeping into his voice. He reached for the remote with the call button, and I snatched it away before he could page a nurse.

"I already told you." I stared into his eyes. "You don't know me. You have no idea what my life has been like. You don't know how many people I've killed. But I want you to think long and hard about what Ace Darrow found on me. My career alone should tell you I'm not the innocent little girl you remember." I opened my jacket, revealing my nine millimeter. "Did Ace tell you stories about Cross Security or the things Lucien Cross has done? Maybe he mentioned my boss's father is the police commissioner. Do you understand what that means?" Truthfully, it didn't mean much of anything. Cross did what he wanted because he found ways to bend or break the law, not because his father let him. But Don didn't need to know that. "You can play your games all you want, Dad," I said the word like it was the ultimate of curses, "but the deck's already stacked in my favor. You lose."

"You're a terrible liar. You always were."

"I'm not lying." I grinned contemptuously. "In fact, I feel relieved. I've had this notion of you and Mom hanging over my head since the day I left. I always wondered if you'd call or write. I thought you'd show up to take me home for winter or summer break. That you would show up at my graduation to apologize and say you wanted us to be a family again. Eventually, I gave up on such childish and naïve ideas. People suck. You taught me that. You taught me that no one will ever care about me. You taught me that it's always about watching out for myself. That I can't trust anyone. That I shouldn't let anyone in because if I do, they'll destroy me the same way you and Mom did. So when you showed up, it threw me. But since I don't want to be cold and calculating like you, I gave you what I had, in case there was a chance at reconciliation, but you squandered it. Now, I'll make sure you get what you deserve." I reached into my jacket.

"I don't deserve this," Don said. "I wasn't lying to you when I said I don't want you to get hurt. I wasn't lying about needing the money."

"What about everything else?"

He stared at the wall, fighting with himself on whether to answer.

"Who really attacked you?" I asked, taking a seat on the edge of his bed. He didn't answer, so I slid my knee up so I could sit sideways to face him. He hissed when my kneecap pressed into his broken ribs.

"You're a bitch."

"I guess I learned from the best."

He scowled at me. "I already told you."

"How about you tell me a different story? The truth would be nice. Who do you owe the $200,000 to?"

"To whom do you owe," he corrected in that obnoxious way he'd always done when I was growing up.

This time, I slapped him across the face, which resulted in a loud shriek. "To whom do you owe the money?" I glanced at the door, but his cry hadn't attracted the nurse's attention yet. I'd have to be more careful. Damn, where was Julian Mercer when I needed him?

"It doesn't matter."

"Yes, it does," I insisted. Don Parker didn't deserve an olive branch. He didn't deserve my help. But he wouldn't give up on getting the money, which meant I had to help him or kill him. If not, he'd go after Martin. I couldn't let that happen, particularly since the police needed a better suspect and a motive. And no matter how many dark thoughts I'd entertained upon entering the room and continued to entertain every time Don opened his mouth, I wouldn't commit patricide. Mark Jablonsky was right. I would do anything I could to protect Don. "Ace Darrow told you Cross Security is one of the best security and investigation firms in the country. I have contacts and resources in law enforcement and in the private sector. I can help you, but you have to tell me what's going on. And you have to leave Martin out of this."

"If you want to help, get me the money."

"No."

"You were always stubborn. You'd rather break than bend. That's why you never improved as a dancer. It's why you couldn't reach your potential. You got in your own way. You—"

I shoved my hand over his mouth. I could feel his hot breath and spit on my palm, but it was worth it to muffle the sound he made. "Whoever is coming after you is close. They broke into Ace Investigators and attacked Ace. The files are gone. The man you owe has everything. You're next." The color drained from Don's face, and I knew my assumption had paid off. Slowly, I released my grip on his mouth. "Let me help you."

His eye twitched, and he eyed the gun beneath my jacket. "Fine, we'll try it your way. But if it doesn't work out, I will take your boyfriend down. Do we understand one another? I can only keep quiet for so long. There's a clock on this. If they don't think I'll get the money, they'll kill you and me."

"What do I have to do with any of this?"

"I had to tell them something, so I said my daughter could get me the money. And since you said they took Ace Investigators' files, you're in their crosshairs now too."

TWENTY-TWO

"Parker?" Heathcliff had been waiting near the front entrance. As soon as he saw me stumble out of the elevator, he moved toward me. "What's wrong? Did your father tell you what happened?"

I brushed my hair back. "It's complicated."

He led me back to the car and cornered me. "Did Martin do this to him?"

"No."

"You're sure?" Heathcliff searched my eyes. "Officers questioned a person at the scene. He described the attacker as a tall man with dark hair wearing a business suit. Another account was given to the 9-1-1 operator when the call was placed. That description also fit, business suit, athletic, with dark hair."

"Can we talk off the record? I need a friend, Derek. Not a cop."

"I hate it when you go off the rails."

"Then don't ask me questions I can't answer."

He sighed. "Tell me everything. I'll figure out what to do with it afterward."

"I—"

"You have to trust me, Alex."

I hoped I wouldn't regret it. "Don's a CPA. He and a buddy thought they could branch out. They'd been researching the stock market and trying to build a portfolio and business. Don went to one of his clients for seed money, but he lied and misrepresented what he was doing with the money and the kinds of returns the guy could expect to receive. When everything started crashing down, his investor wanted to see those returns and profits he'd been promised. Don paid him from his own account for as long as he could, hoping it'd turn around. But it never did. Don and his buddy lost everything."

"Most new businesses tank," Heathcliff said. "The investor should have known that was a possibility."

"Don swore it was a sure-fire thing. He promised him he'd make double within the first year. The guy he borrowed the money from, the investor, isn't exactly the most reputable man. From what Don said, I'd say he's money laundering and thought if Don's sure-fire thing was such a guarantee, he could use that to clean money without taking as steep of a hit."

Heathcliff rubbed a hand down his face. "Did Don know the investor was laundering money?"

"I'm sure he did. Don was his CPA."

"Why—"

"I don't know."

Heathcliff looked the exact way I felt when Don had told me the news. I must have had the same expression, only with a tad more rage.

"Don always let image rule things. He wanted to project success. Working at the same job, in the same position for decades didn't scream success. Starting his own investing firm would have been a step up."

"Like a second act," Heathcliff said.

"You should know, Don Parker's the biggest asshole on the planet. When his investor confronted him about the missing funds, Don tried to turn the tables on him and threatened to expose him, figuring that would get the investor to back off."

"Does this guy have a name?"

"Chad Averly. I searched him on my phone, but the internet didn't turn up much. He might be a lackey for someone more powerful. I texted Jablonsky to look into it. We'll see what shakes loose."

"I'll run the name too," Heathcliff said.

"Great. But in the meantime, Averly wants his investment back with the interest he was promised. Don came to me to get it. But Averly didn't trust Don. He figured the bastard was planning to skip town, so Averly sent someone to keep an eye on Don. I'm guessing that's who put him in the hospital."

"Don didn't say?"

"He won't go on record with it. He's afraid Averly will kill him if it gets out that Don talked to the police." That wasn't Don's only motivation for remaining silent, but I didn't want to tell Heathcliff the other reason was to keep Martin on the hook until I got Don the money to pay back his debt. "I told Don I would help, but he's reluctant. He won't give me his attacker's name or tell me where I can find him. He says he doesn't know, but I think he's lying. All I know for sure is the guy who beat him up works for Averly."

"Averly's getting tired of waiting for his money." Heathcliff rubbed a hand down his face. "What's your plan?"

"I'd like to take down these guys, Don included, but it's not that simple. Don isn't local. Averly went through a lot of trouble to send muscle to follow Don. He wants to send a message that no one steals from him."

"How much does Don owe?"

"Two hundred. That's why he came to see me. He thought he could get me to give him the money. He shelled out that much raising me and paying for college. He figured I owed him at least that much, maybe more. I gave him what I had, but it wasn't even close. That must have been why he met Martin for dinner, to ask for the rest. But Martin didn't want to tell me. He didn't want to upset me."

"Did Martin give Don the money?"

"I don't think so. But I'll find out."

Heathcliff looked torn. "Your dad's in a lot of trouble."

"Yeah."

He squinted. "What am I missing?"

"Don thinks if he doesn't return the money soon, whoever roughed him up will come after me or Martin next."

"Ace Darrow was assaulted yesterday afternoon and his office ransacked hours before Don was assaulted." Heathcliff exhaled. "All right. Let me see what I can do."

"I have to talk to Martin first."

"He's key to the investigation."

"Derek—"

"That's not up for debate, but I'll buy you some time. However, I don't like this. For this Averly guy to have that kind of reach, we could be talking organized crime, ties to terrorism, or a million other terrible things. Someone beat up Ace Darrow. That same person came for your adoptive father. For all I know, the asshole with the hammer could be connected to this." His eyes narrowed. "You already suspected as much."

"I thought it could be a possibility, but I mentioned that to you."

"You left a lot out." He wagged his finger in my face. "I don't like it when you do that."

"We don't know anything for sure, but if the hammer guy wanted money, shouldn't he have asked for it before trying to take my head off?"

"He may have wanted to put you in the hospital instead of Don. He must have figured that'd prove to Don that Averly was serious about getting his money back."

I mulled it over. "I'll have Cross Security go over the footage again."

"I'll make sure the department does the same. In the meantime, find out what Martin knows. Don's assailant may have been nearby when they left the restaurant. Martin may have seen him. If he did, we need to know about it."

"How about you drop me off at my car on your way to Kelsey Savage's place? I'll talk to Martin and find out what's what. We'll meet back at the precinct and exchange notes. Okay?"

"Fine." But Heathcliff wasn't happy about it.

* * *

I parked at the MT building and texted Martin. He didn't

respond. That meant he was in a meeting. Hoping he'd get back to me in a couple of minutes, I called Cross.

"Did you get my text about Chad Averly?" I asked.

"Yes. How did you find Don and convince him to tell you the truth?"

"I didn't find him. The police did."

"Go on."

I swallowed. "Things went from bad to worse. I'll fill you in later. Just tell me your conversation didn't open the gates of hell."

"You mean my phone call with Lydia?"

"What did she say?" I physically braced myself against the steering wheel.

Cross cleared his throat, which wasn't a good sign. "I'll need to dig deeper."

"How bad is it?"

"She had a much different story to tell than Don. According to what she said, he asked for the divorce and made sure she got everything. Since he's the farthest thing from an altruist, I don't know why he'd do that, unless it was a sham. He may have wanted to protect her or as many of his assets as possible."

"Protect her from Averly?" I tried to think through the possibility. "He acts like she's the root of all his problems and our family issues."

"The operative word is act."

"Do you think he loves her?"

"You tell me," Cross said. "He might, or he could be a classic narcissist. Either way, he would have wanted to find a common enemy to explain his bad behavior throughout your life in order to sell the lie that he wants to reconcile and convince you to give him the money. Lydia fits the bill."

That was too much for me to think about. "Did she know anything about the withdrawals?"

"She said Don and his work buddy needed cash to start their own side business. That's why he kept taking out the money. It got to be too much. Before she could say anything to Don about it, he served her with papers. She figured he'd be facing bankruptcy soon enough."

"Did they plan to get back together afterward?"

"That's why I need to do more digging," Cross said. "Her story is plausible, but it's also convenient. One of them is lying."

"Unless they both are."

"Also possible." Cross continued to speak before I could ask any other questions. "As far as she knows, he's still working as a CPA and he's been staying at his buddy's house. Don doesn't have much in the way of expenses. But his bank account is practically empty."

"Which is why he wants me to get him $200,000." But there was one part of the story that made no sense. "Don warned me I would get hurt if I didn't help him. Why isn't he afraid they'll come after Lydia if he fails to pay up?"

"Do you think he'd tell you if they threatened her?" Cross asked.

"Maybe not."

Cross cleared his throat again. "I checked area police reports. She never made any calls. Neither have the neighbors. If someone plans to use her as leverage to convince Don to return the money he took, they haven't done it yet."

"That could be because he offered me up on a silver platter."

"Like I said, I'll dig into it. Is there anything you need in the meantime?"

"I need Martin to get out of his damn meeting." I grabbed the phone and locked my car. "I'll let you know how it goes after we speak."

TWENTY-THREE

"Good morning, Ms. Parker," Jeffrey Myers, MT's head of security, greeted as I made my way to the desk. "What can I do for you?"

"Is Mr. Martin here?" I asked.

"Yes."

"When did he get in?"

"A little before eight. He's been working a lot of long hours lately." Jeffrey pulled out my old MT ID card and slid it through the machine, activating the magnetic strip which would give me access to the elevators and the rest of the building. "He may be in a meeting, but I can find out."

"Please." I took the offered access card.

After a few seconds, Jeffrey put down the phone. "They just got started. Figure forty-five minutes to an hour, but you can wait here or in your old office if you like." Jeffrey leaned closer. "I'm sure he wouldn't mind if you waited in his office, but as head of security, I shouldn't tell you that."

"Don't worry, you won't get into any trouble." I turned, assessing the interior and exterior cameras. Nothing had changed since I made my last security assessment and reviewed their upgrades. I knew just as much about this system as Jeffrey did. "I could use your help with one thing."

"Name it." He folded his hands together on top of the desk and leaned forward, eager to assist.

"Did an older gentleman stop by to see Martin

yesterday? He would have been around sixty with graying hair and a bald spot."

"You just described half of the board members."

I laughed, going along with the joke. "This would be someone you didn't know."

"Only employees and expected guests came through yesterday."

"This could have been after business hours."

"I left at four. Randall covered the evening shift, but today's his day off."

"Can I see the security footage?"

"As long as the boss doesn't mind."

"He won't."

Jeffrey waved me around the desk and grabbed another chair. He set me up in front of a monitor. "Do you remember how everything works?"

"Yep."

Watching the footage on fast-forward always reminded me of Laurel and Hardy, even though the feed wasn't in black and white. After thirty minutes, I'd gone through everything. Don Parker hadn't set foot inside the MT building. So I brought up one of the exterior cameras that covered the front door.

"That bastard." Don had camped out on a nearby bench while he waited for Martin. The moment Martin stepped outside, Don approached him. They spoke for a few minutes. From Don's apologetic gestures, I had to assume he was lying through his teeth. Finally, Martin nodded. Don went down the street, disappearing from view, and Martin pulled out his phone. I didn't know who he called, but it wasn't me.

After recording the timestamp at the beginning and end of their conversation, I turned off the video. Martin should be almost finished with his meeting, but even if he wasn't, this had to take priority. We were on a clock. If I didn't return to the precinct, Heathcliff would come looking, and we had to have our stories straight before then.

"Tell one of the assistants to pull Martin out of his meeting and have him meet me in his office," I said.

"He won't like that," Jeffrey warned. "Can't this wait a

few more minutes? He should be wrapping things up shortly."

"It's life or death. Also, I don't expect this to happen, but if anyone shows up and asks for access to the security footage or any building records, do not hand them over. If the police show up, remind them they need a warrant."

"What's going on?"

"We're taking a few precautions. That's why I have to talk to Martin."

Jeffrey picked up the phone while I made my way to the elevator and slid the card through the reader. After pressing seventeen, I paced inside the empty car. It stopped on the eighth floor and someone else got in. She pressed eleven.

"Today's a nice day," she said.

"Yeah, sure."

The doors opened on eleven. She stepped out, and I resumed pacing.

Finally, I reached the top floor. I could hear Luc Guillot's assistant talking on the phone. Other than that, there was nothing but the hum of the building. Slipping past her open office door, I used the override code on the biometric locks and let myself into Martin's office.

Paperwork covered his desk. But I didn't see anything related to Don Parker. I went into the washroom, relieved when I didn't find any bloody towels or clothing. More than likely, Martin went straight home after the altercation. But I didn't know where it occurred. Heathcliff hadn't told me which restaurant they went to or where the 9-1-1 calls originated. Don hadn't volunteered that information either, so I had to rely on Martin to fill in the blanks.

"Alexis," Martin's voice boomed, a combination of worry and anger, "is everything okay?"

I stepped out of the washroom. "Don Parker was assaulted last night, but you already know that."

He worked his jaw. "Is this why you dragged me out of my meeting?"

"You assaulted him."

"Is that what he said?" Martin shook his head, annoyed

and frustrated. "I should have killed him."

"Don't say that." Crossing the room, I grabbed his right hand, finding it bandaged. His left didn't show any injury or bruising. Unfortunately, Martin was right-handed, which was consistent with the injuries being focused on the left side of Don's body. "There were witnesses. At least two. Don's threatening to have you arrested. He wants to press charges. I don't know if I can get ahead of this. Lt. Moretti will buy us some time, but I have to come up with a reasonable alternative. At least Don's finally talking, but I don't trust him not to stab us in the back. There's no reason he can't get what he wants and," my voice cracked, "take you away from me too."

"Sweetheart," Martin hugged me, "it'll be okay. It wasn't that big of a deal."

"You lied to me."

"I didn't." Martin's eyes darted to the side. He wouldn't look me in the eye. "I left out a minor detail. Before I hit the bag a few times, I hit Don."

I pushed away from him. "Don's in the hospital. He has a concussion. You fractured his cheek and broke his ribs."

"Shit." Martin ran a hand through his hair. "I knew I hit him hard, but I didn't mean for that." He squinted. "How did he break his ribs?"

"You tell me. I wasn't there." I circled. "Did you kick him? I would have kicked him. I would have kept kicking him."

"I didn't kick him." Martin's eyes darted back and forth while the scene replayed in his head. "I hit him once. Right here." Martin tapped the left side of his face. "He staggered backward. I told him to fuck off or I'd fuck him up. And then I got into the car."

"Marcal saw it happen?"

Martin nodded.

I wasn't sure if that would help or hurt. "Why were you anywhere near him?"

"He was waiting for me."

My cheek twitched, and I gave Martin a shove. "Why didn't you tell me this last night? I asked what happened and you lied to me." I swiped at my tears, unable to stop my chin from trembling or the strangled gasps from escaping every time I took a breath. It only made me madder. “Why would you do that? I thought we were in this together.”

TWENTY-FOUR

"Alexis." Martin reached for me, but I pushed away from him, gulping down my sobs and getting my emotions back in check.

"The truth this time," I said.

"That piece of shit has had you twisted up inside since the moment he came back into your life. I didn't want to upset you."

"Great job." I took a shaky breath, biting the inside of my cheek. I had so many questions, I didn't even know where to start.

Martin's phone buzzed in his pocket. He pulled it out to check the display.

"Don't you dare answer that," I said.

Ignoring me, Martin typed out a quick text and put the phone down on his desk.

I turned to face the windows and stared outside. The leather sofa creaked as he sat down. I searched the reflection to find him in the glass. I had always trusted him. Now, I wasn't sure.

"He was waiting for me to leave work. He said he wanted to apologize, clear the air, and explain a few things to me. He suggested we have a civilized chat over dinner."

"Who did you call after Don walked away?"

"Marcal," Martin said. "I told him we were going to the steakhouse a few blocks from here and that he could pick me up there. It was early, so getting a table wasn't a problem. But Don didn't know that, which is why I sent him ahead. I never should have shown up. That man knows exactly how to twist the knife."

"You've accused me of that before."

"Sweetheart—"

I turned to face him, wrapping my arms tighter around my middle and leaning against the glass. "That must be where I got it from."

Martin got off the couch, and I flinched. Holding up his palms, he sat back down. "That's not what I was going to say. I would never say that. He is poison." His expression softened, his eyes passionate. "I am sorry you grew up with that."

"Let's stick to the facts. Did anything happen at dinner? Did you fight? Argue? Threaten to cut his throat with your steak knife?"

"No. We didn't make it that far. He wanted money and was willing to say or do whatever it took to convince me to give it to him. I had no desire to hear his bullshit, so I excused myself. He followed me out of the restaurant and grabbed my shoulder. He wouldn't take the hint, so I hit him and told him to stay the hell away from us. By then, Marcal had pulled up. He got out of the car to help, but I didn't want our exchange to turn into more of a scene, so we left Don on the sidewalk."

"You should have known better. I told you the only reason he showed up was for money. By hitting him, you opened yourself up to criminal charges and civil lawsuits."

"I know." Martin rubbed the bandage on his hand.

"Did you really only hit him once?"

"It took a lot of effort not to whale on him, but despite everything, he is your father. I didn't want to make things worse for you."

"You didn't answer the question."

"I only hit him once," Martin said. "Honest."

I stared at the phone on his desk. "That would have meant more two days ago." Not keeping secrets had been one of my issues that I'd been working on ever since we got back together. Now it felt like that was for nothing. "You knew I was looking for him. You should have told me.

Getting blindsided with the news this morning didn't help matters, particularly when Don said you put him in the hospital."

"Are the police waiting outside to arrest me?"

"No. I explained the situation to Heathcliff and put a nice spin on it. I told him you'd never do such a thing. He barely bought it. As soon as he sees your hand, that story goes out the window, along with my credibility."

"Alex—"

"Tell me what happened after you left Don. Someone else is out to get him. He finally fessed up, but it's Don. It could be a lie. I don't know. I don't know anything anymore."

"Marcal stopped at a fast-food joint. I took dinner over to Bruiser's, ate there, and came home. Once I got home, I hit the bag a few times to burn off some of that anger, got changed, and poured a drink. That's when you came home."

"No other stops?"

"None."

"Did you tell Bruiser what happened?"

Martin nodded. "He knew I was upset, and he spotted my injured knuckles as quickly as you did. He regrets not being there."

"There's nothing he could have done," I said.

"Bruiser doesn't see it that way."

I'd have to speak to him after this. His lunch would be arriving a little late, but under the circumstances, I hoped he'd forgive me. "Run through it again."

"Sweetheart, I don't think—"

"Don was waiting for you outside. I didn't see a car or anyone else on the security footage, but the cameras don't see everything. If a professional is monitoring him, he would have done his best to avoid detection. Did you notice anything?"

Martin shook his head. "I was surprised. You spent all week trying to track Don down. I never expected him to show up outside."

"What about at the restaurant? You said it wasn't crowded."

"It wasn't. There were maybe two or three tables in use. The rest of the place was empty."

"Was anyone eating alone?"

"No, but there was a guy at the bar."

"What did he look like?"

"Tall, dark hair, tailored suit," Martin squinted, "but he had cheap shoes. That was the part that didn't fit."

"Cheap shoes?"

"They were dark-colored and scuffed. No shine. They looked like work shoes."

"How did you notice that?"

Martin smiled. "You must have rubbed off on me, sweetheart."

I wasn't buying it.

"Or," Martin said, "it's because he had one foot on the rung of the stool and the sole of his shoe would make this loud, obnoxious squeak every time he adjusted on the seat. The sound is what caught my attention. Expensive shoes don't have those thick rubber soles that squeak."

"Remind me not to make fun of your fashion expertise." I yanked the notepad and pen from my pocket.

"Did I say something brilliant?"

"I wouldn't go that far." My gut said the man at the bar beat Don Parker to a bloody pulp. "How big was this guy?"

"My height, maybe a little taller. He was built."

"Was he still at the bar when you left?"

"Yes."

"Did you see him again after the altercation?"

"All I saw was red," Martin said. "I had to get out of there. The only thing I remember is Marcal calling to me and getting into the car."

"All right." I held the pen and paper out to Martin. "Write down every detail about the restaurant, the staff, the people eating there, even the little things like shoes and hair color. Whatever you remember, but don't incriminate yourself. The police are on the cusp of bringing you in for questioning. Heathcliff said he'd do his best to delay the inevitable, but I have to provide them with another suspect they can pursue instead."

"Do you think the man with the work shoes is that

suspect?"

"He fits the description."

Once Martin was finished, I took what I hoped to pass off to the police as Martin's statement and left the MT building. Every part of me wanted to go to the restaurant and ask questions, but when the police followed up, I worried they'd think I interfered. However, if what Martin said was true, I had no reason to worry. He hadn't done anything inside the restaurant that would get him into more trouble, and if he only hit Don once and left, he could be facing simple assault charges. A good attorney could plead that down to a misdemeanor or make it go away entirely.

It all hinged on if Martin told me the truth, and while my heart and gut told me he did, my head had other thoughts. Go figure. So I'd have to speak to a few other sources.

After picking up lunch, I drove to Bruiser's apartment. He dog-eared the book he was reading and put it on the coffee table. Once I got his lunch situated on the TV tray beside him, I sat down across from him.

Bruiser opened the bag and pulled out the grilled chicken salad. "You're late. Does it have anything to do with Martin showing up early yesterday?"

"Why don't you tell me what you know?"

"Oh, an interrogation and lunch. It's like dinner and a show." Bruiser tucked the napkin into his collar and stabbed a piece of chicken. "None of that would have happened if I'd been with him."

"Jones," I said, "you can't blame yourself."

"You want to bet?" He snorted. "How many times have I heard you say that under the exact same context?"

"Then get your ass healed so you can get back to work."

He stared at me for a moment, surprised since I'd been his cheering squad and indulging his pity party up until now. "Yes, ma'am." Though he knew I didn't like being called ma'am, he didn't say it to be snarky or disrespectful. He said it like he would have if he was still in the Navy. He'd been given an order and planned to carry it out. "What do you want me to tell you?"

"Everything. Start with what time Martin showed up, the condition he was in, and everything he said to you."

"Didn't you already go over this with him?"

"I did, but the police are going to ask questions. I'd like to have the answers before they do."

Bruiser told me everything. It matched what Martin had said with enough minor differences that I knew Bruiser hadn't been coached and they hadn't rehearsed their stories.

"Did Martin say why he hit Don?"

Bruiser put his fork down, but he wouldn't look at me. "Don said something unkind."

"About me?"

Bruiser nodded. "There's no point repeating it."

I didn't force the issue. I didn't need any more of my adoptive father's hateful remarks circulating in my mind while I was trying to get him out of the jam he'd gotten himself into. "Did Marcal join you and Martin for dinner?"

"Yeah. From what he said, he was outside the restaurant when the altercation happened. He was prepared to jump in and have Martin's back. It turns out he's the original bodyguard."

"Driver, valet, assistant, bodyguard, that man wears all the hats. He's the one we have to worry about if Martin ever decides to replace either of us." I tucked my notepad back into my jacket pocket. "Kick ass at PT today. We may need you back at work sooner than we realized."

"Copy that."

After I left Bruiser's apartment, I called Cross Security. Lucien was busy, so I spoke to Justin. The last time a Cross Security protection detail followed Martin they'd failed to prevent an attack. But I wanted eyes on him. More than likely, whoever was after Don wouldn't turn his attention on Martin, at least not yet, but I wanted to make sure Martin had a continuous alibi from here on out. Also, if Martin were to do something else self-destructive and stupid, which was usually my play, I wanted the protection detail to protect him from himself.

Once that was handled, I dialed Marcal's number. He gave me the same rundown Martin had with one exception.

He remembered seeing the man with the suit leave the restaurant around the same time Martin got into the car. The man with the suit had gone over to Don. Marcal didn't know what happened after that, but he saw the man approach. That would call into question the eyewitness accounts. If the eyewitnesses had looked away for a few seconds, they may have missed Martin leaving the scene and the unsub entering.

But optimism wasn't my schtick. To be on the safe side, I called Mr. Almeada. Almeada was out of the office, but I explained who I was and that James Martin may need to retain his services.

Martin's attorneys could deal with civil fallout, but I wanted to make sure we had a heavy-hitter on the bench if we needed him. Or was it a pinch-hitter? Damn, now I was mixing my sports metaphors.

A knock sounded on my window, and I jumped. Detective O'Connell took a step back, holding up his palms. "Sorry, Parker," he said as I got out of the car. "I didn't mean to startle you. Is everything okay? I thought you'd be with Heathcliff. Didn't he drive you to the hospital?"

"He did, but I convinced him to drop me off here so I could get my car. We split up to cover more ground."

"Moretti said your dad was attacked. Is he okay?" O'Connell scrutinized my face. "You've been crying."

"Can you be a little less detective-y today?"

"Jen asks me that every time she comes home from the mall. The answer is always no."

"I have to catch Heathcliff up first."

"But you're okay?"

"Yeah, Nick. I'm fine."

"In that case, you'll be happy to hear Kelsey Savage has been brought in for questioning. We're waiting on the search warrant for his home, car, and locker at work."

"What did Heathcliff find?"

"A *Zorro* mask. It was on display, along with several other ornate and decorative masks. Apparently, Kelsey thought he could hide the evidence in plain sight."

"Dumbass move. What about the shotgun?"

"We'll see what the warrant turns up."

TWENTY-FIVE

Kelsey Savage wasn't talking. A sawed-off shotgun had been found inside a foot locker in his bedroom closet. When his wife, Breann, had been questioned about it, she said she'd never seen it before but the only person with a key and access to that foot locker was her husband.

"Did you find anything else?" I asked.

"We found clothing that matched what the lead robber wore at both the gentlemen's club and check-cashing place robberies," Heathcliff said.

"Neither of those outfits stood out as unique."

Heathcliff's eyes narrowed. "Planning on working another gig for a defense attorney?"

I pantomimed zipping my lip. "What about the *Zorro* mask?"

"That was the final piece we needed for the warrant." Heathcliff glanced at the clock, but Kelsey's attorney hadn't shown up yet. "Was your afternoon as productive as mine?"

I told him everything I'd learned about the mystery man from the restaurant. "I wanted to follow up but was afraid if I requested additional information about the man with the suit, spoken to the restaurant staff, or gotten a look at their surveillance footage, the PD would think I tampered with evidence."

Heathcliff gave me the same look O'Connell had earlier. "Did Martin hit your father?"

"He didn't put him in the hospital."

"Parker." I hadn't heard that tone in quite some time.

"I told you why someone would want to hurt Don. The man in the suit from the restaurant fits Martin's description. More than likely, he's muscle for Chad Averly or whoever Averly represents. Adding any other details at this point will confuse or slow down the investigation. Right now, the priority has to be identifying the unknown man in the suit."

"You're absolutely certain there was another man in a suit?"

"Yes."

Heathcliff scrutinized me for a moment longer before picking up the phone. He relayed everything I had said to the detective handling the investigation and hung up. "We'll see where that leads. Hopefully, not back to Martin."

"I swear he didn't put Don in the hospital."

"Yet, I get the distinct impression you're splitting hairs."

"Can we go to the restaurant and get a look at the surveillance footage?" I asked.

"You just said you didn't want to risk tainting the investigation."

"I can't if you're there."

Heathcliff pressed his lips together, his mouth quirking on the side. He didn't want to disappoint me. "It's not my investigation either. The lead investigator knows about this. He'll perform his due diligence."

I gave the phone on his desk a pointed look. "When?"

"Soon."

"Now would be better. We could get to it now."

"Alex, come on, you know that isn't a good idea. If you thought it was, you would have already done it. You wouldn't have waited to talk to me. You would have gone straight to the source."

"Maybe I was wrong. Maybe I should go now."

He grabbed my wrist. "Sit down, Parker."

"There's a clock on this. Don's threatening Martin. I can't let my life cause him more harm."

"Give the detective twenty-four hours to gather evidence, speak to witnesses, and figure out what's what."

Heathcliff let go of my arm. "You said you asked Jablonsky to look into Chad Averly."

"Yeah." I squinted. "Why? Did you find something?"

Heathcliff shook his head. "I put a call into the locals, but there's nothing in our databases. However, if Averly is involved in something big, the FBI would know more than we would."

I pulled out my phone, but there were no messages or missed calls. "Don could be lying about that too. I just don't know."

"Are you absolutely certain Martin didn't put Don in the hospital?" Heathcliff was careful to use the same wording I had.

"That's what he said, and I believe him. But I can't do nothing. I should be out there, looking for the big guy in the suit." Except I had no idea where to look. Cross was exploring all the angles. Once he had something concrete, he'd tell me. For Martin's sake, it'd be best if I waited for a lead. "Who knows what he might do next or who else he might hurt."

"Patrol's at the hospital. Martin's got security at work. And you're here. Who's left for him to target?"

"He already attacked Ace. I can't think of anyone else."

"What about your father's business partner or your mom?"

"I don't know. But they aren't local, and no threats have been made."

"In that case, how about a distraction?" Heathcliff pointed to the board where he had photos of the suspects in the armed robberies hanging. "Looks like Kelsey Savage is the ringleader."

"Do you think he'll roll on his accomplices?" I forced my mind to stop conjuring images of Martin's bruised knuckles and reached for the paperwork on Heathcliff's desk. "Has the lab gotten a chance to run the DNA from the *Phantom of the Opera* masks yet?"

"You know how DNA goes. Now that we have evidence, we can compel Kelsey to provide a sample. We'll know if they match once it's collected and analyzed."

I was itching to do something. Anything. "What are we

waiting for?"

"Kelsey's attorney. He refused to answer questions without counsel present."

"I'll see if he's here yet." Without waiting for Heathcliff to respond, I went through the double doors and down the stairs. Every fiber of my being wanted to find the detective in charge of investigating the assault, but I didn't do it. Instead, I spoke to the desk sergeant to see if Kelsey's attorney had arrived.

"He should be here any minute," she said.

"Is Officer Franco around?" Sitting still would make me crazy, so speaking to Franco about yesterday's canvass would keep me busy for a few minutes while I waited.

She pointed to the hallway behind her. "He's updating the watch commander. He should be out in a couple of minutes."

I examined the bulletin board on the side wall. Several notices were posted, along with photos and sketches of offenders who were on the loose. I didn't recognize any of them, which was probably a good thing.

"Ms. Parker?" a familiar voice said from behind.

I turned, surprised to find Almeada with his briefcase in hand. He looked like he'd come straight from court. "Did you get my message?" I asked.

"What message? Was it about the Gibbs case? Did you discover something new?"

"No."

"If you're not working on that, why are you here? Did you get arrested again?"

"I rarely get arrested."

"Are you in trouble?" he asked.

I glanced behind me to make sure we were alone and lowered my voice. "It's not me. It's James Martin. The police believe he may be a suspect in a recent assault."

"Is he here? Have they brought him in?"

"Not yet. They have another possible suspect to pursue." I gave his phone a pointed look. "You should check your messages."

"I'll do that." But he didn't move. "Is that why you're here?"

"No. I'm consulting with the police department on a string of armed robberies." The lines across his forehead deepened. "Don't worry, that has nothing to do with my research into the Gibbs case," I said.

"That's not why I'm worried."

Before I could ask any other questions, Officer Franco appeared behind the desk. The desk sergeant pointed to me, and Franco joined us. Almeada excused himself and stepped outside.

Franco and I stood near the stairs while he filled me in on the details of the canvass. Unfortunately, Franco hadn't found anything else while conducting the search. No smoking gun. No eyewitnesses. No surveillance footage with clear shots of the suspects without their masks. The footage they recovered from near the dumpster where the masks were found didn't show anyone in those clothes or with masks. The men must have changed in the alleyway and split up to avoid detection.

"Tell the detective I want in on the next interview," Franco said.

"Will do," I promised, my attention split between the eager police officer and Almeada, who I spotted through the door, talking on his phone.

I moved closer, catching the tail-end of Almeada's conversation.

"...conflicted out. Call Titus and Reed. Tell them to send someone immediately. Then call Cross and tell him his retainer just went up." Almeada tucked his phone away and continued down the steps to his waiting car.

"Was that Kelsey Savage's attorney?" I asked the desk sergeant.

"I think it was supposed to be, but he said there was a mix-up and another attorney would be here shortly to provide representation."

Confused by this turn of events, I returned upstairs and found Heathcliff grinning as he hung up the phone.

"Did they find the big guy in the suit?" I asked.

Heathcliff wiped the smile off his face. "Sorry, I didn't mean to get your hopes up. That was the lab. The prints on the duck sauce packet weren't in the system."

"No surprise there. Eyeholes acted too much like a first-timer."

Heathcliff pointed to one of the surveillance photos from the grocery store robbery. "He got lucky the first two times. However," Heathcliff peeled off the top sticky note and held it out for me to read, "third time wasn't a charm. We IDed him."

"The credit card?"

"Yep. That was an amateur mistake."

"He must have thought we wouldn't connect the food poisoning to the robbery or connect him to another crime scene." I read the name and address Heathcliff had written on the sticky note. *Ed Mitchell.* "Are we going to pick him up?"

"We will, but first things first. What's going on with Kelsey Savage's attorney?"

"He left."

"What?"

Before I could explain, the phone rang. Heathcliff picked it up. After a few uh-huhs, he hung up. "Looks like we have time to pay Ed Mitchell a visit. Mr. Titus, Kelsey's new attorney, won't be here for another two hours. The desk sergeant said you scared off his previous counsel."

"I guess I did."

Heathcliff slipped into his jacket and tugged the hem loose from his holster. After a quick in and out with the LT, Heathcliff and I got back into his car. I sunk into the seat and took a breath. I'd been going nonstop since waking up this morning. Martin's situation weighed heavily on my mind. Maybe we'd have time to swing by the restaurant, but Ed Mitchell's address wasn't anywhere near there.

"Are you all right?" Heathcliff glanced at me as he drove.

I shook away thoughts of Martin getting dragged out of the MT building in handcuffs or a judge awarding my no-good adoptive father a seven-figure payday. "Kelsey Savage can't afford an attorney from Reeves, Almeada, and Stockton."

"Maybe that's why Almeada left."

"He left because it'd be a conflict to represent someone I

helped you arrest."

"Maybe it was pro bono."

"Almeada isn't into charity. I'm sure his office takes a few on occasion, but I doubt he'd do it unless he was required. It'd be odd that he just happened to choose this case." I leaned my forehead against the cold glass of the window, hoping it'd cool down my emotions. "The guy who attacked Don is the same guy who attacked Ace Darrow. Maybe we should speak to Ace again."

"It'd be hard to get much traction on that when Ace refuses to cooperate. He didn't even want to press charges, claimed it was a hazard of the job, and wanted to be left alone."

"Why won't anyone cooperate?" I sighed and stared out the window. I'd have to speak to Lucien about that. "Is there anything else I haven't thought of that might help?"

"You could get your father to clarify his earlier statement, explain how Martin left, and someone else attacked him. That'd go a long way."

"It won't happen, unless Don gets the money, and paying him off will only make Martin look guilty. What's to stop Don from refusing to recant his statement and from following through on his threats? He'd use the payoff as evidence, if he wanted."

"Tell Martin to come in and provide a statement. If he has an alibi, we won't look twice at him. Then it won't matter what Don says or does."

"I have to find the big guy. That's the only way." But even that could look hinky. "Martin's driver was there. He saw what happened. He could provide an alibi."

"Martin pays him." Heathcliff wasn't arguing, merely pointing out a fact. "What exactly did Marcal see?"

"He saw Martin leave Don outside the restaurant. Don wasn't out-cold or bleeding."

"Martin hit him." Heathcliff turned to look at me, but I kept my expression neutral and stared out the windshield. "I asked you what happened."

"I can't confirm or deny."

"Fine. I know I can't stop you from looking for this guy, but be careful. You're a P.I. It wouldn't be that strange if you found him, but it won't help if we bring him in and your dad contradicts what you say about the big guy's involvement. On the one hand, your father's the victim. On the other, your boyfriend's a suspect. You'd have reason to fudge the details, and your credibility could be called into question. That's not a good place to be."

"No kidding."

"For what it's worth, I believe you," Heathcliff said. "Averly sent someone to rough up Don. Martin happened to be in the wrong place at the wrong time. I'm guessing the offender used Martin's appearance to his advantage to avoid drawing attention to himself."

It was also possible Don had planned this. He knew how to push Martin's buttons. He made sure he got punched. Then he had someone else go to town on him, so he could blame Martin and extort or sue him.

I sent Cross a text, asking him to do everything he could to find the big guy, but he was already searching. Until I heard back, there wasn't much I could do. It's not like Don had told me who the big guy was or where I could find him.

"Are you still with me?" Heathcliff asked after a few minutes of total silence.

"Sure." I rubbed my eyes and tried to clear my head. "What do we know about Ed Mitchell, a.k.a. Eyeholes?"

"He works part-time as a janitor and lives in public housing. No criminal record. He's widowed. No children."

"How recently did his spouse die?"

"A little over three years ago. Their savings went toward medical expenses. He paid everything off, but he's got next to nothing left. He wouldn't make it from paycheck to paycheck without government assistance."

"That's the pattern with our robbers. Wayne and Ed are in dire straits. Kelsey isn't bad off, but his brother is, so he may be doing this to help him. But Eye—I mean Ed, was reluctant to hold up the coffee shop. The money may not be enough motivation for him."

"Ed didn't have the same qualms about robbing the grocery store. Maybe he had performance anxiety at the coffee shop," Heathcliff said.

"I don't know. Ed looked nervous on the footage at the

grocery store too. The witnesses and victims described him the same way at the gentlemen's club. He's our weak link."

Heathcliff checked the address and parked the car a block away. He didn't want Ed to see us coming.

TWENTY-SIX

"Let me knock on the door," I said.

"You're not a cop, Parker."

"He may recognize you." I gave Heathcliff an exasperated look. "If you had let me confront him outside the coffee shop, this wouldn't be a problem."

"So you were right, and I was wrong?"

"That goes without saying." I gave him a playful smile. "But I don't mind hearing it from time to time."

Before Heathcliff forced his point, I hurried up the walkway and rang the doorbell. The door creaked and groaned, requiring a good yank for it to open. The frame had been warped from years of weather and temperature changes. I recognized the man on the other side instantly, even without the ripped beanie over his head.

"Mr. Mitchell, I'm Alex." I offered a friendly smile. "This is my friend, Derek."

Ed Mitchell squinted at me. "How can I help you?"

"Do you mind if we come inside?"

"I'm in the middle of something. Who did you say you were?"

Heathcliff reached for his badge. "Police. We need to speak to you."

Ed's cheeks heated in embarrassment, anger, or a combination of both. He held up his hands and took a step backward. "I didn't have a choice. I didn't know what to do. They made me rob those places."

Heathcliff spun Ed around and cuffed him. Then he patted him down before spinning him back around. "You're under arrest. You have the right to remain silent."

While Heathcliff read Ed Mitchell the rest of his Miranda's, I looked around the apartment. Living room, kitchen, bedroom, bathroom. The open drawer in his nightstand contained a gun, the one he used in the grocery store robbery.

"Parker," Heathcliff called to me, "don't touch anything. We need a search warrant."

I held up my hands the way Ed had while I continued to look around. For a robber, he didn't plan things out. I didn't find any maps or surveillance photos. No rudimentary drawings or blueprints. No research into security systems or police response times. Nothing.

"Where's the money, Mr. Mitchell?" I asked.

Heathcliff had already told him he didn't have to answer any questions, so everything from here on out was fair game. Ed didn't have much in his apartment. The sofa and entertainment center had seen better days. The TV looked new, but it wasn't a name brand. The cash he stole from the grocery store would have paid for two of them.

"Is this what you bought with your ill-gotten gains?" I pointed to the TV.

"No." Ed looked from Heathcliff to me. "Why do you look so familiar?"

"Coffee shop," I said.

Ed's flushed cheeks drained of color, and he stared wide-eyed at Heathcliff. "How did you know we'd be there? No one was supposed to know about that. I never wanted any trouble."

"Is that why you took off?" Heathcliff asked.

Ed looked like he remembered he didn't have to answer us.

"You left your pal holding the bag, and he tried to kill us," I said.

Ed gulped. "I never wanted anyone to get hurt. That's why I took off. I knew it'd be bad. There were too many people inside. Too many possibilities. It was the wrong time. If we'd only waited two hours, there would have been a lull and a full register."

"Why didn't you wait?" I asked.

"It wasn't my decision."

"Who decided?"

Heathcliff gave me a warning look. Pushing too hard would make our suspect shut down.

"I tried to do what they said, but it felt wrong. I couldn't," Ed said. "I never should have done any of it. Everything got messed up."

"How about we go to the precinct and get this sorted? We'll get you something to eat. You can sit down and relax, and we'll take it from there," Heathcliff said soothingly.

Usually, I played good cop in these scenarios, but Heathcliff switched it up since I'd taken point by knocking and asking questions.

"Yeah. Okay." Ed blew out a breath.

"Do you want us to grab your jacket?" Heathcliff asked. "I don't want you to get cold."

Ed jerked his chin toward the closet. "The tan one."

Heathcliff kept one hand on Ed while his other rested on his weapon. I waited for him to nod before carefully opening the closet door. I'd already cleared the rest of the apartment, but it was better to be safe than sorry. No skeletons fell out.

Only three jackets hung in the closet. A faded suit jacket, a tan coat, and a windbreaker. I took out the tan coat, rifled through the pockets and carefully checked the lining before handing it to Heathcliff. He put it over Ed's shoulders.

While he was escorting him to the car, I searched the rest of the closet and checked the other two hanging jackets. I didn't find anything. Donning a pair of gloves, I searched the couch cushions and peered beneath the living room furniture.

Afterward, I went into the bedroom. The dresser contained clothing and nothing else. In the nightstand, beside the gun, I found the beanie and knit gloves. After taking a few photos, I checked the rest of the room. A clear storage tub was beneath the bed.

"Parker," Heathcliff called, "officers will secure the

scene until we get that warrant."

Abandoning my search, I joined the detective outside. Once uniformed cops showed up, we took Ed Mitchell back to the precinct.

"Do you like pizza, Mr. Mitchell?" Heathcliff asked.

"Who doesn't?" Ed replied.

"I'll order a couple of pies, unless you'd prefer something else."

Ed considered his options. "Nah, pizza's good, but can we get cheeseburger toppings?"

Heathcliff glanced at me from the corner of his eye. "I can do that."

"Not so fast, Derek." I turned to look at Ed, secured in the back seat. "We'll get that pizza on one condition. You answer our questions. Deal?"

Ed eyed me, his focus on my previously bruised cheek, as if he could still see the remnants of what Wayne Savage had done. "I don't know much, but I'll tell you what I can. It's not like I got anything left to lose."

Heathcliff told the officer at booking to take good care of our friend Ed and to set him up in interrogation room three when they finished. While Ed was getting printed and photographed, we returned to the major crimes unit.

Lt. Moretti was waiting for us. "I was wondering when you'd get back. Kelsey Savage's attorney finally showed up. Mr. Titus is getting antsy. He's threatening to file a complaint over the delay."

"Wonderful," I muttered.

"We arrested another one of the robbers," Heathcliff said. "He confessed he was part of it as soon as he saw my badge. He says he'll talk. Maybe he'll be able to shed some light on things if Kelsey turns out to be as difficult as his lawyer."

"Do you want to start with this other suspect?" Moretti asked. "I can delay. Titus won't like it, which will make it all the better."

"It'd be better to see what Kelsey Savage has to say first," I suggested, even though no one asked, but they had hired me to consult. So there was that. "Plus, we have to wait on the pizza, anyway."

Heathcliff gave me another sideways look. I'd lost count of how many there had been today. "That's the better play," he agreed. "But first, I gotta find someplace that sells cheeseburger pizza."

"Tony's," Moretti and I said at the same time. The lieutenant pulled out his phone. "What else do you want?"

"Grape soda," Heathcliff said before turning his attention to me. "What kind of pie do you want, Parker? The department's paying."

"Mushroom and extra cheese."

"Cherry cola?"

I narrowed my eyes at Heathcliff, suspicious of his careful attention to detail. "Yes."

"And a pepperoni and sausage." Heathcliff checked the notes on his desk.

"Savage and his attorney are waiting in interrogation room two," Moretti said. "We could offer to bring them dinner too, if you think it'd help."

"Savage isn't a carrot kind of guy. We'll go with the stick." Heathcliff gestured that I go ahead of him, which made me even more suspicious, but I didn't want to cause a scene. I'd save that for when it became unavoidable or absolutely necessary.

Instead, I waited until we were alone in the hallway. "Grape soda?"

"Ed Mitchell's fridge had a half empty three liter inside from one of the bargain stores."

"Good call. You figured that would make Ed more pliable." I sighed. "Is that why you offered me a cherry cola?"

"You're paranoid, Parker."

"Don't gaslight me, Derek. We've been through too much. You've always been straight with me. Don't you dare stop now. I saw you checking your messages when we first got here. Did something happen?"

"I received a text. The hospital let officers question your father again. He hasn't changed his story."

"Don's still saying Martin attacked him?" I'd kill that bastard.

"He said it happened so fast, he doesn't know who

attacked him, but he had been with James Martin prior to the attack. And the man who attacked him was tall, with dark hair, in a business suit. He's not sure it was Martin, but he won't say that it wasn't."

"I already gave you the culprit."

"I know."

Resisting the urge to check my phone, I asked, "Was Martin brought in?"

"Not yet. The detective in charge gave me his word that he'd look into the unknown man from the restaurant before doing anything else. However, he went to your apartment to speak to the doorman about what time Martin arrived home that evening. He thought it might put that possibility to bed."

"Shit."

Heathcliff cocked an eyebrow. "I take it you left something out of your story."

"It was irrelevant."

"The detective doesn't think so. Martin threatened to kill Don a week ago. Building security said you held him back."

"I didn't hold him back. Do you think I could hold Martin back?"

"It doesn't play well."

"That's why I didn't tell you." I swallowed. "Two weeks ago, Don came to me for money. I gave it to him, but he came back for more. That's when Martin and I told him to get lost. I didn't know Don owed money or his life was in danger because of it. I thought he was just being an asshole."

"That's why he wanted to try his luck with Martin."

"Martin wouldn't give it to him either. Either the big guy saw Don's failed attempt and hoped to incentivize him to do a better job next time, or Don set this whole thing up to force Martin to fork over the cash."

"You really think your father would do that?"

"I wouldn't put anything past him. I just don't know how ransacking Ace Investigators and assaulting Ace fits into it. I don't think that would fit into Don's plan, if his entire goal was to create a scenario to force Martin to shell out, unless he said something about this to Ace and feared the private eye would turn him in."

"That's an awful lot of speculating," Heathcliff said. "You have theories and alternatives."

"And alternatives to the alternatives."

"You're spinning."

"I'm speculating."

"Right now, I need you focused here. Can you do that?"

"I'll try."

TWENTY-SEVEN

A perturbed Kelsey Savage sat in the chair beside his attorney. Mr. Titus made sure we removed the handcuffs from his client, which Heathcliff had done as a courtesy. If we gave them what they wanted, maybe they'd give us what we wanted.

"You found a sawed-off shotgun in my client's bedroom closet. It was locked up and kept inside his home. He had it to defend himself," Titus said. "We admit it's considered illegal in the state. However, there have been a lot of home invasions in Mr. Savage's neighborhood. He has a young family to protect. Surely, you aren't going to hold that against him."

Heathcliff smiled, though it wasn't what I'd call friendly. "This isn't about the gun. It's about how Mr. Savage used it."

"I've already told you its purpose," Titus insisted.

Spreading out an array of photos from the check-cashing robbery, Heathcliff took out a red marker and circled the man holding the sawed-off. "Does he look familiar to you?"

Titus sunk back in his chair.

Kelsey Savage glanced at the photo. "Who is he?"

"Are you going to play that game? He's holding your gun." Heathcliff took out a photo from the gentlemen's club robbery and circled the man wearing the *Zorro* mask. "We found this mask on display in your house, like a trophy. Stop pretending you don't know what I'm talking about."

"I have a collection of masks. So what? Tons of people have those. They aren't special. They're a dime a dozen at Halloween."

"This doesn't look like proof," Titus said. "That gun is similar, but you can't prove it's the same one. Can you?" He stared at Heathcliff. "I didn't think so. It looks like you're fishing. I'd even say it borders on harassment."

Heathcliff kept his eyes on Kelsey. "Your brother was arrested for the attempted murder of a police officer after his attempt at robbing a coffee shop was thwarted. Since then, you've been busy. We found the crowd-sourcing campaign you started to pay his bail, but that's a bust. So you had to find other means of raising money."

"Again, you're fishing," Titus said. "Unless you have proof my client's one of these masked men, apologize and cut him loose."

"We have the masks from this robbery." I pointed to the first photo Heathcliff circled. "I'm sure a seasoned defense attorney like yourself knows forensic evidence would be on a piece of plastic worn over a man's face. Skin, hair, sweat, saliva, fingerprints, all sorts of fun things."

Titus narrowed his eyes at me. "You're bluffing."

"No, and as soon as we collect samples from your client, we'll run a comparison that will prove he was involved in these robberies. However, if you'd like to save yourself some embarrassment, we may be willing to negotiate."

"My client's not giving you a sample of his DNA," Titus said.

"The court says otherwise." Heathcliff placed the warrant on the table in front of the attorney. "A tech will be in to collect the sample. But I wanted to give you a chance to tell me your side of the story first," he said to Kelsey. "Your brother's been going through a rough time. It looks like you've been doing all you can to help him out. The situation went from bad to worse. You must have felt like you had no other choice. Those circumstances will be taken into consideration if you cooperate."

Kelsey stared at the table. "It's not fair what happened

to Wayne. He worked hard and always tried to do the right thing. But he never caught a break."

"Is that why he planned to rob the coffee shop?" Heathcliff asked.

Kelsey looked up. "I never said he did that. Pay attention. I just told you Wayne always tried to do the right thing. You railroaded him. You must have forced him into a bad situation or you made shit up. Now he's stuck behind bars because he can't afford to pay. Explain to me how that's fair."

Titus gave Kelsey a sharp look and shook his head. "My client insists he's innocent. Whatever crime his brother is accused of has nothing to do with him."

Heathcliff placed a photo from the freezer section of the grocery store down on the table. "You're right, except whatever scheme your client and his brother concocted involved more than just the two of them. Isn't that right, Mr. Savage?" Heathcliff pointed to the men in the photo. "That's Wayne. That's you. And this guy," he tapped the image of Ed Mitchell, "is in the next interrogation room, waiting to tell me everything he knows. But since we brought you in first, it was only polite to see what you had to say."

"I have nothing to say."

"I guess this was a waste of time." Heathcliff opened the interrogation room door and told the tech to collect samples for the lab.

"There's one other thing you may have forgotten." I pointed to the photo from the check-cashing place. "The masks failed to hide one very specific identifier." I tugged on my earlobe. "You should have taken that out before you decided to play Robin Hood." Without waiting for a response, I followed Heathcliff out the door.

Heathcliff pushed open the door to the next interrogation room. He held it for me, letting me enter in front of him. I went to the back of the room, stood beside the two-way mirror, and crossed my arms over my chest. Alex Parker, bad cop.

Heathcliff took a seat in front of Ed Mitchell and unhooked his handcuffs. "Hard to eat with your hands stuck together." Heathcliff flipped open the waiting pizza box. "Cheeseburger." He gave it a suspicious look. "I can't say I've ever tried it before. Do you mind?"

Ed nudged the box toward Heathcliff. "Help yourself."

Heathcliff took out a slice and waited for Ed to do the same. "Hey, Parker, ask the officer to get us some paper plates, napkins, and something to drink."

I knew the routine. While I was collecting the items waiting in the observation room, Heathcliff continued to build trust with our suspect. We'd need someone to cooperate since neither of the Savages wanted to be active participants.

"Here you go." I put the plates and napkins down before putting a can of grape soda on the table beside Ed. "Anything else, Detective?" I said in an annoyed, bitter tone, playing up the act.

"Nope." Heathcliff finished the tiny slice he'd taken, wiped his hands on the napkin, and rocked back in the chair.

"Now that you're settled, Mr. Mitchell," I put my palms down on the table and stared at him, "it's time you tell us something useful."

"Let the man eat." Heathcliff jerked his chin toward the back of the room. "He gave us his word. He'll get to it in a minute."

"Fine, but it's your ass on the line." I went back to holding the wall up with my back, wondering if Ed was buying any of this.

"Is it?" Ed asked while he chewed. He was already on his second slice. He washed the mouthful down with a sip of his drink and wiped his mouth on his sleeve. "Your ass, I mean. I don't want you to get in trouble." He picked up a third slice and bit off the triangular point. "There's not much I can tell you. I needed cash. Bills are piling up, and I haven't been able to find a second job that fits with the hours I currently work. I can't risk quitting because the janitor job pays better than anything else I've found. That's how I ended up outside the coffee shop."

"You weren't alone," I said from the corner.

Heathcliff gave me a look, warning me to cool the act

now that Ed was talking. “Another man was already inside who had the same idea. You were working together.”

“We were supposed to.” Ed finished his third slice and took another gulp of soda. “I wanted to wait. I told him we should wait. But he said we couldn’t.”

“Tell us about your partner.”

“I don’t know much about him. The other guys knew him better than I did.”

“Other guys?” Heathcliff asked.

Ed looked uncomfortable, almost like he’d lost his appetite. “I shouldn’t. I don’t want to get anyone else in trouble.”

“That’s okay,” Heathcliff said. “Tell us about Wayne. If you don’t know him well, why were you going to rob a store with him?”

“We met at the job postings board near the food pantry. I’d seen him around there a lot. We tended to go at the same times to pick up our groceries and check for new job listings. He said he’d gotten laid off. We got to talking and bitched about how screwed up everything was.”

“I’m really sorry about that,” Heathcliff said.

“Thanks, but that’s life. A lot of people have it rough. Except Wayne was fed up. He didn’t see a light at the end of the tunnel. Actually, he thought it was a speeding train. Anyway, that’s how it went. Whenever we’d run into each other, we’d check in. But nothing was getting better. A few weeks ago, there was another guy at the board. He had on a nice coat and dress shoes. He didn’t fit in. I thought he was there to post a job listing, so I asked him about it. He said he was looking to put a crew together. I thought he might have been in construction.” Ed took another slice from the box and put it down on his plate. “Wayne came over to see what was going on, and that’s when this guy gave us his card. He said if we were interested and knew anyone else who might be, we should show up at the loading doors at a certain warehouse store at a specific time and date. He said he’d have a job for us.”

Heathcliff moved his plate and napkin out of the way and pulled a pen from his pocket. “I’ll need the details on that, but first, what was this guy’s name?”

"He didn't say. His card didn't have anything on it except the location with the date and time."

"And you didn't find that odd?" I asked. "It sounds like something out of a horror movie."

"Believe me, the thought crossed my mind, but Wayne was into it. He figured the guy had the cards printed so he could leave them at the job listings board for anyone interested. I let myself believe that. I wanted to believe it. I just wanted something to work out." Ed finished his fourth slice and closed the box, having reached his limit. "Wayne said he had a couple of friends who'd be interested. I left while Wayne was talking to the guy, but I figured if he was going to show up with some of his buddies, it wouldn't hurt for me to check it out. What could possibly happen when there was going to be so many of us around? Worst case, we'd get roped into listening to an inspirational speaker preach to us how to manifest our desires, worship harder, or pitch us on joining a cult."

"Have you run into a lot of guys like that?" Heathcliff asked.

"Maybe three or four in the last couple of years. It's more an annoyance than anything. But this guy wasn't like the others. He wanted to hire us, and he wouldn't take no for an answer."

"What happened?" I went to the table and helped myself to a slice of pizza. The mushroom and extra cheese was waiting upstairs, but my stomach had started growling, and since Ed had been cooperating, I thought it was safe to drop the act and break bread with the man.

Heathcliff ignored me as I inhaled the slice, his focus on Ed. "Please, we need to know."

"I just...I don't want to make things worse for myself."

"The more you can tell us, the better off you'll be," Heathcliff said. "I'll tell the prosecutor how helpful you were. We have two other suspects already in custody and a growing pile of evidence. We'll find out one way or the other."

"I showed up to the warehouse store and went around the back to where the trucks unload supplies. Wayne was already there with two other guys, who I assumed were his friends. I went over to see what was happening, and that's when the man who'd offered us the job came around the side of a sixteen-wheeler. He had a gun. He forced the driver to open the back doors. Then he shot him."

"He killed him?" Heathcliff asked.

"I don't know. I saw blood. The guy went down. That's when the man turned his attention to us. He forced us to take the boxes off the sixteen-wheeler and load them into a moving truck. He said he'd kill us if we didn't do as he said, so we did. Then he locked us in the back of the moving truck and drove away."

Heathcliff slid the pen and paper over to Ed. "How did you escape?"

"We didn't. He let us out at the container yard. Wayne and the other guys didn't seem nearly as worried, but I wasn't paying that much attention to them. I was sure when he opened the doors, he'd kill us."

"Why didn't you call for help?" I asked. "Surely, someone else must have been around."

"It all happened so fast," Ed said. "He killed the driver. I wasn't going to do anything to step out of line. He would have killed me too."

"Except he didn't." I wondered how true the story was. "Why didn't you call 9-1-1 from the back of the truck?"

"I didn't have any bars."

"Why didn't you report it to the police after he let you go?" Heathcliff asked.

"He had taken video of us stealing the merchandise off that truck and loading it into the other truck. He said he'd turn us in, say we masterminded the entire thing, that we killed the truck driver. That's when he handed us envelopes with a thousand dollars each and said he had a few more jobs in the works and would be in touch."

"He paid you to steal that stuff," Heathcliff said. "Do you even know what it was?"

"Pallets of TVs and tablets."

"Like the one in your house?" I asked.

"I didn't steal it," Ed insisted. "But when I got home from cleaning an office building the next day, it was set up and waiting in my living room with a note that if I went to the authorities, the evidence would point back to me."

"Write it all down. Every bit. I'll make sure you aren't blamed for anything you didn't willingly do," Heathcliff said.

"Did he contact you about the other jobs?" I asked.

Ed nodded. "He left me a phone. I'd get texts from an unknown number with a date and time. That was it."

"Why did you show up?"

"I was scared he'd turn me in for stealing from that warehouse store."

"What were the other jobs he sent you on?" Heathcliff asked.

Ed hesitated. "I'd rather not say. I'll incriminate myself. It'll make things worse."

"Not if it helps us track down the person who forced you to commit these crimes," Heathcliff said.

TWENTY-EIGHT

While I picked the mushrooms off a slice of pizza and ate them separately, I reread a copy of Ed Mitchell's statement. "Are you actually buying this?"

Heathcliff's eyes had been glued to his computer screen since we returned to the major crimes unit. "I can't rule out the possibility."

"Why would a killer let any of them live? If this guy wanted a crew to do his dirty work, he could have found a team of professional thieves. Why did he trick a bunch of nobodies into helping him?"

"For one thing, Wayne and Ed don't have criminal records. No one would ever suspect them. For another, they were desperate. That would make them easy to control with money or intimidation."

"I don't know. It doesn't feel right. It's too simple."

"Simple?" Heathcliff peered around his computer screen at me. "You think this is simple?"

"Would you prefer if I say it's too complicated?" None of Ed's story made a damn bit of sense. "Ed's excuse is too easy. Someone made him do it. Someone forced him and three other men to rob that truck. Then the shot-caller gives them two options. He'll pay them to perform more jobs or he'll kill them. And he kept the video he took to use as blackmail in case they got caught or ballsy enough to go to the police."

"What's your theory?"

"I don't have one yet. But if things happened the way Ed said they did, why did Wayne shoot at us? Why didn't someone on that crew come forward? They saw the shot-caller kill a man. That should have scared one of them enough to seek help."

"We still haven't identified the fourth man." Heathcliff pointed to the surveillance photo of the Savage brothers in the freezer section of the grocery store. "Ed IDed Wayne and Kelsey Savage as part of the crew, but we don't know who the fourth guy is."

"Ed said he appeared to be one of Wayne's friends."

"But Wayne won't talk."

"We could ask Kelsey," I suggested.

"We will." But Heathcliff didn't think that'd get us very far since Kelsey had refused to answer our questions. "Maybe the three of them had prior dealings with the shot-caller. Maybe they knew what was going down. Ed may have been the wild card. The guy that happened to show up that no one was expecting."

"He said he was offered a job opportunity."

Heathcliff thought about it. "Wayne could have been grooming Ed or testing the waters. You heard what Ed said. They'd pass each other at the food pantry. They got to be friendly. The rest of it could have been a set-up."

"Why would they set up Ed? He's the weak link. He'd be the most likely to turn them in." I rifled through the case files.

"Ed said the shot-caller forced him to rob the grocery store to prove his loyalty and to make up for what they lost when you and I stopped the coffee shop robbery."

"Fine, but why can't Ed ID the shot-caller? He's been in contact with this guy for weeks. Shouldn't he know something by now? A first name? An alias? Something?"

"Ed may not have wanted to know. The mystery man gave him a thousand dollars, plus whatever other crumbs he tossed Ed's way that we don't know about."

"Like the TV?"

Heathcliff went back to studying the computer screen. "I can see why someone in Ed's position would go along with it, but I don't know. There are a lot of holes."

"Told you so."

Heathcliff pulled up Ed's financial history and phone records. "The shot-caller gave Ed a burner phone. Once we find it, we'll have access to the texts. We may be able to identify the shot-caller from there." He moved over to O'Connell's empty desk, but he didn't find any notes. O'Connell and Thompson hadn't returned yet from executing the search warrant, so we'd have to wait for them to come back with evidence and answers.

"What about the money? What did Ed do with that?" I asked.

"He used the thousand dollars to pay credit card bills, make rent, and buy groceries. It's not like he had any left over. And he had more bills about to come due. He may not have liked robbing places, but he needed the cash. He had received several second and third notices. Keeping the shot-caller happy and knocking over the grocery store did come with monetary benefits."

"If Ed was that afraid of the shot-caller, he should have taken the thousand dollars and skipped town," I said. "It doesn't look like he has anything keeping him here."

"Innocent people don't run, Parker. Even if Ed tried, the mystery man said he'd turn the footage over to the police and make it look like Ed and the rest of the crew committed the crimes and fled the city. In a way, I see how it could work. Manipulation like that, it's how people end up in all sorts of bad situations, getting trafficked, becoming accomplices, working as mules, moving drugs."

"Paying two hundred grand to avoid assault charges?"

"Yeah."

I shook the thought away. "Where's the dead truck driver? Why was no one else outside the warehouse store when this went down? How come no one found the body or reported the emptied-out truck?"

Heathcliff went back to his computer screen. "A state trooper found the truck and body at the end of an off-ramp three weeks ago. The truck had two blown tires. Cones had been set up around it, and it appeared the driver had set off on foot to get help. When no one came back for the truck, the state trooper had it towed to an impound lot. When someone from the store's corporate office showed up to find out why one of their shipping trucks had gone missing, the cops opened the back and found the truck empty and the driver's body. They figured the truck had been ambushed on its way to make a delivery. The merchandise was stolen and the driver killed by whoever set the trap. The coroner said the driver had been dead for a few days. Cause of death was a GSW to the chest. It fit with the staties' theory, but they have no leads. The investigation remains open." Heathcliff stopped reading. "That would explain why no one reported anything at the store and why we didn't know about this sooner. The body was dumped outside our jurisdiction."

"That means someone else had to drive the empty truck off the premises since Ed said the shot-caller drove the moving truck and the Savages and their friend were locked in the back with Ed." I counted on my fingers. "Now we're looking at a team of six. The shot-caller and five men working for him."

Heathcliff pointed to the check-cashing robbery. "Those could be our two unknowns—the fourth man from the grocery store photo and the other truck driver."

"Or one of those guys is the shot-caller." The math was making my head spin.

"Or Ed wearing a better disguise. There's a lot about this we don't know," Heathcliff admitted.

"The job outside the warehouse store is setting off my bullshit detector. Those places are always busy. Between workers and customers, someone should have seen or heard something, especially a gunshot. If some guy forced Ed to commit these crimes, why would he send Ed and the crew out on these stupid little armed robberies at the coffee shop and grocery store? Clearly, this shot-caller has his sights set a lot higher. The payoff wouldn't be worth the risk at those other places when he could have his crew knocking over more cash-heavy businesses."

"What are you thinking?"

"One of these guys," I pointed to the photo of the four of them in the grocery store, "figured this would be a good way to make a quick buck. They could have found a replacement after Wayne got pinched."

"That would mean one of them killed the truck driver."

"The staties may have gotten it right. The truck could have been ambushed on its way to the store. Did the file contain any details on the weapon used to kill the driver?"

Heathcliff went back to his screen. "Handgun. Same caliber as what I took off Wayne Savage when we arrested him." He reached for the phone. "I'll see about comparing ballistics."

Still, most men didn't wake up one day and decide to become violent offenders. Yet, Wayne Savage's lack of priors indicated just that. Was Ed's story bullshit? What was I missing?

Heathcliff put down the phone. The files the state police had on the truck driver's murder would be sent over, including details on the bullet pulled from the body. With any luck, we'd be able to match it to Wayne's handgun.

"If the shot-caller gave Ed a phone, Kelsey and Wayne should have burners too. Did you find a burner at Kelsey's place?" I asked.

Heathcliff shook his head and picked up a sheet of paper that had found its way to the top of his notes. "You said Wayne had made purchases from an electronics store known for selling burners."

I'd forgotten all about that. "Anything to it?"

Heathcliff read from the report. "Officer Franco followed up. Wayne bought one phone and four SIM cards. The clerk showed him how to install the SIM and where to find the number. Luckily for us, the clerk happened to remember what it was."

"You have the number to Wayne Savage's burner phone?"

Heathcliff nodded. "And a list of calls he made and received, thanks to the CDRs."

I took the paper from Heathcliff's hand, which provided the details on Wayne's call log. "He communicated with four other burner phones," I said. "If he bought the phone and these SIMs. He could be the shot-caller."

"Unless the shot-caller made him do it."

"Now you sound like Ed."

Heathcliff ignored me. "Four SIM cards. Four men." Heathcliff indicated the photo from the grocery store. "Shot-caller or not, this is our crew." He went back to the surveillance footage from the check-cashing place. "Three men went in. Kelsey, Ed, and the unknown."

"Except Ed swore he didn't go inside," I said.

"You already said you didn't believe him."

"I've been wrong before."

"Don't sell yourself short, Parker. This isn't the time to second-guess things. We have a lead. We need to make the most of it. I'll have Wayne Savage moved out of central booking and brought in for another round of questioning. Until then, I want to take another crack at Kelsey. Now that we have a few more facts, we may be able to loosen his lips."

Another thought came to mind. "Who did Wayne hire to represent him?"

"He was appointed a public defender."

"But Kelsey has one of the top paid law firms at his beck and call. How can he afford that?"

"Maybe someone behind the scenes is pulling the strings," Heathcliff suggested, "like the shot-caller. Or Kelsey used the cash from the robbery to cover the expense."

TWENTY-NINE

We returned to the interrogation room where Kelsey Savage was waiting. Heathcliff ran through the facts again, putting a new spin on the situation. "If someone put you up to this, Mr. Savage," Heathcliff said, "it'd be in your best interest to tell me about him."

"No way."

"Are you afraid of the man who's pulling your strings?" I asked.

"My client never affirmed or denied the existence of such a man," Titus said. "He's merely exercising his right not to answer your questions."

"Who's paying you?" Heathcliff asked the attorney.

Titus stared at him. "That is none of your business, Detective."

"This guy's broke." I jerked my thumb at Kelsey. "If he paid you by check, it'll bounce. If he put it on his credit card, I'd say it'll go into collections, but the credit card company would still pay you. So I guess that wouldn't be your problem." I gave the attorney a sweet smile. "But I'm guessing he paid you in stacks of cash. Did they still have the bands around them?"

"This line of questioning is highly inappropriate," Titus insisted. "I should report you."

"I don't work here," I said. "Not usually. They only bring me in on special occasions. This seemed special. After all, you're here, so your client must be someone very special." I glanced at Kelsey. "Except, he doesn't seem particularly special, so I don't think he's who you're representing by being here."

That made the attorney glare harder.

"Mr. Savage, if you or your brother were coerced into committing a crime, that changes the entire scope of this investigation. All you have to do is speak up," Heathcliff said. "We can offer you protection, possibly immunity."

"I have nothing to say. I didn't do anything," Kelsey insisted.

"When the lab finishes its analysis on the masks we recovered, we'll know for sure. In the meantime, maybe your brother will have something different to say. He might since he's staring down a possible murder charge."

"What?" Kelsey asked.

I studied his eyes. He was playing dumb. "The truck driver."

"What truck?"

"It doesn't matter." I gave him a wicked grin. "The public defender on your brother's case is overworked and underpaid. He'll recommend Wayne pleads for a reduced sentence. Maybe facing life in prison will convince him to tell us who's in charge of this little armed robbery spree you've got going on."

"Don't say anything," Titus said. "She's lying to you in the hopes of baiting you."

"Bait means there's something to catch," I said.

Titus scowled at me. "Tricking my client into making a false confession is unethical."

"You'd know."

"That's it. I want her out of here," Titus said.

"She'll remain silent from here on out," Heathcliff said, giving me a stern look.

"Regardless, we're done here," Titus said.

"Like I said, I'll speak to Wayne about this. You may want to stick around in case I have some follow-up questions for your client." Heathcliff grabbed the folder off the table and stood up. "I'd hate to have you make the commute a second time."

"You're serious? Wayne's coming here?" Kelsey sat up,

peering at the closed door like a puppy who heard his owner returning home. "Can I see him?"

"That wouldn't be appropriate," Heathcliff said.

"Please," Kelsey begged.

"You've denied your involvement despite evidence and witness testimony to the contrary. You have no alibi for when any of these crimes were committed. You've given me nothing. You refuse to help yourself and your brother. So why should I do you this favor?" Heathcliff asked.

Kelsey rubbed his nose against his sleeve and stared at the door. "I can't tell you things I don't know."

I glanced at Heathcliff. "You can't keep them apart if they end up in the same holding cell."

Titus watched our exchange, but he had no legal grounds to force the police department to play nice.

"I can make sure that doesn't happen," Heathcliff said. "It won't be too hard. We'll have Wayne brought into an interrogation room and kept in isolation until transport takes him back to central booking. Unless you give me something, Mr. Savage."

"My client has said all he can," Titus said.

Flipping through the file, Heathcliff pulled out a printed photo of the four men in the grocery store. "Tell us one thing, Mr. Savage, and I'll make sure you get some time alone with your brother." He pointed to the fourth man in the photo. "Who is he?"

"How would I know?"

"Because that's Wayne. That's you. And that's Ed Mitchell. Store employees verified it. You're regulars there. They know you. They remember the four of you chatting in the freezer section. So tell me who this guy is."

Mr. Titus leaned closer to his client. "That could have been some random person who stopped to ask if anyone knew where to find the frozen lasagna."

"Were you there, Mr. Titus? Are you the man in this picture?" I asked.

Heathcliff grunted, warning me I was already on thin ice.

"When this is over, Ms. Parker, I'll make sure you never consult for the police department again," Titus said.

I scrunched up my face, resisting the urge to flip him the bird.

"Mr. Savage," Heathcliff said, "this photo doesn't link to any of the crimes. What's the harm in giving us this man's name? You do that, and I'll make sure you get an hour with your brother. Okay?"

Kelsey looked torn, but finally, he said, "That's Jerome Sassen. He's Wayne's best friend."

* * *

While Heathcliff found whatever details he could on Jerome Sassen, I paced in front of the board. My mind was everywhere and nowhere. Lt. Moretti came out of his office.

"Parker, I need a word." Moretti waited for me to join him in his office. "Mr. Titus is unhappy about your behavior in the interrogation room."

"I didn't cross any lines."

"That's not what he said."

"Am I out?"

"Not yet, but this better be the last time a lawyer complains about you. I don't need the DA's office bitching to me."

"The only reason Titus complained was because I was right. Kelsey Savage doesn't have the money to afford his attorney's fees."

"Unfortunately, we're not privy to those details, but he could have a rich uncle."

"How come that rich uncle isn't worried about Wayne?"

"Maybe the rich uncle is on the wife's side of the family."

Pulling out my phone, I texted Kellan, asking him to look into it and see if Breann had family money hidden away. "We both know that's a long shot." I rubbed the worn spot on the arm of the chair. "This mystery shot-caller most likely is made up, a story Ed told us to keep himself out of trouble. Kelsey hasn't copped to it, and Heathcliff gave him every opportunity."

"Heathcliff hasn't ruled out the possibility the shot-caller is paying the attorney's fees. That could be why

Kelsey's staying quiet."

"Which is why I asked the questions I did," I said. "But it's a toss-up. Maybe Jerome Sassen will shed some light on it because I don't expect Wayne to cooperate."

"Do you have any evidence that Jerome was involved?"

"Nothing physical, but Ed should be able to identify Jerome if he served in the crew. That should be enough."

"Good," Moretti said. "I'll see if he recognizes Jerome from his driver's license photo."

"Maybe Heathcliff should do it. After all, Ed's his new best friend."

"Do you want to get something off your chest?"

I exhaled slowly. "Is Martin going to be okay? Heathcliff keeps telling me to wait, but the longer this goes on, the more time the real culprit has to get away. I can't just sit on my hands and do nothing."

"Have you been straight with us?"

"Martin didn't put Don in the hospital. I don't know how many times I can say that. It's the truth. I gave you everything Martin gave me. Look at the restaurant's security footage and speak to the staff. Someone must remember the guy at the bar. That's who attacked Don."

"How can you be certain when your father isn't even clear on what happened?"

"He's clear. He's just spiteful. He wants to hurt me."

"Why?"

I thought about it, but I didn't have an answer. "It's a day that ends in y."

"We got the restaurant's security footage. It'll take some time to parse through all of it. But we should know something by tomorrow. However, witnesses heard Don and Martin arguing at the restaurant, which led to Martin storming out. I'm inclined to believe someone looking for a fight wouldn't walk away when things were getting heated. However, the detective discovered Martin and Don had a prior altercation."

"It wasn't an altercation. Martin didn't get within five feet of Don."

"But he was overheard saying he would kill him." Moretti held up his hand to keep me from interrupting.

"I've gotten to know James Martin very well. There are two things I know for sure. One, he'd do anything to protect you. And two, he can make life very difficult for the department if we were to charge him for a crime he did not commit, again. However, his money and influence will not prevent us from doing our jobs."

"He didn't—"

"I know that's what you believe, and you're probably right. But we have to be absolutely sure. You aren't exactly impartial or unbiased."

"That's why I have to find the guy and prove it."

"It'd be best if you stay away from this. You don't want to face obstruction or tampering charges. I've already made sure the detective knows identifying the other man in the business suit takes top priority."

"Who's in charge of the investigation?"

"It doesn't matter. It isn't this unit or anyone you know." Moretti didn't offer any hints.

"Don has to recant his statement."

"Don't threaten him, Parker. It'll only make matters worse."

Heathcliff knocked on the door and poked his head in before I could respond. "Wayne Savage is waiting for us."

Moretti waved me away. "Get back to work, Parker. Everything will work itself out. Have faith."

The lieutenant liked to watch people sweat, but his heart was usually in the right place. And since he was one of Mark Jablonsky's best friends, I had to assume Moretti would do everything he could to delay Martin's arrest, should it come down to that. But unless Don changed his tune or the police had proof someone else was responsible, the department would have to follow through if Don pressed charges. Right now, the circumstances didn't look good.

"Is everything okay?" Heathcliff asked as we made our way down the hall. "Titus didn't get you kicked off the case, did he?"

"Not yet, but Moretti warned me to tread lightly."

Heathcliff pulled open the door. "I'll take point on this one."

Wayne Savage didn't have much to say on the subject of the armed robberies, his brother's involvement, or any connection he had to Ed Mitchell. Heathcliff barely convinced him to admit Jerome Sassen was his best friend, and even that admission wouldn't hold up in court.

"If the ballistics from your gun matches the bullet we pulled out of the dead driver, you're going to be facing murder charges. Are you sure you don't have anything to say?" Heathcliff asked.

Wayne scowled at me. "If I were a killer, I would have shot that bitch inside the coffee shop."

"It looked like you considered it," Heathcliff said. "Maybe you've done it before?"

"I'm done talking. Send me back to my cell."

Heathcliff didn't say another word. Instead, he urged me out of the interrogation room and back to his desk. "If there was a shot-caller, now would be the time for Wayne to admit it."

"Maybe he thinks you're bluffing about the bullet."

Heathcliff shook his head. "He didn't even ask where we found the driver's body or how. He must have known where the truck was."

"Like I said, Wayne's the one in charge. He bought the SIMs, made sure everyone had a burner, and planned this whole thing with his brother's help." I picked up the printout that had been left on Heathcliff's desk.

While we'd been conducting the interview, Moretti has spoken to Ed and gotten him to ID Jerome Sassen and sit with a sketch artist. But the image the sketch artist produced of the shot-caller looked generic. He could have been anyone. His hair wasn't too dark or too light. It wasn't too long or too short. He wasn't too heavy or too thin. His jaw and nose weren't particularly sharp. According to Ed, everything about this bastard was average. And I didn't believe a single word of it.

"Since Ed and Kelsey IDed Jerome and Wayne admitted that's his best friend, are you picking him up tonight?" I asked, itching to get out of here.

"Tomorrow. No judge wants to deal with signing a warrant at this time of night. And if Jerome's anything like the rest of them, I doubt he'll voluntarily speak to us. A patrol car will keep eyes on him in case he tries to run, but he has no reason to think we're on to him."

"He might, if he realizes Kelsey, Wayne, and Ed are all in custody."

"Let's hope he doesn't notice." Heathcliff checked his watch. "Shift ended three hours ago. There's nothing left for us to do tonight. Thompson and O'Connell found Ed's burner phone in his locker at his regular day job. The call logs match the same numbers in Wayne's phone. Since the search warrant didn't uncover a burner phone for Kelsey Savage, I'll ask his wife about it in the morning. Hopefully, she'll be more forthcoming. In the meantime, I'll have Wayne moved to the same holding cell where Kelsey is waiting. We'll monitor their conversation and see if we learn anything."

"Do you need me to stick around?"

"No need," Heathcliff said. "I'll hang around in case something incriminating leaks out. But I don't see the case breaking tonight. You should go home, see Martin, take it easy."

I leafed through the files again. "Maybe you should toss Ed into their cell and see what happens."

"I was thinking exactly that."

"Then why did you ask me to consult?"

Heathcliff gave me that all-too familiar look. "You're procrastinating. What's on your mind?"

I jerked my chin at Moretti's empty office. "Do you think Martin will be arrested?"

"Not tonight."

"What about tomorrow? You told me to wait until tomorrow. Now you're telling me to go home and see Martin."

"I don't know what's going to happen. But someone will be speaking to Martin soon. You may want to prepare for the possibility it won't go well."

"That's not an option." I'd make Don change his tune. "I'll speak to Don again. Maybe I can convince him to tell me more about the big guy who beat him to a bloody pulp."

"Do you want company or a chaperone?"

"No."

He gave me a long look. "Don't do anything stupid, Parker. Don will be discharged in the morning. If someone is trying to kill him, he'll need somewhere safe to stay, and since he has yet to admit any of these things to the police, there's not much we can do to help. Maybe you could use that to your advantage."

"Thanks, Derek."

"Take it easy," he said. "I mean it."

THIRTY

"You were supposed to tell the cops Martin didn't assault you," I said.

"I said I didn't know who did." Don Parker watched me with wary eyes as I paced in front of his hospital bed. He should have been relieved I hadn't barricaded the door this time. "I'm not going to recant my story until I know I'm safe."

"That's hard to do when you give me half a story. How am I supposed to fix this when you failed to provide any details about the man who assaulted you? A name would have been nice."

"He works for Chad. I think Chad referred to him as Locke."

"Is that a first or last name?" I asked.

Don's brow scrunched together as he thought, which made him wince. "I don't know. Give me the money. I pay off my debt, and that's it. It's simple. You don't need to know his name or anything about him. Why are you making this so damn complicated, Alexis? You always overthink things. That's why you'd mess up the choreography or miss the jumps when you were dancing. You could never do what you were supposed to without questioning everything."

"If you're not going to tell me about the guy who hurt you, tell me more about Chad Averly's business."

"I already told you all about him."

"Who does he work for?"

"He has his own business. He does custom printing."

"Counterfeiting?"

Don looked like I'd suggested something insane. "No. He prints signs, cards, logos, all that stuff."

"It's a front."

Don nodded. "Chad's laundering money. He has investors who order signs under bogus names at a ridiculously high markup. Chad prints the signs, collects payment, and hands seventy percent back to his investors as profits. Then he has me fudge the numbers and move some things around so it looks nice and neat. That's why I knew Chad would be interested in my stock market venture. He was always looking to turn his portion of the returns into a lot more. I really thought I could grow his money for him, and he was more than happy to invest. It should have been a guaranteed investment. But some hedge fund guys messed everything up. So when Chad showed up at the office with the big, scary guy—"

"You mean Locke?" I asked.

Don nodded. "Chad demanded to see his returns. I tried to explain, but he wouldn't listen. I thought I could take care of it, turn it around, but it just didn't work."

"Do you think you could have made a worse decision?"

"Don't talk to me like that."

"How should I talk to you?" I turned away, letting out a huff. "What about your partner? Is he also on the hook?"

"Chad only dealt with me. He didn't know anyone else was involved, or he didn't care. When he gave me the money, he said he expected me to weave it into gold. Me, not anyone else."

"And that didn't cause the warning bells to sound? You are so stupid."

"Enough, little swan," he snapped. "You will show me respect."

"I would if you deserved it, which you don't. You only came here to ruin my life."

Don's jaw clenched, and he stared at the waffle pattern on the blanket.

"Your divorce story's bullshit. Lydia said you gave her everything. You served her with papers and made sure she got every dime you hadn't spent or gambled away in the stock market. She thought it was because you were planning to file for bankruptcy and wanted to protect as many assets as possible. Are you getting back together after this blows over?"

"You spoke to your mother?"

"Answer my question."

"I don't know. We never discussed it."

"Did you leave her in some misguided attempt to keep her safe? Because you never struck me as particularly noble."

"Watch yourself."

I slammed my hand down on the bedside tray. It made a loud, echoing crack that made him jump. It also hurt like hell, but I didn't flinch. "Someone beat you and ransacked Ace Investigators. It wasn't Martin. I've seen the footage. Big guy, dark clothes, smart enough to keep his face covered. I'm guessing that was Locke. Am I right?"

Don nodded. "Give me the fucking money, and I'll tell the cops Martin didn't do this. But to be clear, I'm not telling them Locke did it either. That would be suicide."

"You have to tell them the truth."

"I did." He grinned evilly. "Martin hit me. People saw it. That wasn't a lie. The cops should know he's a public menace."

"You're the menace."

"Give me the money, and I will go away."

That's what I'd been trying to do since the beginning, but it wasn't working. It just made everything worse. "Do I look like a bank?"

"I gave you everything."

"And you took it all away." I swallowed. "Do you honestly think getting divorced will protect Lydia from these people? It's only a matter of time before they use her as leverage against you."

"That's not going to happen."

"Why not?"

"You won't let it."

"You don't know that, and you definitely don't know me."

"I know everything I need to, little swan. You are so

wrapped up in this life you built, in that man you live with, that you will do everything in your power to make this right because you don't want what happened to me to happen to you or someone you care about. Locke was given instructions to do whatever it takes to make sure I get him the money. So far, I've held him off by telling him you'd get it for me, that you needed some time, but when he saw Martin refuse in the middle of the steakhouse, he made sure to remind me that Chad isn't a patient man. Time is running out. For me and for you."

"And anyone else Chad thinks you may care about. I'd guess that would include Lydia and possibly your business associate."

"They are far enough down the list that I know you'll have this taken care of before Chad can send anyone after them. Locke knows to come for you and yours first. That's the reason I'm here."

"Where can I find Locke?"

"I don't know. He finds me."

"Where were you staying before you were assaulted? I know you checked out of the hotel, so don't even waste your breath lying about that."

"My friend from work found an apartment to rent on one of those vacation rental sites. He's covering the expense."

"I need the address and your friend's name."

Don narrowed his eyes. "Are you going to harass him too?"

"Tell me. If not, I'll call Lydia and ask about the guy who's been letting you stay on his couch. She knows who he is. In fact, she mentioned you two were in business together. Maybe I should turn that information over to Chad and let him go straight to the source to recover the money you took."

"Travis Simms, but he has nothing to do with this."

"That doesn't matter to me. You want to destroy the people around me, so I'd be more than happy to return the favor."

A sick smile crept onto Don's face. "I'm impressed. Maybe you did learn something from me, little swan."

I put my notepad and pen on the tray table. "Write it all down."

He picked up the pen and scribbled an address. "I don't see how this is going to help you find the big guy who beat me up."

"What does he drive?"

"How should I know?"

"Ace saw you get out of his car. Lie to me again, and see what happens."

"I'm almost tempted to call your bluff, but that won't serve either of our purposes." He wrote down the make, model, and year. "I don't think it's a rental. It didn't have any stickers or tags."

"How did you get here? To the city?"

"The train."

"You paid cash?"

"Why wouldn't I? It was twenty dollars."

Cross had been right. Flying wouldn't have made much sense since the train ride was approximately four hours. It would take just as long to fly with the check-in, boarding, flight time, and landing. "And this guy, Locke, didn't accompany you?"

"Not that I noticed. He found me once I arrived."

"How?"

"I'm not sure. Ace suggested he could be tracking my phone."

"Is that why you turned it off?"

Don gave me a strange look. "You tried to track me?"

"I wanted to make sure you were gone. You can imagine my disappointment when I found out you never left."

Don pushed the notebook to the end of the tray table. "There's not much else I can tell you. Locke is big and mean. I have no desire to piss him off. He's only here to collect on Chad's behalf. Once I give him the money, he'll go away. That's all I want."

"But you don't know how to find him to give him the money."

"I'm supposed to call Chad once I have it. He'll set up a meet."

That would serve as a last resort because I was pretty

sure Chad would want payment in cash and blood, which meant not everyone would walk away breathing. And I needed the police to realize Locke was to blame for the assault if I had any hope of clearing Martin's name. I had to find a way to track down this guy, or, at the very least, identify him. The name Locke didn't tell me much. Was that a first or last name? An alias? I didn't know, but his car seemed like a good place to start.

THIRTY-ONE

When the elevator doors opened, I found Mark Jablonsky waiting in the hospital lobby. He looked fit to be tied. I looked around, but I didn't see a tactical team or uniformed police officers waiting in the wings.

"How'd you find me?" I asked.

"Heathcliff called. He was afraid you were about to do something stupid. He hoped I could talk some sense into you."

"I convinced Don to tell me more about the man who put him in the hospital." I filled Mark in on everything. "But he won't talk to the police or go on record. He's too afraid, and he wants this hanging over Martin's head, over my head, in order to ensure we give him the money."

"I'll fucking kill him."

"Great, so you and Martin can share a prison cell."

"Marty's too pretty for his own good. He'll need me there to watch his back."

"Oh god." The severity of the situation hit me like a ton of bricks. "Do you think that could really happen?"

Mark dragged me outside, instructing me to put my hands on my head while I circled. "Breathe, Alex. You usually react better to a joke." He stayed close in case I went down or blacked out.

"You weren't joking. Neither was Martin. He wanted to kill Don, and the cops have witnesses who will testify that they heard Martin say it."

Mark hugged me. "I won't let anything happen to either of you, no matter what."

"I hate him. Don, I mean."

"I know." Mark led me to his SUV, which was parked in a space reserved for emergency vehicles. Opening the passenger side door, he jerked his chin at the seat. I climbed in, and he gently shut the door before going around and getting in on his side. He stared out the windshield, noting the security cameras. "Did that asshole have anything new to add to his story?"

"I already told you everything he said."

Mark chewed on a hangnail while he thought about it. "When we first looked into it, we didn't have enough to go on. Nothing popped up for Chad Averly, but if he's cleaning dirty money, we'll have to figure out who has shares in his company. Hartley should be able to pull that up. Don said they were investors. There must be a paper trail."

"How is that going to help Martin?" I asked.

Mark turned to face me. "We get Chad off Don's back, that will get Don off your back."

"He won't care. He's a greedy bastard. He believes I owe him. He'll still want me to give him the money, even if it's just so he can pack it up and start over somewhere else."

"Do you think he would?"

"I have no idea."

Mark fiddled with his phone. "Ace Darrow said he saw Don getting out of Locke's car when he came to pick up the intel. Then Locke went back to get more files from Ace. Do we know what he wanted?"

"More intel on me."

"Locke doesn't believe Don, which means Chad doesn't believe Don. They must think he's buying time, that he doesn't have the money."

"Except Ace dug up plenty on Martin's financial situation."

"Shit." Mark put his phone down and went back to staring out the windshield. "Kate Hartley's keeping a close eye on Chad Averly's personal and business accounts. He wired several thousand dollars out of his personal account to a security solution company three weeks ago. Hartley dug into the company, but they only exist on paper. Funny thing though, the business was called Locke Solutions."

"Send me the information."

"You are not going after this guy, Alex. I forbid it."

I snorted. "You forbid it?"

"Yes." Mark nodded resolutely. "I forbid it. You have a terrible track record when it comes to guys like this."

"Averly must not be that well-connected if he had to hire someone to take care of the Don situation. I'll be fine."

"You could be reading this wrong. Averly may not have told his investors he fucked up because he's afraid they'll do to him what he plans to do to Don. You do not need to get into the middle of that."

I stared out the windshield. "Don's not giving me a choice. Martin's still on the hook for the assault. That's never going to change."

"The police have the surveillance footage from outside the restaurant. The camera didn't catch the actual assault, but it showed a second man leaving the restaurant a minute after Martin did. He was dressed in a dark suit, had dark hair, was tall, and built. It'd be easy for the casual observer or eyewitness to confuse the two. Plus, Marty has his own witness who swears Don was awake and alert when Marty left the scene."

"What about the rest? The threats? My history with Don? Martin's bruised knuckles? Don's statement?"

"Marty needs an alibi."

Martin needed a lot of things. I counted the windows up and over until I found what I thought was Don's room. "Don already said if he doesn't hand over the money, Locke will find a way to get it out of me. Even if we set a trap and arrest him, Averly will just send someone else. This won't end until he gets his money back."

Mark adjusted his holster and smoothed the wrinkles from the front of his jacket, which always looked crumpled. "You know if you turn Locke over to the police, it won't get the target off Don's back. In fact, it could make it worse."

"Getting Martin out of this mess is my first priority. It's my fault he's in this situation."

"No, it's Marty's for taking a swing at Don. He could

have walked away. He knew better."

"Yeah, but Don's in our lives because of me. Martin took a swing at him because something Don said about me."

"That's not on you."

"So what do you think I should do? Heathcliff and Moretti want me to give the police time to investigate and reach their own conclusions, but the evidence doesn't look good. The circumstances are less than stellar."

Mark pressed his lips together. "Does Cross have any suggestions? He and Ace Darrow have history. If he could convince Ace to go to the cops and press charges, maybe it'd be enough to pull the focus away from Martin and discredit Don. If the cops aren't interested in what Don has to say, he'll lose his ace in the hole and be more likely to help us come up with a better solution."

"Cross isn't Ace's favorite person. I doubt we could convince him to do anything without concocting our own blackmail scheme." Cross could pull it off, but Don's words echoed in my ears. I didn't want to be anything like the bastard. Fighting fire with fire wasn't the answer.

Mark checked his phone. "Okay. The OIO will dig up everything we can on Chad Averly and try to build a case against him for the money laundering. In the meantime, I'll assign a car to sit on Marty. I don't want Averly's henchman to go looking for him. Did you get a good look at this guy?"

"I only saw him on Ace's security footage. Locke has no reason to think I'd be able to identify him."

"Let's keep it that way, but if you want, I can have someone keep an eye on you."

"Not necessary. But if I change my mind, I'll let Cross's people know. He already assigned a team to watch Martin, so you may want to tell whoever you have keeping an eye on him that they aren't the only ones."

"The more the merrier," Mark said. We stared at the looming hospital. The lights inside the rooms lit up the building, making it look friendlier than it was. "I hate to say it, but you might have to consider paying to make the problem go away. You give Don the money, he tells the cops Martin didn't attack him, and he pays back Averly.

After that, whatever happens isn't on you. In fact, you'd have nothing to do with any of it."

"I don't have that kind of money."

"Marty would give it to you, no strings attached."

I closed my eyes, wanting all of this to go away. "Don could twist it, make it look like Martin was trying to pay him off to drop the charges."

"Don came here to shake you down for money. If you give it to him, why would he twist the screws?"

"That's Don."

"Is he really that terrible?"

I couldn't believe Mark asked me that. "He put me in Averly's crosshairs, promising him that I had the money. That I'd pay it back for Don. He did that to save his own ass and insulate Lydia and whatever friends or colleagues he has who may have been threatened. He served me up on a silver platter. Now that he knows what Martin's worth, what's to stop him from deciding he shouldn't get a little something extra to help him rebuild his life?" I thought about everything Don had said. "No wonder he wanted to stay with me. He must have hoped Averly's goon would knock me around instead of him."

Mark's expression hardened. "Go home to Marty. I'll do my best to get the PD to back off by telling them the actual suspect is part of a federal investigation, which he is now that Chad Averly is under our microscope. Hopefully, that'll slow them down while we figure out our next move."

"We?"

"You're not doing this alone."

"Thanks."

When I didn't get out of the SUV, Mark nudged me. "Now what's wrong?"

"Martin lied to me."

"I heard."

"You heard?"

"He called this afternoon and said you had a knockdown, drag-out at his office."

"I ranted. He sat there. It felt like old times, but not in a good way."

"Whatever Marty did, he did it out of love. And you've

done enough stupid things for the same reason."

"I know, which is why I thought he'd know better." I gave Mark a suspicious look. "As soon as I get out of the car, you're going inside to talk to Don, aren't you?"

"Go home," he repeated.

"He's a snake. Do not give him anything he can use against you. I don't want him to try to take you away from me too."

"That's not possible. Now go home. That's an order."

"You can't order me around. I don't work for you anymore."

"Parker."

Sighing, I opened the car door. "I better not find you in a holding cell when I show up at the precinct tomorrow morning."

THIRTY-TWO

Going home wasn't an option. Instead, I went to the vacation rental where Don was staying. A security camera covered the walkway and a doorbell camera covered the front door of the duplex. If Locke had been keeping tabs on Don, he must have been here. For all I knew, he could be staying here with Don. I had to find out. I had to find him.

More than likely, the owners had installed these cameras to keep the rental secure when no one had booked a stay. It may have also been to ensure the guests didn't rob the owners blind. However, the system was rudimentary enough that most people with a basic understanding of wireless networks and password-breaking could gain access to the live feed and stored footage.

Since I planned to break in anyway, I came prepared to thwart the cameras. The large cardboard box I'd taken from my trunk and carried in front of my face concealed my identity as I approached the house. Once I was out of sight of the security camera, I moved onto the porch and held the box in front of the doorbell camera, blacking out the video feed. I rang the bell, but no one answered.

Balancing the box using my knee and one arm, I grabbed the roll of black duct tape from the top of the box, ripped off a piece with my teeth, and felt around the side, covering the doorbell camera with the tape. Hoping that I didn't miss, I slowly lowered the box to the ground, finding the tape hanging precariously over the lens. I adjusted it and checked to make sure no one was around. Luckily, whoever lived in the adjacent unit didn't appear to be home or didn't care what went on next door.

After taking my lockpicks out of the box, I went to work on the front door. This would have been easier if I'd gotten the key from Don's belongings, but I didn't want him to know about this. I didn't trust him as far as I could throw him.

Once the door was unlocked, I put my things back inside the box, stepped into the house, and reached around the side to remove the tape from the doorbell camera. In case someone was monitoring the live feed, I didn't want them to get suspicious. With any luck, they'd write off the brief interruption as Don's guest struggling to unlock the door while carrying in her belongings.

The house was dark, and I resisted the urge to turn on the light. Instead, I used the flashlight on my keychain to look around. I didn't hear any beeps or see a panel for a security system. Given that this was a vacation rental, the owners wouldn't want the burden of constantly resetting the code or dealing with the security company and police every time a guest forgot what the disarm code was. That bit of laziness would make my life that much easier.

As soon as I knew the coast was clear, I moved through the house. It was minimally furnished. Not a lot of clutter or knickknacks to get in the way. It made sense. The less things to steal, the less likely someone was to take something. That meant whatever mess I found had to be Don's, or so I assumed.

On the couch was his laptop. Resisting the urge to open it immediately, I placed it gently in the cardboard box. Nothing else in the living room screamed out Don, so I moved into the bedroom. There I found an empty rolling suitcase. Nothing was hidden in any of the compartments or sewn into the lining.

Leaving the suitcase where I found it, I searched the dresser. The only thing inside were several dust bunnies. Closing the drawers, I checked underneath and behind the furniture. Out of curiosity, I turned on the television and scanned for any inputs. Nothing was attached.

I was giving Don too much credit by thinking he'd hide

something somewhere no one would look. But he had been hiding Chad Averly's assets. It didn't appear that translated into more tangible terms. However, it didn't stop me from checking under the mattress and beneath the bed.

In the nightstand, I found Don's phone. It remained off. He had taken the battery out and left it beside the charger. Grabbing all three items, I tossed them into my cardboard box and opened the closet.

The top shelf contained additional pillows. A storage container at the bottom held blankets. A built-in shelf contained half a dozen worn board games. The few items hanging in the closet looked like what I'd seen Don wearing during our previous encounters.

After tossing his clothes into the box, I searched the rest of the closet, making sure he hadn't hidden something with one of the games or buried it amidst the sea of pillows and blankets. I had just shoved everything back where I found it when I heard a car door out front.

It's probably the neighbor, I surmised, but something dragged me to the window. Flipping off my flashlight, I made sure there were no other lights on before peeling the blinds away from the glass. A black sedan had parked a couple of doors down. There was no sign of the driver. From here, I couldn't see the plate. Was it the neighbor, or had my trick with the camera tipped off whoever was watching the feed? Maybe Locke had returned or had the same idea I did.

Deciding it'd be best to hurry things along, I moved quickly through the bathroom, tossing the products I remembered Don using from my childhood into the box as I went. The medicine cabinet was empty. The cabinet underneath the sink contained a stockpile of toilet paper, hand soap, and feminine products. A check of each of the boxes revealed nothing.

Perhaps Don hadn't hidden anything. The linen closet contained plenty of towels and laundry soap. After tossing his shower items into the box and checking behind the toilet and in the toilet tank, I left the bathroom and made a quick stop in the kitchen.

A shadow moved outside the window, making the

already dark room appear darker. I didn't know who was out there. If it was a neighbor, they may have seen me enter and gotten suspicious. For all I knew, the police were on their way. I didn't want to get arrested for breaking and entering. Heathcliff would not be happy about that.

The kitchen cabinets contained dishes and nothing else. The pantry had a few cobwebs and some outdated snack bars. The refrigerator had cans of diet cola in Don's favorite brand, a half-eaten sub sandwich that had been hastily rewrapped, and an open bottle of wine. It was a mid-priced red, the kind of pretentious thing Don would waste money on and sip to appear more cultured. He always drank like that. I doubted he even liked the stuff. It was all for show, like having a daughter enrolled in ballet and training to be a prima ballerina.

Shutting the fridge, I checked the freezer. Footsteps sounded outside the back door. Resisting the urge to look, I grabbed my cardboard box and headed for the front door. If I was fast enough, I could sneak up on the guy from behind. But I had to move.

Opening the front door, I hesitated long enough to make sure no one was waiting for me out front before hefting the box high and darting down the walkway and across the street to my parked car. The cameras would have caught my fleeing back, but I didn't think the angle was good enough for me to be identified on the feed. And I couldn't worry about that now.

Ditching the box on the sidewalk beside my rear tire, I pulled my nine millimeter free from the holster, tucked my hair into my jacket, and moved in a crouch down the sidewalk, remaining hidden behind the row of parked cars. Once I had a clear view into the postage-stamp sized backyard behind the duplex, I darted across the street, taking cover behind the rear of a red hatchback. No one was in the backyard.

I scanned the side of the duplex. But I didn't see anyone. Moving around the hatchback, I stayed hidden in the space between the two parallel parked cars. No one was in front of the duplex either. But I had seen his shadow. Someone else was out here.

Unsure where he'd gone and wanting to make sure I wasn't going crazy, I crept toward the black sedan. The hood was still warm. The car hadn't been here when I arrived.

I checked the front license plate. *Massachusetts.* It was an out-of-state vehicle, which fit perfectly with what I knew about Locke. The car matched the description Ace had given us too. But I had to be certain.

Afraid the driver would return at any moment, I moved along the driver's side of the car. The doors were locked, the windows rolled up to the top. I could break in, but it'd take too much time. Instead, I continued to the rear of the vehicle. Pulling out my phone, I dialed Cross's number.

"I think I found him," I said when Cross answered.

"Who?"

"Locke, the big guy who ransacked Ace Investigators. Did you get the plate number from his vehicle?"

"Only a partial," Cross said. "They're Mass plates. Oh, six, nine."

I looked down at the number. "Yep."

"Where are you?" Cross asked.

"Outside the duplex Don rented."

"Text me the address." Cross didn't wait for me to do it before asking, "Where is he? Do you have a visual on him?"

"Negative. I don't know where he is."

"You don't know?"

"He's close. He was snooping around outside the house while I was inside. I didn't see anything that indicated he was staying with Don, which makes me think he showed up because he's looking for Don or the money."

I peered across the street in the direction of my parked car, but no one was around. I didn't want to leave the box with Don's belongings exposed for anyone to steal, particularly his laptop. There had to be something damning on that.

"Do the police have details on the car?" I asked.

"I gave them the basics. They wouldn't have been able to come up with it otherwise."

"Great. Do me a favor. Call in a tip that the car was spotted. I want the police to see this."

"You want to have this guy arrested?"

"Maybe." With any luck, they'd arrest Locke for assaulting Ace and some digging would reveal he also assaulted Don. That would get Martin off the hook and buy me some time to figure out how to deal with the Don situation. It had been Mark's plan, with a slight adjustment.

"I hope you know what you're doing, Alex."

"Me too." I gave Cross the rest of the plate and hung up.

Once my phone was tucked away, I pulled the switchblade I'd recently started carrying out of my pocket and stabbed it into the rear tire. The blade made it a few inches in before getting stuck. I had to use both hands to get the knife out of the thick rubber tread. A whoosh of air followed the cold steel. It wouldn't take long for the tire to go flat. That should keep the bastard from escaping.

Darting across the street, I hurried to my car. Where was he? I didn't see anyone outside. The houses on the block had lights on. It wasn't that late. No one had gone to bed yet. Maybe he didn't want to cause a commotion and attract unwanted attention, so he stayed hidden.

Unlocking my trunk, I placed the filled cardboard box inside, keeping my head on a swivel, not wanting a repeat of what happened in the parking garage the previous week. Thankfully, no one tried to bash my skull in this time.

Movement in my periphery caught my attention. The streetlamps were few and far between. The duplex didn't have its porch lights on. That had been a perk when I was breaking in. Now, it was a hindrance.

A shadow lumbered along the sidewalk on the opposite side of the street, hunkered over, like a bear. Pausing directly across from me, the dark figure stopped moving. He had finally found me.

He remained where he was. I remained where I was. It was too dark for me to make out anything but a shadowy mass. I didn't think he could see me any better than I could see him. The nearest street lamp was half a block away in either direction. The cars shielded me from the illumination, the same as him.

But I wasn't sure I could get inside my car and lock the

door before he was on top of me. The police were on their way, and with that flat tire, he wouldn't get far. However, he could run.

I could shoot him. That was always an option, but that'd be hard to explain when the authorities arrived if it turned out I was wrong about who this guy was or why he was staring at me from across the dark street.

"What do you want?" I asked.

"You know." His voice was deep, like a rumble of thunder.

"Did you put Don in the hospital?"

He didn't answer.

"What about Ace? What were you hoping to find?"

His gloved hand squeaked against the car as he moved off the sidewalk and between the two parked cars. I kept one hand on my keys, the other on my gun.

"Does Don have the money? Is that why you came here? To give it to him?" he asked.

"Why would I do that?"

"I'm going to need the money. He's past due. No more time. No more extensions."

"Who are you?" I asked.

"Nobody."

"Who sent you?"

"You know."

"That's the thing. I don't."

His laugh sounded like a snarl. "Don said you wouldn't give him the money. So I'm gonna have to change your mind."

"Good luck with that."

I didn't see his gun, but I heard the muffled shots. He had a suppressor. My rear window blew out, and I returned fire, my gun making an echoing boom on the quiet street. But I was shooting at shadows. With only a general idea of where he was and no cry of pain, I had to assume I missed.

The gunfire didn't make him back off. Instead, he barreled across the street. A mass of black against a black background. I ran for the driver's side door, yanking it open and diving inside as another shot went through my back window at an angle, leaving a bullet hole and spiderwebbing my windshield on the passenger's side.

I tried to tug my door closed, but he grabbed the frame. Even with him being this close, I still couldn't get a good look at him. He'd concealed his features with a mask and hood. He raised his gun, forgetting that killing me wouldn't get him his money.

Pulling harder, I hoped to close his hand in my car door, but he was too strong and had a good grip with the one hand. Instead, I let go, causing him to lose balance. He stumbled backward. I didn't waste time on the door. Instead, I started the car from my nearly horizontal position, slammed down on one of the pedals, knocked the gearshift into reverse and was relieved when the car lurched backward. The back tire jumped the curb, making the car bounce.

I took that opportunity to put it into drive. Yanking the wheel in the opposite direction, I stomped down again. My car leapt off the sidewalk and charged forward. I grabbed the wheel and pulled myself into a seated position as the car careened toward the parked cars on the other side of the street.

The bastard in black rolled out of the way before he got nailed by my swinging driver's side door. Jerking the wheel the other way, I straightened out and sped down the street. He fired again. Three shots ripped through my window, breaking the glass and forcing me to cower in my seat.

Angry, I slammed my brakes, knocked the car into reverse and gunned it. He dove out of the way before I could strike him with the two ton battering ram. The daylamps caught sight of him racing toward his vehicle. By the time I aimed, he was inside his car, his brights blinding me as he hurried out of his space.

The flat rear tire shot sparks into the air, keeping him from moving as seamlessly or quickly as he hoped. But that didn't stop him from driving toward me as fast as the three wheels were capable. He held the gun out his window, firing at me and putting more holes in my windshield.

A car turned onto the street behind him. The headlights were joined by a spotlight. Then the whoop whoop of a siren and blue and red flashing lights.

Locke gunned his engine, his nose colliding with mine. I tried to block him in, but we were already at the end of the street. He sharply turned the wheel, knocking down the stop sign before taking off down the cross street. The police car didn't wait for me to move before chasing after him.

Locke only made it another block before he ditched the car and took off on foot. I drove straight down the street, hoping to cut him off at the cross. But I didn't see him. The bastard got away.

THIRTY-THREE

The police took my statement, but I wasn't sure how much to say or how much they'd believe. So I stuck to the facts. I was at the duplex to pick up some things for Don. A man showed up. He said Don owed money and wanted to collect. I wouldn't give it to him, so he tried to kill me.

"Did you arrest him?" I asked.

"He got away. We have a BOLO out, but your description was vague."

"It was the same man who attacked Ace Darrow."

"How do you know that?" the cop asked.

"My father hired Ace Darrow. Ace was assaulted, his files taken. The man who attacked me was looking for my father. He must have wanted to find out where he was staying. He could have gotten that from Ace's records. I know it all connects."

The cop brought up the report. "What's your father's name?"

"Landon Parker."

He typed that in. "Both Ace and your father were assaulted. Now someone came after you." He squinted as he read the details on the screen. "Your father thought he knew his attacker. We have a name. James Martin."

"He was mistaken."

"Do you know James Martin?"

"He's my boyfriend."

"Are you sure your boyfriend's not trying to kill you?

Domestic situations can get messy."

"Are you insane? Didn't you see the plate on the car? Why don't you run it and get the asshole's name? He left his car. I know you have that. You may even have his prints and hair."

"The car was reported stolen two weeks ago. The plates are useless."

"Who reported it stolen?" I asked.

"I'm not at liberty to say."

"Did you check the vehicle for prints?"

"We will. But I don't need you to tell me how to do my job, Ms. Parker." The cop rocked in his chair. "Is there anything else you can tell me about this situation?"

"No."

"In that case, you're free to go. A detective will follow up sometime in the next few days."

"Tell him to save himself the trouble. I'm consulting for major crimes. Lt. Moretti will know how to get a hold of me."

"Great," the cop said sarcastically. "You have yourself a safe night."

When I stepped out of the precinct, Cross was waiting for me. "What the fuck did you do to my car?"

"It's the company car."

"That makes it my car."

"I didn't do it. The asshole who came after Ace, who assaulted Don, he's the one you should blame."

Cross rubbed his eyes. "The police are keeping the car, claiming they need it for evidence. However, I convinced them to let me remove your personal property and mine from the vehicle."

"Your property?"

"My car, remember?" He led me to his actual car. In the back seat was the cardboard box from the trunk. "I hope whatever's in there was worth it."

"Me too." My hands had stopped shaking, but the adrenaline crash was hitting hard. "I found Don's computer. Maybe there's something on it we can use."

"I'm not sure what you're hoping to find."

"Details, leverage, anything that will make this better."

"Don't hold your breath."

I stared out the window. "I won't."

By the time we reached the office, I had fallen asleep. Cross pressed the release on my seatbelt, the click waking me up. "Do you want something to level out?"

"I didn't realize you were pushing tonight."

He chuckled. "I meant espresso, but if you'd prefer, I could give my dealer a call."

"I'm going to pretend I didn't hear you say that."

"It pays to know people in the business, particularly with our clientele." He held the door for me while I lugged the cardboard box out of the back seat and carried it toward the building.

"Espresso sounds good. Thanks."

We took the box up to the lab where Cross's techs cracked the password to Don's laptop and scanned his hard drive. Since I wasn't sure what we were looking for, I figured we might as well check everything. But an extensive review like that would take hours.

While they worked, Cross looked into pulling whatever footage he could find from the vacation rental and the surrounding homes. Most people had doorbell or security cameras. Even though they were closed networks, he was confident he could gain access to them with the right tools or by offering enough incentives. However, the police were out in droves, searching for Locke, who by now was long gone. So we had to wait.

The techs checked the rest of Don's belongings for trackers, but nothing was bugged. Taking the box back to my office, I pulled each item out and checked every nook and cranny. Everything was as it appeared. Nothing had been hidden or concealed. Again, I was reminded Don Parker was not Jason Bourne, which was something I kept forgetting as I struggled to find something useful among his polo shirts and deodorant stick.

Finally, I called Mark and told him what happened. He'd make sure the police looped him in on their findings concerning the stolen vehicle. I didn't know what I'd hoped to accomplish by looking for Locke, but after finding him, the only thing I achieved was pissing him off.

"Didn't I tell you to go home?" Mark asked when I finished my story.

"That's where I'm headed now. Though I'm not entirely sure how I'm going to get there." I thought about calling Marcal, but if Locke had me in his sights, I didn't want to risk any more of Martin's staff.

"I'd offer to pick you up, but I'm in the middle of something."

"Do I want to know?"

"You have no room to talk. You're already on thin ice," Mark warned.

"It's fine." I looked up to find Cross standing in my doorway. "Lucien can do it."

"Make sure he's careful."

"Yep."

"I can do what?" Cross asked when I put the phone down.

"Lend me a car to go home."

Cross snorted. "That's out of the question. Try again."

"What do you want?"

"The car was stolen from a parking garage in Roxbury, near Franklin Park. A place like that should have plenty of cameras. I'll see what we can get remotely. If that doesn't work, I'll make a few calls. Locke must have been caught on some camera at some point. We should be able to find footage of him without the mask or hood, so we can identify him, but it may take some time. Amir is tracking where the vehicle came from on local DOT footage."

"I really appreciate this."

Cross jerked his chin toward the end of the hall. "C'mon, I'll take you home. There's nothing left to do while the programs run."

Cross took a long, circuitous route that took three times longer than necessary to make sure no one was following us. All the while, I wondered if my phone would ring with news that Don Parker was dead or Mark Jablonsky had been arrested. Thankfully, I made it home without incident, choosing to believe that no news was good news.

Martin wasn't home yet. I sent a text to Marcal, who assured me everything was fine. With a Cross Security team and an FBI detail keeping watch on my beloved, I didn't think some muscle for hire stood much of a chance, not with the police searching for him too. But that didn't stop me from worrying.

My mind went back over the entire Don situation. Entering my home office, I turned on the computer and logged into every government database I could access while I searched for details on Chad Averly and anything I may have missed on Landon Parker and the mysterious Locke. When I could no longer see straight and my eyes hurt from staring at the screen, I gave up on the research and crossed into the second floor guest room.

Martin had recreated my old apartment inside the spacious suite. I ran my hand along the back of my couch. The first time Martin and I made love had been in this room, but the furniture had been his.

Shaking that thought away, I spotted a few of the dents in the plaster, a remnant of our break-up and Martin's violent side. When I saw the damage, I knew he loved me. It was the first time I really understood he felt the same way I did. It was the same reason he punched Don and lied to me about it.

Swallowing, I climbed onto my old bed and curled up on my side. How had things gotten so messed up? We were supposed to be better than this. Why hadn't we learned from our mistakes?

The security system beeped, letting me know it had been disengaged. A minute later, it beeped again as it reengaged. Footsteps sounded in the hallway. Then the stairs creaked. A few minutes later, they creaked again.

"Alexis?" Martin entered my room.

I turned, finding him in a jet black suit, black tie hanging, top buttons of his crisp white shirt open, his leather shoes and belt adding a layer of shine, and his dark hair unkempt with the hints of a five o'clock shadow dotting his jaw. Under his arm was a giant teddy bear holding an oversized red heart which may have been filled with fancy chocolates. Tied into the red ribbon on the candy box was a long, black jewelry box.

"Sweetheart, I'm so sorry."

"Is that for me?" I nodded to the bear which was nearly as big as Martin. It could have its own seat on the couch.

"Yeah, I...I didn't know what to get you. You were so upset. I wanted you to know I didn't mean to hurt you. I screwed up. But," he sighed. "that bastard deserved it." He put the bear on the couch and moved closer.

"Did you buy it because you were afraid I wouldn't have anyone to snuggle with once they lock you up and throw away the key?"

"Sweetheart—"

I shook my head. I didn't know what to say. The words wouldn't come.

"Dammit, Alex. I'm sorry. Talk to me. Yell at me. Do something. Don't do this. Don't freeze me out. Don't shut down. I can't handle that right now."

I moved to the edge of the bed and grabbed his hand in both of mine. "I'm terrified, Martin." I stared at the wall, knowing I wouldn't get it out if I was looking at him. "The police still think you could be responsible even though I gave them their prime suspect tonight. I don't know what's going to happen."

"You found the man who assaulted Don?"

"I did, but he escaped. They're looking for him. I'm not sure we want them to find him. In fact, I'm not sure about anything."

"Are you okay?"

"I'm still processing, figuring things out, trying to come up with a plan."

"I never meant to make it worse."

"I know. But that's what Don wanted. He plays games inside of games. He doesn't miss a single opportunity. When one thing goes wrong, he finds a way to use that to his advantage. He's opportunistic. Everything fits perfectly together for him. I don't know how he can see the cards ahead of time."

"He must mark the deck."

I was the one thing Don hadn't predicted. The baby girl he chose who failed to fit into the premade mold he and his wife had picked out. That's when it clicked. It wasn't because I failed. It's because he had been wrong. And he'd been wrong again when he tried to worm his way into my good graces and convince me to give him money. That's why he was being so vindictive.

Martin eased onto the bed beside me, took my face in his hands, his fingers tangling in my hair as he tilted my head back and kissed me like we hadn't seen each other in years. "I love you."

"Not in front of the bear," I said.

Martin glanced over his shoulder, chuckling. "Are we okay?"

"If we weren't, I'd be a huge hypocrite." I swallowed. "We're okay."

"Promise?"

I nodded.

"Then why do you still look so sad, sweetheart?" He combed his fingers through my hair.

"Even though we're okay, I'm afraid you're not. Don's determined to make you pay."

"He does not get to use me as a weapon against you. I'm going to tell the police what happened," Martin said. "I have a meeting scheduled for late tomorrow afternoon."

"No."

"Alex, I hit him once. How bad could it be?"

"Martin, no," I repeated. "The detective investigating may decide the confession means it's open and shut. The police will disregard everything I told them about the man who attacked me."

"Attacked you?"

"More like the company car. Cross is pissed. He has to replace the glass." I tilted my head, placing a gentle kiss against the side of Martin's neck. "You need to wait until you speak to Almeada before you do anything. He'll be able to advise you on how to proceed. Please, don't sacrifice yourself for Don. I don't want to worry about the things that could happen to you in lockup if he presses charges and you get thrown in jail."

"This was Almeada's idea. We spoke briefly on the phone, but we're meeting for lunch to go over specifics before going to the precinct to provide a statement."

"Statement or confession?" I asked.

"We'll see."

I pushed Martin onto his back and laid against his chest. He put his arms around me and we fell silent while I contemplated the possibilities, but none of the scenarios turned out particularly well.

"I think the only way out of this is to give Don the money," I said.

The way Martin's chest rose and his arms tightened around me said he wanted to protest, but he didn't. "Whatever you think is best."

I didn't want to give in. But I didn't think we had any other choice. "It's your money. It's up to you. You can say no."

"You just said it's the only way."

"I've been wrong before."

Martin chuckled. "How does he want it? Check? Wire transfer?"

"Probably cash." I hadn't asked, but given who he owed, I doubted Chad Averly would find a paper trail acceptable, and even if he didn't care, I didn't want the funds to trace back to Martin. This had to be a onetime deal. But Cross's warning played through my head. Don would bleed us dry.

"I can go to the bank in the morning," Martin said.

"Not yet. I have to talk to Mark first. He's working on a plan."

"Is that why a black SUV with federal plates has been following me for half the day?"

"That was Mark's decision, not mine. You called him. It's your own fault."

"And the Cross Security detail?"

"I thought you should be able to establish an airtight alibi from here on out."

"You didn't ask them to protect me?"

"Only from yourself."

"I deserve that. But Don deserved getting his ass handed to him. I only got in that one punch, but it felt damn good."

"Remember that when you're handing the bastard two hundred grand." I pulled away from Martin. "NDAs aren't binding when it comes to concealing a crime, at least not typically, but Almeada may know of some sort of loophole.

If we can find a way to ensure it's enforceable, I'll insist Don signs it before we give him the money."

"That's contractual. My regular attorney could handle it."

"Read him in on the situation too, in case Don decides to sue you for damages should your role in the assault come to light. The ABCs and Reeves, Almeada, and Stockton should be able to come up with some way to protect you if Don Parker pursues criminal or civil recourse after he gets what he wants."

"You don't think paying him off will be the end of it?"

"Lucien warned me it'd never end. That's how blackmail works. But our safety is at risk. Don told the man he owes that we'll pay his debts if he doesn't. One way or the other, Chad Averly plans to get paid. Our hands are tied because our safety is at risk, so we pay off Don's debt. But once this blows over, if it blows over and they don't kill all of us out of spite, there's nothing stopping Don from coming back for more, particularly when there are witnesses who heard you threaten his life and who may have seen you hit him. We won't be in the clear until the statute of limitations on assault runs out."

Martin cursed and reached for his own phone. After setting a few reminders for tomorrow, he put the phone down. "It's late. Are you ready for bed?"

"Can we sleep down here tonight?"

"Whatever you want, gorgeous." He ran his thumb across my cheek and gave me a gentle kiss. "Everything will be okay. I promise."

I got out of bed and loosened the ribbon on the teddy bear's heart-shaped box. Martin moved beside me, his hands brushing against my sides, his lips gently moving along the top of my shoulder. The velvet box contained a beautiful silver bracelet with tiny heart-shaped links.

"You shouldn't have done this. You should be saving your money, not wasting more of it on me," I said.

"Do you like it? It's a little gaudy, but there weren't many stores open this late, and I had to bribe the clerk to let me wander around the storeroom since there was nothing remotely romantic on the shelves."

"You raided their Valentine's Day selection?"

Martin chuckled. "Maybe."

"Well, I love it." I snapped the box closed and reached for the giant box of chocolates. Pulling open the lid, I moved the paper aside, reading the top before finding a chocolate caramel. After taking a bite, I smiled. "If you weren't forgiven before, this would have cinched the deal." I waited for Martin to select a candy before closing the lid and picking up the massive bear. He must have weighed twenty pounds. "Come on, buddy, I want to show you where you'll be sleeping tonight." I put the bear on the living room couch and turned to find Martin standing in the doorway, an amused look on his face. "You know I don't like having an audience."

THIRTY-FOUR

I awoke, my throat tight and aching from the silent sobs that had filled my subconscious. Martin ran his fingers through my hair and held me until I calmed down. He didn't ask what my nightmare had been about, and I didn't say.

After that, I barely slept the rest of the night. Too much weighed on my mind. But in the dark, I could almost pretend we were in my old apartment, that things were good, that Don hadn't come back, and some goon wasn't lurking in the shadows, silently waiting to collect. But when morning came, I couldn't pretend anymore.

While Martin went for a run and came back to lift weights, I took out my aggression on the heavy bag. Right cross, hook, uppercut, uppercut, knee. Hook, hook, jab, uppercut, knee, kick. And so on. I bounced, throwing my hips into every move. The bag danced, swaying back and forth. Each time, I hit it harder, watching it swing higher.

"Alex," Martin called over the constant rat-a-tat of my onslaught, "you have to get ready for work."

I wiped the sweat from my face with my forearm. Rearing back, I did one final combination which made the chain squeal as the bag lurched and bounced. Then I stepped away, tugging on the Velcro straps with my teeth.

"Feel better?" Martin asked.

"Not really."

He took the gloves from me while I unwrapped my

hands and tossed the sweaty strips into the hamper. "Come on, champ. Let's hit the showers. There's one thing that's guaranteed to make you feel better."

"I wouldn't count on that, but it won't make me feel worse, unless you do it wrong."

He gave me a look. "Have I ever done it wrong?"

"There's a first time for everything."

His green eyes sparkled. "I dare you to say that again." The endorphin rush had made him playful, and he chased me up the stairs.

After our shower, Martin left for work. He wanted to stop by Bruiser's to make breakfast before dealing with whatever insanity today would bring.

A quick glimpse outside revealed a black sedan with government plates waiting in the driveway after Martin left. Mark must have assigned a detail to keep an eye on me too. It would have been nice if he'd told me.

Emptying the rest of the coffee into two travel mugs, I went outside to see if whoever got stuck babysitting me would like a cup. The driver's side window rolled down, and Eddie Lucca grinned.

"Good morning." He held his hand out for the cup. "Where's the rest of my breakfast?"

I peered into the car, but Lucca was alone. "What are you doing here? Did Jablonsky put you up to this?"

"Not exactly, but he read me in." Lucca ran one hand in a circle around the steering wheel. "It turns out Landon Parker's your father."

"No."

"No?" He looked confused. "That's how most people would refer to him."

"Most people who know him refer to him as an asshole."

Lucca nodded solemnly. "Anything you need, I'm here. We're partners. I couldn't leave you exposed when a knee-capper expects payment and may come after you again."

"We're not partners." I made a show of looking down. "And I'm fully clothed. Nothing's exposed."

He rolled his eyes and reached for the travel cup again, but I didn't offer it to him. "Isn't that for me?"

"No."

"You're double-fisting the caffeine now?"

"I'm thinking about it."

"Why are you always such a hard ass?"

"Why are you here, Lucca? You have actual OIO business that needs your attention."

"I wanted to make sure you were okay."

"God, Eddie, don't be nice to me. I don't know what to do with that."

"Normal people appreciate genuine concern."

"Fine." I took a step back. "You said you wanted breakfast. Come inside. I'll get you breakfast."

"You're serious?"

"The offer expires in five seconds."

He rolled up the window, got out of the car, and locked it. As he followed me up the steps, he took in the house. "How come you never invite me over? I spent months twisting your arm to get you to agree to dinner, but you and Martin still owe me and my wife a night out. Now that you're back from California, I intend to cash in."

"Don't hold your breath." I led him into the kitchen, opened a cabinet, and felt around the back until I found a box of chocolate cereal with colored marshmallows. "You're in luck." I shook the box. "We still have some of the good stuff."

Lucca stared at the box of cereal like I'd insulted him. "I should have known. You look like an adult, but you don't act like one. The house threw me. It looks like a place that would have real food in the cabinets."

"Fine." I moved the box out of his reach and grabbed the bran flakes. "Enjoy."

"This must belong to Martin. I don't remember seeing anything nearly this nutritious in your apartment."

"I wouldn't call that nutritious. It's the same as this, but without the flavors, colors, and fun."

"God forbid your breakfast isn't fun."

I pulled out two bowls and grabbed the container of milk from the fridge. "Help yourself."

Lucca poured a bowl of bran flakes while I grabbed a spoon from the drawer and poured one of the travel cups into a regular mug for me. I hadn't planned on eating at home, but my morning workouts had left me famished. The cereal would tide me over until I got to the office or the precinct.

Lucca examined the contents of his bowl, stirring the flakes around in the milk. "No raisins?"

"I ate the raisins."

"Is that why you bought the cereal?"

"I like the raisins."

"The store sells raisins without the cereal."

"Yes, but the ones in the cereal box taste different. I like them better."

Lucca stared at me like I was crazy.

Instead of arguing, I grabbed another bowl from the cupboard, poured the good cereal into it, added a decent amount of milk, and slid it in front of him. "Shut up and eat that. I won't tell anyone."

Reluctantly, he picked up the spoon and ate the chocolate cereal.

"You know, it makes chocolate milk when you're done," I said matter-of-factly.

"I have a toddler. I understand the concept of chocolate milk, Parker."

"Great. Drink up." I picked up my bowl, drank the remainder of the milk, and put the dish in the dishwasher. Then I stared at him, expectantly waiting for him to follow suit.

When he finished, he wiped his milk mustache away with a napkin and sipped from the travel mug. "What's on your agenda today?"

"Cross Security, then the precinct."

"I'll drive you."

"Did Mark tell you what happened to the company car?"

"Yeah, but I'm wondering what happened to your car."

"My trunk has a hole in it."

"Did you back into something?"

"Yeah, a guy with a hammer."

Lucca gave me a look. "I'm gonna need to hear that story, and I'm going to insist on driving you to work. Consider it Jablonsky's orders."

"I thought you said he didn't assign you to babysit me."

"Officially, no. Unofficially, you know how he is. I'll be reviewing reports and performing threat assessments for the next six months if I don't keep an eye on you."

"Oh, so you're not doing this out of the kindness of your heart." I winked. "That makes me feel so much better."

Lucca chuckled and waited for me outside. Once we were on the road, I filled him in on everything. At this point, my past, which I'd always kept private, might as well be broadcast on network television. I hated it, but there wasn't much I could do about it.

"We could build a case and arrest Don," Lucca said. "Given what you've told us and Don's known associates, it shouldn't be that hard to find enough evidence or convince someone to cooperate."

"I don't think Chad Averly would cooperate."

"I meant Don's CPA associate, the one who knew about his stock market scheme. What was his name? Travis something..."

"Simms," I said. "Frankly, I wouldn't mind seeing Don go down. However, he owes Averly a lot of money, and he told him I had it. Even if something were to happen to Don, Averly would still try to collect."

"Correct me if I'm wrong, but you don't have that kind of money."

"Martin does. Don's threatening to file assault charges if we don't give him the money."

"You said that bastard wanted to extort you. It looks like he figured out a way to do it." Lucca slowed as we approached the office building. "The only other option is to take down Averly."

"That is the plan," I said. "Mark's hoping to bring him up on federal charges, but it'll take time to do the research and build a case."

"In the meantime, you're still on the hook."

"Yeah."

Lucca stared out the windshield. "Your best option is to give Don the money, make sure he pays Averly back, and wait for us to take them down quietly. That way, nothing blows back. Nothing points to anyone."

"Do you think it's a gamble?"

Lucca nudged me. "Don't worry. We're not gonna let another crime lord come after you."

"Great." I opened the car door and stepped out. "Go to work, Lucca. I'll call if I need you."

"How are you getting to the precinct?"

"Martin's driver can pick me up."

"All right, but be careful."

"I'm always careful."

"That'll be the day."

By the time I made it upstairs, the morning meeting was ending. Cross dismissed everyone as soon as I stepped into the room.

"What did I miss?" I asked Bennett Renner, who was on his way out.

"The usual. You're already working on something, right?"

"More or less."

"Alex," Cross said, giving Bennett a dismissive look, "I have something to discuss with you upstairs."

"Guess I'm in trouble." I fell into step beside Cross. "I'm sorry I'm late. Lucca stopped by for breakfast."

"Jablonsky's concerned," Cross said, pressing the button for the elevator and tucking his hands into his pockets.

"How would you know that?"

"He's waiting for you upstairs." Cross didn't say anything else until we were alone in the elevator car. "Landon Parker's laptop contained the basics on his failed day-trading business. He made some terrible investments and kept throwing good money after bad. It's no wonder the whole thing tanked. But we haven't found any incorporation documents or business licenses. Nothing that indicates he hung a shingle. He may have convinced Chad Averly to invest in the company, but there was no company, not legally, which makes it all unofficial."

"That's why we never found anything."

"Most likely. It also means Don isn't as innocent as he claims."

"I never thought he was innocent of anything," I said. "But I doubt he could be arrested."

"The FBI could look into fraud. If Don misrepresented

himself or his business to investors, they could run with that."

"Who's going to testify against him? Chad Averly?"

"Don doesn't need to know that. You could turn the tables and threaten him with this. It might be enough to get him to back off."

"I see you and Ace Darrow have something in common."

Cross growled, his eyes narrowing. "What would that be?"

"Never mind."

He let out another disgusted grunt but chose to ignore me. Cross kept details about his clients' dirty little secrets. I'd never seen him use that to his advantage unless they threatened him or his company, but I wasn't privy to his actions usually. I wouldn't put it past him.

"Amir determined that before attacking you, Locke had come from the same hotel where Don Parker had been staying."

"Where we spoke to him?" I asked.

Cross nodded. "Locke wasn't a guest, but he was looking for something. He asked if he could see room 213. That he was considering checking in, and that room had sentimental value. The hotel refused. Locke went up to the room anyway, knocked, and forced his way inside. The couple staying there had gone out for dinner and drinks, so they missed him, but when they returned, they reported someone had broken the lock on their door."

"And you know for sure it was Locke?"

"I've seen the footage. The police have a copy."

"He must have been looking for something."

"Whatever it is must have been why Locke shot up my car and wasn't too concerned with keeping you alive. I'd say he believes Don stashed the money somewhere and wants to find it."

"But Don checked out of the hotel a week ago. Locke must have known since he's been keeping tabs on Don. Why would he think anything of value would still be at the hotel?"

"Curious, isn't it?"

I hated when Cross spoke in questions. It usually meant

he knew more than he was saying. But I had no way of knowing, and he wouldn't give up the information until he was ready.

"Do you know if the police made any progress?"

"I haven't heard, but why would I?"

"Have you made any progress?"

"I'm still gathering out-of-state footage, but that is our best bet for now." Cross watched me through the reflection in the doors. "I told you what would happen if you gave Landon Parker money. Now it looks like Locke wants to kill you as a way to demonstrate to Don just how serious he is."

"Or he thought I had what he wanted."

"Did you find anything hidden in the vacation rental or among Don's belongings?"

"No."

"Are you sure you didn't overlook something? A USB drive, a crypto wallet, anything like that?"

"Nothing."

Cross sighed. "This is Ace's fault. I've had a lengthy discussion with him about this. My people are off limits. If anyone hires him to dig up dirt on one of us again, he's to come to me immediately."

"Do you believe he will?"

Cross glanced at me from the corner of his eye. "Yes, which is why I wish you had prepared me for this possibility in the first place. We wouldn't be dealing with these issues now if I had known. And one of my cars wouldn't be in police impound."

"Do you think I knew this would happen?"

"You should have predicted it."

"I'm not a fortune teller, Lucien."

"Regardless," he cleared his throat, "I have no desire to argue with you over this. Everything has already been said and done. Now we deal with the fallout. I've provided the police and FBI composites, three-dimensional renderings, the raw footage, and optimized stills of Locke from each of his three assaults—Ace, Don, and last night."

"What about Martin? Was he on the footage?"

Cross licked his lips. "I saw what happened. It wasn't pretty, but it's nothing I wouldn't have done. In fact, I've done much worse without repercussions. Don goaded James. He wanted to get hit. He wanted to hold this over your head. He needed the bargaining chip."

"I know."

"James did not put Don in the hospital. Locke did. If James had done serious damage, Don would be eating from a straw now."

"It would have been an improvement."

"I'm sure that was James's thought also."

I blew out a breath. "Do the police know?"

"They have the footage with the timestamp. I didn't turn over everything, but if they collect a fresh copy themselves, they may see it. I've informed Mr. Almeada to prepare for such possibilities." Cross glanced at me. "I could make sure the possibility doesn't exist."

"You mean hack in and delete evidence?"

"It's up to you. The police don't need to see James Martin delivering the first blow to build their case against Locke."

"What did Almeada say?"

"He said I shouldn't tamper with evidence. But he can't advise me to break the law. That'd be unethical. However, the smarter play would be to convince Don not to press charges against James. Then it won't matter. The police won't try to make a case without the victim's cooperation."

"That's what I've been trying to do all along, but there's no guarantee I can get Don to cooperate."

Cross smiled, tilting his head down in the hopes I wouldn't notice. "I have a suggestion."

"What is it?"

He licked his lips, forcing his face into a neutral position before looking up. "I'll front Don the money with one stipulation. He leaves James out of this and never darkens his doorstep again. Yours either."

"What?" I couldn't have heard him right.

"It's not a gift. It's an advance on your salary."

"Lucien, you don't pay me enough for that. I'd have to work for free for a decade to pay you back."

"I never realized you were so bad at math. It wouldn't be that long. In fact, I've already worked out a fee schedule and had legal draft a new employment contract for you. You sign a contract agreeing to work for me for the next five years. Every raise and bonus will go toward what you owe. Your current salary will remain the same."

"That math won't work out."

"It will. You haven't been here long enough, but you should know I'm not stingy with raises, and since you agreed to take a fifty percent pay cut when you signed for the ability to moonlight, your first raise will be significant if you agree to the new terms."

"Five years?"

"Is that so bad?"

The elevator doors opened, revealing Mark Jablonsky sipping an espresso while he leaned against Justin's desk. He looked tired and not particularly happy. On the plus side, he hadn't murdered anyone in the last twelve hours.

"I don't do commitment," I said.

"You told her you'd pay?" Mark asked, giving Cross an uncertain look over the rim of his coffee cup.

"I did, but I told you she wouldn't accept."

"Alex, thank the man and sign the papers," Mark said.

I gave Mark a confused look. He never wanted me to work for Cross Security in the first place. The fact that he thought I should sign my life over to Cross for the next five years made me think I was missing something important. "Did you hit your head and get amnesia?"

"Marty could shell out the money, but I don't trust that bastard Don not to spin it to his advantage. Plus, we don't need anyone tracing the funds back to Marty. He can't afford that. You can't afford that. Don sold you out. Pass the buck off to Cross Security, that way Don's story remains intact and the assholes he screwed over will think long and hard before making a move on you or Marty, should something happen."

"Something?" I asked.

"Arrests, raids, airstrikes." Mark winked. "Y'never know. But having Cross foot the bill is the safest thing for everyone involved. His company has a reputation. He has an army of former Spec-ops on his security teams and ties to local and federal law enforcement. It'd be suicide for anyone to wage war against him."

"You and I both know you're not that protected," I said to Cross.

"It's not about truth. It's about perception. It's about threats. And don't think I can't or won't call in favors when necessary. I have on your behalf more times than I'd care to admit."

"So I already owe you."

Cross shrugged. "It's simple. You want out, pay me back." Cross opened his office door. "The contract's on the coffee table. Give it a look."

THIRTY-FIVE

"You can't be serious," I said to Mark as he parked in one of the precinct's reserved spaces. "You hate that I went to work for Cross. You practically disowned me because of it. You made me feel like shit because I disappointed you."

"Given what I know now, I'm sorry for that." Mark rubbed the grit from his eyes. "Your old man made it rough on you. I didn't realize how triggering it was when I did the same thing."

"Don't give me that psychobabble bullshit. Tell me why you want Cross to give me the money. Did Martin tell you he doesn't want to foot the bill? I wouldn't blame him. I already owe him the ransom he paid. If he pays for this, that's almost half a million dollars I will have taken from him." I cringed. "I never wanted a dime. It was never about the money."

"Marty knows that, and he hasn't said a word to me about not paying. In fact, I haven't said a word to him about any of this. The reasoning is sound. Cross and I laid it out for you. It's the best option in this situation."

"Five years."

"It doesn't have to be. Cross pays Don. Marty pays Cross. You get your ass back to work for some federal agency. The DEA would be more than happy to take you."

"I told them to screw themselves."

"Yeah, well, I spent a week in D.C. listening to them talk about how much they could use you. You could write your own ticket. You want to work a desk, they'd let you. You want out in the field, Agent Decker would vouch for you. They have openings in the local office. You wouldn't have to go to California or Florida."

"Mark—"

He held up his palms. "I know. You're not interested, but I had to put it out there, particularly when you're thinking about running away. You have options. Always."

"I'm not running this time. Don forced me out once. He won't force me to give up my home and my family again."

"Good." Mark nodded toward the building in front of us. "We'll go inside. I'll have a chat with Moretti and whoever's looking into the assault. I'll run some things by the detective in charge and do what I can to get Marty's name removed from the list of suspects. It shouldn't be that hard now that we have a lot more facts. In the meantime, Cross and a team of security specialists will wait at the hospital for Don to be discharged. Once he is, they will take him to one of their safe houses. Cross said he has an apartment set up. Don should be comfortable there."

"Not too comfortable, I hope."

Mark smiled. "Cross will work out the terms of the money transfer and provide Don with the cash to pay back what he stole as early as this evening. I don't imagine that will be a pleasant experience for either party. Cross said he'd keep us in the loop, but I'm not on his speed dial, so if you hear from him, call me immediately. Do you understand?"

"Yes."

"For now, it'd be best if you go about your business. From what I heard, you and Heathcliff stumbled upon an armed robbery ring."

"Did Cross tell you that?"

"Moretti did." Mark quirked an eyebrow. "You really think your boss would want to engage in small talk or provide additional unnecessary details to me about anything?"

"That's why I was surprised you knew."

"With everything going on, I figured it'd be best to keep an eye on you."

"No wonder I'm always paranoid."

He chuckled. "I take it you gave Lucca a hard time this morning."

"You haven't spoken to him?"

"Not yet."

"When you do, he'll say I withheld raisins and tortured him with chocolate milk. Don't believe a word of it."

Mark shook his head. "I don't even want to know."

We parted ways, and I headed upstairs to see what kind of progress Heathcliff had made. Thompson glared at me when I entered.

"Now what did I do?" I asked.

Thompson stared at my empty hands. "Really, Parker? You used to bring us donuts and coffee. What gives?"

"No one said it was my turn."

"Ignore him." O'Connell returned from the break room with two cups of coffee in hand. He pressed one into my palm and took a seat at his desk.

Thompson shook his head and focused on the board Heathcliff had set up for our case. "Parker dropped this case in our laps. Usually, that means she bribes us with food."

"Cool it." O'Connell gave Thompson a withering look.

"I don't remember you ever talking this much, especially to me," I said to Thompson. "When did you get so chatty?"

"Forget it." Thompson went back to work.

I raised the mug a few inches and nodded at Nick. "Thanks," I mouthed.

"Don't forget about tonight," O'Connell said.

"What's tonight?"

"Double-date night. Martin mentioned a pop-up."

"Shit."

"You forgot."

"I don't even know what day it is."

"Don't sweat it. I'll tell Jen you've had a lot going on. I'm sure she'll understand."

"I owe you."

"You owe all of us," Thompson muttered.

While I checked the board for updated intel, Heathcliff appeared from wherever he'd been. He stood beside me.

"Did you hear what happened last night?"

"No." I glanced at O'Connell and Thompson, but they were wrapped up in something else.

"It turns out putting Ed Mitchell in the same holding cell as the Savages was akin to placing a zebra in the lion's den."

"Oh no."

"Luckily, officers were moving Wayne Savage out at the same time we moved Ed in, so it wasn't two against one, but," Heathcliff whistled, "we're lucky Kelsey Savage was the aggressor or Mr. Titus would be filing suit against the department."

"Jesus."

"He wasn't there," Thompson mumbled.

I quirked an eyebrow at Heathcliff. "What happened?"

"Let's just say Kelsey has an appropriate last name. He started screaming how all of this was Ed's fault, how Ed abandoned his brother, how if he hadn't backed out, Wayne wouldn't be locked up. It took five cops to break it up. Thompson was one of them. He got two bruised ribs for his trouble."

"I'm sorry, Thompson." Now I understood the hostility. "I'll bring you a few jellies and a large mocha to make up for it."

"Make it a bear claw. And after that, you can bet your ass I'm not signing any damn waiver."

"No one would want to see your ugly mug on TV anyway," I teased.

"Probably for the best," Thompson said. "All those reality dating shows would be calling me up to be a contestant."

"In your dreams," O'Connell said.

I rubbed my eyes. "How is Ed?"

"Surprisingly better than anyone could have hoped. He's got some cuts and bruises, but the man knows how to duck and cover," Heathcliff said.

"He didn't fight back?"

"No." Heathcliff shuffled through the papers on his desk and handed me the medical report. "We're keeping him in isolation for his own protection, but he's fine."

I scanned the page but Ed's wounds were mostly superficial. He'd gotten a broken nose and fat lip. His forearms had blocked the brunt of Kelsey's punches, but that was the extent of it. Thompson and the other cops who'd tried to pull Kelsey off Ed had gotten it a lot worse.

Raising my hands in front of my face, I made fists and held my arms together the same way Ed must have blocked. But that left my middle exposed. I hunched over, but that wouldn't work either.

"He was on his back on the ground. Savage was on top of him," Heathcliff said. "We pulled Savage backward, and he fought us until he realized the cage was open and made a break for the exit. That's when Thompson grabbed him and got rammed into the metal door."

"Ouch." I winced, studying Thompson.

"And not even a damn apology donut."

O'Connell rolled his eyes.

Heathcliff handed me another sheet of paper. "We'll be adding charges to the list of offenses Kelsey Savage is accused of committing. I'd say even if he got out of the armed robbery, he won't get away with assaulting police officers or attempting to escape custody."

"Has Titus been informed?" I asked.

"That was a fun conversation. Moretti's not happy our play backfired."

"I can understand why." I rested my hips on the desk and sipped my coffee. "Did we learn anything from this, besides Kelsey blames Ed for his brother's predicament?"

"Officers overheard Kelsey say to Wayne that he was close to getting the bail money together, that he'd take care of it, that Wayne had nothing to worry about, to which Wayne pointed out that Kelsey was behind the same set of bars and facing charges himself. Now, the Savages are being even less cooperative," Heathcliff concluded.

I flicked a photo of some bullet casings. "Did ballistics come back?"

"Not yet. The lab's still backed up." Heathcliff scanned the sticky notes on his desk. "Breann didn't have any idea her husband had a second phone. In fact, she adamantly insists that he doesn't. I asked her if there were any other places Kelsey kept things. She mentioned he used to keep stuff at his brother's, but Wayne's been staying with them, so that's out. Officer Franco is digging through Kelsey's financials and attempting to follow his footsteps, hoping to figure out where Kelsey may have stashed a phone."

"He could have tossed it after the check-cashing robbery," I said. "That may have been their final score. One last job."

"In that case, it could be anywhere. We didn't find it in the dumpster with the masks and takeout bag, but there are a million trash bins and sewer grates between there and his house."

I read Ed Mitchell's medical assessment. The doctors hadn't noted any other recent injuries or previously broken bones. "What does Ed have to say now that his friend tried to kill him? Has he changed his story?"

"Not even a little bit. I asked if he wanted to press charges against Kelsey, but he said he understood why Kelsey was pissed. Family is family. But he maintains that Wayne made the decision to rob the coffee shop despite his protests that they wait."

"Did Ed say why Wayne wouldn't wait?"

"He said the man in charge didn't give them a choice, but Ed didn't care. He wasn't going to risk someone else getting hurt for a few hundred bucks. He already saw the truck driver get shot. He didn't want to see that happen to anyone else."

"But Ed admitted he had a gun with him that day."

"He never planned to use it," Heathcliff said. "He said it wasn't even loaded."

"It was loaded when we retrieved it from his drawer," O'Connell said.

"That doesn't prove anything," I said.

Heathcliff sighed. "Regardless, Ed's actions at the coffee shop and last night in the holding cell indicate he's a pacifist. We can't say the same about the Savages."

"Do you think they forced Ed to comply?"

"Possibly."

Grabbing a marker, I went to the board. "Ed's the lookout." I scribbled that beside his photo. "Wayne and

Kelsey are the armed robbers." I drew an arrow to the other man in the photo from the strip club robbery. "What does this guy do?"

"He holds the bag," Heathcliff suggested.

I snickered. "You've been spending too much time with me. I've warned you about that." Capping the marker, I took a step back. "There's only one way to find out what role this guy played. Let's ask him."

THIRTY-SIX

"I've got a bad feeling about this." I studied Jerome Sassen's house. The shutters were askew, covered in grime and creaking in the breeze. The walkway to the front door was pitted and crumbling, making it uneven and gravelly. Something was off. It wasn't the outward appearance of the house, but I had yet to put my finger on it.

"We're in luck. That's his car." Heathcliff pointed to a washed-out black sedan, which had turned a drab gray due to the peeling paint and sun bleaching.

"That doesn't mean he's home." I went around the jagged chain-link fence, with its rusted patches, so I could get a better view of the back. A doghouse sat directly behind the front door. It was wooden and painted bright red. *Spike* was written in script above the opening.

"He's got a dog," I said.

"Rottweiler? Mastiff?"

"No idea." I stepped closer to the fence, but the ferocious beast didn't appear. "I don't see it."

"It could be inside," Heathcliff said.

"Let's find out."

Heathcliff waited for me to come around the side of the house and step to the side of the door before he rang the bell. Cocking an eyebrow, he waited a beat before pushing the button again.

"I don't think it works." I looked around, spotting a security camera attached to the end of the porch. Whoever was inside wanted to get a good look at anyone who came knocking. I pointed to the camera and waved.

"He could have a problem with porch pirates."

"Maybe he should invest in a few signs that say *Beware of Dog,*" I said.

Heathcliff rested one hand on his hip, revealing his badge and gaining easier access to his gun before knocking against the door. "Mr. Sassen?"

A deep bark sounded from within. I took a step back, moving closer to the window so I could get a look inside. A brown and black dog approached the door. Either Sassen was a werewolf, or he had one big guard dog.

I reached for my gun. "I hope you're good with animals."

Heathcliff exhaled slowly and knocked again, causing more barking.

"Spike, zwinger," a voice said from inside. The door creaked open, and Jerome Sassen peered out at us through the narrow slit. "Can I help you?"

"I hope so. I was wondering if you could tell me about your friends." Heathcliff showed his badge.

"I don't have any friends," Sassen replied.

"That's not what Kelsey Savage said. According to him, you and his brother, Wayne, are best friends."

Sassen glanced down at Heathcliff's badge. "That's not a crime."

"Did you know Wayne was arrested for armed robbery?"

Sassen shrugged.

"Any idea why he'd do that?" Heathcliff asked.

"Wayne lost his job. The man needed money. 'Nuff said."

"Not quite." Heathcliff moved closer to the door. "It'd be best if we discuss the rest of this in private. I don't think you want your neighbors to hear what I have to say. May we come in?"

"We?" Sassen opened the door a little wider and looked straight at me. He'd seen me on camera, so why the charade? Something about him was familiar, but I couldn't place him. "Who's she?"

"A police consultant," Heathcliff said before I could

offer a more creative response.

Sassen looked me up and down. "What are you consulting on?"

"Your décor," I said.

He opened the door wider. "Spike, fass."

The dog barked once, taking flight as it launched itself from where it had been sitting behind Sassen. It growled, latching onto Heathcliff's arm. In the commotion, Sassen ran toward the back of the house.

"Parker, go," Heathcliff said even as the dog yanked on his sleeve.

Everything told me to help Heathcliff, but Sassen was getting away. So I dashed around them, half-expecting the dog to grab me by the leg and rip me to shreds. But it didn't. It remained where it was, content with its current prey.

Sassen didn't go for the back door. Instead, he veered to the right and down the hall. He entered the room on the end, attempting to shut the door before I could enter.

I threw my shoulder into the door as he pushed it closed. Since the lock hadn't engaged, the door pushed back on him, but Sassen was stronger than I expected. He stepped back with his left foot, angling his body to keep the door from opening wide enough to allow me entry.

Without the momentum, I was at a disadvantage, and I scrambled to gain enough traction to force the door open. Unexpectedly, he let go, sending me tumbling forward. I caught myself with my hands.

The sound of a gun being cocked echoed in my ear, and he pressed the muzzle of a semi-auto into the back of my neck. "Stay down," he warned.

I kept my cheek pressed against the rough carpet, facing away from him. I couldn't see him or the gun. But I knew it was there. And I knew he wouldn't miss. From what little I could see, this guy was a weapons fanatic. He had gun racks mounted on the walls above his dresser. Beneath the bed was a heavy metal case. Grenades? Missiles? Who knew what this guy was into. But my gut said Rambo was his role model.

"You robbed the check-cashing place. You had the

handgun. You provided backup to Kelsey Savage," I said.

He pushed the muzzle of the gun harder into my neck before taking a step back. "Don't move."

"I wasn't planning on it." From what I could hear, he was grabbing something. Maybe packing a bag. I resisted the urge to turn around. Instead, I scanned the area for a reflective surface, but I didn't see one. "If you run, who's gonna take care of your dog?"

That made Sassen falter. "How did you find me?"

"Kelsey Savage gave you up."

"That bastard."

"Tell us what happened. We can cut you a deal."

The window slid up. "Yeah, right."

I counted to five, turned toward the sound, and drew my weapon. Sassen was halfway out the window. The second it took for him to pull himself out gave me enough time to roll out of the way before he fired three shots in rapid succession, each one closer than the last.

Throwing myself against the side of the bed, I returned fire. Sassen ran. I launched myself through the open window, rolling and coming up with my weapon aimed in the direction he'd gone.

He saw me as he leapt over the fence. Once he was on the other side, he fired again. I felt the shot, but it wasn't enough to take me down. I squeezed the trigger, seeing him jerk. Instead of firing at me again, he ran.

The instinct to chase overtook thoughts of self-preservation, and I vaulted over the fence, the jagged metal slicing into my palm. I landed on the grass on the other side.

"Freeze," I shouted, my gun in front of me, my aim unsteady as I rushed after him. But he wasn't slowing.

Tucking the gun into my holster, I raced after him. He made it halfway down the block before almost getting hit by a car backing out of a driveway. Several people had heard the gunfire. A few were standing on their front porches, phones out.

Sirens sounded in the distance, but they weren't close. Help was a couple minutes out.

Sassen diverted around the car, changing course. Seeing

that he was heading across the street, I sped up as he started to slow. I tackled him low, my shoulder colliding with his back and knocking him off balance. He landed hard, his upper body splayed across the sidewalk.

Crawling over him, I grabbed for his gun. Blood dripped down his arm from my bullet. He elbowed me with his other arm, hitting my side and setting my nerves on fire. First there was pain, then numb tingling. Neither felt good. But I fought to stay focused. I had to get the gun.

It was barely within reach, but he was now struggling to get to it, so I batted it away, sending it skittering across the asphalt and into the grass. Then I pulled my own gun and aimed.

"Give me a reason." I stared at him, my hands steady, my breath ragged. "I'm already having a bad enough day."

He made a move, and I took my finger off the trigger guard and placed it on the trigger. The look in his eyes told me he'd risk it. But before we could find out who was faster, Heathcliff announced from behind, "Police. Hands in the air."

Sassen glanced at his dropped gun. He'd be dead before he made it an inch. Even if he was faster than me, which he had yet to prove, he wouldn't be able to avoid my bullet and Heathcliff's. So he raised his hands over his head.

"Face down. On your belly." Heathcliff covered Sassen while I got back on my feet, stepping backward until I was close enough to make sure no one else could grab his gun. Then I covered him while Heathcliff cuffed and frisked him.

"Where's Spike?" Sassen asked. "What did you do to my dog? You better not have hurt him."

"Unlike you, he obeys," Heathcliff said. His sleeve was tattered and a little bloody, but it didn't look too bad.

Sassen looked bewildered as Heathcliff spun him around. "He'd never let you go without my command."

Heathcliff glared at Sassen. "So ist bray. Aus."

"How did you know that?"

"Police dogs, asshole." Heathcliff checked the wound on Sassen's arm where my bullet had gone in but hadn't come out and called for an ambulance.

The German was unfamiliar to me. But once we had Sassen secured and cuffed in the back of the rig with an officer keeping watch, I asked Heathcliff what it meant.

"It's basically good job and release," Heathcliff said. "We use German to train the police dogs the same way they do in the military. I've picked up a few things from talking to guys in the K-9 unit."

"Was Sassen military?"

"Didn't you read the background I put together?"

"When would I have had time?"

A second ambulance arrived. "Detective, let's get a look at that bite. Do you know where the animal is? Animal control will take him in and have him tested for rabies."

"Let's wait on that," Heathcliff said. "I'm sure the vet keeps records."

"He's tasted blood. He could be a danger—"

"He isn't." Heathcliff examined his arm. The dog had drawn blood, but there were only four puncture marks. Nothing significant. "I'll be okay. I just need this cleaned and bandaged." Heathcliff turned to me. "Are you okay?"

The sting at my side and bloody palm said otherwise. I pushed my jacket aside, revealing a tear in my shirt and a red smear. I felt woozy, more from the near-miss than the actual injury, but my head spun just the same. "Maybe not."

"Is that your blood or his?" Heathcliff asked.

"Mine."

Heathcliff leaned me against the side of the car while he peeled the tattered pieces away. I looked down, seeing where Sassen's shot had barely grazed me, but he'd made it worse by elbowing me. No wonder my ribs were perpetually sore. "It doesn't look too bad, but you should get checked out. Something could be broken."

"Nothing's broken," I said. "It just stings." I turned to the EMT and held up my bloody hand. "I'm gonna need to get bandaged too. Do you think we can get a two for one deal?"

THIRTY-SEVEN

"Why is there a dog in the middle of my bullpen?" Lt. Moretti asked.

"He may have information about our suspects," I said. "He also assaulted a police officer, so we had to book him. Right now, Heathcliff's buttering him up in the hopes of negotiating a deal."

Heathcliff glanced down at the cushion he'd taken from the break room that Spike was using as a bed. "He bit me, sir. I wanted to keep an eye on him until the vet verified his vaccination records."

"Did they?" Moretti asked, taking a step back.

"Five minutes ago. He's clean. Officer Rigby's going to keep him in the kennel until we figure out what to do with him. But he's out on a call now. He'll get him as soon as he comes back."

Moretti gave the dog an uncertain look. "You were supposed to call animal control."

"I know, but he's a trained military dog. He was following orders. It didn't seem right."

Moretti crouched down. "Does he have a name?"

"Spike," Heathcliff said.

Moretti held out his hand for the dog to sniff before giving him a few gentle pats. Spike's tail thumped against the tile before he rolled over for a belly rub. "Are you sure this dog attacked you? He's nothing but a big baby."

"Careful, he's a killer," I said. "But lucky for you, he

doesn't speak English."

Moretti finished petting the dog and straightened up, nodding at my bandaged hand. "Did he do that?"

"His owner did."

"He also bites?" Moretti asked.

I shook my head. "Chain-link fence."

"And a graze and an elbow to the side." Heathcliff nodded at the police t-shirt I was wearing instead of the button-down I had on earlier.

"Told you Parker's a magnet for trouble," Thompson said.

Moretti eyed me. "As long as you're all right."

"I'm fine."

"Good." He wiped his hands on his pants. "The department's got enough problems. I don't need the hassle of dealing with a consultant getting killed on my watch."

"I'd hate to make your job harder."

Moretti jerked his thumb down the hallway. "Jerome Sassen's ready in interview room two. I'll keep an eye on our K-9 killer while you speak to him." Moretti handed Heathcliff a folder. "You may want to take a look at that first."

"Yes, sir." Heathcliff grabbed the folder and scanned the pages. "C'mon, Parker." Spike sat up when we stood, his eyes sharp as he watched us. "Bleib," Heathcliff told him.

"I didn't know you were a dog guy," I said.

"I'm not." Heathcliff led the way to the interview room, stopping outside the door. "Ballistics came back. The gun I took off Wayne Savage matches the gun used to kill the truck driver. However, it was an unregistered weapon, believed to have disappeared as part of a military surplus that vanished. Several other guns from that same shipment were found in Jerome Sassen's house."

"Jerome gave Wayne the gun."

"I'm guessing he also gave Kelsey the sawed-off."

That wouldn't surprise me, but it could be hard to prove. "What are you thinking? Go hard on him with weapons charges and offer him a deal if he flips?"

"Maybe. Let's play it by ear." Breathing out, Heathcliff slipped back into being the no-nonsense cop before opening the door. "Mr. Sassen, we have a few questions, starting with why did you sic your dog on me and try to escape?"

Jerome snorted, though it wasn't from amusement. "There's no need to drag this out."

"Fine." Heathcliff took a seat, pulling the other one out for me. "Why don't you start at the beginning?" He laid the photo of the four men from the freezer section of the grocery store on the table. "Tell me what happened at the warehouse store. We know the delivery truck driver was killed, his body dumped in the back of the truck and left on the side of the road. Did you pull the trigger?"

"No." Jerome looked away from the photo and sat back in the chair.

"Who did?" Heathcliff asked.

"Another guy. I don't know his name. We called him Jefe."

"Meaning boss?" I asked, and Jerome nodded. "Look at you. Multilingual."

"What can you tell me about Jefe? Is he Latino?" Heathcliff asked.

"Maybe, but it's hard to tell sometimes," Jerome said. "It could be I just don't see color."

"Where did this Jefe come from?"

"Don't know. Don't care. He wanted us for a job. That's what Wayne told me. He said he found a guy who was looking to hire, and he thought I might be interested in picking up something else."

"What do you do now?" I asked.

"Handyman. It's gig work. Money's always tight. I thought this would work out. Wayne said he thought the guy was in construction. I figured he could use someone like me, and maybe he'd offer a permanent position on his crew. I didn't realize what kind of crew it was."

"Why didn't you report him?" Heathcliff asked. "Were you afraid of him?"

Jerome didn't like the implication he was a coward. "He would have shot us if we defied him. But I wasn't afraid. I've been around a lot worse. Seen a lot worse. We did the job, and we got paid. And since we were already on the hook, he gave us more jobs."

"How'd he communicate with you?"

"Text messages to burner phones. Wayne gave us clean SIMs to put in our phones."

"Wayne was arrested for armed robbery and attempted murder," I said. "How could he have given you a SIM?"

"That was before."

I narrowed my eyes, but Heathcliff bumped his knee against my leg beneath the table. He didn't want me to spill the beans yet. Instead, I stared at Jerome, hoping to figure out why he looked familiar.

"Can you show us these texts?" Heathcliff asked.

"I don't have them. I tossed the SIM," Jerome said.

"When?"

Jerome shrugged. "All I'd get was a location, date, and time. Kelsey always had the rest of the details. At first, Wayne did, but after he got arrested, Jefe put Kelsey in charge of our ragtag group of misfits."

"Who's in the group?" Heathcliff asked.

Jerome tapped the photo. "Looks like you already figured that part out, Detective. I bet they gave you a shiny gold star."

Heathcliff pulled out a photo from the check-cashing robbery. "Ed Mitchell says he acted as lookout. Wayne was behind bars. That's Kelsey," he pointed to the man holding up the clerk. "We found the shotgun in his closet. That leaves these two men. Are you going to tell me I got something wrong? That I'm seeing double? Because the math doesn't add up."

Jerome pointed to the man with the revolver. "That's me. I'm sure when you searched my place, you found the gun."

"We found lots of guns," I said.

Jerome looked at me, a half-smile on his face. "That's my Second Amendment right."

"You gave the sawed-off to Kelsey, a handgun to Wayne, and one to Ed." Heathcliff didn't phrase it as a question, but we had yet to prove it.

"I have connections. I know people. My friends needed protection. Wayne and Kelsey said someone had been lurking around their house for the last few months. I helped them out, so they could protect their home. At the time, I had no idea the guns would later come in handy against Jefe. Jefe was armed. Each time he summoned us for a job, I wondered if it would be our last. Once he was done with us, he'd have no reason to keep witnesses around. He'd frame or kill us. We needed to protect ourselves. Armed, we had a fighting chance."

"You're claiming you committed these robberies under duress?" Heathcliff looked skeptical. "It sounds to me you were planning on double-crossing Jefe."

"Kill or be killed. That's how I survived."

Heathcliff tapped the photo from the check-cashing surveillance footage. "Who's this guy? Is this Jefe?"

"That's Ed."

"You're sure?"

"Yeah, after that job, we split up. I went with Ed. Kelsey went on his own to meet up with Jefe."

Heathcliff turned, giving me a skeptical look. "Do you buy that?"

"Not really." I studied Jerome. "Why would you believe him? Didn't you think Kelsey may have been planning to screw everyone over by taking off with the cash?"

"Hey," Jerome held up his good hand, the other arm remained in a sling at his side, courtesy of my bullet that the hospital had pulled out of his bicep, "I got the text and showed up. I did what Kelsey told me. Ed and I didn't want to risk another run in with Jefe. The last time we met, Jefe killed a guy."

"Jefe killed him." Heathcliff pulled out the report and placed the photo of the dead delivery driver on the table. "You're sure about that?"

"Yeah."

"Did you see it happen?"

I wasn't buying Jerome's story, but from his expressions and mannerisms, he believed what he was saying. "I saw the body. I heard the shot."

"But you didn't see who shot the truck driver," Heathcliff said.

"It had to be Jefe."

"But you can't really describe him."

"He was just a guy," Jerome said. "Nothing special or distinctive about him."

"You said Kelsey Savage gave you your orders." Heathcliff placed a photo from the strip club robbery on the table. "Tell me what happened here."

"Same thing," Jerome said. "Kelsey emptied the register. I collected from the girls and the horny fat asses, and Ed kept watch to make sure the bouncers didn't try anything. But security at that place is a joke. We didn't have much to worry about as long as we were quick. In and out, like the girls prefer."

"You cased the place." Again, Heathcliff didn't bother with questions. With Jerome, statements worked better.

"I was trained for reconnaissance. That's what I'd call it. But I didn't do it. That's what Jefe told Kelsey and Wayne to do."

"And you trusted them?" I asked. "You're the one with military experience. What qualifications do they have?"

"I'd been there before," Jerome said. "I wasn't worried. It was a good place to blow off steam. The girls don't mind making extra money." Again, he looked at me. "Same with the coffee shop. We'd been there before too. That doesn't mean anything, unless you think Jefe was keeping tabs on us."

"You were at the coffee shop?" Heathcliff asked. "Why didn't you help Wayne?"

I searched my mind, recalling as many details as I could, but I hadn't been paying that much attention to the people at the tables. But now that I was thinking about it, two men had been seated near the door. Jerome could have been one of them.

This time, Jerome chuckled. "You're the cop who freaked out Ed. After that, I knew we were blown. But Wayne figured he could get the money and get out without anyone realizing what was happening," Jerome stared at me, and that's when I realized why he was so familiar, "except you spotted him. You're the reason Wayne got caught."

"Is that why you came at me with a hammer?" I asked.

Jerome didn't bother denying it. "You're lucky it wasn't a gun, or you'd be dead and I wouldn't be here."

"Kill or be killed. Why deviate?"

He opened his mouth, reconsidered, and stared down at the table while he collected his thoughts. "I've killed. But I'm not a killer. You were doing your job. It wasn't personal. I heard your name tossed around when the cops were questioning everyone from the coffee shop. That's how I tracked you down. I'd seen you get in your car when you were leaving, so I knew what it looked like, a silver four-door. Originally, I only planned to scare you, hoping if you backed off or changed your story, the charges against Wayne would go away."

"He tried to kill us in an alley. That's armed robbery and attempted murder. Nothing you said or did could change that," Heathcliff said.

Jerome swallowed. "I had to try something. Wayne's my best friend. He was desperate. He had to pull off the robbery. Jefe would kill us if he didn't."

"Funny thing about that." Heathcliff laid the ballistics report on the table for Jerome to see. "The gun you gave Wayne is the same gun used to kill the truck driver. Can you explain how that happened?"

Jerome stared at the report utterly confused. "That's not possible."

"The lab double-checked. It's a match."

"No." Jerome shoved the folder away and shook his head. "Jefe must have taken Wayne's gun and switched them. Jefe threatened to frame us. Of course, he'd do something like that. The guy was crazy."

"The only way things work out for you and your friends is if we get Jefe. The DA will take everything into consideration. You stand a decent chance, but only if we take down the man pulling the strings. Ed's told us as much as he knows, but Wayne and Kelsey haven't said much. Do you think Jefe's still threatening them?"

Jerome jumped at the chance. "Yeah, that must be it. Kelsey has family. Jefe could go after them."

"What about the truck you guys emptied? Who drove that away from the warehouse store?" I asked.

"Kelsey," Jerome said.

"Kelsey?" I cocked my eyebrow. "Wasn't he in the back of the moving truck with you, Wayne, and Ed?"

"No. It was only me and Ed in the back of the truck. Wayne drove the moving truck away, and Kelsey drove the delivery truck. He knows how. He's a professional truck driver."

"Where was Jefe?" Heathcliff asked.

Jerome frowned, his eyes moving from side to side like the carriage on a typewriter. "Maybe I'm mistaken. That was our first encounter with Jefe. I was too busy working on a plan to overpower him when he let us out. At that point, I was sure he'd kill us. But he didn't. Instead, he gave us envelopes with cash and said he'd be in touch."

"Jefe let you out?" I asked. "Are you sure? That was at the container yard, right? Where Wayne used to work."

"No, you're right. Jefe wasn't there. He ditched us. He made Wayne drive the truck there. He gave Wayne the envelopes. That's what happened."

"And he knew you guys wouldn't go to the police or report him?" I asked.

"Somehow, Jefe already knew everything about us. It was weird."

I narrowed my eyes at him. "Did Jefe tell you to track down my car and try to kill me?"

Jerome shook his head. "I already told you that I heard the cops say you were a witness. I just wanted to scare you off. I had a buddy at the DMV run your name against the silver car and he came up with your address."

"Why were you breaking into those other cars?" Heathcliff asked.

"I didn't know which one was hers, and when I saw the building where she lived, I knew I'd never be able to get inside to deliver my message."

"You mean threat."

Jerome glared at me. "You're the reason my best friend is in jail. As far as I knew, you were going to get us all killed once Jefe found out. Frankly, I'm surprised he didn't kill us as soon as he heard."

"I'm gonna let you in on a little secret." I crooked my

finger and leaned in. Automatically, Jerome did the same, though it wasn't a conscious thought. "There is no Jefe. Wayne and Kelsey made him up. They played you."

"No fucking way."

Heathcliff closed the folder. "Think very hard, Mr. Sassen. Are you absolutely certain you saw Jefe?"

"Yeah, he was outside the store. He had on a sports coat."

"Did you see him kill the driver?" Heathcliff asked.

Jerome bit his lip, fighting to keep his shoulders from shrugging.

"Did you ever see Jefe again?"

"No, but—"

"Just think about it." Heathcliff led me to the door.

THIRTY-EIGHT

I stood in front of the board, staring at the photos. Wayne Savage bought one burner phone and four SIM cards. That would explain why we never found Kelsey's burner. He used his regular phone and switched out the SIM. He could have disposed of the card when he ditched the mask and takeout bag. We'd never find anything that tiny.

Spike pressed his wet nose into my hand, and I jumped. He licked my fingers, checking to see if I'd be a tasty snack. I pulled my hand away and crossed my arms over my chest. How did Wayne and Kelsey convince Ed and Jerome that there was a shot-caller when none of the evidence supported it?

Jerome supplied the team with the weapons, including the gun used to kill the truck driver. Wayne bought the phones, and Kelsey called the shots after his brother was arrested. Maybe he'd been calling the shots since the beginning. Out of the four, he was the only one with a prior criminal record.

I spun around to find Heathcliff working at his desk. "Do you think Wayne got someone to dress up and play the part of Jefe?"

"I don't know. Do we have evidence to back it?"

Spike bumped my hand again, letting out a bark.

"The dog thinks so. Does that count?" I bent over to rub behind his ears, which appeared to be what he wanted. Though, I wondered if he was lulling me into a false sense of security before biting my face off. Except his fur was soft, and his big, pink tongue lolled out of the side of his mouth. He looked content, not homicidal.

"I'm serious, Parker. Nothing suggests anyone else is involved."

"Except what Ed and Jerome said. I would suggest letting Jerome hang out with his best bud and his best bud's brother, except the Savages may try to rip him limb from limb."

"Run through it with me," Heathcliff said.

"For starters, Kelsey knows more about the jobs than anyone else on the team. We have yet to recover his burner phone, but I doubt he has one. He may have switched out the SIMs."

"Agreed."

"Kelsey has the best attorney money can buy. He wouldn't go through the trouble if he wasn't afraid he'd be facing decades of hard time." I ticked the points off on my fingers, which made Spike bark, so I went back to petting him. "Third, Kelsey's the only one with a criminal record. He'd be more likely to color outside the lines."

"That's assumptive."

"How did you make detective without realizing that's the job?"

Heathcliff narrowed his eyes. "Let's talk about the truck. Wayne's gun was used to kill the driver. But Wayne didn't dump the body. His brother did, according to Jerome."

That made me pause. "Jerome and Ed were together in the back of the truck. A man had just been killed. They were forced to play along."

"Right."

"What if they have false memories? Trauma can cloud perception. Ed may have seen a man in a suit near the board, but maybe it didn't go down quite like that. Wayne could have pointed the guy out, said he had a job offer for them, and gave Ed the details. Ed shows up. By then, Wayne and Kelsey have already hijacked the truck and killed the driver. Jerome could have been there. Maybe he heard the shot. He could have seen someone else in the parking lot, a manager or someone, and Wayne and Kelsey told him that was the guy who hired them for the job."

"One of the brothers told the story and the other swore by it," Heathcliff said.

"Pretty much. Then when Ed and Jerome are trapped in the back, trying to make sense of what just happened, they share what they know and come up with Jefe."

"Ed never called the shot-caller Jefe," Heathcliff said. "Yet Jerome said that's what they all referred to him as." Heathcliff hit a few keys, bringing up Jerome's military record. "Hey," he called to an officer who'd just come out of Moretti's office, "Sassen had those framed photos from his days in the service. Is anyone still at the scene?"

"Sanders and Nielsen."

"Thanks." Picking up the phone, Heathcliff had dispatch patch him through and asked that they check the back of the photo. "Any call signs?" He waited. "Bag and tag it."

"What?" I asked.

"His unit referred to their CO as Jefe." Heathcliff pointed at me. "You may be on to something. We'll have to get a shrink in here to provide a consult. But Ed and Jerome may be remembering wrong. Eyewitnesses are usually unreliable. I never expected the same from a pair of perpetrators." Heathcliff made some calls while I considered each of their stories.

"There's just one thing," I said. "If Wayne and Kelsey lied to their friends and used them to pull off these robberies, where's the stolen merchandise?" I went through the manifest of the items the store never received that were supposed to have been on the truck. Two pallets of TVs, boxes of tablets, laptops, sound bars, fitness trackers, and video game systems. I scanned the reports, checking to see what the search warrants had uncovered. Kelsey Savage had a game system, the same kind that had been on the truck, but that could have been a coincidence.

Heathcliff put down the phone. "I checked with the staties again. Patrol's always up and down that stretch of highway. They timestamped when they first spotted the abandoned delivery truck. An officer looked around, didn't notice anything suspicious, and left. After several more passes and no movement, he called to have it towed. No one saw anyone near the truck, but since it was right near that off-ramp with the nearby gas station and fast-food place right off the highway, Kelsey could have had his car waiting there. After all, he and Wayne arrived at the warehouse store together. I'll see if we can get footage from near that exit. Maybe we'll spot Kelsey dropping off his car before the truck was abandoned or someone picking him up afterward."

"Yeah, maybe." But I was focused on finding the stolen goods and cash. We'd searched everyone's home and workplace, but no one had the bulk of the goods. Until we found them, we couldn't disprove that a mysterious shot-caller forced them to commit these crimes. And given the growing pile of evidence, that was the only thing keeping us from closing this case. A thought came to mind that had been percolating for a while. "Wayne Savage worked at the container yard."

"You think that's where they unloaded the truck and hid the merchandise?"

"Ed alluded to it. He said they were let out of the truck at the container yard. That would also explain why we haven't found stolen goods stockpiled at their homes. It could also be where Kelsey is hiding the money from their last job."

"They could have pawned the goods. That could be how they got the envelopes of cash to give to Ed and Jerome."

"The shipment would have been too large for one shop, unless they sold it off piecemeal."

"Scattershot. A few TVs and tablets here and there. There's enough pawn shops and swap meets in the area for that to work." Heathcliff grabbed a pen and made a note. "I'll have Franco hit up a bunch of the shops and flash our suspects' photos around. If they pawned anything, we'll find out about it."

My gut said we might get lucky, if my assumption about Jefe was correct. "Ed had one of the TVs. He said Jefe gave it to him. Maybe we could get that dusted for prints."

"The results would be inconclusive. Even if we find Wayne or Kelsey's prints on it, they'd say it was because they were forced to steal the TV. Any random prints could be from the manufacturing, assembly, or boxing. But I'll have someone check, anyway."

"Thanks."

Heathcliff reached for the mouse. "Ed and Jerome agreed on one other thing. They got paid with envelopes of cash. A grand each."

"What did Jerome do with the cash? Can you trace it?"

"There's nothing in his bank statements. However," Heathcliff rifled through the papers, "all four of them recently paid off outstanding bills."

"What about since the last job they pulled? The $50K should have gone a long way to paying off any remaining debts."

"It doesn't look like it. Nothing's changed. No deposits. No payments."

"Except to Mr. Titus."

"We don't know how Kelsey's paying for that or even if he is."

"If there's no Jefe and no rich relative, Kelsey found the cash somewhere. Titus didn't take him on pro bono. He got stuck with the gig because Almeada couldn't touch it. That means Titus is getting paid an arm and a leg for his services."

"You're cynical."

"Only on my good days."

Heathcliff smiled. "Do I want to know what happens on your bad days?"

"Ask Jerome." I paced in front of the board. "I'm telling you, one of the men we have in custody is in charge of this operation. My money's on Wayne, except he got yanked, so Kelsey took over."

"They could have planned these jobs together. Wayne was desperate. He'd trust his brother to drive the second truck and dispose of the body. Jerome is Wayne's best friend. Jerome would believe anything Wayne told him, and Ed was in such desperate need of a cash infusion that Wayne must have figured they could buy his silence if necessary."

"Wayne must have thought Ed would go along to get along, except Ed freaked out when they shot the driver.

And it only got worse when he saw what they had planned for the coffee shop. That's why he ran."

"That would explain why Kelsey attacked him in lockup."

It all made sense, but one thing still bothered me. "How come Wayne doesn't have better counsel?"

"We arrested him before they stole the fifty grand. He didn't have the money for that. Instead, he was assigned a court-appointed attorney. Switching to a top defense attorney after that last job would be too suspicious. Instead, Kelsey hired the best for himself. They could be hoping for a joint trial. In which case, they could share representation."

"I didn't know you practiced law in a past life, Detective."

"No, Parker, but you nearly did."

"Things like that are rare. Usually, the motion is for separate trials. I don't think it works in reverse."

"The DA said they could be given a joint trial if they are brought up on the same indictment. The men we arrested worked in tandem. They committed the same crimes. They could be tried together."

"The joint trial would only apply to the warehouse store incident." I wondered if that'd be enough to get the crew off. It would all hinge on if the judge decided the men had no other choice and agreed with the affirmative defense that they committed the crimes under duress. If he bought their story, he could hand out minimal sentencing or drop the charges entirely. Jury nullification would also be possible, but that was still a gamble. "For that to work, the defense would have to prove beyond a reasonable doubt that Jefe exists and forced his clients to commit those crimes."

"The defense has four different accounts. Each one could insist a man in a suit lured them to a location with the promise of honest work, only to murder a man and threaten their lives if they didn't comply with his demands. That sounds compelling to me. Plus, the burner phones have text messages. Everything we know about how the phones were obtained could be because Jefe ordered

Wayne to buy the phone and SIM cards. After all, where would Wayne have gotten the money for such expenses if a rich and sinister benefactor didn't give him the money and insist upon it? Wayne was flat broke at the time."

"We have to prove the Savages orchestrated all of it," I said.

"That's why I have Franco putting in the legwork as we speak."

"Meaning?"

"He's questioning everyone near the food pantry. He's also collecting security camera footage from the area and everything he can find from the warehouse store. After that, he'll follow up with the pawn shops to see if anyone on our crew made an appearance. We're gonna find out exactly how this went down."

"While you work on that, I'll see what I can dig up." I put my jacket on only to remember I didn't have a car. Slumping into my chair, I contemplated my phone-a-friends.

"What's wrong?"

"I need a ride."

Heathcliff reached into the drawer and pulled out his keys. He held them out, only to snatch them away before I could take them. "What happened to your company car?"

"I'll tell you later."

"Before you go, take a look at this." Heathcliff gestured that I should join him behind his desk. When I made it around to the other side, he paused the footage on a shot of Jerome gripping Kelsey's shoulder and leading him out the front door of the coffee shop. Kelsey kept looking back, like so many others. But unlike the rest of the crowd, he wasn't afraid of getting shot. He wanted to help his brother. "It looks like we missed two other would-be robbers that afternoon."

There was no way a robbery that small would require a four-man crew. "They didn't care about the register. They were going to empty out the place, same as the strip club. I wonder..." Reaching for the witness list, I scanned the sheet. "Did you run everyone?"

"Yeah, they were all clean. But like I said, most cleared

out before the cops arrived."

I thought about the number of laptops and phones I'd seen. Maybe some of those aspiring screenplay writers were actual screenplay writers. "E-mail me a copy of the footage."

"What are you going to do with it?"

"See if anyone special is in the mix. I don't have the faces of every celebrity, influencer, and high-powered businessperson burned into my brain. But I can see if Cross Security can work some magic and get us names for those who fled the scene. For the four of them to hit the coffee shop, they must have hoped for a big score."

Heathcliff forwarded me the file. "Do what you can."

I e-mailed a copy to the techs and asked if facial recognition could identify anyone special in the crowd. I had no idea how long it'd take, but Cross had a look-book of who's who saved on the servers so he could cherry-pick his next client. "No guarantees, but they may find out if any wealthy targets were at the coffee shop."

Heathcliff handed me his keys. "Do what you have to, but be careful. If you need backup, call me. Do not hesitate." He stared uneasily at the keys to his car. "Try not to damage it. My insurance isn't that great."

"I'll treat it like my own."

"That's what I'm afraid of."

THIRTY-NINE

Before leaving, I took a detour to see what was going on, but Mark had left the precinct hours ago. Instead, I waited out front for Martin to show up. When he didn't, I sent him a text. *Do you still have the same lunch plans?*

We're holding off. It may be rescheduled, he replied.

I didn't want to ask too many questions in case our phone records were ever subpoenaed, so I did my best to squelch my curiosity and drove to the container yard. With any luck, Cross's plan had worked and Don was no longer threatening my beloved.

Rows of freight containers created a maze that reached to the sky. Figuring out where to start was half the battle. A large crane would move the containers off the ships. Depending on how the crates were labeled, workers would open them, remove the contents, place them onto trucks, and haul them away. Sometimes, the container itself would be placed on a flatbed and moved. I never understood how the supply chain worked, but this explained a lot.

Finding an office, I checked the address before pushing open the weathered door. A tiny brass bell jingled. A woman looked up from the water-damaged pages she was reading. From here, I could see a brown coffee ring circling the center of the page.

"Going out or coming in?" she asked.

"Neither." I looked around the office, which smelled like salt water, trash, and dead fish, as if all the bad smells from outside had been trapped and condensed in here. "Is this where Wayne Savage used to work?"

"What's it to you?"

"He listed this as his last job. I wanted to see if there were any issues which led to his unemployment."

"Downsizing," she said.

"Was Wayne a hard worker?"

"He fulfilled his duties. Nothing more. Are you looking to hire him?"

I ignored her question, unsure how to play this. "What exactly did he do here?"

"He emptied the incoming cargo containers."

"Does he still have access to any of the containers or storage units?"

She flipped a few pages in the overstuffed binder. "He never turned in the keys to A872. It's possible he could still access it, but I don't see why he would. It's a rusted hunk of junk that was taken out of circulation. We're using it as temporary storage for packing materials."

"Is anything else kept in there?"

"We may stick a pallet in there if it's the closest storage unit, but we haven't used it lately."

I peered out the dirty windows. "Where would I find that container?"

She crossed her arms over her chest, revealing an anchor tattoo on top of her forearm. Either she was a Popeye fan or she'd served in the navy or coast guard. "You never answered my question. Are you looking to hire Wayne?"

"Not exactly."

"What exactly?"

I placed a Cross Security card on top of the curled pages of her binder. "Wayne's been hiding assets. I'm hoping to find them."

She picked up the card and studied it. "Is there a reward?"

"Depends on what I find."

"I want two grand." She studied my leather jacket. "You got the cash on you?"

I reached into my pocket, tired of being shaken down.

Did I look like I was made of money? "How about," I checked the contents of my wallet, finding two hundred dollars inside, "I give you this to start. You tell me where this unit is and give me permission to search inside, or you point me in the direction of the person in charge, who can authorize me to search the container."

"I run this office. That'd be me." She took the money, reached into her flannel shirt, and tucked it underneath the spaghetti strap on her tank top. Then she lugged a second binder out from a lower shelf and flipped it open on top of the desk. After turning to a worn page with faded print and several unidentifiable stains, she pointed. "A872 is in this quadrant. You'll find it five over and three deep. Wayne's got the keys, so no one's accessed it as far as I know. We've been meaning to get some bolt-cutters and cut the lock off, but we haven't needed the extra storage or packing materials. It's rare that we get asked for that stuff." She nodded down at the bolt cutters. "Do you want to borrow those? I can rent them to you for a price."

"That's okay. I'm not into property damage." I tilted my head, studying the map. "Is this where we are?" I pointed to a square with an x.

"Yep."

"So I go out this door and turn left." I faced the door, gesturing with my hand. "Then right and straight."

"Pretty much. You'll know when you've gone too far when you see the decrepit containers waiting to be scrapped. A872 is right before that."

"Thanks."

"Uh-huh." She closed the other binder and shoved it back on to the lower shelf. "Don't forget about my reward." She pointed to the nameplate. "If he's got valuables in there, I should get a percentage, like a finder's fee. Write down my name, so you don't forget."

I wouldn't forget this, but I pulled out a pen and my notepad to humor her. "Thanks, Crystal."

"I'll be seeing ya," she said.

After getting whistled at by two guys who were unloading the day's catch from a fishing boat, I found the container in a secluded area of the container yard,

Truthfully, I'd never have found it without Crystal's instructions, but that information wasn't worth more than what I'd paid for it. Why was everyone determined to get money from me? Had Martin taken out a billboard that he was my sugar daddy? Because I missed the memo.

The container itself was dented and rusted. It looked like something had been dropped on top of it, but it remained solid. Whatever items were placed inside would be protected from the elements.

After making sure I was alone, I took out the case with my lockpicks and unlocked the container. Tugging open the heavy metal door, I stepped back, unsure what to expect. Stacks of cardboard shipping boxes filled the interior, leaving only a narrow walkway.

Pulling out my flashlight, I stepped inside. Though I wasn't particularly claustrophobic, visions of being locked in played through my mind as I read the labels on the boxes. According to the text, they contained dolls, remote control cars, and playsets from a popular toy manufacturer.

I opened the top box to find it empty. I tossed it aside and checked another random box in the next row. Also empty. Three-fourths of the container was filled with empty boxes and packing materials. Crystal said this was used for storage.

Knocking over another row of empty boxes, I found a stack of flat screen TVs hidden amongst the decoy boxes. It was about damn time.

I took a few photos of the items with my phone and sent their location to Heathcliff before continuing my exploration. Scattered among the empty boxes were rolls of clear plastic wrap and commercial-sized tape. Searching beneath them, I found more of the items stolen from the back of the delivery truck. Hidden inside a giant trash bag of packing peanuts were wads of cash and a burner phone.

Some of the money was crumpled and greasy, as if it'd been tucked into g-strings and brassieres, which it probably had been. A stack of well-worn bills had been sorted by denomination and held together by a rubber band. Near the bottom were stacks of hundreds, fifties, twenties, and tens with the bank bands still around them.

Thumbing through them, I only counted forty grand. The other ten must have gone to pay Mr. Titus's retainer and legal fees. My phone rang, but reception wasn't ideal inside the metal box. So I took a few more photos to make the police department happy and went outside to answer the call.

"I'm on my way," Heathcliff said. "Officer Franco isn't far out. He'll get there first and secure the scene. Tell me a judge isn't going to throw this out."

"The property doesn't belong to Wayne. It belongs to the container yard where he worked. The woman in charge told me Wayne never turned his keys in to unlock this unit and no one's used it since. I offered to open it up for her, and she was more than pleased. But she is hoping for some kind of reward."

"Uh-huh." Heathcliff may not have bought the entirety of my story, but there was enough truth in there for him to justify the search. "I'll brief Moretti on the situation. Did you check out the burner phone?"

"The battery's dead. Do you want me to charge it?"

"Leave it be, Parker. We will take care of it."

"Fine."

"Tell me you wore gloves."

"In case you've forgotten, I have conducted searches before. I know better than to contaminate a scene."

A few minutes later, a patrol car pulled up and Officer Franco and his partner got out of the vehicle. They looked like tiny specks from here, but the police car gave away their identities. From where I was hidden in the maze of cargo containers, he'd never see me or find me, so I called him and gave him directions.

"Is this it?" he asked, eyeing the open door.

"Yep."

His partner peered around the other side. "Any problems?"

"None."

"We'll do a walkthrough, make sure it has what you said, and rope it off." Franco took the flashlight off his belt and went inside to look around. He and his partner came out a minute later. “Was it that messy when you got here?”

“I may have knocked over a few empty boxes. It’s hard to search and not make a mess.”

Franco didn’t look pleased. “Okay.”

“Did you find anything out about the robbers?” I asked him.

“A few employees from the warehouse store have dashcams installed in their vehicles. They only record when their cars are turned on, but luckily, one of the guys had left the car running while he went inside to check his schedule and put in a request for a day off. We didn’t see exactly what happened, but his dashcam caught the sixteen-wheeler pulling into the lot. Eight minutes later, it left the lot.”

“Are you sure that’s the same truck?”

“We got a good view of the plates upon arrival and departure. The rest happened out of view.”

“At least we know the truck was there. Anything else?”

“A lot of nothing, which may be something. I spoke to everyone who works at the food pantry and everyone who came to get groceries. At least a dozen people were there around the same time our suspects claimed the man in the suit posted the job offering on the board, but there was no post on the board and no one remembered seeing a man in a suit. I checked nearby surveillance footage, but no one matching that description ever showed up around there. No suits. No sports jackets. Nothing even close to that.” Franco looked at his partner. “We were in the middle of checking with pawn shops when Detective Heathcliff rerouted us, but we may have a possible lead on a shipment of new game consoles.”

“I’m listening.”

“The last pawn shop we visited had just put eight of them up for sale,” Franco’s partner said, “but the owner bought them from the buyer and he wasn’t in. The clerk we spoke to couldn’t find the records.”

“There might not be any.”

“That’s what I was thinking,” Franco said.

“Good job, fellas.”

“It was a team effort.” He nodded to the container.

"How'd you know anything would be here?"

"I didn't. But we looked everywhere else. This was the only place we didn't check, and we hadn't checked because Wayne hasn't worked here in months. But the bastard kept the key, and I'm guessing no one thought it was strange to see him wandering around."

"Or they flat-out don't care." Franco's partner nodded to a few men wearing hardhats and safety vests. "Have you spoken to anyone?"

"Just the woman in charge."

Franco nodded to his partner. "I'll wait here. But we should get a jump on things."

My phone rang again, and I hit answer, assuming it was Heathcliff asking for directions. Instead, it was Jeffrey Myers.

FORTY

"I didn't know if anyone called you," Jeffrey said.

"Why would someone call me?" My heart pounded in my chest. "What happened?"

"Everyone's fine. Mr. Martin is fine."

"What happened?" I repeated. I'd only spoken to Martin an hour ago.

Jeffrey exhaled into the mouthpiece. "He received a disturbing delivery today, a letter with a photo from one of his magazine spreads with crosshairs drawn over his chest."

"What did the letter say?"

"Tell Parker it's time to pay up."

"Did the FBI—"

Jeffrey cut me off. "They know. They've taken the letter and photo in as evidence. Mr. Martin gave them our security footage from this morning."

"What about from a few days ago?" I asked.

"No. Only from today."

At least Martin hadn't shot himself in the foot by trying to be helpful. However, I should be hearing this from him, not Jeffrey. "When did this happen?"

"A few minutes ago."

Just this once, I'd give Martin the benefit of the doubt, but if I found out he'd kept this from me, I wasn't sure what I'd do. "How is he?"

"He's...fine."

"Really?"

Jeffrey snorted. "At this point, it seems old hat to him. He doesn't seem fazed. The FBI agents stationed to protect him are on edge."

"What about the team from Cross Security?"

"They're flanking him from meeting to meeting. He's not pleased."

"Good." I blinked a few times. "Did the letter say anything else?"

"No."

I checked the time, wondering why Mark hadn't called. Did he know what happened? "Is Martin in a meeting?"

"He just went back to his office."

"All right. Make sure building security is on alert. And be careful." I hung up and called Martin.

"Sweetheart," he answered on the first ring, "it's fine. I was just about to call you. I'm fine."

"Not if I kill you."

"Should I pick up plastic sheeting or duct tape on my way home from work?"

I glanced at the freight container. "If I wanted, I'd get it myself. I'd hate to have you implicate yourself in your own demise." I leaned against another container, sinking to the ground. "Did they see who delivered the threat?"

"Big guy. Dark clothes, dark jacket, kept his hood up, wore gloves. What you'd expect."

"Send a copy of the security footage to Cross Security."

"They already have it."

"Did anyone call Mark?"

"Yes." Martin hesitated. "He wants to move me into a safe house for safe keeping. I spoke to Almeada before this occurred. Lucien assured him the situation was being handled, which is why we held off, but now this happened. The police should know. They should be involved."

"Mark will take care of it," I said. "Do what he says. Do everything he says." Protective custody was the best idea I'd heard all day. "We've made arrangements to get Don the money. We'll pay off his debt. I promise I'll find a way to keep these assholes away from you."

"Away from us," Martin corrected. "This isn't your fault, Alex."

"It is. Don's here because of me."

"Don's here because he's an asshole."

I laughed, and so did Martin. I could hear him smiling. "Don't die on me," I said.

"Because you want the honor of killing me?"

"Exactly."

"Okay. I love you."

"I love you more." By the time I hung up, Heathcliff was heading in my direction. Tucking my phone away, I stood up, brushing my hands on my pants. Then I joined him at the front of container A872 and filled him in on everything he needed to know.

Heathcliff went inside and checked everything out. "Until we see what's on that burner phone, we shouldn't jump to conclusions. But it looks like Kelsey wasn't smart enough to get rid of his. This could be our smoking gun," he said. "That money looks an awful lot like it could have come from the check-cashing place. We may be able to pull prints and match them to the clerk they held up."

"That would prove it." I pointed skyward. "Surveillance footage is spotty around here. Not many cameras, but Crystal should be able to shed some light on things. She may have noticed someone she didn't recognize snooping around."

"We'll question everyone who works here and who's been on the premises in the last few weeks. Someone must have seen something. In the meantime, the DA's office has been informed of what you found. We want to make sure evidence collection is all aboveboard."

"I didn't break any rules," I said.

Heathcliff nodded. "We want to be careful. We're already on thin ice."

"Because of me?"

"Because Kelsey Savage hired Mr. Titus. Certain defense attorneys always put the DA on edge, who, in turn, puts the department on edge." Heathcliff jerked his chin at my phone. "You okay? You look upset. Is this about Martin? I expected you to want to do nothing but talk about that today, but you haven't said a word."

"It's being handled. Jablonsky's working on it, but I need to take care of some things. Do you need me for this?"

"We'll need you to write a report."

"Anything else?"

Heathcliff shook his head. "You're not sticking around for the fun part?"

"There's so much shit in there, you'll be buried in evidence collection for the next few days. I doubt I'll miss anything." I held up his car keys. "I'll leave your car at the precinct, along with my report."

"Do you need backup?" he asked.

"You have your hands full, Detective. I'll be fine."

Heathcliff didn't look convinced. "If you don't want my help, you could borrow Spike or ask O'Connell. He's your favorite."

"You're my favorite," I said.

"That's not what you say behind my back."

"You're both my favorite, but I got this. Cross and Jablonsky already volunteered, so you guys can sit this one out."

"If that changes—"

"You'll be my first call." I bumped against Heathcliff's arm and nodded to Franco who looked utterly confused by our exchange, then I hurried back to the car.

* * *

Jablonsky met me at the precinct and drove me to Cross's safe house. Along the way, he briefed me on the situation with Don and Martin. My fingers tapped a beat against my thigh, but I did my best to keep the million questions to myself until he finished.

"Didn't you say you were going to take care of this? Isn't that how we left things when you dropped me off at the precinct this morning?" I asked.

"I wasn't expecting Locke to threaten Martin. Your encounter last night must have put him on edge. He's freaking out. He wants to collect Averly's money and get out of here before the cops arrest him."

"He knows they're getting close."

"He should. A police car chased him. We tracked his vehicle to the hotel where he was staying. We know where he's been. It's just a matter of time before we figure out where he is and who he is."

"Cross is working on that," I said.

Mark nodded, tapping absently on the steering wheel as he drove. "Cross is narrowing it down. I called the Boston field office to assist. They've been talking to the police who investigated the GTA. They have a few leads, but nothing definitive yet. It's just a matter of time before we get his name off the business records from his bogus security firm. Once we do, we should be able to connect him to Chad Averly. They could both be facing conspiracy or murder-for-hire charges on top of everything else."

I paid attention to the turns, wondering where we were going, but Jablonsky didn't seem to have an intended destination, even though I knew that wasn't true. "He didn't kill Ace Darrow, but he tried to kill me last night."

"He left Ace alive in case he needed more intel. You," Mark glanced at me, "pissed him off. I'd say he's got a temper and a short fuse."

"But if I'm supposed to be the source of his boss's money, he should know better than to kill me."

"We don't know what Don told him." Jablonsky fiddled with the temperature controls while we waited at a red light.

"He may have thought I had the money or whatever he wants from Don inside the box I took from the rental. He must have figured he could kill me and take it."

"No witnesses," Jablonsky said.

"Except I don't know what he wants besides the cash."

"That may be all he wants. Was the box big enough to hold two hundred grand?"

"Yeah."

"There you go."

I stared out the window. "That son of a bitch threatened Martin an hour ago. With an FBI detail and Cross Security keeping watch, how did Locke get away?"

"He left the package for Martin at the front desk. He was gone by the time anyone bothered to look at it."

"I need to end this. Now." I watched the side mirror, but no one was following us. After a few more turns, Mark pulled into a private garage beneath an apartment building, pressed the button on a fob, and entered through the newly opened gate.

We got out of the car and headed for the elevator. Mark used a different fob to get the elevator moving. How many keys did this place have? Would it even be enough?

"We have to get the focus off Martin," I said. "Chad Averly needs to know he is a non-player. He has nothing to do with any of this."

"That's why Cross is giving Don the money. We'll make it clear at the exchange."

"Has Don been briefed?"

"Cross said he'd handle it, but I'll make sure we go over everything again. I don't want any miscommunications."

"I should have handled this better. If I'd gotten Don to open up sooner, if I'd listened to him, agreed to go to dinner with him—"

Jablonsky grabbed my shoulders. "Stop. He is your kryptonite. He didn't want to tell you. He lied to you every chance he got. He waited to tell you the truth, and that was only after he threatened to blackmail Marty. It wouldn't have mattered what you did. Don's playing his own game with his own rules. He was only ever going to tell you after he exhausted every other option."

The doors opened, and Mark led me down the hall. He knocked twice and waited. A moment later, Cross came to the door, gun at his thigh. As soon as we were inside, he locked and bolted the door.

"Don's in there." Cross pointed to the kitchen. "I already established strict guidelines on what is to happen and how it will happen. Almeada will be here with the paperwork for him to sign before I hand over a small fortune."

"Did you hear what happened at Martin Tech?" I asked.

Cross cleared his throat and rubbed his chin. "My team's on it. No one will get near James."

"The psycho doesn't have to get near him if he has a rifle," I said.

Cross exchanged a look with Jablonsky. "I offered."

"Yeah, and the last time, you did a lousy job protecting Marty. I know guys who can do better." Jablonsky glanced at me. "We'll get Marty set up in a five-star presidential suite. Top floor, limited access. He'll be safe until this blows over."

"How long do you think that'll take?" Cross asked. "What you propose could be months or years in the making."

"We give Chad Averly back his money," I said, "and make sure he knows this is a onetime thing. No love is lost between me and Don. I can't be used as leverage against Don, and I don't have enough assets for Chad to come after me if he decides he wants more. Martin wouldn't pay and wants nothing to do with any of this, so coming after him will only cause problems. I'll make sure that's clear."

"How are you going to make that clear?" Jablonsky's eye twitched.

"I'm going with Don to the exchange. Give me a clean phone," I said to Cross. "It's time we set up the meet."

FORTY-ONE

The sun had set, but the sky remained bright. Within the next thirty minutes, it'd be pitch. That's why I wanted to get this over with before we lost visibility. But if Locke was smarter than he looked, he'd show up a few minutes late. It's not like we could leave if he didn't arrive on time.

Don held the backpack on his lap. It was solid black. No reflectors. No color. Just like Chad had instructed.

"I hope you realize there's no guarantee we'll make it out of this alive," I said. "The man Chad hired could be watching us through a scope. He could have the crosshairs centered between your eyes. One shot. Your brains go splat on the wall behind you. You'd never feel it. You'd never even know it happened."

"Is that supposed to be comforting or creepy, little swan?"

I gave Don a sideways look. "Neither."

I had been watching everything, including him. Cross Security had a team of security specialists scouting the area. Mark Jablonsky was checking nearby buildings for sniper's nests or vantage points. Mark had wanted me to be wired, so he could better monitor the situation. But I couldn't risk it. The point of this exchange was to ensure Chad got what he was owed. It was the only way to make sure Chad didn't send any more goons to collect from Martin or me.

Don put his hand on my knee. "You always had a strange sense of the world."

"I must have picked that up from the people I lived with."

"Why are you so angry?"

"This bastard tried to kill me last night. He threatened Martin this afternoon. Actually, he may have threatened you by using Martin, but either way, I don't like it."

Don's smile was bright enough that I could see it in my periphery despite the growing darkness. "You love him. How long have you been together?"

"I don't. We aren't."

"A father knows better."

"Name one guy I had a crush on in high school."

"You were too busy studying to notice boys."

"What was I studying? Do you know what my favorite subject was? Or my worst?"

Don exhaled. He didn't concern himself with me once my life stopped being about ballet. "Does James Martin take care of you?"

"I don't need anyone to take care of me."

Don kept smiling. "You swore you didn't need me and your mom either, but I bet you found someone else to mooch off of after you left us. Let me guess. A professor? That would explain your high scores."

"You're a sick fuck."

"Teaching assistant?"

My phone buzzed. *Don't let him in your head. Stay focused.*

Mark had sent the message. I wasn't sure where he was, but he was watching, possibly listening. I wasn't sure if he'd bugged the area or had a parabolic mic, but I wouldn't put either past him. I put the phone back in my pocket and looked to my right.

"Is he here?" Don asked.

"No." It was almost dark. I didn't like the delay. It felt like a trap.

I'd been in the room when Don made the call. He'd spoken to Chad. We'd forced him to put it on speaker. Don said he had the money and would be back in the morning to return it. Chad told him not to bother. He'd have someone pick it up. No name. No other information. But Don knew who he meant. We all did.

Chad set the terms. Don was to be at this location. Originally, he was supposed to come alone, but I insisted on tagging along. I told Chad exactly what I thought of Don and wanted to make sure the bastard didn't sneak off with the cash my boss had given me to give to Don. That's when Cross came on the line, gave Chad his terms, and said the next time Don screwed up, Chad better find somewhere else to collect his pound of flesh. I seconded that, telling Chad if he had any other problems, he should kill the bastard because I was out of money and patience. Chad didn't seem to care one way or the other. All he wanted was his money back and what Don promised him. My connections and I were just a means to an end for him.

Don nudged me when a sand-colored four-door parked at the end of the street. A big man in black climbed out of the driver's seat. Locke was here. He'd gotten another car, one equally inconspicuous to use as his getaway vehicle.

After making sure the coast was clear, he approached us. He didn't realize the last thing I wanted was to see him cuffed or dead. I needed him to do his job first and deliver Chad's money.

Locke stood twenty feet away. "Do you finally have the money, Mr. Parker?"

"Ye-yeah," Don stuttered.

I'd never seen him act timid before. I found it disconcerting. I stood, my hand in my jacket. Locke reached for the holster on his hip, but I didn't take my hand out of my pocket. "Are you alone?" I asked.

"Are you?" Locke retorted. "The terms were no cops. No one else." He glanced around.

"It's just me and this giant pain in the ass." I gestured with my free hand toward Don, glad that I'd changed out of the police t-shirt before showing up to the meet.

"Where's the money?" Locke asked.

Don held the backpack in front of him. It wouldn't make him bulletproof, but it would increase his chances of survival if someone shot him through a stack of cash. "I have Chad's money. Every cent. Right here. All twenties, like he asked."

The big guy looked around, gesturing for Don to come to him. Don looked at me, and I nodded. As soon as Don took a few steps forward, the big guy took a few steps back. The cross street to his right was a dead end. Most people used it for parking and not much else. No one had any reason to go that way, unless they were getting their car, which seemed unlikely given all the empty spaces.

"I'm sorry it took so long to put this together," Don said. "Alex couldn't get me the money as easily as I thought. It turns out her boyfriend couldn't give a shit about her."

"He's not my boyfriend," I hissed.

"No, he's just some asshole you let use you in exchange for a place to stay." Don snorted. "My daughter, the mistress. I guess it's a step up from twirling around a pole."

I let it go. All that mattered was no one ever came after Martin. However we achieved that feat should be considered a win, even if the words made my blood boil. No wonder I'd always had so much self-doubt when it came to my relationships.

"Enough." Locke couldn't care less about our drama. All he wanted was to finish the job. "Bring it here." He held out his left hand, his right near his holster, but he never made a step toward Don to take the bag. He wanted Don to come to him. That set my radar buzzing, but I couldn't warn Don not to do it. We had no choice.

"I offered to bring this directly to Chad, to save him and you the trouble, but he didn't want it," Don said.

"He doesn't want to see you ever again." Locke didn't take the bag from Don. Instead, he unzipped it to check the contents while Don kept the bag strapped to his chest, like one of those baby carriers.

Don shrugged. "Things weren't supposed to turn out this way. The market wasn't supposed to nosedive. Our business model was sound. We should have—"

"No one needs to hear your excuses," I said. "Shut up and give him the money."

Locke fixed me with a stare. "You came up with the money somehow, huh?"

"No."

"Don't make me laugh. My ungrateful child wouldn't lift a finger to help me," Don said. "But since I knew where she worked, I appealed to her boss's business sense and convinced him to help me out."

"In that case, why are you here?" Locke asked me.

"I wanted to make sure Don didn't run off with the cash or feed you or your boss any more lies. The last thing I want is for you or the next muscle-for-hire to come after me or mine again. I don't know what kinds of lies Don's been spreading. But we aren't close. We haven't seen each other in a decade and a half. Don had no way of knowing what I was doing or if I even had that kind of cash, which I don't. But you made it personal by coming after me and the people I care about. I wanted to make sure that wasn't going to happen again."

"It wasn't personal," Locke said.

"Last night felt personal."

"It was business. Don broke the rules. He kept stalling. I had to make sure he knew I was serious. The beating didn't quite get the message across."

"You should have hit him harder," I said.

Locke snickered. "Do you expect me to believe the tough gal act? He's your father."

"We share a last name, but that's it. He's not my real father."

"Yet, if it hadn't been for you, he wouldn't have gotten the money, and he'd be dead right now."

"The money's from Cross Security. Lucien Cross footed the bill. If you don't believe me, call him and ask," Don interrupted.

"How did you swing that?" Locke zipped the backpack and yanked so hard on the strap that he tugged Don forward a few feet when he failed to let go fast enough.

"That's where Alexis works," Don said.

Locke kept one eye on us while he inspected the other pockets and outside of the bag. "Trackers?"

"No," Don said.

"Marked bills?"

"No. I followed Chad's instructions. The last thing I

want to do is upset him again," Don said. "We've been doing business together for years. This was all a misunderstanding. I want him to understand that there are no hard feelings."

Don remained too close to the guy. I wanted to tell him to step back, to stay out of striking range, but doing so might confuse Locke into thinking I cared what happened to Don. Right now, that was the last thing I wanted.

"Are we done here?" I asked.

"Almost."

He rushed Don, grabbing him behind the collar and tossing him into the wall. Don tripped on the curb, screaming when his broken nose smashed into the brick. I fought my instincts to pull my weapon. Cross's team was close. Jablonsky was too.

"Shut up." Locke tossed the backpack over his shoulder and pulled a gun. He pressed it into Don's battered ribcage.

I looked around, but the streets were empty enough that no one heard Don's pained scream or rushed over to help. However, I wasn't certain the people at the other end of the street or one block over weren't calling the cops to report a disturbance.

Don whimpered and grunted. He didn't have a lot of experience with physical pain. Maybe he should have learned how to dance on pointe or practice until his toes bled.

Locke whispered something to him that I couldn't hear.

Don shook his head vehemently, but he didn't struggle or fight back. "I won't do it again. You have my word. Tell Chad I promise."

"Do you believe him?" Locke asked me.

I didn't want to answer. "You collected Don's debt. If there isn't anything else, you should get out of here before someone reports hearing screams."

"Collecting was only half my assignment." Locke took a step back, his gun still aimed at Don, who remained facing the wall, blood dripping onto the sidewalk in a steady stream. "But you're right. I wouldn't want the cops showing up in the middle of this. Help me get him in the car."

"You don't want to do that."

"Why not?"

"He'll bleed all over the seats. If the police find the vehicle abandoned with blood inside, they'll link it back to you. You don't want that. You're already in enough trouble after the stunt you pulled last night."

"It's a different car. Only you can connect them both to me."

I raised my palms and stepped backward. "Not my business. I have nothing to do with this. You do what you have to. I'm just offering my advice."

Locke shifted his aim to me. "Not so fast. I was supposed to pop you too. You first, then him."

"You wanted to make Don watch, so he would suffer, except you realized we're not one big happy family. We aren't even family. We're nothing. But if you try to kill me again, we're gonna have a problem." I pulled my piece and aimed. "Do what you have to, but I want no part of this."

"Alex?" Don sounded scared. This wasn't part of the plan. This wasn't what we'd discussed before the meet. "You'd really let me die?"

"Shut up." I tilted my head from side to side while I studied Locke, wondering what he'd do next. I had no way of predicting his behavior since our prior encounter had made him seem erratic.

"Why did your boss give Don the money if you hate him so much? Why didn't you stop him?" Locke asked me.

"Self-preservation. Don lied and said I would pay off his debt, which I can't and won't. But I knew you'd never believe that. So when Don begged my boss to help him out, I didn't think we had any other choice."

Locke snorted. "I was told Cross Security means trouble."

"All kinds," I said, "which is why you may want to reconsider killing me. Cross hates having to look for new employees."

"Chad doesn't want trouble. Don's caused him enough. The last thing he wants is for this to cause him even more grief. I'm to provide a solution, not another problem."

"In that case, you should get going," I repeated. "You got what you came for. Chad should be pleased."

Locke jerked his chin toward Don's trembling back, where he remained against the brick wall, too afraid to move. "I'll make you a deal. Since you hate Don so much, you kill him. And I'll let you live. If not, I leave you both on the sidewalk. I bet I could paint a nice picture for the police of a murder-suicide."

"Alex?" Don's voice cracked, on the verge of hysterics. He tried to turn, and Locke shifted his aim, urging Don to go back to kissing the brick.

Locke pointed the gun at me. "What's it going to be? I'll give you five seconds to decide. Four. Three."

"I want your word that you'll never darken my doorstep again."

"Fine."

"Alexis," Don panicked, "please don't. I love you, bab—"

"Shut up." I fired one shot into the center of Don's back, and he went down.

FORTY-TWO

I pointed my gun at Locke. "Now what are you going to do?" He hadn't put down his weapon, which meant I wasn't putting mine down either.

Locke jerked his chin toward Don who lay on the ground. Blood spreading on the sidewalk around him. "Let's make sure."

I moved closer, aware of the big guy at my flank, and fired a second shot into Don's back. Before I could fire a third, Locke put his hand on my gun.

"You're one cold bitch," he said.

"I hated him."

"It shows." Locke tossed the backpack over his shoulder and holstered his weapon. "Our business is concluded. You'll never hear from us again."

"If I do, that'll be you," I warned.

Locke nodded. "Understood."

I held my ground, the shock of what happened forcing me to remain in place. After Locke got into the stolen car and drove away, I sucked in a deep breath and went back to the bench. The police would have a field day with the forensic evidence. Blood. Shell casings. Bullet fragments. As long as they didn't try to pin any of this on Martin, I didn't care what they found.

The adrenaline surge triggered an endorphin rush, not that dissimilar from a runner's high. I exhaled slowly, surprised by the feeling of relief. It was finally over.

Cross strolled casually down the street and joined me on the bench. "I bet that was cathartic."

I took another breath, feeling queasy. "Not really."

"Not even a little?"

"What kind of monster do you think I am, Lucien?"

"You're human." He glanced at Don's body. "Do you want me to check for a pulse?"

A moment later, Don's pained gasp filled the air, accompanied by several moans.

"Don't react," Cross instructed. "We have to be sure Locke didn't set up any surveillance." His phone chimed. "No foreign signals." He sent a text and received an immediate response. "Locke's heading for the highway. We're in the clear." He sent another text. "Stay still, Don," Cross said, even though he continued to face the street, "my medical team is on the way, but Alex is an excellent shot. I'm sure she only hit your vest. There's nothing to worry about." Cross nudged me. "Get out of here. Jablonsky's waiting for you at the extraction point. I'll take care of Don."

"What about the cops?"

"Jablonsky's already worked something out with major crimes."

Getting up, I moved on shaky limbs down the street, turned, and kept walking. At the end of the next block, I spotted Mark's SUV. Opening the door, I climbed into the passenger's seat. "How close did an FBI sniper come to taking me out?"

"Not as close as they came to almost taking out Locke when he pointed the gun at you."

"Now what?"

"We'll keep an eye on him, make sure Chad gets his money, and Don's demise becomes front page news. Maybe in a few days or weeks, we'll start putting our case together against Chad. After all, now that Don is dead, he has no choice but to cooperate if he wants the perks and benefits of WitSec."

"You already worked that out?" I asked.

"I ran it by the Marshals this afternoon."

"But we never discussed the possibility that I'd shoot Don."

Mark snorted. "You made him wear the vest. You knew Locke wanted to kill him. I've spent too many years watching you work not to know what you'd do to save Don's pathetic life."

"Maybe I forgot he was wearing a vest. Maybe I really wanted to shoot him. For all you know, he could be bleeding out right now. Did you see the blood on the sidewalk?"

"That was from his nose."

"That could be fatal."

Mark rolled his eyes. "It's okay that you care. A part of you is always going to love him, which is why you hate him so much. If you didn't, you'd be indifferent. None of it would matter. But it matters a lot. That's why it hurts so much that he isn't the dad you want or need him to be."

"Will it ever not hurt?" I asked.

"Probably not."

"I'm glad I have you," I said.

"Me too, kid." Mark gave my knee a squeeze. "Once Cross's team makes sure Don's okay, we'll get rolling on getting him into federal witness protection. Moretti's got case files, crime scene photos, and evidence waiting to go. We'll make sure to custom-tailor it to fit what Locke witnessed. Chad will never think anything different. And once we build a case against him, we'll arrest him. Don will testify, and then he'll be permanently relocated. You won't have to worry about this ever happening again."

"I have trouble believing Don will stay hidden." I swallowed, feeling my lip curl in disgust. "He'll want me to support him, or he'll try to blackmail Martin again."

"Contracts were signed," Mark said. "None of that is possible. If he refuses protection, Chad will kill him. He already tried once. He won't fail again."

"In that case, Don would take me down with him."

Mark grabbed my wrist. "Enough of that." He waited for me to meet his eyes before letting go. "Chad Averly knows not to come for you. As long as he remains convinced Don's dead, he won't expect anything to bounce back on him. We'll investigate his money laundering and murder-for-hire and build a rock solid case. Once he's arrested, Don can go back to doing whatever the fuck he wants, just as long as he stays the hell away from you."

"That could take years."

"It won't. Hartley and the rest of the forensic accountants have already found dirt on Chad's money laundering and details on his alleged investors whose money he's cleaning. Once we get Locke's full name, the locals will arrest him for the GTA. Chad's going down. They are all going down."

"You plan to flip Locke?"

"I plan to try." A thought flitted across Mark's face, but he didn't share it with me. "I got this."

Mark circled the block a few times before pulling directly into the garage at one of the nicer hotels. He parked behind several other cars and made sure no one was around before opening his door. Then he escorted me to the private elevator that led directly to the top floor, slid the keycard into the slot, and pressed the button.

I slumped against the wall, resting my elbows on my thighs and putting my head in my hands. "How long are we going to be here?"

"The weekend, at a minimum. It depends on how long it takes shit-for-brains to get the money back to his boss. But I already told Marty he could go back to work on Monday. Let's hope Locke doesn't make a liar out of me."

The doors opened, and Mark flashed his credentials at the armed agents waiting in the hallway. Mark introduced us and made me hand over my identification for verification.

"Right this way." The lead agent led me to the door and unlocked it. Two other agents were positioned in the living room, near the doorway. The windows were covered. No one could see in or out.

"Where's the asset?" Mark asked.

"In the master suite."

Mark jerked his chin toward the closed door. "I'll let you handle that while I take care of everything else. I'll be back to pick you up on Monday morning. If it's not me, it'll be Lucca. I'm not sending anyone else. You got that?"

"What about Bruiser?" I asked.

"I'll check in on him and make sure he's got whatever he needs, but I'm sure Marty already arranged for regular meal deliveries. He has that odd obsession with feeding people."

I laughed. "That's so true."

* * *

I put a large box of donuts and an extra large mocha on Thompson's desk. "The bear claws and jellies are for you. The sprinkles are for Nick." I took the vanilla latte out of the drink carrier and put it on Nick's desk. "Where is he?"

"Do I look like his keeper?" Thompson asked, doing his best not to acknowledge the donuts, even though he was itching to reach into the box.

"You're his partner. It's your job," I said.

Thompson snorted. "He's helping Heathcliff out with an interrogation. Shouldn't that be your job? We had a pool going on when you'd grace us with your presence again."

Since Thompson had yet to touch the donuts, I opened the box and took out a chocolate crème and an old-fashioned, placed the old-fashioned on Heathcliff's desk, along with a black coffee, and helped myself to a napkin before I made a mess. "I want to ask you something," I said. "And I want a serious answer."

"Can I stop you?" Thompson asked.

I shook my head. "Do you really despise me?"

He looked up at me like I was crazy. "You drive me insane, Parker. Haven't I made that clear?"

"Yeah, but this seems like more."

Thompson grunted, turning his focus to the box and scooping up one of the bear claws. Then he popped the lid off his coffee and dunked the oversized pastry into the cup. "You left us."

"For the weekend."

"No, Parker. You took off for months. We weren't sure when or if you were coming back."

I smiled. "You missed me."

"Heathcliff and O'Connell were worried. I don't like it when they worry."

"You were worried too." I poked him in the arm, grinning. "You like me."

"Shut up."

"You really like me."

"I like it when you remember to bring donuts and coffee. That's about it."

Before I could rib him some more, O'Connell and Heathcliff returned from the interrogation rooms. O'Connell picked up the latte and took a sip, nodding good morning to me, while Heathcliff gave the donut on his desk a confused look before pushing it to the side and taking a seat.

"You're here bright and early." Heathcliff opened a desk drawer and pulled out a few folders. "Is everything okay? I thought you would have called to tell me what happened."

"Didn't Moretti tell you?"

Heathcliff nodded. "I'm sorry about Don."

"Yeah, me too." I brushed it aside, knowing I had to carry on the charade but confident my friends knew the truth. "Shit happens."

"Yep." Heathcliff pushed the folders toward me. "Since you had that to deal with, I took care of the armed robbers. Evidence collection finished with the freight container yesterday afternoon. Almost all the stolen items were accounted for. The few that were missing have already been located at various pawn shops. We verified they were from the same shipment via the lot numbers."

I flipped the pages, scanning the photos before getting to the reports. "Officer Franco found eight of the ten stolen game consoles at that pawn shop."

"The owner identified Kelsey Savage as the man who sold the hot merchandise to him. He gave Kelsey four grand for the game consoles, which explains where the envelopes of cash came from. The ninth console was found in Kelsey's home. Kelsey gave the tenth one to his nephew for his birthday."

"I didn't think Wayne had any children," I said.

"His wife's sister's kid," O'Connell clarified around a mouthful of donut.

"What about the burner phone I found?" I asked.

Heathcliff indicated the other folder. "Keep reading."

Inside were texts from the phone I'd found. The number matched the burner that had sent instructions and locations to the other four phones. This phone should have belonged to the shot-caller, Jefe. Each text laid out the time, place, and date for their next robbery. Those texts had been sent to Wayne, Ed, and Jerome. The more detailed texts, which included detailed plans, who to hit, where to hit, and how to execute the hit, were sent to Kelsey's burner.

I hadn't expected that. "You mean to tell me Ed and Jerome were right? There is a fifth guy who forced them to commit these crimes?"

"That's what it looks like," Heathcliff said, "except when we dusted the phone and swabbed it for DNA. The only person who used the burner was Kelsey."

"He had two phones?"

"It looks like it. We think he used the SIM Wayne bought in his own phone to receive the instructions, which is why we never found a burner phone in his house. And he hid the other one in the container with their scores, figuring we'd never find it, but if we did, it'd implicate someone else."

I rocked in my chair, reading the reports I'd missed while I'd been hiding in a fancy hotel room. The epithelial cells pulled off the *Phantom of the Opera* mask were a match to Kelsey. That had been his mask, as if we ever had any doubts. He and Wayne had orchestrated all of this. The only question remaining was whether Ed and Jerome were in on it and feeding us the bullshit story about the shot-caller, or if they actually believed it.

"Have you gotten anyone to flip or confess that they knew what was going on?"

“Not yet.” Heathcliff broke off a piece of donut and chewed. “They’re sticking to their stories. Ed hasn’t deviated. The psych eval we gave him indicates he believes it, but he could be lying. There’s no way of telling which is which.”

“But he’s not delusional?”

Heathcliff shook his head. “None of them are. Though, Wayne has antisocial tendencies and issues with authority.”

“I could have told you that, and I don’t have a Ph.D.” I read over the interview notes again. “Ed seemed like our weak link, but you heard what he said.”

“He has nothing left to lose.”

I put the folder down and checked the floor. The cushion was gone. “Where’s Spike?”

“Officer Rigby found a spot for him in the kennel. He’s okay.” Heathcliff gave me a curious look. “Want to tell me what you’re thinking?”

“Kelsey and Wayne are behind this. They won’t deviate from their plan. If they do, they’ll go to jail. No passing go. No collecting any more money. We can’t break them.”

“Kelsey has a wife and kid. That should mean something,” O’Connell said.

“He could be doing it for them,” Heathcliff said.

“Jerome will talk. I know what he wants.” I just hoped the police department would allow a man they had in custody some visitation.

FORTY-THREE

I sat across the table from Jerome. His arm remained in a sling, but it didn't seem as sore or stiff today as it had the last time we'd spoken. By now, the wound had started to heal. The cut on my side had scabbed, but the bruise remained.

Heathcliff and I went over the facts and pointed out the discrepancies in Jerome's story a second time. This time, Heathcliff brought visual aids to prove our point.

"See this?" Heathcliff played the footage from outside the fast-food restaurant. "That's Kelsey's car. Note the date and time." He pointed to the top corner of the screen. "Why would his car be parked here when he was nowhere near this location? Weren't the four of you busy unloading that delivery truck right around now?"

Jerome took an uneasy breath. "Maybe Breann had the car. She travels for work sometimes. She could have stopped for an early lunch."

"Sure." Heathcliff fast-forwarded the footage. "Can you tell me who this is?"

Jerome's eyes went wide, but he tried to cover his surprise. "So?"

I rubbed my eyebrow, wondering how long he could hold on to his belief. "Last time we spoke, you said Kelsey drove the delivery truck away from the store. Here he is roughly forty-five minutes later, walking back to his car, which is near the same mile marker where the delivery truck was abandoned."

"Right, Jefe made him do it." Jerome shrugged. "What's the problem?"

"How did Kelsey know he'd have to drive the delivery truck and dump a body? How did he know where to park his car?" I asked.

"Maybe Jefe gave Wayne instructions before we met."

"Not possible," Heathcliff said, "unless you failed to mention that Wayne knew what was going to happen ahead of time."

"He didn't. He got the business card from Jefe about the job, same as Ed did. Wayne was told to bring along friends, which he did. He didn't know what was going to happen. He'd never be involved in something like that. He's a good guy. He wouldn't knowingly drag us into this."

"Then how do you explain Kelsey planning ahead and leaving his car there?"

"It could have been a coincidence. Maybe he and Wayne got breakfast before showing up at the warehouse store, and instead of driving separate, they left Kelsey's car."

"Wayne's staying at Kelsey's. If they left together, why would they drive separately?" Heathcliff asked.

Jerome growled, the frustration getting to him. "I. Don't. Know."

"They set you up," I said. "I'm sorry. It sucks. Being betrayed by the people you love, there's nothing worse."

He looked up, the sincerity in my voice catching him off guard and breaking through his defenses.

"They used you. They don't care what happens. They're hoping your story will get them out of trouble, but if it doesn't, if the judge sees through it, if the jury hears what we have to say and sees these inconsistencies and discrepancies, the four of you will be blamed for everything. You'll be an accessory to murder, and you said you weren't a killer."

Jerome's cheek and nose twitched. "They're my brothers."

"They aren't," I said.

"You gave Wayne the gun that was used to kill the driver, and you provided the weapons used in the other robberies. Luckily, no one else was seriously hurt, but you were there. That's felony murder. However, if you'd be willing to testify, the DA's agreed to take that off the table. You'll do time on the weapons charges, but that's it," Heathcliff said.

Jerome didn't look convinced. "How long?"

"That depends on a lot of factors, but possibly less than five." Heathcliff went to the door. "Maybe Spike can help you decide."

The dog had been sitting outside the door, his head cocked to the side. But he remained still, waiting for Officer Rigby to give him the command. Once Heathcliff nodded, the K-9 trainer said something and Spike raced into the room. He ran to Jerome, his tail wagging as he put his head on his owner's lap.

"What's going to happen to him if I serve time?" Jerome asked. "If I go away, they'll euthanize Spike."

"I won't let that happen," Heathcliff said. "You have my word."

"If you give us everything we need, you could plead down to a year. Spike will be waiting for you. The vet said he's only three. He's got several years ahead of him. Do you want this to be the last time you see him?" I asked.

Jerome tapped his leg, and Spike jumped up with his front paws so Jerome could hug him with his one good arm. "I'll tell you whatever I can."

* * *

I finished the paperwork and stretched. "I'm glad we got it sorted. I can't believe Kelsey and Wayne would use people like that."

"Wayne was desperate," Heathcliff said. "Kelsey concocted the plan after watching one of those court shows and seeing the defendants get off because no one could determine exactly who was to blame."

"Someone should have told him that was fiction, not real life." I thought about Ed's story. "Do you think Ed knew the truth?"

"He needed the money. Even if he suspected, he let himself believe he had no choice. He wanted to have no choice."

"But he didn't want anyone to get hurt. He must have known that would happen if they tried to rob everyone in the coffee shop."

Heathcliff put some things in the drawer and logged off his computer. "Did Cross find any lucrative targets from that footage I gave you?"

"No, but the number of laptops would have made up for it. More than half the people inside were working on their computers."

"Figure that would have been a few grand."

"Plus cell phones and cash." I laughed. "That's the last time we go to breakfast."

"It was lunch. And we agreed. I pick from now on."

"That's right. I almost forgot." Taking the paperwork, I knocked on Moretti's door and placed it on his desk. "It was nice working with you again."

"Glad we could benefit one another." He winked. "Take care, Parker."

Heathcliff was waiting to walk me out. I wondered if someone else would attack with a hammer, but I didn't want to bring it up. I'd agreed to pretend that didn't happen for the sake of gaining Jerome's cooperation.

"You still don't have a ride?" Heathcliff asked when he spotted Jablonsky's SUV parked in a reserved space.

"Cross wanted me to finish working for the PD before he gave me use of the company car. He's tightening the reins on a lot of things." I didn't want to think about it, but I owed him. And I'd rather owe him than become more indebted to Martin.

The side door opened, and Officer Franco exited, holding Spike by the leash. "Detective Heathcliff, I just got tapped for the detective's exam. Thank you, sir."

"No problem." Heathcliff took the offered leash from Franco. "You need help prepping, let me know."

"Thanks." Franco nodded to me. "Have a safe one."

"You too."

Franco disappeared back inside, and I knelt down to pet Spike. His tongue lolled out, and he looked up at me with big brown eyes. For once, I was pretty sure he didn't have plans to use me as a chew toy. "I thought you weren't a dog guy."

"I'm not." Heathcliff looked down at him. "But I had to do something to convince Jerome to cooperate. I know a retired dog trainer who fosters abused animals. She's agreed to take care of Spike until Jerome gets released."

Mark honked the horn, which made Spike bark. "I should get going. Have fun with your new roommate."

"He's not mine," Heathcliff said.

"Whatever you say."

*   *   *

Mark parked in the garage beneath the federal building. The place had been closed off and secured. Don Parker was being moved into federal witness protection. He'd requested that his ex-wife be allowed to go with him. Lydia agreed. She'd be picked up and transported to meet Don at a later date.

"Alex," Mark nudged me as I watched Don from across the parking lot, "if you have anything to say, now's the time."

I got out of the car. Don turned at the sound of the door closing.

"Alexis," he didn't smile, "are you here to see me off?"

"I wanted to make sure you were okay."

"How is giving up my entire life okay? You didn't give me a choice."

"I saved your life."

He winced, the bruises on his back still fresh. "That's debatable. Some would say you wanted me dead."

"You're safe. If you cooperate, you'll be taken care of. You'll start over. I heard Lydia will be joining you. Doesn't that count for something?"

"I guess."

"Yeah, well, now maybe you can create the life you want. Ask the Marshals to give you a daughter you could be proud of, one who met all your expectations, who never disappointed you." My chin quivered, and I swallowed. "I want you to know that I always tried."

"Not hard enough."

"No, Don. I tried too hard." I walked back to the SUV and got inside. "It's time to go home."

* * *

Martin's town car was parked in the garage when I let myself in. I'd invited Mark to stay, but he had paperwork. More than likely, he was afraid I'd get emotional and didn't want to deal with it. Instead, that would be Martin's problem.

I trudged up the steps, spent from the last few weeks. I didn't think I had anything left. All I wanted to do was curl up on the couch and watch TV.

"Parker," Bruiser's voice caught me off guard, "I see I've been replaced." He was sitting on the couch beside the giant teddy bear. "The new guy doesn't say much, but he's got amazing focus when it comes to monitoring the security feeds."

I laughed, fearing the sudden emotional high after the low would make me cry. "What are you doing here?"

Martin stepped out of the kitchen. "I invited him for dinner. I figured he could use a change of scenery." He moved across the living room and kissed me. "Are you okay? Did you see Don off?"

I nodded. "He doesn't matter anymore. I have my family right here."

DON'T MISS THE NEXT INSTALLMENT IN THE ALEXIS PARKER SERIES.

CHECK OUT HOSTAGE SITUATION (ALEXIS PARKER #26).

ABOUT THE AUTHOR

G.K. Parks is the author of the Alexis Parker series. The first novel, *Likely Suspects,* tells the story of Alexis' first foray into the private sector.

G.K. Parks received a Bachelor of Arts in Political Science and History. After spending some time in law school, G.K. changed paths and earned a Master of Arts in Criminology/Criminal Justice. Now all that education is being put to use creating a fictional world based upon years of study and research.

You can find additional information on G.K. Parks and the Alexis Parker series by visiting our website at www.alexisparkerseries.com

Made in the USA
Middletown, DE
11 May 2025

75405339R00196